a New Lu

Laura Castoro

a New Lu

RED
DRESS
I N K
™

First edition March 2005

A NEW LU

A Red Dress Ink novel

ISBN 0-373-89514-3

www.RedDressInk.com

Printed in U.S.A.

To the Writers Colony at Dairy Hollow
in Eureka Springs, AR.
Thanks for the food, shelter and,
most importantly, the uninterrupted creative work time.
What more could a writer ask for?

February

The stupid crazies are those moments in your life when you go for broke.
Sometimes you win.
Sometimes you lose.
But you just *hadda* do it!

—"The Midlife Crazies"
CUE LU!

Prologue

Sex for the very last time. That's what I was thinking.

It's not unusual, for a single woman of fifty, to contemplate life without sex. Notice how even Oprah's sassy smile grows a bit rickety when she boasts about the big Five-O? That because she ain't talking about Hawaii.

For the year Jacob and I have been separated I've had lots of time to think about just how long a no-sex ever after could be. I'm not proud of what I've just done. I'm not even defensive. Chalk it up to the stupid crazies.

The weekend was to be about closure. Understand, this word was not in Jacob's vocabulary until he started counseling fifteen months ago. Neither were formal separation nor divorce. He didn't even tell me there was a counselor until the second sentence in the paragraph that burned down the roof of my life. The paragraph began, "I think we need to separate."

Thankfully, the pathetic excuse of another woman wasn't written into the script of my modern life. Yet, after a year of talk and tears, I can't say that I understand Jacob's reasoning much better than I did when he completed that fateful paragraph. Maybe a few key factors got cut in the dress rehearsal with his counselor.

What stuck in my mind was the part in the middle of his goodbye speech about his "need to be needed," which I was no longer supplying. I didn't have a comeback for that. Still don't. It's hard to recoup from a first blow that stakes out the best emotional ground.

Every other base we had already covered, twice. Drift, too many business trips, insomnia, the dead bore of routine, desertion of college-bound children…and, of course, aging. Jacob is against aging.

He thought his three-days-a-week trips to the gym and swimming laps the other two weekdays would be enough to stave off time. Then a couple of years ago a golfing buddy teased him about how the sun had bleached his temples white. The very next day he came home with a box of Just For Men. Said he needed the color for a psychological edge in the marketplace.

I, on the other hand, promised myself that when the time came, I would allow nature to take her course. No lifts, tucks, lipo or dyes. Many friends began pulling out silver hairs in their early thirties. I was forty before the first one caught my attention, forty-five before the word *graying* could be attached to me. Even then I developed streaks, one above my right brow, another over my left temple. *Striking,* my hairdresser called the changes. *And you have such a young-looking face.* So, why deny that I have lived long enough to earn my "stripes," as Jacob once affectionately called them?

Jacob. It has been a while since I could attach the term *affection* to Jacob's attitude toward me. Despite my bravado, I'm not finding one good thing about the half-century mark that looms in the middle of this year. When I look in the mirror, what my age looks like on me no longer makes me smug. I suspect Jacob noticed, too, and disapproved.

Yet there he was last Wednesday, appearing suddenly at his ex-door of his ex-house, a nervous smile on his face. Once his crooked grin was enough to ignite a frisson of affection at thirty paces. Now it makes me feel guilty. Furious at him, sure, but guilty because I can no longer be what he needs. He said he'd been thinking, and he thought we needed to be sure we're doing the right thing. Divorcing. I said I had already signed the papers. He said he had, too, but wouldn't it be a mistake not to be certain? He said he thought maybe we should go away for the weekend, just to talk things over one more time. How about somewhere in the Caribbean? I said I couldn't afford an island getaway. He said he'd pay. I thought, boy, that's generous of him. But I'm not crazy. I said, separate rooms. He said, fine.

Okay, I needed a vacation. But that's not why I said yes. Guilt still works as my motivation. The truth is Jacob's leaving hurt, but it didn't shatter me. I had drifted out of range.

There's got to be more. Those words echo in my mind with the familiarity of a self-evolved mantra.

Maybe if I just lie low for a few years, until I reach the big Six-O, the urge for something more will go away. So said a letter to the editor at *Five-O* magazine last year. Okay, I wrote the letter.

We needed an intro to an issue devoted to the restless years of midlife. Being the lifestyle editor as well as monthly columnist of CUE LU! for *Five-O* magazine, it fell to me to set the tone. Putting into words the vague dread that has plagued me on the journey from forty-five toward fifty now seems prophetic. Sleepwalking is exactly what I was doing until Jacob walked out.

Second reason: our children. Dallas and Davin haven't given up on the possibility that their parents will one day wake up and be over it, whatever "it" is. So I feel I should give "it" every opportunity. I don't want to be held accountable for not trying hard enough.

A free trip to the Caribbean in February came in third.

Our three-day idyll began as a measured reflection of our accomplishments. Married in 1977. Two great children: Dallas Patrice Nichols (25) and Davin Jacob Nichols (20). One's a graduate of the University of Chicago's business school. The other struggles at Carnegie Mellon. Jacob and I have two decent careers and, after the first sixteen years, a nicer-than-decent house in northern New Jersey.

But I digress.

Sex for the very last time.

This evening, the last night, began innocently enough. Two Bahama Mamas each—heavy on the rum—and no dinner. Looking at the end of the road while it's still in front of you can be hard to swallow. The cues of familiarity kick in. A lift of his right eyebrow; always an invitation. The sudden warmth of my own sexual response. Maybe he is only flirting with the thought. Maybe I am only intoxicated with the possibility of something soon to be taboo. This makes the possibility of "we" more interesting. After all, this could be, for me, sex for the very last time.

He suggests a nightcap.

I suggest, in my room.

Married sex is about comfort and routine. The comfort of knowing what is coming next. It's like Twister played again and again with the same partner. After a while one anticipates, compensates, knows where the body parts can and can't go. If the kisses are fewer, the duration shorter, the move to the main event quicker, you give a mental shrug and lay the complaint on the altar of married sex. There is the comfort, the ritual of routine. That should count for something.

I tell myself this as Jacob is groping my right breast as if it's an overripe mango he's thinking about purchasing. He doesn't like very ripe fruit. Says it reminds him of aging flesh. *Hmm.*

Somewhere between the second tweak of my left nipple and the fingers invading my body, sensations revive that have been absent for thirteen months. No, to be honest, it's been more like eighteen, nineteen months. The end that came with a whimper, not a bang.

We don't exactly go at it like minks but we do a credible job. There is a lot of bed shaking and creaking and the giggles that come with the realization that the guests next door might hear you. And then it's over. The last quick butt wriggle that is Jacob's trademark, and it's ever-after time.

So here I lie in the bed, which he vacated with surprising speed, and stare at the not-quite-painted-over water spots on the ceiling. He didn't really spend much money on this closure weekend, after all. I'll bet he got one of those travel.com quickies. You don't know until the last minute what your five hundred dollars will get you.

"Let's be spontaneous," he'd said, not wanting to tell me where we were going. That out-of-character romantic intrigue now looks like his way of keeping his options open on the cheapest availability.

Okay, so that's Jacob all over. Cheap, and selective about his fruit.

This reminder of two of his annoying flaws inspires other thoughts. This could be the rekindling of the rest of our lives together. Or just a big fat mistake. Despite the sexual flush I'm trying hard to hold on to, I don't know what I'd do if he changed his mind about the divorce.

There's got to be more.

One thing is certain. I am alone in the afterglow. Of sex for the very last time?

April

I'm fifty years old, recently divorced.
Now I'm about to be an unwed mother.
And you thought you had issues....

—"Knocked-Up But Not Out"
CUE LU!

1

The offices of *Five-O*—the magazine for the mature woman—are sandwiched between a ground-floor bagel emporium and a third-level hard-body gym in Upper Montclair, New Jersey. Five days a week, employees are prisoners to the energetic soundtrack for lissome flesh competing with the mother-comfort aroma of fresh bread. In other words, we play dodge ball with the driving forces of life: pursuit and happiness.

I'm part-time. Monday and two other days of my choice.

"So? How was your weekend, Lu?" Babs is *Five-O*'s receptionist and Kmart-style greeter.

"Brilliant!" I tend to adopt phrases from favorite TV shows, movies and books. Just now I'm hooked on BBC America and *Changing Rooms,* the British version of neighbor-to-neighbor interior design. Of course, *Absolute Sh-t* would work, as well.

I'm bloated and dehydrated after a weekend of too much fun and drama in Atlantic City with my buddy Andrea. Well, she had fun. I had the drama—a case of indigestion that kept me far from the gaming tables because I couldn't stray from the loo. Don't know what I ate but I'm convinced it had battery acid in it.

Babs hands me a sheaf of memos. I fan them out and grimace. Two from my darling daughter, Dallas. It seems she no longer trusts e-mail and phone messaging. She's resorted to third party intervention.

"You should do something about her encroachment on your time." A stern look meets mine over the tops of Babs's glasses. "You don't look so good."

I smile. "If Dallas calls again before noon, tell her I'm in an editorial meeting."

"You should be so lucky you are in a meeting for the next month."

I don't call Babs on this impertinence because at *Five-O* we venerate our elders as an affirmation of our own futures. And, because she is old enough to be my mother. And, because she is right.

Six months ago Babs Kern was rusting out in a retirement village when our recently deposed editor-in-chief, Sarah Mann, decided we needed to act on our mission statement: "To seed our futures by our present acts." Sarah hired a receptionist from the riper side of sixty-five. (There's no correlation between the hiring of Babs and firing of Sarah, since Babs is still with us.)

For the *Five-O* woman, there's no such thing as retirement. We simply adjust to rising circumstance. In other words, we will work until all options evaporate, mind and body.

Don't be fooled by Babs's penchant for dangling earrings, blue eye shadow and upsweep of impossibly red hair with an inch of white roots showing at her nape. "The Radish" is an affectionate nickname. Truly. Once a private secretary for a Manhattan banker, Babs retains a mind that can keep tabs on everyone's production schedule, as well as recall without prompting the birthday, anniversary or upcoming celebratory event for each of our fifteen employees. She's even learned the menstrual cycles of the women in the office, and can predict who'll call in sick when.

The fact that Babs uses a motorized wheelchair to get about hasn't slowed her in any meaningful way I can think of. Right now I'd trade my body for Babs's mind.

I flip through Dallas's messages and realize I've forgotten who her caterer is, where the wedding consultant's office is and what the Lorrie Kabala creation she's chosen looks like. The cost is, blessedly, not my problem.

My brilliant firstborn is getting married in five months. The plans have been in the works for more than a year. She and Stephen hoped to marry sooner, but the perfect location for the reception was booked eighteen months in advance. Now, I know I'm from another generation, yet the short attention span of the young would seem proof of my thinking. Any marriage that can wait eighteen months on the booking demands of a reception doesn't seem to have much oomph!

They don't even live together anymore. She's moved in with two girlfriends in the city, while Stephen has moved back to his teenage bedroom in his parents' home. I assumed saving money was at the bottom of this development. Wrong. Dallas says that since their engagement she and Stephen have adopted "celibacy as a psychophysical state" in order to strengthen the more spiritual aspects of their union before marriage. The mom in me is proud. The woman in me is wondering, *"What?"*

I've never wanted to know the particulars of my children's sex lives. Somehow it's as icky a thought as what Mom and Pop were doing upstairs on those quiet Sunday afternoons.

Not that my children need wonder any longer. In my briefcase are the final papers from my divorce. One needn't even show up for the legal coup against the eternal sovereignty of love anymore. Notice comes via the post from one's attorney. In this instance, six weeks to the day after Jacob and I headed for that closure weekend.

Jacob seemed so proud of himself as we waited for our respective flights back to the States—I was right about the cheap fares! He even managed to pat my sunburned shoulder as he said how much he appreciated my support of his needs during the weekend. I'd given him the closure he needed. He was leaving. "Free. Able to move on, to put what we had behind us."

It's not as if I expected or even wanted him to fall on his knees at the airport and ask me to marry him all over again. Still, I felt—feel—used. He didn't need to think it over. Was the sex that bad?

Depending on who you ask, divorce is just one of those "everybody has one" items or a frontal attack on American morality. I tend not to ask.

Slump-shouldered with fatigue, I slink away from Babs and pass wide expanses of spotless floor-to-ceiling windows that line the eastern corridor of our hallway. This design gives the illusion of air and space to the row of glass-walled but windowless offices opposite them. The architectural brilliance is meant to inspire. Safely on the eastern banks of the Garden State, we Jerseyites can still gaze out across the Hudson and dream Big Apple dreams. Too bad, I haven't had an inspired thought in months.

The power of persuasion has deserted me. The two CUE LU! columns I carry with me read like loser-compensation packages. Once I was proud to be a *Five-O* woman. Today I feel like I'm AWOL in my life.

I stop to gaze out toward Midtown backed by an April-blue sky. Jacob didn't approve of me taking this job. "Fashion and lipstick for women with whiskers," he calls *Five-O*. Not that his own situation is safe from satire. Jacob is an executive for a fast-food chain, international division.

"You're going to hawk lousy nutrition to the world?" Davin responded when his dad announced his decision to take the position two years before.

I kept my thoughts to myself, for Jacob had been downsized out of his last place of employment eight months before this opportunity came along. Luckily, I had just begun with *Five-O*. A man without a career—well, it might have been the beginning of the end.

Yet I remain stupefied by a perspective on the world that suggests the best way to bring equality and egalitarianism to nations beset by ceaseless civil strife is to offer them the possibility of answering that American-classic question, "Want fries with that?"

But what do I know?

Remorse is sometimes a difficult emotion to pin down. Swipe the last cookie and you know why you feel toadhigh when the theft is discovered. But spend a weekend with your about-to-be ex and the self-reproach is more elusive. Six weeks later and I still feel as though I may just have escaped unscathed from…

"Oh, there you are. Tardiness is not a virtue."

A stranger is standing in the middle of my office. Well, "middle" would be a generous description of the three feet between the door and the chair before my desk.

For one irrational second I think, *The unsuspected other woman!*

This one would certainly fill the bill of middle-age female nightmare. She's impossibly tall and thin, both attributes accentuated by the yardage of legs exposed beneath her coral sweatshirt with hood and matching short shorts. And blond. Or rather, the pale gold thick bob scissored off at her nape still manages the volume of bimbo hair. Spiky cut, her heavy bangs nearly tangle in her eyelashes.

She extends a hand, lean and bronzed to perfection as the rest of her.

"Tai."

"Lu."

One syllable each and we've sized each other up. This is Tai Leigh. My new boss. Oh, joy!

"We weren't expecting you until midweek." I know that's true because I read that memo.

She smiles but it doesn't quite evaporate the frost in her bottle-green gaze. "I was in the city for a 10K run and thought, *Why not pop over, get an early look-see?*"

Impossibly trendy Tai Leigh is known and loved as a marathon runner for causes, in her spare time. I once walked a 5K. Promised myself to lie down if the urge ever overtook me again. But she's speaking.

"—your columns."

What my columns? Nothing to do but play along. "I'm flattered."

"Really?"

Damn! She must have insulted me when I wasn't listening. That's what I get for letting my mind drift. But I'm accustomed to dealing with a disaffected reader. "It's an opinion column. I don't expect to win over everyone. But while reading me, that reader is at least giving thought to a different idea."

"A different idea. Yes." I swear she bats her lashes at me. One slow sweep of mascara spikes.

She's good. I'm on the defensive before I've had a chance to be really annoying or snide. I could ask the media-buzz question of the moment in the magazine world. Why did Tai Leigh leave *Bling,* the youth-thing magazine where she made her name? *Five-O* is "an age-conspicuous backwater," if I correctly quote *Vanity Fair.* That is, we don't tout consumption over quality-of-life issues. Tai was thought to be bounding for Tina and Anna territory. Gazelles don't usually tread bayous. She must have ticked off the wrong person. I can see how that could happen.

It's amazing how little of three feet of space she takes

up, I note as I slip behind my desk. "CUE LU! is quite popular." I casually reach for my top file cabinet. "Perhaps you'd like to see our recent poll results."

Her gold mop swishes a quick left-right. Before I realize her plan, she picks up the portfolio I laid on my desk, flips it open and reads aloud the title of one of my columns. "'The Joys of Solitude.'" She lifts the page. "Oh, dear. 'The Middle-Age Tummy.'"

Good. She's entered my bailiwick. Research is my game. "Did you know that tummy tucks don't last? In fact, for women over fifty, the results can disappear faster than the profits of a day trader. Now, that's throwing good money after bad genes."

She genuinely smiles, looking at me like Trinny and Susannah on "What Not To Wear" after they've pushed their latest victim before a 360-degree dressing-room mirror. I am immediately aware of every bulge, roll and wrinkle. And that's just my clothing. We're casual at *Five-O*. My oversize sweater, long skirt and mules usually pass as esprit bonhomie. In Tai's gaze I am reflected as bag lady.

"I read your last half-dozen columns coming in on the train this morning. All that old-school feminist ambition! It's just so—dreary, isn't it?" She replaces the portfolio. "To be frank, your views no longer fit the profile of our readership."

"I *am* the profile."

"Yes. And you do write your age."

To my astonishment, she kicks off her sporty Ferragamo suede mules, lifts a brown leg as thin as my arm to anchor her heel over the back of the nearby chair and does a deep bend from the waist.

"I took a poll of my own via our online service. My numbers show that while women may say they accept fifty or even seventy as reality, they still want to pass for ten or fifteen, even twenty years younger."

As she comes upright, pretzel-stick arms bowed over her

head, she says, "Our readership wants to make age irrelevant."

Make age irrelevant! I wrote that column, too. She knows that. She knows I know, so— Damn! She's pulling rank, and we both know I'm the subordinate clause.

Then it hits me. She's here to do some preemptive snipping. I could be *numero uno* on her hit list. By Wednesday, when she makes her triumphant entrance, I could be history. Unless I salute her flag.

But I've had a rough few weeks. I've gone beyond the pale, rushed in where angels do not tread, burned some bridges and—well, I've made my point, and I'm woozy with cliché. Now I stand to lose a job as well as a husband in the same week. I should back down. But I feel the pressure of rising stomach acid. It perfumes my words.

"If you think a thirty-year-old can dictate how a fifty-year-old should live, you're mistaken. We hate being told how to dress by our children."

"That's cute." She comes up again, drops her leg and lifts the other into place. Down she bends, so limber her knee hyper-extends as she touches her forehead to kneecap. On a great day I can do three-quarters of that stretch.

She turns her head, gazing at me from beneath an armpit. "I'm here to boost flat sales. Demographics indicate this should be easy. You Boomers are lemmings for trends! That's why I'm going to save your butt."

She rises, drops her leg and slips back into her shoes before turning to me. "Perfect honesty? Readers will look at me and be reminded of the women they once were. You, on the other hand, are a known quantity, and obviously no threat." She's noticed not all my bulges are puckered fabric. "Therefore I propose we unite."

She's offering a merger. Albeit a sneaking, self-promoting, condescending merger. And here I was expecting the boot.

"A sort of ying and yang approach?" I ask.

She consults her watch. "I'm offering you the opportunity to be *Five-O's* poster child of change. You've let yourself go. But I see potential." A small smile flickers. "You've got good genes. Of course, you'll need to start a genuine health regimen. With a little effort on your part, we can work miracles. You'll need a new byline. Something like 'A New You.'" She looks up, eyes going so wide her green irises look like kiwi slices. "No, make that 'A New Lu!'"

I almost laugh in relief. "You want me to hang out at a spa and write about it?"

"I want everything."

Her gaze fixes on a spot behind my left shoulder, pupils expanding like black holes. "You'll document the whole process of your middle-age rebirth, from personal trainer to nutritionist to shrink, if need be. You'll need lipo. That middle-age tum has got to go. A face-lift, perhaps. Definitely, work around the eyes. We'll see what the experts recommend. Perhaps you can try a chemical peel and Botox."

Before I can muster more than a shocked "You're not serious," she's off again.

"For the readers' benefit we'll need month-by-month photo documentation. Finish up with a full photo layout. Make that a shopping-spree spread! If we get going, your unveiling can be the focus of the spring issue. Think of all the opportunities for product placement and tie-ins? Advertising will wet itself over the idea!"

She blinks, coming out of her now-famous "Tai moment" trance. She looks at me with a genuine smile. "The tab's on us. The time off for procedures will be considered paid vacation."

I'm seldom at a loss for words, but Tai has just suggested that weeks of surgery and recovery qualify as a holiday. All I can think of are my aunt Marvelle's parting words last time I visited. "You need to stop being a walking advertisement for that damn AARP and get your color done!"

Maybe I have been carrying the gray-hair thing too far.

The *shrrrr* of Babs's motorized vehicle precedes her appearance. "There you are. Everything to your satisfaction, Ms. Leigh?"

"In due time." Tai turns to me. "Take a week to think it over."

I'm tempted to say "I quit" and stalk out, but I was born with my mother's practical gene. I have bills. A snide comment will have to do. "When Gloria Steinem announced that she was fifty, and the disbelieving suggested she'd had some work done, she replied, 'This is what fifty looks like.'"

Tai smiles. "Gloria also said she'd never marry. We all have our breaking point."

Gone. The light tread of her shoes in the hallway is the only proof Tai didn't simply turn sideways and vanish.

"That went well?" Babs suggests.

"Depends. How soon is one eligible for social security?"

"Mom! Where have you been?"

"Stuck in the dryer with the missing socks."

The tiny pause on the phone line is meant to remind me how much my daughter doesn't appreciate my humor at moments of high stress. Trouble is, lately she seems to have no other moments.

I thumb open the pop top on my diet soda as I say, "What's wrong, Dallas?"

"I was worried." The sulk of neglect seeps through in this slightly longer silence. "You haven't returned my calls."

"Honey, I'm swamped." Two new columns to write before Tai reappears. "Having lunch at my desk. Can this wait until evening?"

"You said you'd be available last weekend to help me. Lucy, Amanda and I were sampling dishes from three caterers. I sent you times and directions."

"Oops!" I search my mind for a memory of that promise. Lately I'm having trouble concentrating. Just now the sight of a bit of wilted spinach stuck in the corner of the plastic lid covering my lunch salad sidetracks me. It looks too much like a squashed bug for my touchy stomach to deal with. I shove the salad aside.

"Mom?"

"I'm sorry, Dal. I thought my presence was optional since Lucy and Amanda were there to help." Lucy is the wedding coordinator and, I suspect, the main reason for my daughter's heightened state of alarm these days. Amanda is Dallas's best friend and maid of honor. "I went to Atlantic City."

"Really?" Suddenly there's butterscotch in my daughter's tone. "Another weekend with Dad?"

"No." Why Jacob told her about our getaway weekend I'll never know. His response is in the opened manila envelope lying at the corner of my desk—which I'm left to deliver. "It's official, Dallas. The papers came today. The divorce is final."

"Oh."

After a year I still haven't found a way to speak without wincing to my grown children about the implosion of their parents' marriage. "I'm sorry."

"Don't worry, Mom." Her tone is now empathetic, solicitous. Got to admire her variety of emotions, as well as the whiplash shift of them. "He's not serious about the divorce. There isn't even another woman. I checked."

"You *what?*"

"Nothing as demeaning as a private detective." She goes on as if my squawk of disapproval has no merit. "There are signs, if you know how to look for them. Be patient. Men get stupid at your age. I sent Dad several books on the subject. I know he's read them because I asked questions. It's just taking longer than I expected for him to admit he made a mistake."

"You could try to get him on *Dr. Phil,*" I offer in annoyance.

"Thought of that." She didn't skip a beat! "But as you know, one of his sponsors has a contract with our agency."

I can't count the ways I'm appalled by the last minute of this conversation. I almost feel sorry for Jacob. No wonder he spilled our beans. He must have felt against the ropes with a daughter who never pulls emotional punches in the clinch. With a writer for a wife he had something of a chance. Sometimes I need a week to perfect the perfect comeback.

"So, Dal, about the caterer—"

"A complete fiasco. Lucy asked for the unpredictable, and what do we get...?"

Dallas is a marketing dynamo at McCann Erickson. A force of nature, according to her boss. Fast on her feet, never at a loss for words. With bonuses, she makes in a month what I not so long ago made a year. Thanks to Lucy, the wedding coordinator, Dallas was encouraged to approach her wedding with a fervor heretofore reserved for a really big client. I fault media with their constant barrage of high-end celebrity knot-tying, those *Good-Morning-America* weddings designed by online voters, and cable wedding shows starring ordinary people who want, for once in their lives, to be the stars in their own Blockbuster moment. But Dallas, who is usually a sensible person, has allowed her natural competitiveness to be overlaid by a kind of giddy neurotic enthusiasm one usually sees only in Oscar nominees.

For weeks last fall, my desk was regularly papered with Polaroids of her posed in every high-end wedding gown available in the tri-state area. Once I made the mistake of asking the price of a particular confection. While I recovered from a near swoon, she stood over me with the look of a disgruntled five-year-old. "I'm paying," she said when my eyeballs stopped rolling around.

"Everyone will be looking at me," is her strongest argument anytime I try to insert a vein of reality into the white-fondant monstrosity that threatens to be her wedding day.

So, I listen to the disaster of pairing asparagus au gratin with spinach pesto—who knew?—and why ancho chilies in raspberry infusion won't work as a dressing for both cold salmon and grilled tuna, and cluck in sympathy. I keep telling myself if I offer no opinion, advice or help, I cannot be held accountable for the outcome.

"By the way, Dad's going to Kosovo for a few weeks. I'm sure that when he gets back he'll have a different perspective on things." Finally Dallas takes a breath.

I guess this is as good a time as any to mention my own plans. "I'm going to put the house on the market."

"Going to or have?" The professional is back.

"We already discussed this."

"But you promised you'd think about it. Do nothing rash."

I love my daughter dearly, but her parents' divorce has completely undermined her opinion of us as wise and mature beings. We failed to hold up our end of her need for us to exist as a united example of wedded bliss and traditional family structure on the eve of her own foray into eternal commitment. My motives are all suspect.

"No matter what, Dallas, your dad and I will walk down the aisle hand in hand on your wedding day." That is usually the mollifying statement in these conversations.

"There's one other thing, Mom."

Time makes my mom nerve endings tingle. The sensation is usually a prelude to news that has included such things as, "The kitchen is on fire," "The dog ran into the street," and "How was I to know he wouldn't see the car parked there?"

"Stephen's mother has a really good friend, Mrs. Lakewood—practically family. She wants to throw a party for the mother of the groom and her friends the week before the wedding."

"You're concerned that I'll be offended if I'm not included. Don't be."

"You are, Mom. It's a sort of spa day."

"You mean I am invited, but it's going to cost me a fortune to get a pedicure?"

"I'll cover the expense. It's a Botox party."

Now I read the paper, watch TV, and magazines are my life, but I still have to ask, "What, exactly, do you mean?"

"Mrs. Lakewood thought it would be fun to go as a group and get a 'freshening up' before the big day. Everybody's doing it. Since the injections last three or four months, she's alerting the invitees well in advance, in case they already have a schedule with their own doctors. That way, they can pace themselves if they want to be included."

"In the stick-me-in-the-face-with-poison party?"

"See, I knew how you would react. I'll decline for you."

"No, no, this is my day for just such invitations." I begin to stutter with the laughter bubbling up within me. "I—I must get a better bathroom mirror."

Long silence. "There is one other, small thing."

"Optional chemical peels?"

"Do you know anyone who might give them a good deal on a group rate?"

"Dallas, why would you think I would even know a Botox doctor?"

"I didn't," she admits. "Still, you *are* in the image business."

"I'm in the business of aging gracefully." I glance up at the door, half expecting to see Tai standing there with a sneer on her face. "For the time being."

"Well, it was just a thought."

After we hang up, I stare at the salad I don't want, and wonder why I ordered it. Yet I know the answer.

As contemptuous as I am of Tai's opinion that the pursuit of ageless longevity is a valuable use of one's time, energies and money, a tiny bit of me would like to know what it's like to live in a body like Tai's.

Not worth thinking about! You have to be born that long and lean, with a bird-size rib cage and knees two-thirds up your legs. No amount of salads will buy me back a single worn-out cell. It will keep those still operating working awhile longer.

I reach for the plastic box, rip off the lid and toss it into the wastebasket without glancing again at the suspect splat. At my age it's about not giving up ground recklessly.

"Whatever happened to pedicure parties?" I murmur to myself.

The moment the words are out, I shove the question-able salad out of my sight and turn to my computer. There's a column in that thought. Even an old-school feminist can appreciate shell-pink toes!

About 2:00 p.m. a pale face topped by a thatch of dyed-black hair pokes in through my doorway. "Grab a cup below?"

I nod and wave him off as I am inputting the final para-graph of my new column.

Curran MacAdoo is the only full-time staff photogra-pher, and male, at *Five-O*. For major photo layouts we hire out. He does the day-to-day and in-office photos. This is only a phase for him, he assures me. Curran has a master's in fine art from the University of Iowa. He abhors gloss work, on principle. Yet New York City is an irresistible lure to certain psyches. Women's-magazine work across the Hudson was as close as he could come on a first try.

He's been here a total of nine months, trying his damnedest to develop an urban veneer. The learning curve has been steep. He lost a camera, a bike and a gold-fish his first week on the East Coast. Now he locks up everything, even to take out the trash.

I warn him that it takes longer than that for Iowa to wear off. After fifteen years in New Jersey, I still often feel like a Virginian interloper. At least he gave up trying to sound like outtakes from *The Sopranos.*

"There really is a mafia in New Jersey," he confided after a scary run-in with a neighbor not long after he arrived. I related my experience when we moved here. We were told that while trash pickup is private, you couldn't hire any service but the one the "organization" has assigned to your neighborhood. Just to test it out, Jacob called another service. We were told not to call there again. He was impressed. Me, too. Forget the Christmas envelope and you will pick up your own trash *twice* for months, once inside the house, once outside.

When I show up in the bagel shop ten minutes later, Curran pops up from his chair and fans a pair of tickets before my eyes. "*Belle Du Jour!* Catherine Deneuve. Treat me nice and one of these could be yours."

"How nice?" I offer him my best imitation of a come-hither glance, which always cracks him up. I think it's embarrassment, but he laughs it off as a joke.

He tucks his angular body back into a narrow chair. Long and thin as a coat hanger in black jeans and T, he reminds me of a raven given a spin in the blender. Odd bits of gelled and feathered black hair stick out from his head. He uses black mascara to make his red eyebrows and eyelashes match to achieve his current Goth look.

The ever-present camera bag slung over his shoulder betrays his profession. Otherwise he could be mistaken for a high school dropout.

"So, Ms. Tallulah, you ready to get your party on for Saturday night?"

Now I have to back up a sec. Yes, my given name is Tallulah. And, yes, it does make one wonder why a loving mother would name her only daughter after a drinking, drugging, foul-mouthed southern diva known for her notorious nymphomaniac, bisexual excesses.

Mom loved Tallulah Bankhead from the moment she saw her in *The Little Foxes* on stage at the National Theater during her first trip to Manhattan. Even critics hailed Miss Bankhead's performance. Mom was only thirteen. What she saw and what she's always believed was that Tallulah was a role model, the first woman in her experience to be more than a match for the three men in her life. In 1940, that was an admirable trait. Consequently, she never believed, when she was old enough to finally hear the lurid gossip, tales of the dissolute hellion Tallulah really was.

"Celebrity gossip," she would say with dismissive certainty. "Stars have to keep their names in the public eye."

At fifteen, I fully realized the implication of the mantle I had inherited when a want-to-be boyfriend offered me gin and a joint, because he thought that was how to lure me into sex. When I refused to participate, his taunts went from "*Lu*-sen up!" to "*Lu*-natic" to the standard from my elementary school days, "*Lu*-ser!" I pointed out to my mother—after she'd repeated the celebrity-gossip bit—that Tallulah could have opened orphanages or backed a Children's Hospital if she wanted publicity. She was a slut, and I hated my name.

Mom broke into tears. What's a dutiful daughter to do? I looked up the origin of the name, certain it was made up. Surprise! *Talula* is Choctaw for *leaping spring,* the joyous sound of running water meant to gladden a saddened heart. It was 1969. Cher, part Cherokee, was famous—for the first time. A Native American name I could live with. I told Mom this, and we both felt better.

Which brings me back to the present. Only Curran is allowed to use my full name. Not even Jacob had that privilege, unconditionally. It requires too much explanation at a simple meeting of strangers, who never allow the name to pass unquestioned. In public, Jacob uses Lu. Lu doesn't require a dossier.

Why Curran? Because we share a passion for black-and-white photography, old movies and Catherine Deneuve films. A name like Tallulah was bound to have some repercussions. It could have been much worse.

"Mocha cappuccino with whipped cream, and an onion bagel with a smear. No lunch," I add for Curran's benefit. Then I stifle a yawn.

"You're not sleeping well?" He looks concerned. He's appointed himself guardian, of sorts. Doesn't think much of "any man who'd walk out on a fine woman like you." As I said, I like Curran. But I suspect his attachment to me has more to do with the fact that, poor as he is, most young women won't give him the time of day. I'm a substitute gal pal until he finds true bohemian love.

"I sleep fine," I assure him. "I took a nap before lunch."

He reaches for his camera. "Mind if I take a few shots?"

I shrug and reach for my bagel. Curran has a serious shutterbug jones. Any excuse, and he's snapping photos. I'm one of his models because he says I don't pose. That I allow this invasion of my down time is another reason I'm his favorite of the moment.

"Yeah!" he says to himself as his camera whirs with the automatic advance. "We could do some serious work, some respectable work."

"We?" This sounds more like "werror" because I have a mouthful.

He pauses to grin at me over the top of his camera. "Older women, they're, like, amazing. My favorite fantasy is an hour alone with Isabelle Huppert or our Catherine—and my camera. Try to squeeze into a single frame the lives they've lived. Cannot be done, Jack! Only collage can capture the elusive essence of a mature woman."

I smile, nod and swallow. "Too bad our new boss doesn't share your view."

"I heard about the makeover. Bummer about the outcome. But Tai said I'd be doing some real honest photography for a change."

I pause in mid-sip of my cappuccino. "You've been talking with Tai?"

He lowers his camera and reaches for his latte with skim milk. "Offered me a job, extra pay, a full layout."

"Doing…?"

"You." The vivid blush that washes through his face is enough to embarrass me, too.

"She told you about her proposition to me?" Why are we suddenly speaking in suggestive language?

"Bummer about the outcome." He's repeating. Young men have a very limited vocabulary for disappointment. "After all that work, your face won't have any genuine character. But think of the 'before' images? A record of the real you! I'll do you very Georgia O'Keeffe. Stark lighting. Facial lines etched by shadow into dry riverbeds. Lids like awnings. Sweet!"

"No." His unique perspective of my "maturity" may be a compliment, but I can't dredge up any enthusiasm for the project as a whole. "I'm not undergoing any reconstruction that involves scalpels and collagen."

"Good on you!" Curran can't keep his cool when he's excited. "Screw it! I don't need a new Nikon macro lens or a shearling coat or even a twelve-speed bike."

"That's not on par with Grandma needs an operation," I deadpan.

He grins. "Can't fault a guy for trying. I mean, I think you're beautiful just as you are. But let me mourn a moment my fifty-Benjamin high."

"Tai offered you a five-thousand-dollar bonus for before-and-after photos of me?"

"If she liked them. But, like, what's not to like? Right?"

It's not that I don't think Curran could produce pictures worth the money. But I was once a reporter, a real newspaper reporter, and I smell a rat. Tai obviously isn't just waiting for me to think over her idea. She's hedging her bet. Offering Curran the opportunity to have a spread in a major magazine! She's working on him, so he'll work on me. And, of course, that makes me the villain if I nix his dream. But how did she know Curran and I are friends?

That woman's dangerous.

"What's wrong with Dallas?"

My conversations with my son have no preamble. I sit up on the sofa where I fell asleep in front of the evening news. "PMS."

"Oh." Davin is not big on discussions of "girl" things.

"Premarital syndrome, Davin."

It takes him so long I begin to wonder about my darling boy before he breaks into a snicker. "Pre-*marital* syndrome. Good one, Mom!"

That's my boy!

"Look, Dal called me, and while I don't give a flying f— Well, anyway, who cares about asparagus au gratin?"

"You won't be required to eat it." I glance at the clock. It's half past seven. I was out cold.

"Listen, Mom, the thing is, you can't sell the house. Dad loves that house. He'll eventually get tired of apartment life. Then he'll want to come home."

"I suppose I should be thrilled with the thought your dad might resettle for me if I come with the house of his dreams."

"You're getting weird on me, Mom."

"No, Davin. Groggy."

"You've been drinking?"

"Sleepy. I fell asleep."

"Unassisted?" Really, where did my children get this idea that I can't function without supervision?

"I'm clean and sober. I'm not suicidal or despairing or

even deep-down hurt about the divorce decree, Davin. All I need is time to figure out the shape of my immediate future and a nap. Preferably in reverse order."

"You sound okay to me." This was in doubt? "Dal says you're not yourself."

"Have you done your laundry this week? Finished your paper for Black Studies? Told Angie you need your space?"

He chuckles. "You're fine. Got to run. Love you."

"Me, too."

3

"If I agree to change my column, won't I be caving in, folding my tent, reneging on a principle—"

"Bending over and taking it?" Andrea suggests this as she picks her way through a bin of Villeroy & Boch ramekins at the Liberty Village Outlet Mall in Flemington.

"You know I hate male-inspired homophobic expressions."

Andrea pauses in her count of ramekins. "'S'cuse me, Ms. PC."

"You're right. That was an absolutely bitchy thing to say."

"Can I say amen without you blowing your whistle again?"

Andrea Fábregas-Prem is half Puerto Rican and half Thai. Thanks to a childhood in Brooklyn, she's all urban sass. And gorgeous. Not tiny gorgeous. She's got more curves than rigatoni pasta. Then there's that Asian-Carib salsa-slide to her walk. Men literally trip over their feet when she walks by. I'm never bored in her company.

"2005 is the Year of Me," she announced in January.

At thirty-eight, she's dedicatedly single and totally self-absorbed, except when it comes to her family and friends. Which is not to say she isn't looking for Mr. Right. There are just so many clauses in her personal prenup that no mere mortal man could ever hope to pass the inspection. She owns three weighty engagement rings but never had a groom. "The price of taking up my time," she'll proudly say as she displays one.

She's also the closest thing I have to an unconflicted ally.

Other friends have studiously avoided the Nichols clan while we divvied up our marriage. Who wants to get caught backing the wrong party? Andrea knows Jacob by sight. She never chose to improve on that level of acquaintance, which makes her invaluable to me these days.

"I say, take Ms. Leigh up on her offer. Did you see what they did for that woman with the split lip on *Extreme Makeover?*"

I shudder, remembering the too-graphic operating-room footage. "It's one thing to correct a deformity. Another to believe that one less wrinkle in your eyelid or abdomen will make you a better person. That's so shallow."

"But that's me. *Muy somera!*"

We both laugh. I've known Andrea since she bought a huge fixer-upper in Upper Montclair five years ago. Years earlier, Jacob and I had settled on a less-expensive proposition a few blocks away. We met when she stopped to ask who was repointing our chimney. When I told her the cost, she exploded in a combination of Spanish and Thai that did not need translation. After that, we swapped numbers and comments on the various contractors who poured in a steady stream in and out of our lives. Jacob always went with the cheapest bid. Andrea taught me how to get the best cheaply, a notable distinction.

That's why I'm spending my free Friday two hours from home, strolling through outlet stores in the central part of the state. She needs a matching set of ramekins for her Easter soufflés. There are closer outlets but Andrea says it's worth the drive. I wanted company—this the price of hers.

Andrea is a corporate attorney, the first person in her extended family to finish college. Her separate journey began after she won a regional spelling bee at age twelve. Her intellect attracted the attention of two benefactors who wanted to help an inner-city child. Andrea parlayed that interest into college tuition at Columbia, and then Yale Law School. She is grateful, but proud of her achievements. She once told me, "I needed a leg up, not a handout. After tuition and books, I paid my own way."

She worked as a cook while in college, then as a caterer throughout law school. She calls her method Thai-ribbean cuisine. My favorite is her black beans with ginger and lemongrass and just enough chilies to make the top of my head sweat.

She is all business when she needs to be. The rest of the time, she plays hard. On summer weekends the neighborhood vibrates with the sounds of her Brooklyn family on holiday in the Garden State. They earn their keep. Uncles, brothers, cousins and nephews build, repair and refinish. Sisters, aunts and nieces sew, paint, reupholster and plaster. Her place now looks like one of those chi-chi B and Bs. During the winter months, she lays out a monthly spread for a select group, sumptuous enough to satisfy the snootiest gourmand. As a result she's the A-list hostess in our area, knows everyone. But she's no fool. Complain about her exuberant relatives in July, you will not be sitting down to beluga with lime as a first course in December.

"My folks are in the restaurant business," was all she said as she offered blue-point oysters on the half shell or fresh sockeye salmon in mid-January.

"Mafioso," Jacob often murmured.

I don't know if there's a Puerto Rican Mafia, let alone a Thai one. I rather suspect she's got connections in the restaurant business. I do know she can make a dollar go farther than a Sosa home run. Thrift and extravagance, she makes it work.

While she pays for two dozen pieces of matching porcelain at fifty percent off retail, I wander out into the crisp afternoon air and over to a village shop window displaying shoes. All my shoes have shrunk. Right now even my Keds feel like vises gripping my toes. I have gained five pounds. Unaccounted for. Where was the wanton abandon to calories that's supposed to accompany unwanted weight?

A sharp pain twinges in my left shoulder as I heave a shopping bag full of Andrea's other purchases onto a nearby bench. A hand from behind snags my purse strap as it slips from my shoulder toward the ground.

"You're losing something."

I turn my head in reflex annoyance at a stranger's daring and meet the nicest smile I've seen in a while. My frown softens into a flirtatious smile. "Thanks."

He nods. "You're welcome, ma'am."

Ma'am? And he isn't even that young. Thirty-five or six?

"Same thing happened to my sister last year," Andrea responds when told of the incident a few minutes later over lunch. She dips her goat cheese and tomato wrap into pesto sauce and takes a healthy bite. Sustenance for the drive home. "Face it, you could be going through the change. That'll make *men's* interest *pause* before it gets to you."

Andrea can be so reassuring.

"Out of luck and soon to be out of work. Story of my new life." I sip my chai tea. Food seems suddenly to come only in varieties of greasy, smelly or green.

"So, you're serious? This is a moral issue for you?"

"I'm willing to do a lot for a job but that doesn't include mutilating my body for column inches. Tai made it clear at her first editorial meeting yesterday, it's her way or the highway."

"*Phom/di-chan sia jai ka.*"

Andrea is frowning, but that's not why she has my full attention. She doesn't know much Thai. Her father didn't think it was useful for an American girl. For her to pull it out now means she has something serious on her mind.

"I got to say this, Lu. You look bad. I mean, I know you, right? We're tight. You can take a truth. You look beat down, girl."

"I'm just tired."

"You slept all the way out here." She leans in for a closer look. "Maybe you need to see a doctor."

This kinda shakes me up. Andrea is a strict believer in herbal remedies. "You don't approve of physicians."

"That's me. You're a Western medicine baby. You got to go with what you know."

I glance down at my watch and remember I have a date. "Are we done here?"

Andrea puts her hand on my arm to stop me collecting things. "Got to give you credit, Lu. You handled yourself beautifully during the divorce. But even stone will crack, put under enough pressure." She pauses for emphasis, black eyes wide with compassion. "You need to take time off."

"That bad, huh?"

She sighs and nods.

"I can't just take a holiday. Tai might discover how dispensable I am."

"That's just when you gotta disappear. Let her know you're not afraid of her."

"But I am. I desperately need this job."

Andrea doesn't believe in microexpressions. When she's emotionally involved her whole body gets a workout. She throws up a French-manicured hand and rolls her head back on her neck. "Then get your belly suctioned and stop complaining. Or tell this Tai woman to kiss your ass-sets, and then make sure the door doesn't smack you in the behind on your way out. Either way you gonna lose something. Oh-kaaay?"

No wonder she's an attorney. Andrea does have a way with words.

"I'm sorry, Cy."

"Not half as sorry as I am. But I understand."

I've taken the cowardly way out, calling instead of knocking on my neighbor's door. "It's just that I'm bushed. Maybe I'm coming down with something. Wouldn't want to expose you."

"I should be so lucky, catching something from a pretty girl at my age."

If you ever need a pick-me-up, try Cy Schelgel. "Can I have a rain check?"

"I'll have to check my schedule."

"You're a sweetheart."

"Tell all your friends, the single pretty ones."

"Thanks."

"Lu, you need anything tonight, anything at all. Even in the middle of the night. I'm here. Now, lock up tight."

I hang up feeling worse, if possible, than after my conversation with Andrea. I know how much Cy looks forward to our monthly outings. He probably got a haircut today and his shoes shined in town.

Cy is my neighbor and movie companion since shortly after his wife died three years ago. We have a standing date, third Friday of the month. Amazingly, it was Jacob's idea. Cy's seventy-two, the semiretired owner of a prestigious architectural firm that still benefits from his name on the door. He and his wife always went to the movies on Sunday afternoons, until she became too ill. After Esther's death, Cy became all but a recluse. His children tried to pry him loose from his home, but he wouldn't budge. Then they sicced the grandkids on him.

One day, after yet another trip to Six Flags Great Adventure, Cy confided to Jacob, "I get lonely but I'm too old to date. And I feel foolish squiring my granddaughter to dinner. What's an old man to do?"

I could rarely drag Jacob to the cinema, but he thought me going with Cy would be okay. And that's how it began.

Since Jacob left, Cy offers me financial advice in exchange for homemade pie. He says his wife—God rest her soul—never mastered the knack of flaky pastry. My maternal grandmother thought no woman was complete without the skill. He likes apple, peach, cherry and blueberry. But when I want to make his day I make lemon meringue. I owe him one for tonight. I'm just too tired to nod off in a dark theater.

As I slip a spoon into the double-fudge-brownie sundae I picked up on the way home from Andrea's, I wonder where I could afford to go for a week to rest. There is the possibility of just staying here, pretending to be out of town. But no, that would worry Cy. If I curled up in my house and didn't come out, he would have the volunteer emergency squad over here after three days to break in and save me, sure I'd had some sort of collapse.

As I suck creamy goo off the end of a plastic spoon I realize that I'm eating something I never eat—ice cream. And chocolate. I looove chocolate. But as the saying goes, might as well apply it directly to my thighs. Tonight I didn't hesitate when I saw the option. So much for the intention of buying a grilled chicken sandwich.

I pull my feet up on the sofa and take another bite. Heaven.

A cheap vacation means family. If I call my mother I'll have to explain things. Lots of things. Dallas gets her interrogation tactics from Mother. She loves me, worries about me. I need a not-worried person in my corner.

Aunt Marvelle! The French say Mar-*velle*. I've always called her Marvel, like the comic books. Aunt Marvelle lives on eastern Long Island. She wouldn't think of prying into my life. She's too busy living her own.

4

"I don't want an old man. They smell. Yes, they do. They don't bathe, don't change their drawers. All they see when they look at a woman is a cook and a nurse!"

Marvelle Harrington flashes a toothy seventy-five-year-old smile. Her jewelry, a combination of gold charms and diamond tennis bracelets, jangles as she reaches for her martini. "You get to my age, you look for some fun! Someone who can take you places. Dancing."

"That's right." Cleo Watley nods her perfectly coiffed head. "I'm not interested in caretaking some old fart."

"And about all that farting." Grace Clifford frowns. "What is that radioactive stuff they produce? Turns my rooms blue."

Jane Simmons wags her finger. "If you want companionship, you should try a senior cruise."

"I never would do that." Marvelle turns to me. "Last time I was down in Florida, Jane talked me into going to a dance at an assisted-living residence. But the only people dancing were women with women. They got all dressed up to dance with one another! What men there were were sitting in their chairs. When I walked in, a pair of old souls, trying to be gentlemen, started to get up. Now, I said, 'Don't get up. That's all right. I'm just passing by.' But they were bound and determined. Lu, I had to stop and pat my foot it took them so long. Creaky old men! What am I supposed to do with a man who can't even get out of a chair?"

I'm halfway through my second martini and more than silly with laughter. It feels good, really good to laugh. Aunt Marvelle lives the life of a merry widow, together with a few select friends. For the last six days I've been their guest and their audience.

Cleo sniffs. "Never go to an old folks home. All they do is talk about their ailments."

Marvelle nods vigorously. "And who died."

"I don't want to talk about illness." Grace gives an olive on a toothpick a ride through her martini. "They're half dead, but then we all are. What's to talk about?" Said olive disappears between her coral lips.

We are holding forth before the fireplace near the bar of Maryjanes, an East Hampton restaurant, at two in the afternoon. Ladies in their seventies and eighties don't go out much after dark. It's April, but there are enough fur coats present to keep an Eskimo family happy through a winter. Spring is being coy on the eastern end of Long Island.

"You're so lucky," Jane says with a wink at me. "You're still young. You have plenty of time for love."

My smile curls sheepishly when I realize all eyes have turned to me. After only a week in the company of women a generation older, I feel practically like a teenager. This is my going-home party. Tomorrow I return to my real life.

"Jane's right." Grace smiles benevolently at me. "You're pretty, too. You'll have many lovers. But you may find you're happier single."

"Speaking of single. Did you see Nicole on *Entertainment Tonight?* All splayed fingers and awkward schoolgirl gestures." Cleo waves her hands about to demonstrate her point. "Someone should tell her she's too old for that giggly sex-kitten act."

"Meg Ryan, too." Marvelle nods. "Used to like her but she seems stuck in adolescence."

"And, really, has Goldie looked in the mirror lately? There's more collagen in her lips than in her bustline."

"She never married that guy, right?" Jane chuckles. "Better than a divorce, like Nicole."

"Now see, I disagree." Marvelle is in her element. "Tom walking out was the best thing could have happened to her. Look how her career took off. A bad divorce is sometimes better than a good marriage, if you ask me."

"Maybe. So what about Demi? What happened there?"

"Oh, she acted a fool. Now she's gone and got a full-body makeover—and a young lover. Didn't recognize her on the *Tonight Show.*"

My aunt and her friends discuss movie stars and other celebrities as if they knew them personally, and as if I should.

"So, then, you don't think I should have a little work done?"

"Work done?" Grace looks at Marvelle. "Does she mean surgery?"

"Your aunt was talking about stars. You're not a star," Jane answers. "You've still got your looks, mostly."

Marvelle nods vigorously. "I told Lu, join a gym and hire a personal trainer. A male personal trainer. A female, with her perk young butt, will only make you mad, but a male trainer will get you to try things the wildest night of passion wouldn't."

"Tight is better than skinny." Cleo pats her firm round cheeks for emphasis. "Lose too much weight after forty, you will sag. Wrinkles are worse than pounds. Take Meryl Streep and Susan Sarandon. They're aging beautifully. Contrary to what you read in women's magazines, men don't mind a few pounds. Means you're real."

"And most probably cook!"

"Not that again!"

I laugh and reach for the last of the plump pearly oysters on the half shell we ordered. It goes down cool and salty-sweet.

A waiter approaches, deftly catches my eye and offers a smile meant just for me. "You'd like something more?"

His name's Kiri. He's Serbian. He's got dark and dangerous eyes and a mischievous smile. I'm smitten, for the afternoon.

Grace has noticed our flirtation and leans forward when he's gone with our lunch orders. "Don't be taken in by these local fellows. Any man available this time of year has less than two nickels to rub together. Or he's married. Hausfrau in the old country."

"That's a truth." Marvelle drains her glass. "Charm is cheap!"

Each of them has buried at least one husband. Only Jane first lost hers to a younger woman, eight years ago. When the time came to bury him last year, Wife Number Two came to Jane for help. Aunt Marvelle told me the story the day I arrived.

"She didn't know Bruce was Episcopalian. Didn't know his favorite flower. Didn't even know what family he had left. That man-stealer had run through his money, and didn't know his brother's name! Jane said she realized then that she'd had her revenge on Bruce since he left, only she didn't know it. Of course, Jane saw to it Bruce was buried properly. Said it was the least she could do since her children bear his name."

But this is not a bitter group of women. They appreciate life in a way that is rare. They live it, day by day.

The noise in my own head has subsided in their company. And I've made a few plans.

Later, when Aunt Marvelle and I have returned to her house, I decide it's time we talked. "I am going to sell my house."

"Oh no, Tallulah." Marvelle looks stricken. "Not your lovely house."

"It's too much house for one."

"But the children?"

"Dallas is living with friends. She and Stephen have found a place to live after the wedding. Davin didn't spend but six weeks at home after his freshman year. He's already got a lead on a job in the Catskills for this summer. He'll be home even less."

"There's something you're not telling me. But that's fine."

Aunt Marvelle doesn't have to pry. After five days in her company I want to come clean.

"Jacob and I don't want the children to know. But the months he was out of a job took a toll on our savings that we haven't been able to recoup, thanks to the stock market. Davin is only halfway through school, and we don't want to have to pull him out. But tuition has to come from somewhere. Jacob gave me the house with the understanding that if it became necessary I'd sell."

"And?"

"My job is in jeopardy."

Marvelle smiles. "So, come and live with me."

I smile but shake my head. "I'd be a drag on your social life."

Marvelle shrugs. "I'm about to tell you this because I don't want you to make the same kind of mistake. I was fond of Jacob. But my fondness stopped the day he walked out. I'm through with him! Don't let a man who hurt you come back. That's what happened to Jane.

"Bruce led her a merry dance! Ever since they met in

college. Could have married half a dozen times, good men, too, with nice jobs. But Jane was a fool for Bruce. And didn't he marry twice before he offered for her hand? She was thirty-five, almost too late for her to have children. Should have heard what her father had to say about that! Bruce was not husband material. We all tried to tell her he'd break her heart. But then… There're a lot of ways to go to the devil."

I can't argue with that.

In the distance, I hear faint sounds of waves lapping the shore of the harbor. We are sitting on the small patio of Aunt Marvelle's modest bungalow, one of many in the beachfront community of Azurest. Built half a century ago as a summer retreat, this Sag Harbor community has become the retirement place of Marvelle's Marvelous Matrons, as I've dubbed them. The interior furnishings are Danish modern, circa 1950s, a bit worn but more than serviceable. Not much has changed. Amazing to think a house could remain essentially the same for what is my lifetime.

All at once I want to cry. Nothing in my life will ever have this kind of permanence. I envy the Marvelous Matrons the continuity of their lives.

"I may not do anything about the house for a few months. We'll see. But it's April and prime selling time. I can't wait long."

"That disposes of the house and the children. What is in your future?"

I blink hard. Aunt Marvelle doesn't approve of emotions on display. "Oh, I don't know. A dalliance with a gigolo?"

"Serbian waiters are for women of a certain age. You are too young."

My face creases into a wide smile. "I came here feeling a hundred."

"Pooh! Nothing some color in your hair won't put

right. The salt air is good for you. Stay another week and you will have your choice of men, good men. City men."

A hiccup escapes me. And then another. The pitch from the pleasant dizziness of the afternoon into the maudlin affairs of my future has taken a sickly turn. "I think…I think…I'm going to be sick!"

"I don't need a doctor. It was the martinis. Or the oysters." Just the thought of them makes me wobble as I'm sitting cross-legged in bed.

"You look about as green as a scallion. You were up three times at night, heaving and retching. I counted."

Aunt Marvelle is right. Now the sky is a washed-out pinky gray. I feel about the same, clammy and sticky besides.

"I'm calling my clinic, soon as they open. They know me—they'll work you in."

"No, really, I'll see my own doctor if I'm still sick when I get home."

Aunt Marvelle gives me a look that would back down a drill sergeant. "You think you can drive three hours when you can hardly walk a straight line to the bathroom? I'm driving you to the clinic."

I want to protest, but I've gotten a whiff of bacon. Who's cooking pork at this hour? It's enough to send me sprinting again for the porcelain throne, though there's nothing left to come up, unless my toenails count.

5

The waiting-room walls at the Bridgehampton Geriatric Clinic are a warm, inviting coral. Roman shades are raised to matching height so as not to disturb a mind that has substituted compulsion for neatness. Brass rails at chair level steady a hesitant step and prevent a stumble. The playful sound of a waterfall soothes with the universal code among mammals: this is a life-giving oasis. The tightly woven carpet with bold shell designs won't snag a walker, wheelchair or heel. It takes only a moment to realize that the coral scallops lead to the receptionist's station, the turquoise whelks to the door to the examining rooms and the gold starfish to the handicap rest rooms. "Helpful hints" for the faulty memory.

No wonder Aunt Marvelle dropped me off out front as if I were a dope delivery. I'm sure the car did not come to a full stop. She knew what I would find inside those deceptively benign double doors.

Some are Fifth Avenue habitués. Others are clearly blue-collar townspeople in stretch tops and pants, gimme caps and jeans. I'm mildly surprised at this mix-and-match patient list in an area of Long Island known above all else for its class distinctions. I recognize a couple of those high-profile profiles. Rene Panek, the writer who's been working on a follow-up to his Pulitzer Prize play for, what, eight years now? And there's Jaime Kronenfeld, the Manhattan restaurant maven. Three seats away sits the owner of Aunt Marvelle's favorite Chinese take-away place. Same business, worlds apart.

Then I realize that they have something in common. In one form or another, the illness of decay has brought them together.

"I distinctly said, not before noon!" A wizened woman in a Chanel suit waves a gnarled hand weighted with a yellow-stone ring the size of a doorknob at the uniformed chauffeur who has just entered. "Noon!"

All eyes turn instinctively to the wall clock, the size of a harvest moon. It is 11:57 a.m. The townies snigger and exchange knowing glances. The upper crust continues conversing in voices that carry their requisite name-dropping.

The door to the office interior opens and a spry gentleman in a gray suit with green bow tie hobbles out, a grin shoving his trim white mustache up to his nose. "Polyps are gone!" he announces to the room.

I recall what the Marvelous Matrons said about growing old. *"We're all half dead. What's there to talk about?"* Plenty, it seems.

During the hour and a half I've waited, I've heard more than anyone should about impacted bowels, drained abscesses and shunts. There has been plenty of time to notice other things, too. Like the fact that a good face-lift can make Ms. Kronenfeld appear astonishingly youthful, until you glance at her hands. They are like chicken feet, the creped skin shrink-wrapped to ropy blue veins and knotty joints.

I shift uncomfortably in my seat. I can't shake the reality of looking my future in the face. The journey from thirty, the real age of modern adulthood, to fifty was a luge ride of excitement and achievement. Fifty to seventy looks more like downhill skiing. Even if one manages to maneuver past the tree line and boulders of injury or wipeout, the reward is the bottom of the valley. Is Tai right, that we should fight aging with every yellowing tooth and nail? Or is my mood just the result of a lousy oyster?

The doorway to the doctors' inner sanctum opens again. This time two people are framed there, a nurse and a doctor.

Now I remember why a part of my brain thought this might not be a totally terrible experience. Dr. William Templeton.

Aunt Marvelle swears he single-handedly pulled her through her heart attack. I was there and know it took a handful of specialists to do the job. Yet Dr. Templeton made it his business to come see her every day she was in the hospital, to answer any of her questions and concerns. By the end of the week, the Marvelous Matrons were timing their visits to his. What I remember best about him is that no matter how outrageously they flirted, trying to tease out details about the private man, he humored them without revealing a thing. Except that he was married.

Now, wait. What was Aunt Marvelle saying about him on the ride over? Things were still touch and go with my stomach.

Oh, yes.

"William's had a lot of tragedy in his young life. That pretty wife of his was killed in a boating accident last year. Then his only child, a lovely girl, married a hellion, one of the townies. Poor sweet man. He keeps it all to himself. You know how people like to talk. We'd know otherwise. Stoic, that's what he is."

He doesn't look stoic to me. In fact he looks really good, better than I remember. Big and solid with an easy grin and a hint of gray at his temples—exactly the sort of smart mature man a *Five-O* woman would have a lech for.

When he finishes conversing with her, the nurse turns back to the waiting room and briskly inquires, "Mrs. Nichols?"

Another half hour drags by while I sit in a paper robe and nothing else, in a space the temperature of a meat locker.

A quick knock and then the door opens with the briskness of a man on a mission. "Hello, Mrs. Nichols. Long time no see."

Yes, that's the voice, the gentle baritone that says everything's going to be all right. Close up he's even more attractive. And it's not just because he remembers me.

"Hello, Dr. Templeton."

He smiles. "How are you?"

"Pretty well." Better by the second.

"And your children. You have two, right?"

Oh, this man is unbelievable. Or, he actually read the paperwork I filled out before he came in.

"Yes, Dallas and Davin. And you, a daughter, right?"

He nods. "Married last year." I don't detect a single trace of emotion other than fatherly pride. That's nice.

"Dallas is getting married, in September."

"You and your husband must be very proud."

"We are. Separately."

He lifts a brow.

"Common story. Divorce." Oh, damn! Now he'll think I'm coming on to him. "How's your wife?"

His fractional start is enough to ignite a furious blush that stings my face. "Oh, that's right. Aunt Marvelle told me. I'm so sorry."

"Thank you." That is a period to a subject if I ever heard one!

He must be still grieving. Of course he is. He's left-handed, and his wedding band can't be missed as he flips open the chart he carries. "Why don't you tell me what's wrong today?"

I go through my complaints and then answer questions about my medical history, repeating most of what's on the form in his possession. He stops me occasionally to ask a question, really listening to the answers. He's got a big head, a strong, wide face like a lion or a bull that seems to demand one's full attention. He's also got brown eyes, and a nose that's pitched slightly to the right, a sign that it was once broken.

While answering, I try not to think about the fact that he is going to examine me. For while I know he's free and I'm free, it's still not okay to let him know where my way-ward thoughts are taking me. This is a professional situation. I don't usually react this way to men, even handsome, flattering ones.

At last he puts the chart aside. "Why don't we take a look?"

"I always get a bit nervous in an examining room." I need a cover story for when he listens to my heart. "Probably why my blood pressure's up."

He *umm-hmms* me and, as the nurse enters, sets to work examining me.

The natural reserve of the physician is in place when he returns to the room after the preliminary exam. He's holding the same clipboard. I try not to notice his hands. I've just banished the sensation of those warm fingers gently probing my abdomen. But the look on his face makes me take a deep breath. Something is not right.

"There's a problem?" I can't take the suspense.

"Not at all." He looks at the board again and then at

me, a bemused expression on his face. "I haven't had a chance to say this since I left general practice. Congratulations, Mrs. Nichols, you're pregnant!"

"I'm *what?*" It's a reflexive answer. Then I start to laugh. "Good one. You had me going."

He tilts his head to one side, watching me. "I assure you, I would not kid you on such a matter."

I start to speak but suddenly I can't think of any words. Instead, laughter yowls forth from my open mouth; it's loud and off-key, like a cat pulled backward through a screen door. I don't blame him for the half step back. Me? Pregnant? Funniest line I've heard since…since…

Gulping air, I try for control. "Jacob's gone. Walked out a year ago. The divorce was final a week ago. So you see, it's not possible."

He frowns and strokes his upper lip with thumb and forefinger. "I don't know quite what to tell you, Mrs. Nichols."

Mrs. Nichols! *Mrs.* Nichols! The appellation mocks me. I'm not Mrs. anybody anymore.

Then it hits me. The awful truth! Morning sickness and the overpowering sleepiness. My last period was in January. Sex for the very last time, February!

I don't cry often. I'm terrible at it. But the laughter is gone and tears are rising fast. "But I can't be pregnant! I can't!"

He breaks into a tolerant smile. "I assure you, you can be."

"No, you don't understand." Awful, lurching panic seizes me. "Yesterday. At lunch. It was at a going-away party. I drank three mar-*tinis!*" I'm so ashamed, but I can't stop myself. "Oh! And I ate raw oysters. There's the potential for botulism poison. *Ohhh!* Poor pickled poisoned baby!"

I'm crying, in open-mouthed gulps. Tears race down my face and dribble onto my chest. A reasonable person would back off from the rabid-dog image I invoke.

Dr. Templeton does the most extraordinary thing. He plucks several tissues from a box and begins dabbing at my chin. Mortified, I snatch them from him and try to muffle my crying.

To his everlasting credit, he smiles and opens his arms.

To my everlasting shame, I go into them and sob until his green lab coat has a three-inch soggy patch just above his name tag.

"Feeling better?"

"Quite. Thank you."

When I ran out of tears, Dr. Templeton left me to dress and collect myself. Then a nurse led me to his private office, a woman of my years whose manner told me she knows all too well what's wrong with me. I've had a strong cup of real coffee while I wait. Now he's here, smiling that imperturbable smile.

As I perch on the edge of the chair before his desk, I am so sober and self-contained my eyes ache, and my head feels so hot and tight it may explode.

"I'm very sorry for my earlier behavior. Truly. I can't think—" Well, maybe I can. "I am deeply embarrassed."

"Don't be." He sits down and leans forward, the desk safely between his fresh lab coat and me. "I understand how this news could come as a shock…at this time."

"You mean because I'm about to be fifty."

He takes his time. "Among other things. Yes. It's rare but not unprecedented."

"You've had other cases?" Okay, the "fool factor" may be mitigated if he delivers this kind of news occasionally to other hysterical women.

But instead of an easy reply, he blushes beneath his cedar tan. I wonder what accounts for that particular shade? Italian? Jewish? Portuguese? "Actually, we don't see cases of this kind here. Collapsed uteruses, yes. Ripe ones, no." His smile edges back. "To be perfectly frank, Mrs.

Nichols, I had to send across the street to the pharmacy for a pregnancy-test kit."

"One of those over-the-counter do-it-yourself job-bies?" I can just imagine what the nurse had to say about that errand!

He nods. "We're not equipped here for that sort of test-ing."

"So you could be wrong." Lifeline, thank you! "This isn't your field. It could be a false positive. A menopausal thing." That last statement drives me to my feet, giddy with the possibility.

"See a specialist." His expression is meant to be reas-suring as he stands and offers to shake my hand. But the tender amusement playing at the edges of his smile says he knows he's right.

If so, I'm screwed. Twice.

6

It's Sunday evening. I sit on the edge of my garden tub amid the crumpled boxes and paraphernalia of pregnancy kits. The line, the stripes and a window with *Yes* in some cheerful script have all looked out at me with proof. The "EPT"—evidence proven true—of my indiscretion makes it "ClearBlue Easy" to see now that the "First Response" of my libido should never have been "Answer"-ed. I am preggers.

The image of myself in the wall of mirrors above the vanity is of a woman deflated. Her shoulders are hunched into a spine curled in defeat. Her hair— I look as if I'm wearing a skunk that's been run over. While I don't quite qualify as Amazonian, I stand five nine in my bare feet. The scale will say I'm twenty-five pounds overweight. Dressed as I am in oversize gray sweats, it looks like more. Okay, it was thirty pounds before permanent morning sickness set in. I'm sallow. Looking at me I now understand what that word means. A bloodless beige. Even my lips, one of my better facial features, look drawn and pale.

It's as if I'm staring at a very old Polaroid, fading before my eyes.

I keep picturing Dr. Templeton's sweet-sad expression as I left his inner office, as if he wanted to tell me that everything would be all right. But he knows better. No matter the outcome, a certain amount of damage has been done, if only to my sense of how the world should work. The good doctor might never know squat about my future, but he knows it won't be quite as simple as before.

Aunt Marvelle was suspicious of my bloodshot eyes and quivering lip, but she didn't say a thing when I told her the diagnosis was bad shellfish. As quickly as I could, I loaded up my car and headed into the sunset of New York City-bound traffic on Friday afternoon.

Then the real torture began. Every thought in my head was a double-entendre or pun. Even with my fertile imagination I could barely conceive the truth of what I'd been told. One thought begot another. The crawling highway traffic mocked my efforts to outdistance the news that had been delivered. Like how I'd been laboring under the false assumption that the menopause stork was on my doorstep. I jammed one of Davin's forgotten CDs, by Run DMC, into the player just to stop the noise in my head. But when they began singing "Walk This Way," I envisioned a line of ninth-month mothers-to-be, waddling like fattened Christmas geese through the aisles of Toys "R" Us.

And yet, between the fits of fear and disbelief that have accompanied my discovery, and every sane argument against it, I keep finding myself inexplicably smiling.

Pregnant! A new life. The beginning of something wondrous, and enormous, and special! Who would have thought this was an option at my age? Fie on Tai's opinion of me as in need of drastic measures to stall my slide down into doddering wrinklehood. The fertility goddess has winked at me!

And then reality slaps me like a wet mackerel in the face. Pregnant. Babies. Diapers. Midnight feedings. Diapers. Colic. Croup. Diapers.

Okay, I'm smart enough to know the difference between being pregnant and having a baby. At best, a significant portion of the treacherous territory of the first three months of pregnancy still lies ahead. I don't need a doctor to tell me that, at my age, the chances of losing the pregnancy are high.

I suppose I should take Dr. Templeton's advice and see a specialist.

I feel sick again. It's not hormonal this time. Of all of events of the past two and a half months, two of the ten minutes I'd most like to take back are those at the Bridgehampton Geriatric Clinic. The other eight? What else?

The first attractive man I encounter as a single woman, and what do I do? Come to him with the news I'm pregnant, blurt out what sounds like a lurid lifestyle to explain it, and then do a bimbo number by crying about it on his shirtfront. Where was that accumulated sophistication of fifty years of living that should have allowed me to merely lift an eyebrow at the startling news, then shrug it off with a enigmatic, "Do tell?"

He might have thought I was mysterious or coy. He didn't have to know I was so pathetically foolish as to give my ex a clear parting shot at me, so to speak.

Jacob. No. I can't even think about that conversation just yet. First, I need to know how deep I'm in. And what this means.

The math is easy. Acted a fool in February. It's April. Seven weeks, two days, and two hours into the gestational period—give or take seventy-two hours. Sometimes the details matter. I need information, from a reliable source. Google!

I rush to my computer and type in the most obvious search: Late-Life Pregnancy.

Okay, I'm now officially freaked. The first site that comes up is a notice about how couples will have to agree to sterilization if they want to be cohabitants because some health-care facilities can't be responsible for the complications of "late-life pregnancy."

I didn't know there were such places with such rules, or that people would agree to them in exchange for a place to stay. But as my mother likes to say about any idiot-sounding offer, they must have some takers or they wouldn't be advertising it.

It's pretty much downhill after that.

"You look so good I don't know what! And who's lost a few pounds?" Babs is eyeing me with motherly pride as the rest of the staff within hearing distance looks up with smiles or smirks. She shoots up alongside me, her motorized vehicle purring. "Didn't I say what a week at the shore would do for you?"

"You were right." That and the one-hundred-and-forty-five-dollar color job I had yesterday instead of showing up for work. My gray is now cellophaned in shades of almond, toffee and butterscotch. I feel like a very expensive candy bar.

Babs's gaze lingers, searching, then she smiles. "That's a new skirt."

"I thought I needed an update. Like it?"

She nods. As I said, The Radish doesn't miss much. She knows that I know we're talking about my hair, but Babs is old school. The only woman who mentions in public the dye job of another is your mortal enemy.

I do feel better. I don't know why I ever hesitated with the hair color. It's nothing dramatic, but the face that looked back in the mirror this morning seems younger, more vivid. More like me. The faded Lu has retreated, for the moment.

As for the pounds, I've been on a saltine-and-herbal-tea diet for the past four days, that and big, fat prenatal vitamins Dr. Templeton prescribed for me until I could see an ob-gyn. Could the pills be any bigger? The one this morning turned sideways in my throat. I thought I'd have to give myself the Heimlich maneuver before it dislodged. Even then, with the coating dissolved, it scraped down my esophagus like a Roto-Rooter tool. I soothed the raw feeling with live-culture organic yogurt. Thankfully it all stayed down.

The vitamins are just a precaution. It's clear to me after a weekend on the Web reading about my "condition" that nothing need be done, as it is more than likely to resolve itself any day now. I've waded through case histories of women in their thirties and forties who went to incredible lengths to conceive, and lost. I feel chastised and grateful all over again to have two children of my own.

By comparison, Dallas and Davin were a breeze, only the usual pregnancy stomach heaves, and first-trimester migraines with Davin. But I was still practically a kid myself. *Strong as an ox,* as my grandmother fondly called my statuesque physique. This is entirely new territory.

In fact, at my age I'm an anomaly at seven weeks and counting. I don't need to think about a baby. I'm too old to sustain one. This pregnancy is a passing fancy.

To be honest, I'm relieved.

After all, it isn't as if I'd been on any special regimen like those women a decade or three younger than I am are admonished to begin months before they try to conceive. Since Jacob left, good nutrition and I have also been estranged. I'm not physically prepared to carry a child. Mother Nature has been temporarily fooled. And you know what they say about fooling Mother Nature.

I will do nothing harmful—drinking and shellfish are two of the items off my diet for the time being. Yet there's no sense in preparing myself psychologically for the nearly impossible—that I will remain gestational. Soon, this will be one of those memories one doesn't share, even with a best friend.

I stop short at my office door. Well, what was my office. It now looks like the warehouse of a cosmetics company. Boxes are piled knee-high on the floor and chest high on my desk, bearing names like Body Bistro, Aveeno, Clinique, Botanicals and a dozen other names less familiar but obviously pricey.

"We've been busy in your absence."

I'm beginning to hate the way Tai appears like a hologram in my life. This time she's materialized just behind me, wearing a thigh-high shift embroidered and beaded in a vaguely ethnic pattern. "You're just in time for the editorial meeting."

It's clear from the opening comments that the editorial staff has as many concerns about this change of approach at *Five-O* as I do.

"I've been canvassing a focus group," says Rhonda, our style editor. "Long-time subscribers say they stay with *Five-O* because we've made them comfortable with who they are."

"We can always strive to be better," Tai answers matter-of-factly.

"If we go all *Lucky* on them at once, they will scatter," predicts Crescentmoon, our resident aging hippie and health editor. Her impressive silver-fox ponytail reaches down to the middle of her back. She can still tuck her ankles behind her ears, and cuss like a drill sergeant. But most of the time, she speaks in the soft, measured tones of a young girl. "We've been in service to our readership's desires. We must not now appear critical of their choices."

"Easing the passage of maturity is our mission," adds our beauty editor, and youngest staff member, KaZi. At twenty-seven, KaZi's already had a varied and successful career. Assisting her father, a leading Broadway makeup artist, she's helped make up most of the stars over forty treading the boards today. She has a gift of making complexions look—dare I say it—younger. Why she insists on the Kabuki look for herself, I'll never know. The orange-sherbet hair is cute, though.

"In these tight times, with pensions and IRAs drying up faster than a box of prunes, we should be pushing the new economics of aging," declares Gwendolyn, our financial columnist, and occasional business-and-finance feature writer. With her tied-back brindle dreads, she looks more like Toni Morrison than Toni herself. She's just as unapologetic about her opinions. She's got the financial chops to back it up. She came over last year from *Fortune* as a bridge to her own retirement from the magazine business, and stayed. Even Tai realizes how lucky we are to have her.

"Give me six ideas on how to rebuild a broken nest egg," Tai responds quickly. "I'm looking for a year-long approach to re-solvency."

"I did get a request for another article about older women with much younger men. It's been two years." Rhonda chuckles. "I, of course, volunteer for the research."

Crescentmoon nods. "And more on sexual preferences of the mature. So long as it's not a crass 'Sex In Senior City' type article." I smile at her because that's the title of a tongue-in-cheek article I wrote my first year here.

There's a mocking glint in Tai's gaze as she turns to me. "What do you think?"

"Great ideas."

Her gaze narrows. "You've done your hair. I wish you'd consulted us first. And, there's something else different." Her smile widens. "You went to a fat farm!"

It isn't that I want to dislike Tai. She just makes it so damn easy. Too easy. However, I'm still employed here, and I'm not giving her an excuse to make it otherwise.

It strikes me that those boxes in my office of night cream, moisturizers and retinin-based refreshers could mean that Tai has changed her mind about the slice-and-dice approach to a new me.

"Might we consider a less-extreme approach to the 'New Lu' idea?" I ask.

"Let's call it a soft start." She actually looks pleased. "Once we can satisfy our readership that there is only so much repair cosmetic care can accomplish, we'll proceed as planned. Go through the boxes in your office. Take your pick of as many as you like. Use them for thirty days. Keep strict records of when and how much you use, and the results, if any. Your opinion of these restorative products will be the first 'New Lu' column. Meanwhile, begin doing profiles of women who've had the procedures you are considering, ones who are satisfied with the results."

I can't resist. "Do you know that forty-four percent of cosmetic surgeries are performed on people thirty-five to fifty, but only five percent on people sixty-five or older? Our audience begins at fifty."

"That says to me they've just given up." Tai's eyes pop wide. "And that we at *Five-O* need to do a bit of cheerleading."

I give up.

Tai issues several other quick assignments, including both suggestions by Rhonda and Crescentmoon.

"I want the August issue to premier our new outlook." Tai says this when everyone is looking validated. Expressions quickly shift to panic-stricken.

"We usually begin work five, even six months ahead on special issues," Crescentmoon reminds her. "The organic dynamic is better if unforced."

Tai nods. "It's a lot, and time is short. But I have every

confidence that each of you will do your part. Am I right?"

Who's going to risk a job in this market by objecting?

Finally Tai turns her attention to the far end of the table, and smiles at the lone male in the room. "Curran's been waiting for Lu's return so he can take 'before' shots. I hope you're ready to shoot today."

"Most def!" Curran grins at me.

"Lu?" I meet Tai's tropical gaze dead on a second time. "Wish you'd waited on the tan and hair but…" The sigh that launched a thousand snide remarks. "Check your date book. You have an evaluation appointment at one-thirty with Rodrigo."

I don't have to ask who Rodrigo is.

"Lucky bitch!" Rhonda whispers, and pats me on the back as the meeting breaks up.

Rodrigo is the owner of the gym upstairs. When it first opened, the unmarried staff of *Five-O* used to take turns leaving the building when we saw him coming up the street to work. Whatever the weather, he walks to work. That way, each of them would have a chance to bump into him in the hallway or on the stairs. He never takes the elevator. He's not bulked up the way body builders used to be. He's lean with Lance Armstrong calves, and gluts as tight as those imported cigars that are said to burn forever. He's also married, with a wife who looks like Penélope Cruz, and two bambinos who are miniatures of their parents.

"By the way, your little vacation has agreed with you." Tai smiles as if it's a bit of an effort, and moves quickly past me and out the boardroom door. "Babs!" She sounds efficient and annoyed as she moves down the hall.

Rodrigo and me. The absence of caffeine in my new morning routine makes me sit down with a little thump when I reach my office.

I wait thirty whole seconds, watching the sweep of the

hand on my desk clock, before I pick up the phone and ask Babs to connect me with Rodrigo's.

"Yes, a spring cold." I pinch my nose for a congested affect. "The seasonal swing in temperature gets me every time. Heavy clothing, really? Denies the body healthy circulation and sunlight. Who knew? Vitamin C, one thousand milligrams? And B$_{12}$? Hold on, I'm making a note. Yes, thank you, Rodrigo. I'll call when I'm better. Oh, and can this be our little secret? Tai is anxious for me to start. I wouldn't want her to think I'm not equal to the task. She asked you for weekly updates on my performance? You can tell her I won't release them for thirty days." That should buy me a few days. "Oh, you're a doll. Bye, Rodrigo."

Meanwhile, I try out a few of these beauty remedies. I select a box at random and pull out a blue pearlized tube. The going price in retail for this three-eighths-of-an-ounce serum is a cool one hundred and thirty dollars. But free to me! Now that's an assignment I can handle.

Tai signed off on Curran's desire to use black-and-white film, mostly because he convinced her that it would compensate for my newly acquired tan.

Curran is standing over me, adjusting what seems like a full set of interrogation spotlights placed in sunflower array.

I reach up to swipe away a drop of perspiration. "I'll be done in thirty minutes, if you baste me."

"Too hot, huh?" He flips a switch, which douses most of the wattage. They will flash as he clicks, now that he has them set up correctly.

I feel pretty silly, sitting in a pair of gym shorts, for comfort, and an off-the-shoulder portrait top Curran says he found in a flea market.

"It makes for a retro forties *Photoplay* look," he assures me.

"I'm not that old," I grouse.

Acting as his assistant, KaZi has used body foundation to even out the tan lines on my shoulders from my swimsuit. My hair, usually worn loose and wavy, has been pulled back into soft poufs on either side of my face, held with big tortoiseshell combs. In place of lipstick she's dabbed baby oil. A little more on my cheekbones and eyelids. "Except for two applications of mascara, that's it," KaZi says.

"Stay natural," Curran has kept repeating under his breath.

We begin with classic poses. Chin not quite resting on the back of a lifted hand. The lean-in pose in three-quarters profile, eyes gazing upward. Full-face smile. No smile. Head down slightly, to the side, pensive. "Think Bette! Veronica! Marlene!" he encourages.

Again and again, we move through the repertoire in Curran's mind as he changes cameras, changes lenses, dancing around me as if I were a block of marble whose grain he is trying to memorize. Ten, fifteen minutes tick by as I'm repositioned, tugged and tucked. Then another set begins. Another break for prop changes, a genuine cashmere shawl, and then still more shots. Curran's burning up film like a pro. I hope Tai bankrolled him.

The weight of the last few days drops back on me from nowhere.

Suddenly I feel like crying. Tension trembles my chin. The torque of will on muscles pulls the corners of my mouth down. I shut my eyes against the flash of lights. Try to shut out Curran's elated, "Yeah. Yeah. You're doing great, Lu. *Ms.* Tallulah! Head back. That's it. Think profile. Neck. Ah! Sweet!"

This is so foolish, unnecessary, so ridiculous. As if I will really go through with this. Any of this!

All at once my eyes open, and I turn my head to say something unkind when the strobe lights catch me completely unready.

"That's a wrap." Curran lowers his camera, grinning like

a kid who's just won his first applecart derby. "You were great." He pats his camera.

I'm gaping like a fish jerked out of water. "I—I don't think I can—"

"We need dinner. Cuban!" Curran says with all certainty that his twentysomething stomach is cast-iron reliable. He glances at KaZi, who's slim as a reed in funky capris and a shapeless vest that still manages to convey that she's not wearing a bra, and possibly needs one. "Want to come?"

"You paying?" KaZi's standard comments to Curran are always framed as a challenge. I suspect she likes him.

The tips of Curran's ears turn a painful pink. He's broke.

"On me," I say. Someone may as well enjoy a meal.

Later, in bed with a carton of Healthy Choice ice cream, and wondering at what point in its consumption does it become an unhealthy choice, I ponder my day. I've lied, cheated, pretended and cried in the shower, and it's only Tuesday. At this rate I won't make it through the week on my own.

I reach for the phone. Who can I call?

Halfway through dialing Jacob's number, I realize I truly do not want to speak to him. I hang up and reach for the TV remote.

Ingrid is telling Cary how she doesn't need him in her life anymore. She's married now to Claude Raines. She's fine—better than fine. Any fool can see she's lying. But he's a man, and he hears what he needs to hear so that he can leave her to her fate.

Sometimes a woman is better off alone with her own thoughts.

May

Women know that passion doesn't end with aging.
So why sit around fanning and thinking,
wouldn't it be nice if...?
That heat from within will smother you if you try too hard to resist.

—"Late-Life Sex and Then Some"
CUE LU!

7

Two weeks and nothing.

My skin is creamier. I've had my pores vacuumed, helped by the array of new night-and-day and in-between creams I'm using. From now on, a monthly facial will be part of my routine. And I've decided I should exercise. Nothing stressful. I looked it up on the Internet. Doctors recommend something easy for pregnant women, like a beginner's yoga class.

"Have you ever done yoga?" Andrea asks this in a tone that suggests I know nothing of what I'm getting myself into. I've brought her along for moral support. Besides, it was my turn to pick our outing.

"Sure. About fifteen years ago." For eight weeks, before life took over and yoga went the way of many things in a working mother's world. Since then, I've tried lots of different exercise classes. But I suffer from interest fatigue. It doesn't take long for me to tire of the same old thing.

"You don't want to do this." Andrea's voice drops to a conspirator's murmur as she leans toward me. "Trust me.

Laura Castoro

Yoga looks pretty but it can destroy your soul." Some moral support.

We have our rolled rubber mats slung over our backs, as do all the women and a few men in the line inching its way down a narrow corridor toward the designated classroom. Andrea is wearing a fuchsia sports bra, and black shorts that make the most of her dimensions in that area. J. Lo would be proud. I have a turquoise T over my bra and stretchy ankle-length yoga pants.

"Think of the alternatives." She leans in. "We could be sitting in a bistro, saluting the demise of a pail of mussels in butter and broth with shots of vodka."

Pregnant women shouldn't eat a lot of shellfish, I remind myself. Out of the side of my mouth, I say, "The last shellfish-and-alcohol combination made me sick."

"Then barbecued lamb riblets and lemonade," the serpent in my ear suggests. "We don't even have to turn around. Just slow down, let these people flow around us. Then, when we're at the back of the line, we'll turn and make a break for it!"

"You said you'd be my ally in this."

"I thought you meant something reasonable. I took yoga for one whole summer in Bombay." She rolls her eyes. "It messes with your moral compass."

I turn resolutely away from my tempter. "I am here to learn, to relax, to find inner pe—"

Andrea shoves me from behind so hard that I involuntarily step on the heel of the person in front of me. He turns, frowning. He's tall and tanned, with streaked blond cornrowed hair. His T-shirt reads Saint Barnabas Medical Trauma Unit.

"Sorry," I say.

"You okay?" he asks.

"Oh, she's fine. Hi." Andrea says. "You come here often?" That's when I realize that I was her excuse to speak to him.

"No, first time." He nods at the young woman standing in front of him. "Deb says it's good for tension. Thought I'd try." He shrugs manly shoulders. But what registers with me most is that he seems young enough to be my son. I can't help it. I see possibilities of my child-who-probably-won't-be everywhere. The suspense of the inevitable collapse of that possibility is killing me.

"Let's compare notes afterward." Andrea is a woman with no fear of rejection. Why should she?

He nods. "Cool."

The breathing part seems easy enough.

I start to lose consciousness before I realize that while all this fresh air might be good for the body, the brain takes a nap when thoroughly fumigated with oxygen. Lulled by vaguely Indian-sounding chimes and gongs played at low volume for atmosphere, my "Tree of Life" pretty soon looks like a sapling caught in a stiff breeze. I weave, sway, my head bobbing back and forth between my arms like a Hindu dancer's. Finally, it's landing gear down before I topple.

Our instructor has already told us that there is no such thing as perfection in yoga. We are to do what we can. That to strive is to lose the purpose. Every effort is its own reward. Hmm. Yoga is not a competition or an exertion in achievement, but a ritual attempt to effect peace, each in our own way. Yeah. Right.

My "Rising Cat" and "Descending Dog" poses remind me of how long it's been since the illustrations in the "Karma Sutra" looked like a fun time.

Midway through the class, I leave the "Warrior" pose for one that has me with my legs so wide open that, when I bend forward and down, the top of my head nearly touches the floor. This is my singular moment of vile western-influenced sense of achievement. Who knew such things were still possible?

As we are gazing inward, each through our own "Arch of Life"—my description—I begin to hear the labored breath of a fellow straddler. I try to orient myself, upside down. The source of great distress comes from over my left shoulder, upside down. If I were upright, it would be facing forward to my left. That's where Andrea placed her mat. Deep, sudden intakes of air increase in volume, like someone is going under water repeatedly. No one else says a thing. I hear desperation in that heaving. I can't stand it. I think, Andrea's having a heart attack!

I arch up and put a palm flat on the floor to steady myself as I seek her out.

But Andrea is not the gasper. She's gazing at me through her spread legs with a big fat grin on her face. Okay, my need to mother is satisfied. Some other neophyte yoga student is on her own.

By the end of the hour, I'm so tired I don't uncoil with the rest of the class. I sit slumped for a full minute while mats are rolled and eager acolytes gather around our instructor to question the specifics of a pose. Finally I lift my head, proud just to have survived what looked simple enough. Andrea's right. My poise and ego will never be the same.

Our instructor is back on her mat, demonstrating a maneuver that draws sighs of approval from her students.

"Double-jointed ho!"

Andrea has this trick of being able to throw her voice. Those nearest her turn in the opposite direction to glance in disapproval at a sweet young thing in a red thong. Only I see Andrea's wicked grin as she comes toward me.

Andrea, beautiful even with her face oiled in sweat, helps me to my feet then hands me a towel. "Did you hear that breathing in class?"

I nod, toweling off sweat that feels like cold cream on my skin. "I thought it was you, having a heart attack."

"Girl, it was Dr. Yummy!" She jerks her head toward

the sculpted medicine man. "That was worth the price of admission."

I smile, too. To think he could be in such good shape, and yet lose control of his breathing at the moment of my personal triumph. Maybe there's hope for me yet. I wink at Andrea. "Want to come again on Tuesday?"

"Wouldn't miss it. But first I'll see if he needs a little mouth to mouth."

She's back in two minutes, rolling her eyes. "Medical resident. Can you imagine his loans? It'll be years before he's in my league." Andrea doesn't do poor.

"I got to think of my future. I am an example for my family," she once said to me. "We need to start trading up, and staying up. Sex is fine, in its place. Mergeable assets are essential."

The first time I heard Andrea speak like this, I thought she was a little cold-blooded. But I've since heard enough stories of her childhood, growing up poor with both immigrant and minority situations to deal with, to sympathize with her attitude. What's that saying about money? It doesn't guarantee happiness, but it sure makes a nice cushion for the bumps and scrapes of life.

"Now can we eat?"

"I don't think I'll be going back to yoga."

"Why not?" Andrea is sitting behind a vegetarian Thai salad stacked like a beehive. "Who knew it would be a place to pick up men?" Andrea charged on, answering her own question. "Women, of course. Natalie says gyms are better places for picking up women than men. Uncle Tito would disagree." Andrea has a bisexual female cousin and a gay uncle. I have yet to see any situation stump her for long.

I fork several pieces of baby spinach and munch a few moments. "I'm not looking to pick up anything anytime soon."

"You say that now. But once you realize that the men you see are all fair game—" she pauses to glance around, as if to show me how easy it all is "—you'll soon be feeling twenty years old all over again." Every man in the bistro does seem to be aware of her presence. She starts doing the cha-cha in her seat. "You gotta get your groove on, girl!"

I spear a grape tomato. "I'm afraid that's already happened."

Andrea stops chewing bean sprouts. "Get out! Who was it?"

"That's not important." I contemplate the idea of a tomato the size of a Thompson grape and wonder if this qualifies as a genuine agricultural achievement. It sure tastes good. "What's important is that I'm not going to be doing any more screwing around anytime soon."

"You screwed him?" Andrea's face brightens up. "You didn't even say you were dating."

"I'm not." I give her a quick glance.

"A one-night stand? *Mi'ja,* you got to be careful with that."

"Wish I'd talked it over with you first."

"That bad, huh?"

"The worst. I'm pregnant."

It just comes out. I guess I was dying to say the words out loud to someone.

"What would you do if this happened to you?"

"It wouldn't."

"But what if…?"

"It wouldn't."

C'mon.

"*Dios!* Okay." Andrea takes a breath, the usual indication that her considerable brainpower is kicking into fifth gear. "First I'd track down the soon-to-be-unemployed pharmacist who sold me the defective birth-control patch. Then I'd find out the brand of the condom that went wrong. Then I'd inform my partner that he has bills coming due from a doctor of my choice. Meanwhile I'd line up one of those sleazy no-payment-till-we-win-the-case-type attorneys to sue the pharmaceutical company, the condom manufacturer and the sperm donor for reckless disregard for my health and extreme mental anguish. After that, I guess I could retire to San Juan to write the novel I carry around in my head."

My mind boggles at her ability to home in on the essentials. "A condom."

"You did use a condom, right?" Andrea is watching me like a hawk.

Now, why didn't I think of that? Because I'm a married—ex-married woman who hasn't had to think of that particular accessory since...

"I've been on the pill. So when my doctor suggested that I give my body a rest last year due to what we thought were premenopausal signals, I didn't hesitate. Jacob had already walked out. My next scheduled checkup—jeez, it's next week!—we are supposed to discuss hormone patches, not birth-control patches. I'm turning fifty next month, for crissakes."

"Lu! You didn't use protection?" Andrea is getting agitated, which means she's using her hands to talk. "I mean, forget getting pregnant. A man who takes a woman to bed just like that, he's going to be doing a lot of screwing around."

"I don't think so."

"You better believe it. So what, you've been married more than half your life. You've got to know STD and HIV aren't cable stations."

I reach for my yogurt smoothie and take a long pull on the straw. Nothing. A blueberry is caught inside. I shove it away. Here's the harder admission. "I know this guy. Really well."

"That's what all nice women think."

"No, really, *reeeally* well."

I've finally managed to shock Andrea. "You've been sleeping with your ex!" I shush her. She doesn't shush. "What were you thinking?"

"Remember the weekend getaway? Well, one thing led to another."

"Uh-huh." Andrea is waiting for the lead-in that will be worth the punch line that's already been delivered.

I stare at her for a second and see only a beautiful brilliant younger woman who, if I wasn't such a balanced person most of the time, I could dislike with jealous intensity. Two men in the booth across from us have taken turns staring at her while the other one talks. Andrea is aware but she doesn't play up to them. She's such a guy-magnet she takes it in stride. A woman like her cannot imagine the thoughts of an average middle-aged female. Sex for the very last time will occur to her about five minutes after she's inside the Pearly Gates. But we are friends, because Andrea sees no difference between us.

That complete faith in her sparks the truth. "I was thinking it might be the last sex I will ever have. Did you know that I have a better chance of being struck by lightning than meeting another seriously-interested-in-fifty-year-old-me male?

"That's some WASPy *menudo!* You believe that? Look at you. Any man here would be glad to take you to bed." I know she means well, but she's in her "Your Honor" mode, and her delivering voice has half the diners staring in our direction.

"Thanks."

"No, let me prove it." Andrea gets up and walks over to the two guys in the booth who grow tremendous grins at her approach. She puts a hand on the shoulder of the lucky one, then aims a prosecutorial finger at me.

"Look at my friend. Doesn't she look like someone you could take to bed? I'm not suggesting you ask, you understand. This is a survey, so don't get any filthy ideas or nothing. I'm an attorney, so what you say can and will be used against you, if I have to. Now tell me, don't you think she's sexually attractive?"

The poor guys can't help giving the answer she wants to hear. "Sure. Sure!" they say, and glance at each other, then at the server who's come up behind Andrea holding a pitcher of water hoping, I suppose, that he has something useful to contribute.

"I'd do her!" a lanky, complexion-challenged youth calls from a back booth. His two friends hoot and stomp for emphasis.

"Thank you very much," I reply in a smothered tone as Andrea comes back to her chair. "Now I'll have to find a new place to get smoothies."

Andrea is unfazed. "I just want to prove a point to you. You can do better than Jacob Nichols."

"At the moment, I have other, more pressing issues."

It hits Andrea all over again. "*Dios!* What if he's been fooling around?"

"Jacob?" I had thought about that, a lot, during the first months he was gone. And then, well, I didn't see or hear anything that would seem to confirm it.

"You really think he'd go a year without? You know him better than I do."

"He went the last six months of our cohabiting without." He better have. "He's not dating anyone. Dallas checked." Who knew that would turn into a comforting thought?

Andrea shrugs. "A year is plenty of time for him to find a meaningless hump, or even pay for it. My cousin required only a weekend to get into trouble, when his wife was out of town last month. Lu, tell me you did think of that?"

"I'm beginning to believe I haven't had a rational thought in years."

"I could smack you around a little, if it would make you feel better. But, truly, you better see your doctor, *pronto!*"

"Any other advice?"

She nods. "Don't have it. That's what I'd do. But I'm not you."

"Meaning?"

"Meaning that if you're sentimental enough to forget to use protection, you're crazy enough to think this is your just deserts, and won't even ask Jacob to foot the bill."

"Well, of course not. I—"

"Or!" She knows how to break a train of thought. "You're hoping he will come running back on his own to cheerfully take care of the little baby you're going to provide as proof of his enduring *machismo.*"

The way she slurs that last word really hurts. "I didn't deliberately get pregnant." I'm whispering because the full company of diners now seems to think our conversation is open for public consumption. "It was an accident. Like a car wreck. With an ambulance and fire truck and everything. Okay?"

Andrea's beautiful face hardens in glorious disdain. "You're a fool. *Estupida!* You're lucky you got me for a friend because most people would just nod their heads a bit for your benefit, and then run out so they could talk about you behind your back. I'm talking to your front, Lu. *Estupida!* You hear me?"

"Conversation with you is always edifying."

But I know she's nearly as shocked as I was, am. Despite her spitfire delivery of abuse the look in her gaze is one of pained sympathy. Clear-eyed bias is her strong point.

I stare out the window for a long moment. "I didn't think of getting pregnant. The furthermost thought from my mind. You think it was an unconscious desire. It doesn't feel like that."

I look back at her. "It feels like I made a mistake."

Andrea shrugs. "All I can say is, with this divorce it's like you just got outta jail. Why go and commit another crime?"

"You mean by having a baby?"

"You catch on quick. Let's look at the facts." Up goes the first finger. "One, you are single. Single parenting is hard. Two, you're employed part-time. Even that income is in jeopardy because you have job issues with your boss. Three, you've earned some Me time. You're at an age when you should be taking long leisurely weekends in the country, curled up in a B and B canopy bed with a good book or a stack of DVDs or, let's be honest, a man who's your equal in intelligence and culture, and sexy as hell."

"I had visions of that, yes." Didn't know how it would happen, but a girl can dream.

Andrea throws up the hand she was counting with. "Do you see any of this happening if you're constantly on call to change stinky diapers, scoop pablum into a toothless mouth and walk the floor all night with a colicky baby?"

"Dallas and Davin were colic free. Mostly."

Andrea is unimpressed. "For the next three years you'll go everywhere burdened with diaper bags, bottles of formula, jars of baby food, car seats, strollers, sippy cups and the twenty-four-seven demands of a tiny tyrant. Do you remember Dallas at sixteen?"

I can't help but gasp.

Andrea nods. "That's what I'm talking about. This time you'll be sixty-six, Lu. Sixteen and sixty-six!"

Andrea attacks her salad with renewed vigor, chewing like a heavy-equipment grinder. It's easy to see this discussion is chafing her determination to never long be burdened by life's difficulties.

Her cell rings. She checks the number and smiles before answering. "Andrea, you got her. Yes. No, not tomorrow. No. No good. What about tonight? Isn't it? I'll meet you. Where? Ah, I like that place. Bye!" She grins. "Our doctor friend has the whole day off. Isn't that cute?"

"I thought you said he was a nonstarter?"

"It's a date, not a lifetime commitment."

I can't help it. She's mauled me pretty good. "Isn't he a little young?"

She arches a brow. "As long as you can reel them in, they're legal size." She has a point.

As we exit the restaurant a sudden cramp catches me down low. Could this be the beginning of the end? I feel a sickening lurch near my heart. Not morning sickness, but fear. Despite Andrea's reasoning, I'm not sure I want it to end like this. I slow my steps as my heartbeat accelerates.

Reluctant to put any strain on my lower back, I lower myself carefully into her car and lift my legs in one by one after me. Maybe that yoga class wasn't such a good idea. The seat belt now seems a hostile device so I slip my hand between it and me, and surreptitiously rub the stitch in my side.

Andrea laughs at one of her own remarks, throws the car into gear and pulls away from the curb as though she's been at a pit stop.

The ache quickly subsides. I don't feel any wetness in my panties as we zip along. But I'm brooding about what that pain could mean, only half listening to Andrea's speculations on how her date will be with Dr. Yummy.

Finally, even she notices. "I'm trying to keep it light, here. What? You don't look so good."

I meet her gaze, letting her see just how seriously unlight I feel. "Did you really mean it when you said you wouldn't have the baby?"

She shrugs. "I take care of business every time because I'm too shallow to deal with exactly what you're into. But you?" She shakes her head, her profile etched with impatience. "Do you believe everything I say?"

"Pretty much."

"*Dios!* You're really considering having it!"

She pulls into my driveway, leans back at an angle and folds her arms across her gorgeous bosom. "So, what are you going to do?"

"I don't know. See a doctor."

"Good." Andrea straightens up. "You call me after you do that, then we'll talk again."

Once in the house, I practically sprint into the bathroom to check on things. Nothing.

I'm so overwrought I slump down on the tile floor. After a moment, my eyes focus on the grout around the toilet bowl, which looks suspiciously mildewy. Soon, I'm on my knees with Jacob's old toothbrush and a spray bottle of bleach. I do this for me, for the unknown, for the future.

9

"Another vacation?" Cy frowns as he speaks.

"To work. I do my best work away from my desk. Friday gets me a start on a marathon work weekend."

"But why out of town?"

I shrug. "You know how it is."

He nods, his balding head peeking like a baby's bottom through the cotton fluff of his thinning hair. "Too many memories in the house."

"Yeah."

We've just been to see Harrison Ford's latest, not his greatest, movie. It doesn't matter. It's a warm mid-May evening. The lengthening of the days adds to my pleasure, for the sky is still violet at the western edge. We took in the 6:00 p.m. showing, and now amble up the block toward a local Italian place. A crowd is there ahead of us, waiting on the sidewalk.

"It's okay to go away." Cy shrugs. "Just don't hide."

"I'm not hiding from Tai." I've explained to him while

we waited for previews to start all about my new boss, and what Tai expects of me.

"I'm not talking about work. I'm talking about life." He jingles the change in his pocket with a hand, a sign that he's thinking deeply. "You need the company of a man."

I grab his arm and squeeze it. "I have the company of a man at this very moment."

He blushes, pleased. "Me, you don't have to worry about. My libido isn't dead, but these days my body doesn't often get the memo. You need the kind of man who can be trouble."

From anyone else, I would have a hot and ready answer to this "you just need a good screw" advice. But Cy means relationship trouble, not just a hot lick. "Maybe we should get more serious." I say this lightly as we come to a halt at the back of the line of patrons.

"Promises, she makes me." He winks at me. "At least I can take you out in public without my children squawking."

"I'll bet you can't say that about all your sweet young things."

The couple just ahead, clearly past forty and clearly working hard to keep that taut, overly tanned look of money, possibly just returned from a Miami holiday, turns to glance at us.

"It's not what you think," I say brightly, and cuddle closer to Cy. "It's September/November, not May/December love."

The woman gives me a quick smile that's more like a muscle tic. The man simply looks away.

"How is it you've remained single?" I lean in to Cy this time so I won't be overheard.

"Lucky for you, I am still single," he answers with a broad grin. "These days, who else can afford your tastes?"

He means my addiction to calzones. Since the morning sickness subsided, they're all I want. But the curious woman ahead of us half turns again before her companion says something under his breath that stalls her.

"You're just too generous—that's your greatest fault," I say a bit loudly, and then when she can't resist turning her head, I plant a big squeaky kiss on Cy's cheek. In flats, I top him by two inches.

"Don't I know you?" The woman's voice is a contralto with a dollop of cream as she smiles at Cy. "Of course, you're the architect! Schelgel, right? I'm Pam Jeffrey." When this doesn't get a reaction from Cy, she fakes hurt. "You don't remember me."

I'm getting all kinds of gold-digger vibes from her. The jewelry is a little too much for a New Jersey bistro on a Thursday night. Her makeup, done with an expert hand, creates a face she doesn't own. The possessive grip she's had on her companion until she recognizes Cy, a well-known rich prospect, slackens. "The autumn soiree benefit for the hospital last fall! You were with—" Her eyes cut my way. "Someone else."

"My daughter," Cy offers in what I know is perfect truth. I had the gig until I came down with the flu.

"You two married?" Cy inquires.

"Oh, no." She answers too quickly to be polite, a fact reflected in her companion's expression. To compensate, she pat-strokes his arm as if it's a lap dog. "This is Rick—Richard."

"How you doin'?" Rick-Richard is Jersey through and through.

Cy reluctantly shakes the hand he offers. When Pam offers hers, Cy says, "You should be married. You act married."

I laugh because I cannot help it. It infuriates the woman, amuses the guy, and Cy, well, Cy has started reading the menu posted in the outside window. "I've a taste for lamb," he says after a moment. "I hope it's nice and tender. I don't like mutton."

And that's why no one messes with Cy Schelgel.

Aunt Marvelle is in the city for the weekend. She and the Marvelous Matrons have tickets to Ralph Fiennes's latest foray onto Broadway. Then on Saturday they plan to hit the newest exhibition at the Guggenheim. Lunch at Café des Artistes, and then a jazz concert at Lincoln Center.

"I sure was glad to hear his name pronounced 'Ray-*ff*' because I surely would have thought his mother lacked sense, naming a boy that pretty some old ugly 'Rall-*ff*.' But you come on and use the place, anyway. You have a key and know where everything is."

I do. Including the ob-gyn clinic where I've made an appointment for 2:00 p.m. today. This time I used my own connections on the island and still had to wait nine days to be worked into a too-full schedule.

I wasn't about to see my own doctor. Not only because I'm likely to run into someone I know there, nor do I care what people say about the confidentiality of doctors, but because the nurses are a problem. I love Sue, Dr. Bernard's nurse, dearly. She talks to patients as though they are personal friends. And friends do discuss friends. I could about count the minutes from the time she learns I'm pregnant until I'll hear about it on the street. Didn't we all know that Joan Dawson had caught the clap before her straying husband learned he'd been busted? That's because Ellen Jenkins, the unofficial town crier for Upper Montclair, overheard Sue talking to the receptionist about Joan's situation as Ellen walked up. Next thing you know, we all know. Nurses can't keep a secret. Okay, so maybe most of them do, perhaps ninety-five percent. I can't afford to be outed by the leaky five percent. I'm going back out to the island to have the pregnancy confirmed. If Aunt Marvelle finds out, well, that's a chance I'm willing to take.

The bad thing about being worked in is that you get worked over first in the waiting room. No chatty elders this time. The ob-gyn shares waiting-room space with one other, and two pediatricians.

Over the next hour, it's clear that playing block-and-check with the preschool set is a young chick's game. Mothers are in constant motion while they wait to see the physician. The kids must all be here for wellness check-ups. I haven't seen so much unconstructive energy confined in a single space since I once wandered into the locker room of Davin's lacrosse team to bring the jersey he had forgotten. Though the waiting room does smell better.

When my name is finally called, I shake my head slightly and pick my way past children and strewn toys, heading for the peace and quiet of another meat-locker-temperature examining room.

I've heard the heart beat! It's strong and fast as a squirrel's! The image looks like a bigheaded shrimp in a blurry Jacques Cousteau film, but that's enough for me. I've met my child-to-be via sonogram.

"You are correct in your assumptions." Dr. Reynolds is curt, nothing touchy-feely in her approach. "You are approximately twelve weeks pregnant."

"Okay." I take a deep breath. It's official.

"This is an unnecessary risk to your health, at your age. You do understand that?"

With the help of the nurse I've levered myself into a sitting position. "Are you saying I'm not strong enough to bear a child?"

Dr. Reynolds looks impatient. "You may make it through the pregnancy with minimal effects, if you take excellent care of yourself. But you must consider the child, and the next ten or twenty years."

"You mean my life expectancy?"

She glances at me over the tops of her narrow-framed reading glasses "You'd be sixty-five with a teenager."

"Now, there's a deal breaker." I say it with a laugh, but she doesn't crack a smile. Andrea was a friendlier opponent.

"You should consider your options seriously, Mrs. Nichols, for the good of all parties involved."

So far, if I count correctly, that's a total of one. Me.

She hands me a brochure. "I'll give you a moment to look this over, and then I'll be back."

It's titled "Middle-Age Childbirth: A Commentary." I've read a lot on the subject, but I scan the essentials. *For many, middle age is the beginning of chronic illnesses that can make it difficult for a woman caring for a toddler. Mothers of late-life children will require support, financial and emotional, and even help with child-rearing at a time when she may well be living on a reduced income, or even assisted living.* Jolly thought!

It goes on, this euphoria-inducing read, to list the financial cost for nannies, nurseries, day care, surrogate care, after-school care and summer programs, with the presumption that a late-life parent is a working parent. Then there is mention of the problematic only-child syndrome. I thought we'd kicked that theory to the curb years ago. A brat by any other name is still a brat. This is a diatribe, not a presentation of options.

Turn the page and the real fun begins. The risks of late-life birth. Birth defects. Low birth weight. Brain damage. Gestational diabetes. Difficult delivery. Down's syndrome. Spina bifida. There's the recommended diagnostic testing for late-life pregnancies: chorionic villus sampling, amniocentesis and percutaneous umbilical blood sampling. Each procedure is followed up by cost analysis, which it says are not always covered by insurance.

I toss said brochure in the wastebasket. But I'm rattled.

"So then," the doctor says, returning as though our

conversation had been put on pause, "what do you think?"

"I think that so-called helpful-hints pamphlet paints a broad target for people's fears. I have no chronic illnesses, and last time I checked my medical insurance was fine."

She quirks her mouth. "You've got good genes. Otherwise, we wouldn't be having this conversation. But senior citizens use up a disproportion of medical and hospital resources as it is. If women your age continue to become regular consumers of obstetrics care, that will finish us. The risks are too high, and my malpractice insurance couldn't stand the inevitable suits from high-risk pregnancies that should never have been encouraged in the first place."

Whoa! When did I become an object of Medicaid (or is it Medicare?) scorn? I don't even qualify yet.

"I really didn't think I had a chance that the pregnancy would take. But seeing the sonogram, and hearing the heartbeat—" I can't help it, I'm smiling so hard my face hurts "—I'm going to be a mother, again!"

"You know the odds are against you delivering a normal child?" She pauses. "At your age."

Just like that I'm chilled to the bone, as if she's injected ice water into my blood. "Have you noticed something wrong?"

"No. The sonogram looks fine. Of course, we'll need to do an amnio to check. But why wait for expensive test results? It's best to end what you've told me was a mistake. I can set up an appointment with a nearby clinic. Is next week soon enough?"

Soon enough? The only "soon enough" I can think of is the need to leave here. The only mistake is that I won't be able to get out soon enough. "Let me think on it." I slide off the examining table and reach for my clothing.

"Don't wait too long. Ten to fourteen weeks allows for the least complications."

I stop trying to dress and turn to look at her. "There's nothing 'least' in any of the complications of my life. But thanks for handling it with such tact and discretion."

She looks faintly offended. "I'm offering you my medical opinion. That's my ethical duty."

"And here I thought you were playing god—small *g*—with patients' lives."

She smacks her lips in the time-honored fashion of a superior being who realizes she's dealing with an unenlightened but stubborn inferior. "I think we're done here. Please see the receptionist on your way out. You may leave an address to have your records forwarded to a physician of your preference."

I let her have the last word because I can't fasten my bra for trembling hands. Damn hooks.

Okay, so I got the doctor from hell. Nearly everybody comes up against one eventually. Burnout, clearly. From malpractice suits? Maybe she'd just opened her new insurance statement before she saw me. I've heard the premiums are running ob-gyns out of business nationwide.

I'm walking stiff-legged into town, after a quick stop at Aunt Marvelle's to change into drawstring-waist pants and an oversize linen shirt. The days of normal clothing are dwindling rapidly. Furious with myself for letting the doc throw me for even an instant, I decided to work off my anger with exercise.

But the doctor has thrown me. I drove back to Aunt Marvelle's in a white-knuckled fury. Thank goodness she was off staring at Ralph, or I would have told her everything on the spot. Instead, I'm in pursuit of comfort in the form of something sweet, cold and gooey, and preferably chocolate.

My thoughts swing wildly as I realize traffic in town has picked up considerably, with city license plates sprouting everywhere. That's the trouble with Paradise. Everybody wants a piece of it.

Who will take care of my child if something happens to me? I hadn't thought of that. Is it genuinely more of a concern than for a parent of twenty or thirty? My life expectancy is seven-five years. For the very first time, I lay my hand on what is still a fairly flat stomach and sense that I am not alone. Twenty-five years would give this tot the chance to grow up, marry and make a grandmother of me.... I don't smoke, or drink heavily. I could lose the rest of the damn excess thirty pounds, if I wanted to. I do exercise. Well, I will exercise more. Eat right, too.

My stomach gurgles. I'm hungry.

I turn into the doorway of the appropriately named sandwich shop, the Paradise, and bump into a crowd of toned and tanned weekenders just leaving. Good, I think. I'm in no mood for reminders of home, and obligations at Rodrigo's. No yogurt today. I need real eggs and cream and sugar consolation.

Sometimes the rain just keeps falling. There at the back table is Dr. Templeton in earnest conversation with a beautiful younger woman. Not cute. Beautiful. She's leaning across the table toward him, a ribbon of shiny black hair flows down her back to touch the seat behind her. She's slim and exotically dark, and she's gripping his outstretched hand for all she's worth. They wear identical intense expressions. This is love, if I've ever seen it.

Bloody hell.

10

Slipping into a chair near the front, I am annoyed with myself for being annoyed. Why should I expect Dr. Templeton to be different from any other free, good-looking, disposable-income male? She's quite lovely, really. Even if she does appear to be Dallas's age.

It's a slow moment in the afternoon. The waiter comes right over. Rather, he makes his way in a leisurely I'm-just-doing-this-until-my-real-life-comes-along pace.

"Chocolate malt, heavy on the syrup." Sleeping doesn't seem to be a problem these days, caffeine or no. Besides, I'm still reeling from my appointment with Dr. Feelbad. Doctors are springing up in my life like weeds, irritating and uninvited.

No, I won't even glance at them again. This is the Hamptons. Young things and older males are so commonplace it's boring. It's the beginning of a warm spring weekend. Sure, that's it. She's just out from the city. That's why the Marvelous Matrons didn't know about her. She was under their radar, not likely to walk through his office door, except to bring in Grandma.

I'm still obsessing when the waiter returns with what passes in my world these days for a stiff drink. At least the straw stands up in it.

But then the words of Dr. Reynolds come back to me. "You know the odds against a women of your age delivering a normal child?" Yes, I do.

"Excuse me!" I lift a hand to bring back the slim young man who'd begun to drift away. He pivots, heel and toe. A model, I don't even have to ask. I hold out the malt. "This really isn't what I want."

He doesn't touch it. "You ordered it."

"I'll pay for it. Just bring me a banana split. Pineapple, strawberry and caramel toppings." I'm giving up—alas!—chocolate.

He takes the malt between two fingers, as if it's contaminated.

I pull out the scanned picture of my little stranger. It's still the photo of a shrimp, but my heart swells three times in size. "We're in this together," I say to the grainy rendering. "You better get used to regular food, though. Okay?"

"Well, hello."

Sometimes the heart pounds for other reasons. Standing over me are Dr. Templeton and his sweet young thing. He smiles easily. "I thought that was you."

No need to lie. "Hi. I didn't want to disturb you."

My gaze moves casually to the young woman. Could be I'm supersensitive, but I spot in a second what could not be noticed while she was seated. This chick is pregnant. Four months at least. *Ooo-kay.* No wonder he had sympathy for me.

He puts an arm protectively around her shoulders, for the second thing I notice is that she has been crying. "I'd like you to meet someone special to me."

I smile, but my eyes say, you old dog!

"This is Jolie Katz, my daughter."

The shoe has dropped, squarely on my dumb-ditty-dumb-dumb head. I rise as if I've been introduced to royalty. "I'm Lu Nichols. So glad to meet you."

Her hand is cool, her touch gentle but not unfriendly. "Hi. Dad says you are a friend of his."

Does he? The look I cast him causes the most amazing thing. A blush! Or something like it. His naturally tanned skin deepens a shade.

"Jolie's not feeling so well today," he says. "She's expecting."

"Oh, may I?" She's noticed my sonogram picture lying on the tabletop.

"Yes, sure." I hand it to her.

"This is yours?" The question carries no pejorative sting.

"As a matter of fact, yes. Remarkable, huh?"

"Oh, no. My aunt just had her seventh, and she's probably older. She's forty five."

I like this girl. "Wow. Seven. But this is your first."

"Yes."

"Congratulations. I hope it all goes well."

She pales and bites her lip. I've struck a nerve I didn't know was exposed.

Realizing we've hit an impasse, Dr. Templeton says, "I'll call you later, Jolie. You've got a key. Just make yourself at home. We'll sort it out when I come by."

She smiles and nods, says goodbye to me and adds, "I hope things go well for you, too. It's a darling picture."

Instead of following her out, Dr. Templeton indicates the chair next to mine. "Mind if I…?"

"Please." Yes, as a matter of fact I am. *Very pleased.*

"What brings you back to town?" He frowns. "Mrs. Harrington is well, I hope?"

"Doing Broadway with her friends this weekend."

He smiles and nods as the waiter sets my banana split down in front of me. "That sounds like fun."

I grin and dig in. I'd be lying if I said it didn't cross my mind that I might run into him. Lying if I said I wasn't hoping to. But now that he's here, big as life in a black windbreaker and khakis, I don't know what to say.

He orders bottled water with lime, which means he's planning to stay awhile. Then he reaches for my sonogram shot and looks at it, smiling. "Just when a parent thinks all his problems are over, reality sets in. Jolie's four and a half months pregnant."

"That was my guess."

"Problem is, she's just walked out on her husband." His sighs are like everything else about him, big and deep. "She found out he was fooling around. Packed a bag and here she is, without warning."

"You going to kill him for her?" I'm only mildly joking, but the look on Jolie's father's face is dangerously serious.

"I'd like to bust his head wide open," he answers, then shrugs. "But she loves him."

I nod and continue consuming ice cream.

"Ever since my wife died, I've been at a loss with Jolie. This business of being both parents to a child, even a married one, is hard. She needs a mother's touch, a woman's point of view on this one. I tend to want to throw things and curse."

"Do you?" This could be useful information.

He laughs. "I take it to the gym."

"So what did you say to her?"

"I told her she's pregnant. She's got to think of the baby. A baby needs a father. Jon's an ass but I think her reaction, packing up and driving out here, is a bit extreme. She says it's never happened before."

"Hmm."

"I'm trying to be supportive, but I think she's overreacting to a one-time transgression."

"So says a man."

He looks up from the lime he's been squeezing into his water. "You think she's right?"

"It's none of my business, okay?" I grin as his face goes blank. "You still want my opinion?"

He relaxes and nods.

"I think if your daughter's unhappy now, it will probably get worse. Men tend to exhibit their true natures early. She's pregnant, a very vulnerable time for a young woman. And hubby's catting around. I can't imagine a worse time for that to happen. She may be doing the right thing, leaving now instead of later, after more damage has been done to her sense of self-worth."

He's staring at me, listening with that big-head intensity of his. Embarrassed, I shrug. "But what do I know? I can't even give my own daughter advice that she will listen to. She's so wrapped up in her wedding. I don't think she's thinking one minute past the honeymoon. That worries me. Stephen's a nice guy. But from what I've seen, he's a simple person. Dallas is about as complicated as women get. He won't ever want her to change, and she hasn't even finished growing up yet. She needs to think about how to cope with the future, not how many forks to use at the reception."

"Like Jon and Jolie!" He wags his head. "Always did sound more like a road movie than a marriage. Jon's a local kid. I don't mind that, believe me. But Jolie's mother reared her to expect the best of everything. They met a couple of summers ago, when Jolie was home from college. Linda never approved of Jon, who was struggling to make a go of his computer service business in Sayreville. When Linda didn't approve of something or someone, she had a way of undermining things so that doubt would creep in, even when you were sure you were right."

The man is talking to me, really talking. And he hasn't

asked me a thing about myself or my situation. I'm flattered, and relieved.

"Maybe, in this instance, she saw something you didn't. About Jon, I mean. They say a woman goes into marriage with the idea of improving her spouse." He groans at this. "And a man marries what he wants, and doesn't want that to change." This time he grunts. "I suspect that the bigger problem in a marriage is the second one. Not changing is much harder than changing. It's impossible."

He reaches for the photo again, then looks up at me. "Is that what happened to you?"

He means Jacob, no doubt. "A version of that."

He nods. "So, everything all right?" He taps the picture with a finger.

"Depends on who you ask." I tell him briefly of my doctor visit. I'm very circumspect because I expect him to vouch for a colleague's expertise, especially a local one. Birds of a feather, it happens in every profession.

"Crap!" he says at the end of my recitation. "You have just as good a chance of carrying this pregnancy to term as a woman in her thirties. Better than a first-time mother in her late thirties. That's because you've had two successful pregnancies. And this was a natural conception, no drugs or procedures involved. You've nearly completed the first trimester, usually the most dangerous time. Of course, you'll need to be screened for a few things. That's standard these days."

My eyes fill. I can't believe how grateful I am to hear these words from him. But I'm not going to make rain on him again. I sniff so long and hard I can feel air entering my tear ducts. "That's only part of my concern. My child will have a grandparent for a mother, if I live that long."

"I predict you'll live to see this child marry. But what if you don't?" He folds his arms on the table and leans forward. "My father died when I was ten. Jolie's mother is gone. Hell, how many children survive divorce, desertion or single parenthood? At least you are willing to be there as long as possible. That's all the probability anyone gets."

"That's just it. If something should happen to me in the next eighteen years, my child won't have anyone."

"Your husband?"

I know what he's asking, but I also know how I feel. "I don't have a husband."

He stares at me a long time. Just stares. I can't tell what he's thinking or what he's not saying. Then he says, "You won't be alone for long."

It's the kind of trite statement everyone says to someone who's divorced or widowed, after a decent interval. It's meant to be a pat on the back. Somehow, in his deliberate tone, it doesn't have that hearty quality to it. It sounds like an oracle's pronouncement. The hairs on my arms actually stirred when he spoke. *You won't be alone for long…unless you choose to be.*

I shouldn't let him know how he gets to me. I smile. "I guess that's true, since I'm subletting even as we speak."

His bark of laughter is bright and sharp, like a woodpecker's cry, and higher in register than his speaking voice. His amusement quickly descends into deep chuckles in his chest. I like this man!

"You want something else?" The waiter has returned.

I glance at my dish. Where did all that ice cream go?

"You can't want more?" Dr. Templeton is looking at me with a mixture of humor and astonishment. "Tell you what, I'll pay for that one if you'll take a walk with me."

We start out at the harbor. While it's only May the yachts have begun to arrive. Sleek numbers, some with sails, that one can imagine owning if only in a dream life. A few remind me of the saying about "having more dollars than sense." On the water it's mild even in the sun, yet the decks of the yachts are dotted with the requisite babes in thongs. From rap artists to movie moguls, the world of the latest-model filthy rich has changed the vacation face of eastern Long Island. I can't decide if it's poetic justice for the shunning of everything not Anglo-Saxon for so long, or just a dirty damn shame that the harbors are polluted, the dunes eroding and that vast stretches of sea grasses are mowed into suburban lawns sprouting steroidal houses. If you demand access to everything you have in the city, what's the point of leaving it?

Mostly this is just fodder for the chat between us. He checks his beeper a couple of times. Once he even apologizes for having to make a call. Even on his day off, the doctor is always in.

I'm calling him William by the time we decide to slip off our shoes to walk up the beach, away from the noise of town. Near the water's edge there's more of life, and less of lives. I have to explain the origin of Lu to him, but it doesn't feel like a drag this time. Maybe because he asks, what few ever do, how I felt about the name. How, if at all, it's shaped my life. Not even Jacob thought of that question.

"I tried to call you." William interjects this into the short silence of our stroll.

He keeps surprising me. "I didn't get any messages."

"That's because I didn't leave any."

"I see." I suppose, since I was such a wreck in his office, he wondered if I'd made it back home in one piece. His call was probably an extension of his bedside manner. But the thought that he called appeals, I must admit.

He bumps my shoulder with his and, when he has my attention, says sheepishly, "I didn't know what I was going to say until I heard your voice."

That's a compliment, I tell myself. He was unsure of himself. And now, not afraid to reveal that.

"So, here I am." The laughter in my voice betrays my giddy pulse rate.

"Yes. Here you are." He takes my hand. I'm thinking *how romantic is this guy?* until he pulls me to a halt with "Watch out for the jellyfish. That kind stings."

There on the sand one stride ahead of my bare feet are the gelatinous remains of whatever earlier washed up on shore. I gingerly step around it.

Funny thing is, he doesn't release my hand. I don't let go, either.

We continue to talk of nothing special until we are at the far end of the deserted beach, nearly to where the land curves away to the north, forming the crescent shape that makes this a natural harbor. My feet are sandy. Each time I smile my cheeks wrinkle with a thin crust of sea salt carried by the breeze. I smile a lot, happy as a kid.

"Want to rest for a while?" William points out one of the large boulders protruding through the sand of an otherwise flat expanse.

With his assistance, I happily haul myself up onto one. He lounges on an elbow beside me. "There's going to be a great sunset. You'll enjoy it," he says, as if it's a performance we've come here for.

I glance at my watch. It's later than I thought. But I have nowhere to be or anyone to report to.

I sit back and glance up. An *ah* of delight escapes me. William only nods. Like me, he doesn't want to draw his gaze from the spectacle of the setting sun on this May evening.

The ever-changing light is impossible to capture in words. But because I am a writer, I try to recompose images as thoughts that might later be transferred to the pages of the journal I keep. Sometimes…when I remember. I will remember today.

We are part of a Monet waterscape, repainted again and again as the minutes pass. On the western horizon the sun

does a fan dance behind a blaze of cerise and molten gold.
Overhead oyster-shell chalkiness thickens the clouds
while rosy moon-shell and whelk coral tint the under-
sides. Shades of sea glass and pearl, tumbled amethyst and
frosted rose quartz emerge. Everywhere there are blues:
aqua, turquoise, lapis, azure, indigo and smoke, at the harbor's mouth drawn from and reflected onto water so still
that the sky slips into sea without a ripple. Time pauses;
only the sinking sun moves. To the Northeast, the seam
of open water and sky, the occasional white sail passes in
the distance.

Even I, a landlubber, sense that such moments are rare.
The sky goes on forever, yet pools at one's feet where it
can be dipped into by a toe. The day's anxieties desert me.
I am as reluctant to let go of this contentment as a child
after a day at the beach, even as darkness edges across us
and into the water, now beginning to curl with the rising tide.

Finally the rich magenta and egg yolk of the final blaze
ignites the western fingertips of now umber-darkened
clouds.

Finally I realize that William is not looking at the sky
but at me. How long has he watched me? A bit embarrassed to be caught gaping in wonder like a beached floun-
der, I dig my palms in and lever myself down from the rock.
As I do, I hear a faint hum growing louder with every moment.

All at once a hectic dark cloud envelops us, full of tiny
high-pitched drills that bite into our faces and necks and
arms. Beach gnats.

William reaches for my arm as I flail wildly. "Come on!"

He hauls me by the upper arm up the beach, instead
of back toward town.

"Where are we going?" I ask between clenched teeth,
because I hate gagging on gnats.

"My place."

11

Of course he has a place nearby. I just didn't know it was so close to Aunt Marvelle. Does she know about this?

"It's a rental," William informs me as we trudge up a trail between the dunes. "Last month of off-season availability. Wanted to see if I like beach life well enough to drop an obscene wad on this property, or one like it."

"Obscene. I see." Elder care is a growth industry.

The moment he points it out I see why he'd consider the place. It's right on the beach, but up a steep slope meant to keep even hurricane-driven seawater at bay. From the beachside, it looks enormous. But as we climb wooden steps across the sea-grape vines up to where a grassy lawn begins, the perception changes. It's still a big house, two stories, plus a ground-level garage, but not ostentatious. In fact, the gray siding that looks like wood weathered by the sea and the slate-colored roofing make it seem historic.

The interior contradicts that assumption. The main floor is open-room modern, not tiny bungalow rooms like Aunt Marvelle's half-century cottage. The living room and dining room flow together, the kitchen separated only by a floating bar. Wide-planked flooring is smoothed to satiny perfection.

"Are you hungry?" William moves to open the blinds at the line of windows extending across the back of the house, which allows the bay to be on full display.

"Sure." Maybe I should not sound so enthusiastic. "My treat."

He hesitates. "I'd planned to have dinner in, if you don't mind. It's nothing fancy."

"Even better." A man who cooks. Lucky me.

He shucks off his coat and slings it casually across a chair. Not anal-retentive about his clothing. "I just need to make a few phone calls first."

Right. He had other plans. The lucky lady was to be someone else.

I pop up from where I just sat on the sofa. "Listen, let's do this another time. You've been more than kind, and I really appreciate the company. But I'm sure you had your evening planned."

He stops moving across the room to listen to my speech. An expression like exasperation crosses his face. "Do you want to go home?"

"No." I give in. "I'm having a really good time."

He smiles. "So sit down and let me make my calls."

He's gone a total of five minutes. I don't even try to overhear who he's talking to. I lucked out, and I'm not going to feel guilty. However, if she's giving him hell, I may pay the price with a burned meal.

I sit and think, not a bad wind-up to a day with a hellacious beginning. But then I've begun to suspect that any day with William Templeton in it would be a good one. *Don't get any bright ideas, Lu!*

When he comes back in he looks happy. "Jolie had gone to bed. She says she's fine. But I'll drop by later to make certain."

I look up to the second floor. "I thought she'd come to stay with you."

"She said she wanted to sleep in her old bedroom. And that being alone will give her time to think."

"Oh." We're alone. How about that? Or maybe the other woman is fuming at the very idea.

"I've got fresh halibut. Picked it up at the market this morning. Though I was buying for one." He reaches into the refrigerator, pulls out a package wrapped in butcher paper, and unrolls it. "You think that's enough for two?"

I chuckle. "It's plenty." Half of his serving sounds much better than all of someone else's. The idea that there was another woman vanishes from my mind.

He makes broiled halibut and serves it with home-made pineapple salsa, a mixed green salad and hot rolls.

"I'm impressed." I don't lie. I make short shrift of my portion. Sea air gave me an appetite.

"Thank you." He leans on his forearms and surveys my empty plate with satisfaction. "I'm teaching myself to cook, thanks to the Food Channel."

I've just consumed the most excellent results. "I hear lots of men—especially those who haven't cooked more than ribs and steaks before—are hooked on the Food Channel. I guess you men like tell-all exposés of a subject so dear to your hearts."

"Second-best activity on the planet." He doesn't even bother to leer in my direction. The little smile he's keeping to himself is enough.

I can't fault him for being a man when I'm noticing how much I like his even teeth and how his ears lie close against his head. In fact, everything about the man who's filled up the last few hours of my life is just fine with me. It's the most pleasant evening I can recall in years. I'm not being a wife or a mother or a colleague, or even a friend. We are not friends yet. The road to discovery, if we want to travel that path, is still ahead.

"What are you smiling about?"

"I was just thinking that I'd almost forgotten what it's like to simply be Lu."

"Nice feeling?"

"Oh, yeah."

He stands up. "Let's finish our drinks on the deck. It's late enough that the gnats should be gone."

I pick up the lemonade he served us and follow him out.

The night is now velvet black, with few lights to connect the dots to reality. Yet the merest sound echoes across the harbor. The happy cry of a reveler onboard a cabin cruiser entering the sound is as clear as the noise of the surf curling onto the sand below us. We lean, elbow to elbow, against the railing for a time, looking out at the oily black water.

"So what do you think? Would a child like this?"

For a moment I'm completely thrown. Then I remember, he's going to be a grandfather. Or maybe he's thinking about remarriage. "Absolute bliss."

He doesn't answer, but I see him nod. The warmth of his arm brushing mine feels good. I fantasize for a second that he will put that arm about my shoulders in a friendly, camaraderie way. That would be nice.

After another minute he turns to me. "I need to check on Jolie. I'll be back in an hour. Will you wait?"

Wait here? For what? For him? What kind of signal would that be? "Okay."

It doesn't take me five minutes to fall asleep to the jazz from the university radio station in Southampton. They're playing Clark Terry as I drift off. It's Lionel Hampton, and the clock says two hours later, when the crunch of tires on gravel awakens me.

I manage to sit upright on the sofa, but I'm still yawning as he comes through the door. My night-owl days are long behind me.

He comes in in a hurry, as if he expected something— that I'd be gone? He looks relieved when he spots me. "Sorry. Jolie needed another cry. She's fine now."

He slips off his jacket and rubs his hands together. "Now that that's taken care of, how about some herbal tea?"

"Lovely." The chill of the night has invaded the room. I head for the bathroom to splash water on my face and rinse my mouth. Some date I make, all gummy-mouthed and bleary-eyed.

When I return he is standing, arms akimbo by a lit fire, like a Boy Scout who's just earned a badge. "Thought this might be fun."

I hadn't noticed the fireplace before. "This place has everything."

"So it seems." He hands me a mug of tea. "Hope raspberry's okay."

Next thing I know, we're sitting on sofa pillows in front of the fire, while I'm feeling as if I've left my life and stepped into the pages of a very nice romance novel. Except for the fact that... Bloody hell!

"That was some sunset." Got to talk about something other than my predicament.

He chuckles. "I don't know any other woman who could sit still for half an hour without speaking."

"There were no words for that sunset." My journal entry will sound overwrought.

"Exactly." Offers me a look it's hard not to interpret as sensual. "You were wise enough to understand that."

He's watching me again, as though he wants to say more but can't make up his mind. Okay, my turn.

"Why did you call me?"

"I wanted to reassure you."

"Because I'd made such a fool of myself in your examining room?"

"Okay."

What kind of answer is that? "I was having an awful day until we ran into each other. Those things you said earlier, about the possibility of me having a normal pregnancy helped. You did some research on my condition, didn't you?"

He smiles but seems more serious than when he left. I remember him saying that Jolie needed another cry. I know how it is when your child's in pain. "I don't like to be caught short when a patient's well-being is at stake."

"Thank you."

He looks away first. *Hmm.*

I decide to follow his lead. He's not talking; I won't, either. When I start to doze again, I'll leave.

"I don't know what you've heard about me."

I smile into my cup. Oh, that. "Only that Aunt Marvelle thinks you walk on water." He shrugs, gaze still on the fire. He knows more than he should about my life. Let's see what he'll say about his. "And that your wife died tragically not long ago."

"Eleven months ago."

"I'm sorry."

He continues to look at the fire. So much for that conversation.

"Linda's death is the only reason I'm not divorced."

"I see." I don't, of course, but my own fifteen rounds in the divorce ring have made me cautious of the idea I might understand anyone else's experience.

"I had a general practice for years in New Rochelle. It was a compromise. Linda wanted to be near the city. I wanted to be where I could do the poor the most good. About six years ago, I noticed that my patient profile was aging. I was giving more and more referrals to specialists. I started thinking I should know more about how to adequately care for patients who don't require a specialist, but have chronic problems common with aging. So I took time off, went back for additional training in geriatrics at New York–Presbyterian." He glances at me. "Linda thought that it was completely unnecessary. But when I was done, I knew I had found a new calling."

"One of the lucky ones," I say.

"I was offered a position at Wake Forest in Winston-Salem, South Carolina. Linda lost it. Said she wouldn't move even to Jersey. She was a New Yorker."

"Compromise time."

He nods. "I looked around and found a notice about a Bridgehampton physician who was retiring and selling his practice. I bought it and haven't looked back. That was three years ago."

"Cushy spot."

He looks at me, clearly annoyed. "That's what Linda thought. That's why she encouraged me to take it. But even this end of the island has more hard-working poor than vacationing wealthy. They oil the wheels of the cushy life."

"Touché."

He puts a hand on my knee. "Sorry. I know you didn't mean it that way. But Linda did. She liked the Hamptons address. She just didn't like the fact that all my patients are elderly, and that I don't cater strictly to the upper end."

"I've seen your waiting room. Prince and pauper, cheek by jowl. You must be good."

He grins. "I'm very good at what I do. But I'm in a practice that loses patients. Linda called what I do living at the edge of the grave. That's the point of it, to make the end easier."

I don't quite know what to say to that. That his attitude is noble or selfless or even rare would be true, but trite. Thankfully, he doesn't seem to expect a comment.

"I thought it would work, but Linda felt betrayed by my new practice." He removes his hand from my knee. "I knew she was afraid of growing older. In fact, she was obsessed with staying young. You name the process, she had tried it—before forty."

"She must have been beautiful." I'm thinking of Jolie. If I'd ever looked like that, I might be a little more willing to sacrifice to maintain it.

"She was, and always would have been, to me. But she changed." He pauses to give me a knowing look. "Being a man, I didn't like the changes."

"And that should teach me to keep my smug mouth shut!"

"There are at least two sides to every issue." He rubs his brow. "I'm sure, if she were here, Linda could make you see hers. She just couldn't adjust out on the island. The summers were great. Winters in a summer resort can be very lonely."

"If you don't have a life of your own."

He nods. "I work a lot of hours, even more now that I'm in an unpredictable field. The elderly, like the very young, get sick quickly and inconveniently." He looks at me again, the fire reflected in his dark gaze. "Sometimes I attend a funeral a week."

And that says more about him than anyone could tell me. He sees his patients all the way to the end of the line.

"Within a few months Linda was miserable. By then Jolie went away to college. Finally, I was miserable. A few days before the boating accident she'd told me she was leaving me."

I think about all those expensive yachts in the harbor, and wonder if the owner or renter of one of them contributed to the alienation of Linda Templeton's affection for her husband. Why I have that disloyal-to-the-sisterhood thought, I don't know. Something in the pain crimping the corners of his eyes is a hint. But I don't ask.

"I regret her death. But to be honest, I was mentally already out the door of the marriage."

"Then why do you still wear a wedding band?" I'm a woman and I need to know.

He looks down at his hand. "Protection. There are a lot of lonely women in my practice."

I chuckle. "Lots of wealthy lonely women."

"Remind me of that in a couple of years, if I'm still sad and lonely." He slips off his ring and puts it in his pocket, and then he turns to me in a motion I don't recognize until it's complete.

He kisses like he does everything else, with amazing poise and concentration and skill. But there's nothing practiced in it. He kisses as if it's been a long time, too long, and it's something he really enjoys, and has missed. Or maybe that's me.

"Okay, that's behind us," he says when he pulls back.

"Good." He's left me breathless, and just a little loopy. I don't know whether to reach again for my tea, or him. This is teenybopper stuff, but I'm loving it! Yet I've lived long enough to be wary. Of my emotions. Of making another mistake. Of misreading the signals.

Because he does, I, too, reach for tea. I don't know what I'm doing, or maybe I do. It's just flirting. "I had a thing for you three years ago."

"Really?" He looks pleased. "Why didn't you say something?"

Because we were both married is the right answer— and the truth. Instead I decide the evening calls for a deeper truth. "Because you're perfect."

"Yes, that makes sense." He strokes his chin. "I certainly see perfection when I shave every morning."

"Come on, a doctor? Please! You are everything every mother wants for her daughter. You're smart, well-educated. Fairly good-looking." I laugh at his doubtful glance. "You're a doctor, *numero uno,* in career-choice husband material."

"You never heard of Bill Gates?"

My turn to laugh. "I grew up not wealthy, but we weren't hurting. I had no desire to marry up. Jacob was blue-collar, had to work his way from the bottom. I liked that, wanted that experience. But the needs and desires of a twenty-year-old have less in common with those of a fifty-year-old than I ever dreamed. Understand?"

He nods, then stops. "No, I don't get it. What happened?"

I meet his gaze. "Have you ever had the feeling that you were wrapped up so tightly by your previous choices that nothing real or new could get in?"

"Linda wouldn't even visit my new offices for fear someone would mistake her for a patient. Wouldn't even visit!"

I don't know if that qualifies, but he's sharing a deep hurt, and I do understand feeling unappreciated and rejected.

"My needs changed. Jacob's never did. Eventually, I wanted something…something more."

He leans toward me. "More than perfection?"

"I didn't leave Jacob, if that's what you're thinking. He left me."

I've surprised him. "So why are you…?"

"Preggers?" Deep breath. "I think they call it pity sex. It sure is a pity I did it the way I did."

He stirs his tea before he says, "Where are you and Jacob now?"

"Jacob is out of my life. I'm free and breezy, at last." The look he gives me forces me to add, "Of course, nothing kills sex appeal like morning sickness."

"That's easy enough to disprove." He puts down his tea. "Want to?"

I'm shocked. I admit that. I haven't been propositioned since—well, a very long time. Surely, he's kidding. But he just kissed me, and he looks more than half-serious, but that could just be me reading what I'd like to see reflected in his gaze, even if I wouldn't very well take him up on—

"You're thinking." So much space for the tenderness on his face. "That's not how it works."

"It?"

He reaches up and touches me with just a forefinger pressed below my collarbone left of center. Even through my linen shirt his finger is warm. "You don't make a decision about these things. They just happen...or they don't."

These things. How many things has he had? Andrea's attitude has become my own. "I'm pregnant."

"I know how it works." He's prodding me ever so gently for emphasis. I've gone all tingly inside. Is this some new erogenous zone I've not known about? "I've been with a pregnant woman before."

I'm taken aback a second time. He seeks out pregnant partners? Oh, right, he's a father. Bound to have had a pregnant wife in his life, and in his bed.

"Is this safe?" Hey! He's the professional here.

"God, I hope not."

As he leans in to kiss me again I notice my shadow on the wall, and it's shaking its head.

He must notice my head movement, too, for he stops and pulls back. "Fair enough. But what's that line? 'Life is a banquet yet most poor suckers are starving to death.'"

He quoted a line from *Mame!* He must like theater, or old movies.

Should I grab for all the gusto? No, that's a beer commercial. The best lines these days are written to sell beer. We no longer have a compelling vocabulary for our relationships with other people—only for things, possessions or would-be possessions. We can feel for the moment, but seldom for the person.

And yet I'm feeling all kinds of good and wonderful and scary things about this man just at this moment. Thinking only of him.

Does he think I'm easy, the kind of woman who'll sleep

with anybody, even her ex? Dumb enough to get knocked up, I'm now safe and easy prey?

He's right. I can't think my way into this, only out of it.

I reach and take his face in both my hands. It's a broad face. Warm and smooth with hardly a prickle of an evening shadow. His cheeks firm in my hands as he smiles. "Are you going to kiss me?"

I try to buy time. "Are you Greek? Portuguese?"

His gaze dips for a moment. "I grew up on the Shinne-cock reservation near Southampton. I'm Montauk, Shinnecock, Irish, African and, yes, Portuguese. Is that an issue?"

"Not even a small one."

"Good. Now, where were we?"

I hold him off with my palms. "Your girl—ladyfriend?"

"No one since Linda." He says the words separately, as if each is a full statement in itself.

The second kiss is better than the first. He drags me into his lap, and though I'm no petite package, I feel right at home in the circle of his legs and arms.

The man can kiss!

He's slow and thorough, and while his hands are slid-ing up and down my back, his lips and tongue are mak-ing love to my mouth. I feel dizzy when we come up for air. But he's a man on a mission, and he isn't mistaking slowness for a need for a rest stop. He's turning me, and I'm so overwhelmed with sensation that I'm on my back before I quite realize how it was accomplished. My big linen shirt, oh! It's sliding up my torso thanks to his hands. They meet my bra, rise up over it and palm both my breasts at once as his mouth again finds mine.

I am anxious, but I'm not always a fool. This is no time to break off and then wonder what might have been. I reach around, find the back of his shirt, and start pulling it out of his pants. His back is broad and solid, and I find myself kneading him like bread dough. He thumbs my nipples through the lace, and I can't help it, I gasp.

"That's what I'm talking about," he whispers into my ear. "Just go with me, Lu. Just be with me."

I mumble an affirmative into his neck, and then nip at his earlobe. He groans. Ah, he likes that! I lift my head and suck his lobe all the way into my mouth, tugging and sucking until I'm satisfied, and then I stick my tongue into the hollow of his ear. He gives a grunt, almost like pain, but he doesn't pull away.

When I'm done, I realize he has opened my bra. He lifts it and ducks his head beneath my shirt.

Oh, now, wait! I wasn't prepared to feel this much, reveal this much. But that mouth and tongue of his are magic. It takes only the briefest thought of what he might do elsewhere with his talents, and I'm shuddering.

"I never come this fast," I say in wonder. Not untouched in strategic places.

All I get in reply is a chuckle. And then he's reaching for the drawstring of my waistband, and I'm no longer thinking, but hoping, praying, yes, oh yes, oh yes!

Some prayers are answered. Some dreams satisfied. I don't mean to sound flip. I mean to sound grateful.

Finally, half-exhausted and delirious with pleasure, I reach for his waistband, slide his belt loose and try to lower his zipper. But he's come up astride me and his trousers are pulled taut. So I go for what I can and stick my hand inside. He sucks in a breath, giving me access, and I find the length and strength of him.

I am impressed. His penis is like a shaft of copper pipe. How old is he? Whatever it is, it's the perfect age. At twenty, he'd have killed me.

Now it's my turn to try to please. Maybe it's him or something I'm doing, but I've hardly begun before he pushes me away, saying, "I don't want to spoil it for you."

I look up, flash my version of a wicked smile, and say, "My treat."

It goes both ways, when you're with the right person. Pleasure begets pleasure. When he comes, I'm overcome with sensation, too.

After that, it's pretty much a love match, a little of this and a whole lot of that.

We end up with me on my knees and him behind, one broad arm reaching 'round to make certain I don't miss one moment of pleasure. I vaguely understand this keeps pressure off my abdomen, but I'm pretty certain if he suggested hanging me up by my big toes at this point, I might be considering it.

I come in hard shudders that rack my body scalp to toenails, make my womb dance, and I think, *Oh baby, baby, ooh baby, baby!*

I feel him come, like tidal waves crashing on my shore, and it's so damn intense that afterward we kind of collapse sideways from the strain. Even then, his arms are there to steady and cushion my fall.

He pats my sweaty back and kisses my shoulder, then says in a fake southern drawl, "Ah sure am grateful for the pleasure of yawr comp'ny this eve'in', Miz Ta-*lu*-lah!"

When my heart stops racing and my eyes uncross I turn my head toward him, grinning. "What did you put in that tea?"

He swivels his head toward me, his expression lazy. "Equal."

I'll say!

12

I can't believe it. Here I lie on the floor—naked! And I'm not cringing.

I have not thought once about my middle-aged body, my stretch marks, my droops, my saddles, my wrinkles or my pores. Why should I? I'm wise enough to know that no alteration in them could have made this evening any better. In fact, I'm in love with the real me all over again. Look what it got me!

There's a man lying next to me, whom I genuinely like, smiling back at me. And to think I thought I had given Jacob my best. My best hasn't been on display in years!

No, scratch that. It's the best sex I've ever had! And I didn't even have to wax my legs.

I hope I didn't say that out loud.

He cups my face. "You're a surprise."

"You don't know the half of it." I shocked myself. Got to be the hormones!

Although... I remember pregnancy sex as uncomfortable, and not particularly satisfying. Jacob was always afraid

he might do the baby harm so we kind of rocked ourselves to a so-so climax. William has only to kiss me to
set me off.

The best sex ever. It's official.

"What are you thinking?" He taps my forehead.

He didn't use a rubber! And then I remember the
crackle of foil. Yes, he did.

"I'm glad you were prepared."

He looks surprised by the first words out of my mouth.
Uh-oh, not a good sign. Brain-numbing sex is wearing
off. Pretty soon fifty years of pretty righteous living is
going to start its inquisition.

I wait a heartbeat. But I don't feel guilt or dread, or even
the shilly-shally of regret in the wings of my joy. Good.
Later is better, much later.

His beeper goes off. I had completely forgotten the possibility of that kind of intrusion. But he's on his feet in a
flash, and after a look at it, he says, "Excuse me," and pads
away into the next room.

Was that a naked man I saw? Why yes, oh yes, that was
a naked man I saw.

I roll over onto my back in laughter. Reduced to nurs-
ery-rhyme humor by giddiness! I'm pathetic. And he's
cute, even from the rear.

After a moment, I sit up to look for my shirt. The smile
on my face feels so broad I have trouble seeing much past
my nose. Yet I manage to find it, put it on and button it
up before he returns.

From somewhere he has snagged a pair of shorts and
pulled them on. He's frowning as he enters, but the moment he sees me, his expression softens. He comes right
up to me and pulls me up from the floor, and into his
arms for another kiss.

After two or three more I can feel the stirring of interest, but he reaches up and captures my face between
his hands. "I'm sorry, but I have to go out."

"Someone's ill?"

He hesitates. "Someone's died. It was expected. But…"

"Of course." I turn and begin to gather my things. He stands and patiently watches until I've found them all, then I head for the bathroom.

When I come out again, in more or less normal order, I see he's completely dressed, too.

He approaches as if he has more bad news. Maybe my conscience absconded to lecture his, because it sure isn't making any waves in my head. Then I remember his lost patient. "I'm so sorry you have to go, and under these circumstances."

He shrugs. "It's what I do."

But when I try to walk past him, to pick up my wallet, he reaches out and halts me with a hand on each of my shoulders. He redirects me back in front of him, but this time he doesn't try to kiss me.

"You said earlier that Jacob was out of your life. Even though he knows you carry his child?"

I really don't want to talk about this now. "He doesn't know."

William's hands drop from my shoulders. "Then you aren't over."

"Of course we are." I feel ridiculous trying to explain my position to a man who's just known me in about every biblical sense. "This wasn't some pitiful ploy to trick my husband back into my life. It is—was a mistake. I don't want him back."

William says nothing.

"You don't believe me?"

"I believe that's what you think today. But you haven't heard what he has to say about your condition. You're angry and hurt. Embarrassed. All of that will wear off in a few weeks, a month."

"When I'm big as a house, you mean?"

"I don't mean anything." He shakes his head. "I can't talk

to you about this. I can't be the one to influence your decision."

"Oh, I get it." He is having the second thoughts I wasn't
having.

"No, you don't." He shoves his hands into his pockets
when I know he wants to touch me again, because I want
him to. "I won't insult you by making any promises, even
to call you. You've got some very important things to deal
with. I don't want to mess that up for you."

"Sure. No hard feelings."

"No, Lu." He steps into my path again. I can smell,
faintly, "us" rising from him. Or am I just that sensitive
to anything to do with him now? "Plenty of feelings. But
feelings are what brought you to where you are. You've
got to stop feeling and think." He says this roughly. "I
know you know that."

He's right, but it hurts more than I expected that he
can be practical when I don't want to be. "I hate it when
men get all superior."

"I don't feel superior." He slaps a hand to forehead and
rubs and rubs. "This feels like I may have just made a big
mistake."

I don't know what I expected. Not this cowardly backing away. I feel as if he's put a foot on my chest.

I step off. "I am not asking or expecting anything of
you, William. I have no claim on you. Don't want to
make any."

"That's what worries me." He moves quickly, grabbing
me and then kissing me, hard and briefly.

I can breathe again. He's afraid I'll be the one not to
call.

"I'll call." I put a hand to his cheek. "It may just be a
while."

He looks away. "We'll see."

It would be so easy, here and especially now, to tell him
he's wrong about the outcome of my conversation-to-be

with Jacob. But that isn't realistic. Reality is, I'm pregnant by another man. The best sex in the world can't change that.

I can't have an affair. No, even at first blush this feels like something much more. So then, I can't start another relationship. I can only get the hell out of Dodge before I make another complete fool of myself by barfing through the afterglow.

Queasiness doesn't react well to so many switches of emotion in so short a time. Besides, I have someone else to think of. There is someone here who didn't ask to be brought to the party. He/she must be my first concern.

My hand slides unconsciously down my front until I notice William's sober gaze following it. "Are you okay?" He looks even unhappier.

"I'm fine. We're fine. More than fine."

"You should put your feet up." He's looking around for a place. "Tell you what, why don't you lie down on my bed? You're welcome to spend the night."

"Not here."

He looks at me for a short while. "You're right. I'm sorry."

He drops me off at Aunt Marvelle's before heading to the hospice. He doesn't kiss me again, and I can't ask him to. But he does walk me to the door, flip on the inside lights and check the hallway before I enter. Old-fashioned caretaking. He's sweet. Too bad it isn't a simple matter of desire between us.

By the time I crawl into bed, I've made a decision. I won't shower until the morning. It's the only way I know to hold on to him a little longer.

13

"Hi, Jacob, it's me." I've driven all the way to Brooklyn before I felt able to make this call.

"Oh, hey, Lu." There is a quality in his voice of someone who didn't expect a call, as if it's been so very long since we last spoke. Then I realize that's true. It's been nearly three months. "How're you doing?"

"Fine. And you?" Who'd believe this sort of formality was necessary after twenty-seven years?

"Good. Good. It's nice to hear your voice. Nice." Yet he seems distracted. I've probably interrupted his Sunday afternoon baseball game.

"Listen, I know it's short notice but I need to talk to you about something."

"I see. Well, I've got a hell of a schedule these days. Flying out to Bogotá on Wednesday. Could this wait a week or two?"

"No." It can't wait even another day.

"Fine. Then we'll talk Tuesday. Coffee or drinks?"

This sounds irksomely familiar: my overture, his retreat

and counter. But this is nonnegotiable. "I need to see you today."

"Everything's a crisis, right?" His laugh sounds awkward, embarrassed. Where did that come from? "As long as we're already talking, why not just tell me about it?"

Oh, he's back on track. First the delay, followed by the quick trivializing of my "crisis" into a phone call Band-Aid remedy. How many crises—the real kind—did I handle while he was away on business, blithely reassuring me that I could and would find a solution? I know this is Jacob's way. But today it feels like manipulation.

"I don't want to talk about it over a cell phone."

"Top-secret business, huh?"

As reply he gets only the rush of air in his ear from my end.

"So, okay. This is not a big crisis, right?" He sounds friendly again because he's gotten the upper hand, or so he thinks. "Want to at least give me a hint?"

Boy, do I. "I've just been to the doctor."

"Shit."

He knows. My heart lurches, thumping wildly like a trapped jack-in-the-box against my ribs. Or he suspects. All of a sudden I'm more scared than I've ever been about this.

The ugly blare of a horn and screech of tires makes me wrench the wheel, steering to the right. I was drifting. A cab speeds by. Even though I don't usually look, I see him flip me the bird while shaking it like a fist, and yelling at what must be the top of his lungs. I hope his passengers are local. The average tourist would be cringing on the back-seat floor.

"Lu?" Jacob's voice sounds half its original size. "You better come over."

"I'll be there by three."

Jacob lives in a furnished apartment with brand-new furniture that looks like the kind they advertise on those rent-to-purchase commercials. Just now he's sitting on the sofa staring at the floor in dejection, as if I've come to repossess for nonpayment. Or, more likely, that I've come to repossess his freedom. My news dropped him like a rock.

He looks up at me. "So, what do you want me to do?"

"Don't you think you've done enough?"

"Oh, come on, Lu. You were there, too."

"Right. I was. And I never thought a thing about it, either."

I was so nervous just before I rang his bell that I started shaking. But the moment he opened the door, the moment I saw that his back was up, that he was ready for trouble instead of full of potential concern for whatever might be wrong with me, I went icy cold inside, muscles locked and under control. If I'm not the victim, then neither is he.

"Right, so then, here's what we'll do." He stands up, begins to pace. "I have you on my insurance so— No wait. We better pay cash." He sends me a weak grin. "I don't want to do any explaining I don't need to, you know?"

Better than he does. But I'm going to be doing a lot more explaining before this is over. And so is he. "I can take care of the bills."

"You can? I mean, it's going to cost a few thousand."

"All right. You can help. Fifty-fifty. They have these new installment plans now. A fourth down on diagnosis, then even payments until the delivery. Usually it's all paid up before you get the prize."

"Now wait a sec!" He approaches me for the first time since I arrived. "You can't keep it. I mean, at your age. You can't possibly be thinking of having it?"

It. Not baby. Not child. Not even kid. *It*. "Yes, I am keeping the *child,* after I have the *child*. The doctor says I'm strong as a horse." Okay, the doctor did sound more like Jacob, but it's the spirit of the point I'm trying to make. "I just came to make certain you knew first."

"First? First!" He's losing ground faster with every second. "You're going to actually tell people about this?"

"In a couple of months even strangers will know." I make an arc motion over my belly with my hand.

He pales and backs off. "Jesus H. Christ!"

"I never liked that phrase, Jacob."

"Holy shit!"

Not a lot better, but why quibble? "I'm giving you a chance to get your feet under you about this. I don't expect anything from you—"

He snorts at this.

"I don't. Hear me. I do N-O-T." It's juvenile to spell, but I'm feeling pretty schoolyard-bullied right about now. "But you are the father and I thought you should be the first to know."

"Who else would you tell?" Just about the time that challenge is out of his mouth, he thinks of two. "Dallas and Davin. Jes— Shit. You can't tell the kids. What will they think?"

"That they have idiots for parents. I think they had a suspicion long before this."

"No, I forbid it. Absolutely forbid it." Red-faced, he comes huffing up to me again, finger pointing at nose level. "Do you hear me?"

I look at him a long time. He's angry, afraid and unprepared. What the hell did we think we were doing in February that was worth this moment?

I don't know why, but I look past him and notice a bowl of fresh flowers on his kitchen table. Jacob never bought fresh flowers. He always said he didn't know what to buy. Besides, they are damned expensive for something you couldn't use, and didn't last very long. So then, who's responsible for the flowers?

"You're seeing someone." Statement.

"How do you know?" He looks so guilty I expect her to pop out of the bouquet.

I'm so damned slow! "What's her name?"

He sticks out his chin. "Sandra."

"How long?"

"A month, yeah. What of it? I'm free." But the bluster doesn't last. "Christ. What am I going to say to Sandra?"

I sidestep him and go to perch on a nearby chair. Icy disdain doesn't last forever, and I'm afraid when I thaw I will collapse. "I won't tell the children immediately. You need time to adjust. But I have a couple of things pending at work that make it imperative that I tell my boss very soon about my condition."

"Oh, yeah?" I see derision enter his expression. "What the hell kinds of things do you have pending at work that require you to reveal your condition? You write a damned magazine column."

"I've been offered a free face-lift and lipo in exchange for writing about the experience."

He looks genuinely surprised. "You think you need a face-lift?"

"Do you?" I can take it, I really can.

He wags his head. "You got a couple wrinkles, maybe, but that's all. Nothing worth that kind of grief and dough."

"I'm not sure whether I should be flattered that money enters into your consideration, but thank you."

I stand up and turn toward his door. "I need to go."

"Now, Lu." He rushes up to intercept me, but stops just short of touching me. "You need to think about this. This has got to have been a shock for you. I'm freaking out, thinking about it."

I soften. "I know. Me, too." I touch his cheek. "I'll wait until you come back from Bogotá. Then we can talk to the kids together, if you want."

He flinches back. "Did you do this on purpose? Because if you think I'm going to just pack up and come..." He can't even finish the thought before choking.

I look at him. He's thinner, his hair is darker, but his expression makes him seem a hundred years old. He can't handle the idea of a return to before. Neither can I.

"I don't want you back, Jacob. I mean it. If you want to be part of your new son's or daughter's life, I would like that. But that's all."

"Yeah, sure." He's nodding, but his gaze dances all about, looking everywhere but at me. "Shit! I thought you had cancer."

"What?"

He glances at me, looking sort of funny around the eyes. "It's what happened to Rod's wife. Six months after the divorce, she developed breast cancer. The guys at the gym say it's what sometimes happens to older women who can't cope with the idea of a future alone. They develop life-threatening illnesses, so the husbands have to go home."

"Doesn't look like being alone is going to be my particular problem."

"Yeah, well, cancer would be easier to explain to people."

And just like that, I know I'm done here.

I move past him and put my hand on the doorknob. "I'll call you when you get back."

"Don't do anything crazy, Lu." He tosses this line at my back as I leave.

He's three months too late with that advice.

Jacob was totally shocked by my news. It never even occurred to him that the old girl might have it in her, at least while he was in there.

And what was that crack about women developing cancer to get their exes to come back? This is what passes for locker-room talk among middle-aged men these days? Bloody hell!

The only part of his thought process that doesn't throw me completely is the news that he is seeing someone. Sandra. I can't be angry. I have—had—could have... Oh damn!

Once out on the sidewalk, the strangest thing happens. I realize that my face is getting wet. Big fat hot tears run down my cheeks until once again, though not quite uncontrollably, I'm sobbing.

I really didn't expect Jacob to take me into his arms and promise me that everything would be all right. I knew he'd be shocked and upset and very unhappy. I don't know where it came from, that tiny irrational hope that he'd kiss me and say, "I'm here for you now, okay? Let's just go home and forget about the past year."

I didn't want that. Wouldn't have agreed to it. But it would have been nice to hear, all the same.

"You told him? Just like that? Why, Lu?"

I'm sitting in Andrea's kitchen. I couldn't face going home to an empty house just yet. When you need neutral territory, you go to a girlfriend's place. Even to one who thinks you're royally screwing up your life.

I'm nursing the cup of chai tea she insisted I drink before I told her why I showed up with a tear-soaked face at 7:00 p.m. on a Sunday evening.

"I needed to make it real, Andrea. As long as no one knew—" I offer her a sour smile. "You know what I mean. No one who had the power to make me deal with it. As long as I was safe, it was like a game of make-believe. Now it's real."

"It's real, all right." Andrea sits back and crosses her arms. "So, how did Jacob take it?"

"He said it would be easier if I had cancer instead."

Andrea sputters in gutter Spanish...and the Thai, I don't even want to think!

"So this is the man you married. *Pttthhoou!*" She actually spits! On her spotless Italian marble kitchen floor. "He's worthless. For you, I am sorry, but for him—"

"He's just upset," I answer, as surprised as she that I'm defending him. "He's not good at coping with personal crises."

"Don't you defend him! Look what he did to you. You think sex was your idea. But, *mi ja,* I got news for you. Sex was on his mind before you even agreed to go with him. He's a man. It was on his mind. But he didn't even think to protect you. That's what you've got to remember."

I'm sure she's right. But Jacob and I came of age in an age when a condom was still a thing people giggled and whispered about, and that was the guys. A woman with a condom in her purse was a slut. I went on the pill in college, which was easier to deal with than packets of latex, and neither of us, to my knowledge, ever had much experience with condoms since.

"So, what are you going to do now?" Andrea has gotten out the antibacterial cleaner and is spraying the spot she spit.

"Keep living my life. The thing is, I—"

The doorbell rings.

"Can you get that, Lu?"

I open the door. It's Dr. Yummy.

"Hi." He looks past me. "Andrea here?"

"Sure. Come in."

"Baby!" Andrea's voice tells me all I need to know about this relationship.

I turn around so he can't see my face as I mouth *I thought he was too poor.*

Andrea grins and moves past me to drag him in the door by the arm. "You remember my friend, Lu. This is Mark. He's doing a fellowship in heart surgery."

Ka-ching!

14

"You're seeing Dr. Templeton? Why didn't you tell me?"

Aunt Marvelle believes in privacy, but the fact that someone beat her to the punch with gossip about her own niece, well, that's practically family disloyalty. I suppose I could have left a note tacked to her fridge. *Great weekend! Screwed your doc. Thanks for the use of your place. Lu.*

"There's nothing to tell, Aunt Marvelle." Nothing I want to tell, anyway.

"Now, listen to me, Tallulah. Any time an eligible man is seen in the company of a new woman, it's news in this town."

I have just walked through my door after spending the night at Andrea's. She thought I was in no shape to be alone after my run-in with Jacob. So I lay in bed in one of her guest rooms until 11:00 a.m.—total slug—marveling at the perfection of the crocheted flowers in the bed canopy. My grandmother could whip up a crocheted sweater with a day's notice. She reared three daughters who could complete a layette for triplets in a week. I'm the maternal embarrassment. Projects completed by me are like life: uneven, full of holes and never according to plan.

As I lay there thinking this and other totally irrelevant thoughts, it never occurred to me that I might be the subject of salacious speculation in an area that usually gets its gossip from real celeb sightings. But perhaps I exaggerate my importance. The phone message from Aunt Marvelle said she had heard from Cleo, who had it from the owner of the Paradise, that I had left said premises on Friday afternoon in the company of Dr. William Templeton. That involves only four people. Still, I was intrigued enough to call her back.

"We bumped into each other, Aunt Marvelle. Dr. Templeton was with another woman. A much younger, truly gorgeous woman. My date was a banana split."

"I see. Of course, you don't have to tell me anything you don't want to, Tallulah."

I can see where this is heading. The less I say the bigger the traitor I become. "Dr. Templeton was with his daughter, Jolie."

The rarely glimpsed daughter is so good a topic that I am able to shamelessly distract my aunt from the subject of him-with-me. The clincher in the gossip diversion is that Jolie's pregnant. I stop short of reporting the estrangement with her husband. That would be disloyal to William's friendship.

Aunt Marvelle hangs up, satisfied that she now possesses her circle's top news morsel of the day. At least for about five minutes.

My phone rings again, just as I'm relieving a bladder that seems to have shrunk to the size of a pea. I survived two successful pregnancies with no bladder repercussions. This youngster seems determined to rectify that good fortune in the first trimester. A phone in the bathroom was to give me access from the tub. I would never admit this to anyone, but I sometimes pick up from my seat on the throne.

"Tallulah!" Aunt Marvelle again. "Jane just dropped by. She had an appointment with Dr. Templeton today, and I think you should hear what she has to say. Now, just hold on."

"Tallulah, sweetie. Marvelle's just been telling me about you and Dr. Templeton. You sly thing!" No need to correct Jane. I won't be believed. "That's why I thought you should know that you've got some competition for Dr. Templeton's favor."

I love the language of the elder set. For them, men still pledge their favors, the knight-in-shining-armor kind. "Really?"

"Luckily, I had just arrived for my appointment when a deliveryman brought in a huge bouquet of flowers. Huge! And expensive, in a very showy kind of way. There were roses and peonies and snapdragons and tulips in that arrangement, not your standard mums and daylilies. The nurses made such a fuss Dr. Templeton came out to the waiting room to see what was going on. Are you ready for this? After he read the card he just smiled and returned to work, leaving the bouquet out there for all prying eyes to see."

You've got to admire the way these women tell stories. It's the way they play bridge, cards held close to the chest as they wait to see who will trump who with what.

"Did someone else read the card?"

"Who didn't? I would never have actually touched it. That's just not done. But when I stopped to get weighed, the flowers were there on the counter right next to the scale. The card was in its plastic holder, facing out."

"Wow. What did it say?" I feel like the straight woman in a comedy routine.

"The thrill! The rapture! Life is a banquet, after all!

Your secret admirer." Cleo whispers the last, as though it's obscene.

"Gee." It seems a like-minded kind of response.

"I tried to finesse a confession out of Dr. Templeton while in the examining room. Pretended I was jealous, for fun. Tallulah, he didn't turn a hair. Just smiled that inscrutable smile he has, and told me that as long as I kept our quarterly assignations, I will never lose his favor! Now, what do you think of that?"

That you've got to admire the savoir faire of a man who's being leaned on by a seventy-eight-year-old flirt. "I had no idea he was so popular."

"That's what we were just saying. The nurses swear they don't know who he's seeing. So, I stopped at the florist who'd made the delivery to make some inquiries. I said I wanted to order a bouquet exactly like the one they made for Dr. Templeton. I was certain the girl would tell me who ordered it. Merchants out here like to brag on certain clientele."

"Don't tell her that," I hear my aunt Marvelle say in the background. "She'll think we spy on people!"

"No, she won't. Besides, I couldn't get a peep out of the clerk. Probably a summer hire. Personally, I think the sender's married. Or an actress. You get all those aging Broadway types moving out here, looking for a little tea and sympathy."

"Give me that phone!" I listen as a short, dignified scuffle, accompanied by jangling jewelry, takes place on the other end before Aunt Marvelle says, "Jane never gets to the point of anything. Tea and sympathy!"

"That means sex!" Jane calls out, in case I might be in doubt.

"Cleo didn't tell you the most important part. Subtlety is not her strong suit. That's why she prefers musicals to dramas. Who cares about the flowers? Women are always throwing themselves at Dr. Templeton. The point is, Cleo says Dr. Templeton wasn't wearing his wedding band when he examined her." I have to admit this tidbit makes the hair stand up on the back of my neck. "Was he wearing a wedding band when you saw him last Friday?"

"I particularly noticed that he was." At the beginning of the evening.

"I knew you'd notice. That's because you're related to me. I'm going to say this only once, Tallulah. If he's made up his mind to start looking for companionship, he won't stay in the market long."

Wonder if William knows he's being talked about like a side of beef with an expiration date on the wrapper? "Thanks for the advice, Aunt Marvelle. But I really just finished dealing with one man. I don't need another in my life right now. Bye."

Time to fess up. I did one other thing while lying in Andrea's guest bed. I ordered flowers and composed that "mash" note. It was the least possessive way I could think of to say thanks to William for the resuscitation of Lu Nichols.

And to think I wondered if I was being paranoid to tell the florist I did not want that bouquet traceable to me. Marvelle's Marvelous Matrons are dangerous.

William isn't wearing his wedding band! I feel the ancient seminal female urge to confess to my indiscreet weekend to my best girlfriend after all. But how can I gush to Andrea about my Dr. Yummy after she sacrificed a night with her doc for me?

I think of calling Mom. But she had a bad week last week, what with the news that she needs a double root canal. If you don't know someone with a real and true phobia about dentists, you can't imagine what that news did to her, or what my father has been dealing with since. He's offered her a Hawaiian cruise as amends for being born with such mutinous teeth. This is not a woman who needs to hear that her eldest child is pregnant by her ex, and sleeping with abandon with a stranger who makes love as if he invented it!

The wage of this sinning must be that I have to bear the guilty pleasure of it alone.

I wander into the breakfast room where the mail and weekend newspapers that Cy picked up are neatly arranged on my kitchen table. He's such a good friend. Too bad his kids would have him committed if he tried to marry again.

He will absolutely understand my situation. I think. I hope. When I tell him. But I have to tell my family first.

I pick up the phone and call Dallas's home phone and leave a message, inviting her to spend Saturday night of Memorial weekend with me. Davin will be home by then, serving his one-week parental duty time before heading off to his summer job in the Berkshires. We'll make it a family sleepover.

15

"Hey, Lu. Waz up?"

"Not— Oh!" My hand rises to cover my mouth as I behold the sight in my office doorway. I almost don't recognize Curran with his sandy-red brows and lashes, minus black mascara. More than that, his head is covered with little inch-and-a-half bundles of matted hair, held together with red rubber bands at the scalp and tip. "Curran, you look just like Binky the Clown."

Curran scratches his chin where a few scraggly reddish hairs have sprouted since last week. "Who?"

"A doll I once had." Binky was a Raggedy Ann-type scarecrow with a clown face and hair made out of orange yarn knotted at the scalp. Curran looks just as silly to me as that clown but I won't contribute that thought. "You, ah, got—"

"Dreads." He grins and nods. "I found a shop in Newark that does Caucasian hair. The stylist is K'Shonde. Gave me props for checking out her stuff. Told her I'm too dope to try weak shizz like chemicals, or peanut butter and toothpaste. My stuff is tight."

He's been working on his hip-hop language, too. So far, I'm barely keeping up with the syntax.

I remember my youthful suffering for beauty's sake—sleeping in hard curlers, wearing spiked heels and pointy toes. But as I touch one of Curran's tightly bundled dreads I have to say, "Those rubber bands look like they hurt."

"No doubt. It takes eight or nine months to create dreads, but only four or five weeks for the hair to lock up. Then I can take off the scalp bands."

I can't help it. Looking at them makes me scratch my scalp. "Don't they itch?"

His head nods forward as he casts me the doubtful look of a young conqueror who's begun to suspect he's laid his booty before an unappreciative audience. "You're misconceptualizing, Lu. Peoples are misled to think it's about dirty hair. Clean hair is the secret of phat dreads."

At the moment KaZi stops at my open door, her hair today so vivid a pink a Mary Kay consultant would blush. "Hey, Lu. I brought you the mock-up for the revamped August issue."

Curran leaps off the edge off my desk at the sound of her voice and spins around to face the doorway. "Whot's up, KaZi?"

"You got dreads. Cool." KaZi deadpans these words, but I can tell she's impressed because she actually walks up to him and examines one little thumb of hair. "Don't do something stupid like put conditioner on them."

"A brother's down." Curran actually preens as he begins rolling a clump of hair between his thumb and fingers. "Using beeswax and tea-tree oil."

KaZi shrugs. "Nice fragrance." She turns and hands me the layout pages. "The art department thinks they need work. They also left room for your column. See what you think. We've got until Monday morning to make adjustments."

"That's what I came to tell you." Curran pats the layout stack. "Your 'before' photos are in here. Tai e-mailed her final choices from Lucerne yesterday. I'da made the same, but for one. The layout's dope!"

KaZi nods.

"Thanks. I think." I have seen the negatives under the light using the magnifier, but not the cropped and touched-up final results.

My fingers nervously run the scales over the top page. Though they have both seen them, I don't want a lot of witnesses as I look at my magazine-size images for the first time. In fact, I want to share this moment only with Curran. After all, his reputation and my self-esteem are tied up in these photographs.

I look up at KaZi, who's paying an unusual amount of attention to her cuticles, and hope she gets the hint.

Finally she glances sideways at Curran. "You got panty hose yet?"

He dumbly shakes his head.

"You need them to wash dreads. I'll buy you a pair at lunch. But you got to pay. For lunch, too."

"That's cool." Curran bops his head. That must mean Tai ponied up the bonus she promised him if she was pleased with his work. My stomach clinches at the thought of what Tai would consider good shots of the "before" me.

As she turns to leave, Curran says to KaZi, "I'm hittin' the shore this weekend. Dip my dreads in the ocean. Drying in the sun will tighten 'em down quick. You down for that?"

KaZi comes close to smiling. "Probably."

"Cool!" He leaps forward to follow her.

As they wander away from my door in the too-cool slouch of a matched set, I realize I've just witnessed a twenty-first-century mating ritual. I feel somehow deserted.

It's not that I hadn't had in the back of my mind thoughts that KaZi would make a great East Coast girlfriend for Curran. I could just have used a few minutes more of his best-bud adoration to get me through the ordeal of the photos. In return I would have bought him panty hose.

Okay, I didn't understand the connection between washing dreads and panty hose, but I don't have to. This is not my generation.

Ah, love.

Ah-*choo!*

As I wipe my nose I tell myself this is not a real cold, but a reaction to the stress of the last weeks.

I've had a few days to compare my weekend dealings with the two men in my life. Well, the two men I dealt with over the weekend.

William handled things remarkably well, considering. More than the physical, he showed me the possibilities of my future. His methods might be unorthodox, but he punched a big crack in the wall of my life. For the first time in a long time I see the sunshine on the other side.

Still, I'm too wise in the ways of the world—okay, too old—to attach romantic destiny to the magic. Men look a lot better if you don't tack *forever* over their snapshots. William had a great moment just when I needed someone in my life to be great. I'm too grateful to expect more. So, just as he suspected, I won't be calling him, but not because of the reason he feared.

Things with Jacob haven't gone so well. We've talked on the phone three times in the two days since my announcement.

He called Monday evening to apologize for not "being there" for me. Then he told me how he had had a chance to think things over, and while it would be nice to think about another child, it wasn't practical in any sense.

I made the mistake of agreeing about the practical part. Before I knew it, he was planning doctor visits and making a payment plan to cover his share of the not-having-the-baby expenses. I told him thanks, but those weren't the expenses I hoped he would bear. I said I thought he might want to be part of the baby's life. He said I was trying to control things. Not giving him options. It went downhill from there.

I shouldn't count call number two because I had hung up on him to end call number one. He was still shouting, and so I hung up again.

The phone didn't ring again until late afternoon yesterday. He was at the airport, heading for Bogotá.

"Lu, be reasonable. Think what this could do to your health. Now, don't take this the wrong way, but turning fifty means you're grandmother material. Many a twentysomething single mother can't cope. I don't want you to be a victim of Post Blue Baby syndrome."

"I assume you mean postpartum depression." He and Davin share this tic of wrong-word association.

"Yeah, that's it. Besides, you have a career to think about. I know you can't afford child care. Jeez, Lu. A baby stuck in day care at six weeks! Think of the harm you'd be exposing it to."

"You're not winning me over, you know that."

"I'm trying to consider what's best for all."

"Including me? Because the best thing for me would be unconditional support for whatever comes."

There's a long silence. "Don't do this, Lu. You will regret it."

I think about this, and almost say that of all the things I really regret the one I regret the most is that closure weekend in February. But that's no longer true. I'm excited about the prospect of being a new mother again. Coping with family and friends is another issue altogether.

I reach for the portfolio. Somehow it is now easier to face my face in print than to entertain thoughts of future conversations with Jacob.

It comes as a shock when I spread out the layout pages and see my face. It is mine, surely. But I don't quite recognize myself. The images are black and white. But more, they are truly old-fashioned glamour photos like those Curran hoped to emulate. While the subject isn't quite an aging classic beauty—say Katharine Hepburn or Lena Horne—Curran saved me from the Bette Davis/Joan Crawford spooky painted look.

What I notice first is not the ravages of time—as Tai so kindly dubbed the concept of the "before" pictures before she even saw them—but the life within my face. I didn't realize I have a jaw that angular, or cheekbones that prominent. Yes, the shadows reveal fine-line wrinkles, but more, they show a depth of things I haven't noticed before. There seems to be wisdom in those heavy-lidded eyes, an acceptance of life in the softening of a generous mouth. I look content. Until the last photo.

I remember the moment, when I thought to myself, *I can't do this!* That is an image I recognize. That startled expression is the shape of my life these days. It could be titled "Home Alone—And Other Middle-Age Atrocities."

I fold up the layout and push it away.

The good news is Tai is out of town for the week, at an Italian Alps run, slogging through air-deficient regions of Italy. What a waste of a great vacation. But I do not begrudge her one exhausting moment of the trip. For it's giving me the breather I need to take care of some personal business.

I look down at the want ads I just managed to tuck away when Curran entered. There are a remarkable number of low-paying journalism-type jobs available. Who's going to hire a pregnant woman? That's the real question.

Because my days at *Five-O* are numbered, given Tai's ultimatum and my decision.

She said we'd talk when she returned. It will no doubt go something like this.

"You're ready for lipo?"

"No."

"Face-lift?"

"No."

"Surely, Botox."

"No, and never."

"You're fired."

"I figured."

Realizing that I'm rubbing my tummy, I stop, hoping no one saw me. Had to tell the Radish it was indigestion when she caught me at it this morning. But that story won't fly much longer. At three months and counting, I'm outgrowing even my elastic waists. My bras are bulging to an embarrassing degree. So, before the word is on the street, I plan to hit both my fledglings with one big mother of a stone this weekend.

16

Dallas is letting her hair grow. Lucy, the wedding consultant, told her that all *New York Times*-hopeful brides wear their hair long or up for their portraits, giving them a timeless look. An up-to-the-moment fashion image quickly dates itself. This decision was made a week after the Oscars and three days after Dallas got a Halle Berry pixie cut. It's been over a year, yet Dallas is still a long way from flowing locks. Her hair has reached yet another unmanageable stage. As she enters, carrying a leather backpack for our Saturday-night sleepover, she looks like a Hobbit.

"I know," Dallas says after she's hugged me at the door and I've swept back a thick chunk of hair from her brow before giving it a kiss. "My hair's a mess. Lucy says that if by my portrait date it isn't long enough to be slicked back with a chignon hair piece, I should consider extensions."

"Why can't Lucy just admit that you have a face made for short hair." I watch her finger-comb the same chunk of hair back from her quite pretty heart-shaped face. "All that hair overwhelms your delicate features."

"Yeah, like a rat in a wig." Davin lounges against the doorjamb to the entry hall.

"Stinker!" Dallas cries in delight at the sight of her brother.

They hug but pretty soon it's clear they are really trying to outmaneuver each other in some sort of karate match-up. I don't care what they say about the leveling effect of martial arts. At five four, Dallas is about two-thirds her brother's six-foot size. When all else fails, Davin simply grabs her about the waist and lifts her a foot off the floor, upside down.

"The male again dominates the female in the age-old struggle!" he pronounces from deep in his chest.

"Put me down!" Dallas says this with as much dignity as a person can manage while being suspended headfirst.

I help Dallas right herself. "And to think I thought I'd be glad when you were grown."

"Yeah, Dallas. Act your age." Davin is grinning, looking so much like his father did in his twenties that I do a double take.

"You started it," Dallas says, swiping hair from her eyes.

"You started it!" Davin mimics.

I'm not usually emotional, but this sniping and one-upsmanship nearly brings me to tears. I start blinking so fast I can feel the breeze of my lashes on my eyeballs. As the big empty house echoes with familiar voices, I feel deep-down warm in a way that I thought I might never feel again.

We're having this sleepover so that I can pretend for one night that they still belong only to me. The truth is, Dallas is about to pledge unending love to a man I like but can't say I really know. Davin is in full blown "I'm an independent being who sprung full-grown from a stone" mode. He loves us, but right now he doesn't want his parents to cast even so much as a shadow in his direction. I thought this was preteen stuff until I had an eighteen-year-old college freshman who lived on his own—on our money. He threatened to leave campus if we showed up for parents weekend. To have him voluntarily come home for a week? Priceless.

I turn away quickly so neither glimpses the tears that come into my eyes. I guess I'm feeling extra maternal these days. "How about a glass of wine, for the grown-ups?"

"Now we're talking." Davin rubs his hands together.

"You wouldn't know a pinot grigio from a watermelon spritzer." Dallas is busy adjusting her capris and crop top.

"Wrong! I know all about the grape, and its varietals. I took a course."

"In wine drinking?" Dallas and I ask in unison as we all head for the kitchen.

"It was a nonacademic elective. A mini course in wine appreciation."

"How could you take it?" Dallas is clearly onto something. "You're not of legal drinking age yet."

Davin ducks my *oho* expression. "They never checked."

Dallas rolls her eyes in my direction. "You see, that's what's wrong with the law. It's enforced unequally. I have to pull my driver's license out every time I order, even when I'm entertaining business clients. Waiters do it just to embarrass me. While wild man here doesn't even have to prove he's eligible for a class!"

"If you'd get a grown-up haircut and stop looking like a Rugrat maybe they wouldn't do it." Davin offers this sage advice while I busy myself reaching for the cheese board I readied to go with the wine.

"Dallas, chardonnay or pinot grigio?"

Dallas frowns. "The pinot should breathe after opening."

"That's only true of pinot noirs. The grigio is fine served immediately." Davin gives her a superior look, then sets about making a racket while looking for the corkscrew.

We talk right through wine and cheese. I have a club soda, saying that I'm trying to lose a few pounds. It doesn't seem right to bring up booze and baby in the pre-amble of the evening. Okay, I'm stalling. But timing is everything, as they say. First we reminisce and then we'll talk of our respective futures.

Dinner is moussaka, Davin's favorite, Greek salad and bread. Dallas is partial to my homemade fudge brownies. I bought ice cream to go with them. I notice that while Dallas said she can't eat much, with her wedding dress about to be fitted, she consumes nearly as much as Davin.

"This is wonderful. I had forgotten what real home cooking is like," she says more than once.

I'm reassured. Tonight, she's happy. I watch her face, animated by her brother's dorm stories, and remember when she was happy all the time. Well, she was a teenage girl. Happy most of the time.

"Hey, what about your wedding dress?" Davin points out when he and Dallas reach for the final helping at the same time. "Sure you can handle thirds, orca?"

"Thirds?" Dallas pulls back, flushing a deep rose. "With all the talking, I wasn't paying attention."

"So, how's the *boy*friend?" Trust Davin to broach the subject in a way most likely to change his sister's mood with one sideswipe remark.

Why she feels the need to defend Stephen each and every time his name is brought up is beyond me. But she does. She looks like someone stuck a coat hanger up her back. "My *fiancé* is fine. Great. Wonderful."

"You guys still living apart?" Davin forks moussaka into his mouth as if it's his first serving.

"Of course. We have found celibacy to be quite instructive." Dallas turns to me. "My productivity has ac-tually increased. Stephen says he's able to concentrate bet-ter, too."

Davin snorts like a racehorse. I try to signal him not to,

but he pounces. "Oh, so Stephen thinks a sexless relationship with you is a good idea?"

"What a stupid question!" Dallas glares at him.

"So it's you." Davin crosses his arms on the table and leans in with a cheesy grin. "Is your hero a big zero in bed?"

I thump Davin on the elbow. "Leave Dallas alone."

"What did I do?" He manages to lounge in a straight-backed chair. "She's the one going all sour. I think it's unnatural to be happy about not having sex."

"Is that so?" Dallas says in an oily voice. "Then why don't you tell us about your newest girlfriend? Or haven't you known her long enough to get her name?"

"Yeah, that's it. I don't know her name."

"What happened to Angie?" I have wanted to ask, but couldn't until now.

"Angie." Davin looks like he's trying to remember losing his first tooth. "Oh, she was into, like, marathon relationships. I had to tell her I'm more of a sprinter."

"Maybe if you slowed down long enough to take notes, you'd know your girlfriend's name *and* get decent grades."

Davin sits up. "What do you mean?"

"Dad says you're letting your grades slide. Again. And what's with taking just twelve hours a semester? Don't you plan to graduate before you're thirty? Or do you expect to live off our parents until social security kicks in for you?"

"Stop." I put up a hand. "No character assassinations in my house. I just had the rugs cleaned." I turn to Dallas. "Will you clear the table?"

"Yeah, woman's work!" Davin jeers.

"Davin, you can dish up the leftovers." I'm so sure Dallas sticks out her tongue at her brother that I don't bother to look.

For no particular reason I can think of, Davin adds,

"And just for the record, I can't collect social security unless I've had a job!"

A child growing up as a singleton will be spared these heart-warming moments, I remind myself as I'm forced to recall the main reason for this family gathering. Maybe after dessert.

It's impossible not to notice that Dallas's carefree mood has deserted her. The clang of flatware and bang of pots is alarming as she sets about clearing the table. The one time I dare sidle up to her at the sink and ask what's wrong, she reacts with predictable defense.

"Nothing's wrong." I see hurt and something else in her quick glance. "What could be wrong?"

Good question. "Just so you know, if you want to talk..." I let it trail, for she doesn't even nod.

I try to think how to segue into the subject of the evening. "Did I tell you your mother's about to become a crusader? Breaking new ground, in a way."

"In what way?" Dallas asks.

"For one, I'm about to put my job on the line as being against any radical measures to regain a youthful appearance. All this preoccupation with lines and wrinkles seems another way of making women feel they need to deny the lives we have lived. My job dilemma might serve as an instructive lesson for women of your generation, Dallas."

"You're not serious, Mom?" I wish Dallas sounded more amused than annoyed.

"I guess that did sound a bit pompous. My thoughts were more along the lines of adding to the general body of passed-on experience."

"I took a history course about your generation last fall. It was called 'The Sixties,'" Davin offers helpfully. "I didn't learn much except I can 'really groove—'" he does finger quotation marks "—on your motto, Make Love, Not War. Right on."

Dallas shakes her head. "The point is, your generation tried to have it all. Now that it's fallen apart, you're whining. Don't worry, Mom. We don't want to be like you. *Five-O* is practically a manual of how–not–to become like you."

Davin, who's started dishing out ice cream to go with the brownies, whistles softly and shoots his sister a "boy, you stepped in it" glance.

"I didn't mean you, personally, Mom." Dallas looks apologetic as she rinses the wineglasses. "I mean, for instance, those women profiled in last month's issue. They were so busy being professionally fulfilled that they waited until forty to try to have children. Now they expect the rest of the world to mourn their lack of reproductive opportunities."

"Yeah," Davin chimes in. "What if you'd waited until now to have a child? It just wouldn't happen."

My moment. "Funny you should bring that up. What if I were pregnant now? What would be your reaction?"

"Pregnant? At your age?" Davin snickers. "Sorry, Mom."

"No, seriously. What do you two think about me having another child?"

Dallas shakes her head. "You can't expect me to react to an impossibility."

"It's not impossible. It is a fact."

I wait for them to both turn startled glances my way and then nod. "I'm going to have a baby. In November."

17

"Maybe it's a hysterical thing."

Dallas swings around on Davin. "What are you talking about?"

"You never heard of hysterical pregnancy?" He's looking smug to be the bearer of knowledge his sister does not have. "It happens to stressed-out women. Happened to a friend last week."

"What friend?" Dallas and I chorus in identical suspicion.

Davin's expression slips into vague mode, the kind he adopts when his father asks what he's been doing with his time, or his money. "A friend of a friend, okay? This guy's girl thought she was pregnant, having all these symptoms, you know? Only it turned out she was major stressed over finals. The infirmary said that kind of thing happens every semester. Women get emotional, right? It affects things. Female things. I'm just saying with Mom going through the divorce and all..." He shrugs. "Hysterical stuff happens."

Dallas looks back at me in disgust. "Do you hear the kind of chauvinist you've reared?"

"I'm not responsible for your brother's warped understanding of female biology."

I reach for one of the bowls of ice cream Davin has filled and plop a still-warm brownie on top. "This is not stress. I have four pregnancy tests and a doctor's examination to back me up."

Two exclamation points appear between Dallas's brows to punctuate her surprise. "You've seen a doctor about this?"

"Two physicians, actually." I drop a thin curl of vanilla ice cream onto my brownie. The truth has given me a powerful new appetite.

"Jeez, Mom!" The same look of utter bewilderment is on Davin's face as when he was four years old and his ice cream fell off his cone onto the grass.

Dallas, as always, takes command. "Is there something we don't know, Mom?"

About half of my life. A mental image flares through my mind of me flat on my back at a beach house, draped with nothing but the doctor-on-call. But this is not the time to inform my children about how much I can deviate from the person they think I am. "Your father and I made an error in judgment a few months back—"

"The Caribbean trip!" Davin chimes in at last, grinning. "I hear the tropical beach scene is a real turn-on."

"The point is, we didn't mean for this to happen."

"Didn't mean…?" Dallas looks stunned. "After all those books you made me read in junior high about safe sex and birth control, and then write reports about…"

"Yeah, and those dumb lectures at the YMCA," Davin chimes in.

"Mom, what were you thinking?"

"Obviously she wasn't thinking 'no glove, no love.'" Davin snickers. "So Dad's still got it in him. Awesome!"

I hereby promise myself to never *ever* have another discussion about my sex life with my children.

"Does Dad know?" The tone of Dallas's question could be termed insulting. I remind myself that she's trying to absorb a shock, and choose to accept it at face value.

"Certainly. He wanted me to wait—"

Dallas launches herself across the room to embrace me, cutting off my prepared speech. "But this is great! So great! Isn't it, Davin? Dad and Mom are getting back together!" She's hugging me so tight I can't get in a word. "Oh, but, Mom, at your age, you'll need to look after yourself." She releases me and turns to her brother. "Davin, get Mom a stool for her feet."

"I'm fine, Dallas, really. Look." I plop down on a kitchen chair. "I'm sitting."

"Are you sure? Because if you need anything, *anything*—" She pauses to inhale an incredible breath. "This is just soooo great!"

My daughter is too happy. It's the kind of instant euphoria that's so over the top you just know the person is going to crash and burn. I should have waited. Should have had her father here to catch her as she falls.

But for the moment her hyperactivity has kicked even her brother out of energy-conservation mode. Davin snatches up the footstool I use to reach the high shelf in the pantry, and puts it before me. Then he lifts each of my feet with the care I wish he'd use when he handles my Waterford crystal, and places them on it.

Dallas actually puts another curl of ice cream on my brownie before she hands me my bowl. All the while she's babbling about new starts, the joys of life with renewed purpose, and how glad she is that her parents have come to their senses.

Finally she pauses and stares at me with such concern that I suspect she's about to drape a tea towel around my shoulders to ward off the possibility of an ice-cream chill. I decide a bracing dose of the creamy cold stuff is just what I need. As I bring a mouthful of brownie and ice cream to my mouth, she reaches out with a napkin to catch a drip.

It's too much.

"Stop! Sit!" The tone of voice, accompanied by the hand command I learned at obedience school when we had a cocker spaniel, works perfectly with children—certainly better than it did with that dog. They resume their chairs at once.

I put my bowl aside and stand up. The general always stands to charge her troops. "First, I'm touched by your enthusiastic response to my news. However, the situation is not that simple. To begin with, your father isn't at all happy about it. In fact, he's very clear that he doesn't think I should have this child."

"Dad's just in shock. Who wouldn't be? At your time of life? " Dallas is nothing if not tenacious. "But he will come around, won't he, Davin?"

Davin shrugs, still clearly out of his depth. At a later time I must ponder his ease with the notion of hysterically pregnant women but not truly pregnant ones.

"Listen to me. This is very important. When your dad returns from his business trip, I don't want either of you to pressure him. He is a free man, after all. All decisions and responsibilities concerning this child are mine."

Exclamation marks reappear between Dallas's brows. "You mean to have it even if Dad disapproves?"

The word "it" is beginning to bug me. "My *child*, Dallas. And yes, I have every intention of seeing this pregnancy through. Alone."

"Oh, my God!" The hysterical edge is back in Dallas's voice, minus this time the euphoria. "What do I tell Stephen? What will he say to his parents?"

At last, Davin finds his footing in the conversation. "Tell them the truth. Dad knocked up Mom after their divorce."

Dallas turns on her brother. "That's—disgusting!"

Davin cackles with laughter. "Better get used to it. Remember the belly on Stephen's sister Lucy last Christmas?"

Dallas's gaze lowers to what is still my fairly flat middle section and her eyes buck wide. "Oh, Mom! He's right. You'll be a blimp by my wedding!"

And the blessings just keep coming. I never liked the mother-of-the-bride ensemble she chose for me. She calls it goldenrod. Looks Teletubby yellow to me. "You can tether me to the church's front pew like a Macy's Thanksgiving Day parade balloon."

Dallas backs away from me as if I've grown Buffy-the-Vampire-style fangs. "I know you don't take my wedding plans seriously, Mom. But I don't understand how you can laugh at me when it's *you* who seems to have lost all sense of decency." She pronounces these words as if they were a judicial pronouncement. "My family has turned into one big joke and embarrassment!"

"I'm not embarrassed," Davin volunteers.

"That's because you don't have a grasp of the situation," Dallas shoots back. "I do."

"It's not about you," I interject before she can begin the barrage sure to follow this martyrdom preamble. "This conversation is about me. Okay? I shared my condition with you out of love and respect. You do not get a vote on how I handle the matter."

"So maybe I should have asked this first. Are you certain it is Dad's?"

Talk about your pregnant pauses… My daughter has a mean streak. From Jacob's side of the family, I'm certain. I feel myself vibrating like a too-tight violin string before words come thrumming out of me. "Your private snooping missed something, Dallas. Her name is Sandra, and she's partial to yellow tulips."

"You've been checking up on Dad?" Davin shakes his head. "That's cold, Dallas."

"Why?" I turn to him. "Did you know about her?"

Poor Davin. He turns bright red. "He might have mentioned seeing someone. Been a while since he was, you know, out there."

"Dad's been calling *you* for dating tips?" For once Dallas's indignant shrill matches my own exasperation. "I cannot be here now."

Dallas turns on her heel, a move she perfected in drill team, and heads for the exit. She's found her backpack and made it to the front door before I catch up.

"Dallas, wait. Where are you going?"

"After all I've done to help Dad see his duty—and he calls Bimbos Anonymous for advice!" She manages to look both devastated and brave at the same time. "But that isn't the point, is it, Mom? This plan of yours to try to win Dad back—I don't understand why it's not working."

"For the last time, I wasn't playing Baby Roulette." Yet I have a feeling this is not the last time I'll have to say this to the people in my life. "The only thing more horrifying to your father than the fact that I'm pregnant by him is that I might have the baby."

"Then this is a horrible mistake, one that is hurtful and—dangerous to the family, to you. I won't pretend otherwise. I'm leaving, Mom. I need to think, alone."

When she has closed the front door, Davin says from behind me, "Way to break up a party, Mom."

I turn to him. Amazingly, he's again smiling.

"How long have you known about Sandra?" I know this is breaching the father-son confidence clause but I've had enough ugly surprises for one season.

"It's not like that, Mom." He shakes his head quickly. "I didn't know Dad was seeing someone particular. But don't worry about Dad dating, Mom. It's just something men do. Doesn't mean he's serious. I mean, you're going to have a kid, right? If it's a boy, Dad will come running back."

That's too much honesty, even for me. But Davin is on a roll, feeling the need to comfort as he follows me back to the kitchen.

"Think about it, Mom. Dad's always on my case. Says I'm not living up to the standards of a son of his. Another son might deflect the heat— Whoa! Hold up. What if Junior makes me look bad?" Davin's thoughts snap him out of his slouch. "Give Dad a new son to rear and he might just write me off!"

As I've said before, Davin's smart. He's just sometimes a little slow on the uptake. I reach for one of the dished-up bowls of dessert that has started to melt.

Davin is suddenly a man with a plan. He comes up and hugs me from behind. "You can't have another one of us, Mom. It's always been a perfect balance. One boy, one girl. You can't mess with the family arithmetic."

"Mother Nature can, and has."

He releases me. "Whose side are you on, Mom?"

Doubt and a genuine sense of betrayal lurk in his soulful gaze. "Do there have to be sides?" I pat his cheek. "Come on, have a bowl of ice cream."

But as I slide one toward him, Davin backs up a step. "I, uh, need to make some calls."

I wonder if he's going to call Jacob. I can't really afford heart-to-hearts via Bogotá, but the price of parenting comes steep these days.

My ankles are throbbing by the time I've cleaned up after dinner. I feel uncomfortable in the middle, too. Two extra bowls of ice cream and brownies could account for that. Sometimes comfort requires a lot of calories.

When I sit down on my bed and kick off my shoes, it looks as if I'm wearing bobby socks under my hose. Sadly, those are my ankles.

"More water, less ice cream," I mumble to myself as I head toward the bathroom for a glass of water. A pregnant woman needs lots of water. She doesn't need a daughter who thinks she's been betrayed by her mother's fertility. Or a son who thinks he can be replaced by a sibling whose sex has yet to be determined.

Maybe I haven't made the smartest moves lately. Perhaps I could have done a better job tonight. But I can't go back. Don't want to.

If I had to do my life all over again, I'd sit down and cry. Who knows that different choices wouldn't mess up the good parts entirely?

I reach for the phone to call William. I said I would. I've wanted to. I've been debating doing it for days. It just didn't seem right to call him before I had told the family about the baby.

Yet as I scroll through my Blackberry to find his number, it occurs to me that with my family in turmoil perhaps I shouldn't complicate my life further. I've just seen how unhappy Dallas and Davin are about things so far. *Mom's got a boyfriend* isn't going to go over well. I don't want to hurt them. Now, if I could just keep him a guilty secret...

I put down the phone. Since when could I keep anything as wonderful as William a secret? Maybe in a couple of weeks, when things settle, I'll call.

18

Despite her "stay-and-sleepover" hosting of nearly two weeks ago, I didn't expect Andrea to keep our bimonthly shopping date. After all, she had to put out Dr. Yummy, er, Mark, to accommodate me, something she was quite vocal about once he'd left.

She hasn't called or answered any of my messages. Not even when I left her a detailed rant about just how unwisely I handled Dallas and Davin. I didn't bother her with last night's call from Jacob. Dallas had called him. Woozy from a twelve-hour flight from Bogotá, he still packed an impressive amount of curse words into each sentence. I hung up on him, of course.

Davin left for his Catskills summer job Monday. He swears he'll call regularly to check on me. This is to show he's technically on my side, but I suspect it's only because technically he still lives with me.

But here Andrea is, on Thursday morning as usual,

standing in my bedroom while I try to find something decent to wear.

"So, am I going to be a godmother, or what?"

"I thought you didn't approve of my lifestyle choice." I say this while trying to hold in a stomach that wants to be free to express itself.

Andrea shrugs elaborately. "What's to approve? You're crazy. I'm crazy. We just have different crazies. This kid is gonna need a lot of help."

Once she's watched me complete the marvel of zipping up my pants, she looks alarmed. "Promise me you won't look like a bag lady for the entire nine months."

"Too tight, huh?" I'm trying to perfect breathing tiny sips of air so my zipper won't pop.

"*Dios mio!* Come on!" She grabs my arm.

As she pulled me through my house, she says, "Pregnancy is the perfect excuse for guilt-free shopping. If there's ever a time to say there's nothing in my closet, this is it!"

Shopping is Andrea's therapy for everything. There is no problem so intractable or tragedy so overwhelming that it can't be eased by the acquisition of apparel. Shoes are her particular weakness. The last time she broke an engagement with a guy, I watched her spend $600 at a discount designer shoe store in SoHo in a single afternoon. The cash layout might not sound like a lot in these days of Jimmy Choos. But what Andrea bought for that price is. Twenty-five pairs! That's because she wears a size six. Something fabulous is always left over in the smaller sizes.

"It's summer," she said in answer to the cashier's amazement. "You can't wear sandals but a season. They get those greasy toe prints on the leather."

"Gourmet baby food. Twist-top throwaway bottles." Andrea's on a roll as we pile into her car. "Furniture, strollers, car seats. And the clothes? Are you ready? Carolina Herrera is doing maternity fashions! I'm going to show it all to you."

I'm not sure I can get into the maternity-fashion mood. Clothes haven't meant much to me in a while. Big-tent clothing seems even less appealing. Besides, the wallet is shrinking with the prospects of unemployment. News of Tai's "tragic accident" on the icy slope of some minor alpine peak is all that stands between me and unemployment.

I try to explain all this to Andrea as we drive up to the first stop.

She stares at me as if I'd suggested *W* stop publishing. "You're giving up on the woman in you!"

She's got a point. The image in the bedroom mirror wasn't wonderful. Maybe I do need shopping therapy.

"You're going to love this. There are lots of improvements in styles since you had Davin." Andrea is marching toward the first store, only to halt and turn when she notices I've fallen behind. "How come you're walking like John Wayne?"

"Sitting in these pants cut off circulation to my thighs."

The first store Andrea pulls me into is an education in itself. Pregnancy trends change from decade to decade. Since Davin is twenty, it appears I'm a couple of generations behind.

I'm feeling pretty good about the advances in maternity clothing until I try on the under belly pant. I pull them on and let go. They slide down around my hips. I try to lift from the front but there's only a couple of strategic inches of material that keeps my bum from showing. "I don't get it."

Andrea heaves a big sigh. "My sister Inez has two pairs. It's for when a woman's huge. The backside takes up the slack in the back while the belly swells over."

"You mean my—stomach will show?"

"That's a really fashionable summer look with younger women," the salesclerk says from the other side of the door. I try to believe there's nothing snide in her tone. "A little halter top and you will be set for the beach or sight-seeing or whatever."

Whatever is right. The sight no one will be seeing this or any other summer is my naked belly, pregnant or not.

After I purchase a few practical items for every day at the discount store, Andrea insists we check out an upscale maternity boutique. I say it's just for grins but I should know better. In spite of my resolve just to look, I'm enthralled by a sleeveless black silk sheath whose polka-dot shear overdress ends at the knee in a flounce of feathers. Put my hair up, give me a pair of big dark sunglasses and a cigarette holder—no—a pair of long black gloves and I'm pure Holly Golightly. All for $495.

"You need this." Andrea's voice is an unqualified yes. "As your mother-of-the-bride dress." Andrea opens the door so fast the clerk nearly falls on her face. "We'll take this," she says to the stumbling woman, and points to me.

"Andrea!" I say in a warning voice, for I don't have the money for something this extravagant that I'm destined never to wear.

"You've got layaway?"

The clerk nods. "Thirty percent down. The rest within sixty days."

"If you don't want it, I'll buy it and give it to my pregnant cousin," Andrea says as the clerk bags it up.

"Which one?"

"Who knows? Someone's always pregnant in a family the size of mine."

"I wish you the best of luck with your upcoming event," the clerk says when I've plunked down the first installment.

My brows shoot up. "You don't think I'm too old to be having a child?"

She smiles serenely, her commission safe. "It's nothing unusual. We get a lot of forty-year-old mothers in here."

I smile. *Forty.* A decade regained. Take that, Tai!

June

Once a woman has "ripped her breeches,"
as my grandmother would say, with family and friends,
what they think just doesn't matter anymore.
She will, however, often form a closer alliance with the truth.

—"When a 'Good Woman' Goes Bad"
CUE LU!

19

The tone is set before I even glimpse Tai. The moment the elevator doors glide open onto the offices of *Five-O* I feel the frost of perfection.

It often happens at successful galas, fetes and other all-important events. Someone arrives, and for a perceptible moment, there's the sense of snow falling from a bright July sky. How can this be? And yet there it is. Those in the know count the number of times this freeze-frame of interest galvanizes the jaded throng—and use it to sell everything from CDs to soap.

"She's back," Babs mouths at me as I approach. Uh-oh. We're down to pantomiming on the first day of Tai's return. Not a good sign. Just how "terrible" was the accident that kept her out of work two weeks?

"Editorial staff meeting at ten o'clock." This Babs manages in audible tones as she scoots down the hallway toward the boardroom.

My watch reads nine-forty-five. I'm technically not

late. Good. Want to get this over with before I turn on my computer. I'll just pop in on Tai for a sec.

Just as I reach her office the door swings open. Out she comes, accompanied by her male equivalent. Once such men were called pampered. Now they are "metrosexuals"—straight males whose grooming habits are so particular that they will walk up to the women's cosmetics counter in a department store to buy Kiehl's or Clinique for Men. His pale hair is Ralph Lauren perfection. No way to gauge the age of that chiseled-chin, sharp-nosed attraction. Every inch is custom-tailored.

Tai smiles at me but prevents my "hi" by saying to her companion, "See what I mean?"

She must mean me because he turns his head in my direction. I'm observed for the nanosecond the truly sophisticated will give a subway token lying in the street as they pass it by. A sketch of a smile, and they move on.

As they walk away in perfectly matched strides, I think, *Fine. Have it your way. We'll have an audience for the showdown.*

I'm feeling myself again. Morning sickness is a rapidly fading memory. My mind is functioning and eight hours is again enough sleep. Best of all, the results from the first round of screening tests came back negative!

My regular ob-gyn, after picking her chin up off her examining-room floor, has promised her office will be discreet. After today, it won't matter.

I check my watch. If I hurry, I won't be late.

Tai is in full stride when I appear in the boardroom doorway. She conducts meetings while in motion behind the imported Italian leather chair she requisitioned for the boardroom. She holds up an arm to show she's wearing a cast on her right wrist, one of those Velcro-tabbed removable ones that leaves her fingers free to gesture and type.

"The sprain completely ruined my concentration," she

says as I move on to find my chair. "Absolutely excruciating! I could barely eat or sleep. Running was impossible." She touches the corner of an eye with the pad of the middle finger from said afflicted arm. "I'm sure I show signs of the strain."

As Crescentmoon, Babs and KaZi reassure her that that is not so, Rhonda and I exchange glances.

"Hard to get worn out in a Swiss spa," Gwendolyn murmurs under her breath.

That's when I look at Tai again, really look, and am struck by how incredibly wonderful she looks. It's something I can't put my finger on. She's lit from within, as if she swallowed a halogen light.

Even when basking in attention, Tai doesn't overdo it. The pacing resumes. "I've called this meeting to introduce our new design strategy." She pauses behind Mr. Metro. I tell myself that he's not smirking.

"It came to me while I was away that what *Five-O* lacks most is a male point of view of today's woman." Tai lays her injured wrist on the man's shoulder. "No one knows the male mind better than Marc Kazanjian."

She pauses a fraction of a second, expecting applause, perhaps. She gets a fraction of a second of silence. She goes on. "It required all my persuasion to lure Marc across the country. He comes to us with amazing credentials. *Details, Maxim* and most recently *Trends.*"

"It's against our mission statement." Crescentmoon's soothing voice flows through the room. "We are by and about women."

"And who knows more about women than men?" Tai counters smoothly.

Other women, I think to myself, and hear Rhonda murmur something too low to be picked up.

"This is whack," Curran says more audibly.

I sense recalculations taking place around the table. We're a small staff. That means we've already worked out the "you're in my space" rules of office etiquette. The intruder looks as if he's accustomed to a lot more room than we collectively own.

"Our mission statement precludes males in major positions," Crescentmoon reaffirms. Her little-girl voice sounds prissier than before.

"That's why Marc is on loan." Tai's irises are dancing. "He's here to coordinate our 'New Lu' series. Over the weekend Marc evolved a design strategy for the series and tie-ins that are just fabulous. We've been so off the mark." She turns to look at me. "And Lu obviously needs close guidance. She's not kept a single appointment with Rodrigo."

In other words, Marc's being here is my fault.

All eyes turn to me. Got to hand it to Tai. She can deflect a hit with the skill of a Beltway spin doctor.

"What do you say about all this, Lu?" Tai asks.

Under cover of the table Gwendolyn pats caution on my thigh. Am I spoiling for a fight? I'm maggoty with it. But I can be mature and above the fray. As long as I don't have to address Tai directly.

I look at Marc. "I'm sorry, Marc, but you'll have to count me out."

Tai takes a moment to fold her arms beneath her perfect small breasts. "Lu. *Lu.*" Could any name sound more pathetic in her mouth? "I see you've beefed up a bit while I was away. Are you afraid you can't recover your premenopausal self?"

Gwendolyn jerks her hand away.

Oh, thank you, Jesus! In my head I hear Tina Turner's gravelly voice talking about singing "Proud Mary." We're going to do this nice and *rough!*

"Funny you should mention fertility. Not, by the way, that I was ever tempted to participate in your slice-and-dice-Lu marathon. But the truth is, I'm not even close to menopausal. I'm going to have a baby."

"You're what?" Tai's expression is one of perfect disbelief.

"I'm preggers, Tai. Sprung, with child, in a family way, knocked up?"

"You can't expect us to believe that."

"Oh, but it's true. If this is a problem for you, I'll quit."

"What?"

"Consider me gone—" I rise and turn sideways to give her the full thrust of my sixteen-week pregnant profile.

"Shit!"

I have to give Tai credit for her appropriate word choice.

Then it hits me. She punctuated that word with a thump of her injured hand on the back of Marc's chair. She didn't injure her arm. It's a cover for some beauty enhancement treatment she underwent in Switzerland.

"You really should do the column yourself, Tai. Challenge women to become 'Fit to be Tai-ed.'" I can't help it, I do the finger quotes, guaranteed to tee off anyone with an IQ above sixty.

Having a roomful of shocked gazes lock on one gives a person a moment of razor clarity. This must be what it feels like to be shot out of a cannon.

I don't make eye contact with any of them as I move. I just let their collective shock levitate me right out of the room.

I'm halfway down the hall when it hits me. For the first, maybe only, time in her professional life, Tai has let someone else have the last word.

20

It's ten-fifteen in the morning and I've already bought more maternity underwear than I'll ever wear out. Damn Andrea, the fashion witch! She flipped my vanity switch and I'm OD-ing online.

I had supposed the English would have a mature and practical take on what constitutes maternity wear. That was before I found JoJoMamanBebe.com, where I discovered that the pregnant tummy is called a "bump," and Elle Macpherson fronts a line of expectant undies.

Look at her, all lush and lanky, single-handedly unclipping the drop cup of a nursing bra! The pose is the female equivalent of 007's trademark smirk. Who can resist such self-satisfied bravado? I bought three: black, lilac and oh-so-hot pink. The thongs I left alone.

Reluctantly I refocus on the job at hand: help wanted ads in the *New York Times*. After ninety-five hours and twenty minutes of silence from the offices of *Five-O*, I assume I'm unemployed.

Out of work. That has an interesting ring to it. But

what exactly does it mean to me? I don't feel desperate yet, though goodness knows I should. I must have been out of my mind to walk out on a job that was mine to lose. I loved working at *Five-O* B.T. (before Tai, that is).

The doorbell only marginally nudges me into action. I take so long to unfold from the kitchen chair and shuffle to the door in a ratty caftan and booties with most of their rubber traction strips peeled off that I expect the would-be visitor to have found something else to do.

No such luck. Cy stands on my porch, trying to peer the wrong way through my peephole. He knows I quit my job. No doubt, he's checking because I haven't drifted beyond my doorway since.

I open the door. "I'm in a bad mood, Cy. You may want to think about that."

He shrugs. "I'm an old man. Abuse me and I'll call the proper authorities."

"In that case, come in."

He's not taken more than three steps inside my door before I say, "There's another thing you should know. I'm pregnant."

For a moment his eyes go perfectly round behind his rimless glasses. "You aren't happy about this?"

"No. I am." I ruffle my unwashed hair. "Really."

A big grin splits his face. You'd think I'd told him I was having his grandchild.

He offers me a quick, hard hug. Afterward, we begin to dance. Well, not dance exactly, it's more an impromptu waltz. We join hands and begin a slow twirl around my hallway, lilting and spinning until I'm laughing, and he's grinning from ear to ear.

Finally out of breath and feeling just light-headed enough to resist the temptation to continue, we stall out.

"You've seen a doctor? You're taking vitamins? You're expecting no complications?" Each time I nod in the affirmative, Cy adds another question until he seems satisfied. "So, when is the grand event?"

"November." And I realize this is the first time anyone has been absolutely pleased by my news.

"Come, come, let's sit and have a glass of milk." He ushers me into my kitchen as though it's his and pours me a tall one. He doesn't comment on the empty ice cream carton in the sink, or the Dove bar wrappers on the counter. He does try to mash down the tuft of hair I haven't combed since I returned from *Five-O*. I'm living hard these days.

"Have you thought of names?" He's standing over me, to make certain I take a healthy swig of milk. "Do you want to know the sex?"

I shake my head firmly no to both questions, too amazed by how refreshing the milk is to speak. I should have been doing this before.

"You're going to need a nursery." Cy perches on the edge of a nearby stool. "I haven't designed one of those since…" The joy in his face dims, and I remember how dejected he was three years ago when his youngest son's wife rejected out of hand his gift of designing a nursery for their first child.

"I won't have your father in charge of what should be my prerogative," I'm told she said. Of course not! Who would want a world-class architect to gift them with a nursery? Some people's children still need a spank now and then.

"I'd love to take you up on the offer, Cy, but I can't afford any renovations."

"Why? Did Jacob lose his job again?"

"In a matter of speaking. He isn't going to be the father of this child."

This time Cy's eyes stay wide.

"Let me rephrase. Jacob's the sperm donor, but he's made it clear that that's the only contribution he plans to make to this enterprise."

"I see." At seventy-two, a person recoups from surprise quickly. I guess there's not much time to waste. "And this is all right with you? No job? No husband?"

"It's fine, Cy. I'll be fine," I say when the milk is gone. "I'm making arrangements to put the house up for sale next week."

He just looks at me. I know how he feels. But again, he doesn't address the issue directly. "You should celebrate the news of this new life coming into the world. Have you done that?"

"Not exactly." A memory of William Templeton's bare buttocks comes to mind before I can stop it. He will forever be in my fondest-memory category. If only the timing were different!

Blessedly ignorant of my wayward thoughts, Cy bounds to his feet as nimbly as a man of forty. Tai chi is amazing. "Then we must celebrate. Tonight. I will call for you at seven."

I'm ready a few minutes early, thinking that Cy will expect me to do the driving. He gave it up years ago when he realized, he said, his life was worth a great deal more than the amount it cost to hire a driver. He had begun driving through red lights while contemplating complex structural ideas. Now that he goes into the office only a couple of times a week, he doesn't even bother to keep a car.

So I'm a little surprised when the doorbell rings as I'm picking up the phone to tell him I'm ready.

For Cy's benefit, I'm flossed, blow-dried and shaved. I'm also wearing the pale-blue-sleeveless-top-and-below-the-knee-skirt maternity set Andrea assured me makes me look fresh and feminine. I pat my "bump" and say, "Nice going, kiddo."

"*Ah!* You look fine," Cy says warmly, when I've opened the door.

When we first started "dating," as he told his children, they were worried until they got what he calls "a good gander" at me.

He hands me an armload of delicate blue irises and pink snapdragons wrapped in florist's paper and says, "Blue for if it's a boy, pink for if it's a girl."

After I've put the glorious bouquet in water and given them the place of honor on my dining room table, Cy leads me out the door to a waiting car. A limo.

"What's all this?"

Cy looks as pleased as a child on Christmas. "We're celebrating. I hope you're hungry?"

"Am I ever not?"

He nods and offers his arm.

"I'm really fine," I protest.

"Independent women," he mutters in halfhearted disapproval as I take his arm.

The restaurant he's chosen is in Manhattan. I'm glad I decided to put on my wedding rings, just in case we draw stares. I couldn't care less about my reputation. At this point, I'm not sure I have one. But Cy is another matter. His children see an old man when they look at him. I see a man who knows a lot about life and living, and how to handle both with grace and charm. I wouldn't hurt him for the world.

He's a wonderful storyteller with a sly sense of humor. By the time we pull up before a discreet numbered awning on a tree-lined side street in lower Manhattan, I've forgotten just how unhappy and miserable I am—or was, or should be.

No surprise the maître d' greets Cy by name. This is one of those quiet, tucked-away places for those in the know. The small dining room glows with pale yellow candlelight. Tables are set with silver, crystal and bone china, atop linen cloths so thick they look like pads. The clien-

tele speak soft words and laugh in muted tones, the tinkle of glasses and flatware are dampened by a draped ceiling. This is a golden-eye view of what life can be like.

No surprise then that our table is in an alcove where a
bottle of Diamant Bleu champagne is chilling for us.

"I shouldn't," I say reluctantly, though I do so love good
champagne.

"One small glass of the very best won't hurt." Cy signals the pouring. "A toast to new beginnings. To a new
Lu."

"A new Lu." It was meant to be a new column, but now
it will be a pledge to myself.

We contemplate ordering a disgusting amount of
things. Cy believes that, if it sounds good, it should be
sampled. We are in the midst of ordering half the menu
when the maître d' comes over and says, "Perhaps you
would prefer a taste of the kitchen."

Cy and I smile and nod like those bobble dogs in the
back windows of certain vehicles. Anyone who loves to
eat well will tell you nirvana is a place where the chef pre-
pares a little of everything from the menu, and serves it
to you in mini portions that leave room for the most sin-
ful of desserts.

When we are done ordering Cy turns a suddenly serious look my way and takes my hand between both of
his.

"You are a proud, strong woman. This I know. So I
won't insult you by suggesting that you need a man in
your life. But a child? A child's needs must supersede even
the independence of the mother." He pats my hand. "Lu,
at a time like this, you should have no worries. If you need
the cash, then put your house up for sale and move in with
me. I have rooms enough for five babies. There, it's settled."

"Because you'll buy my house for more than it's
worth."

He blinks as if surprised I thought of that. He forgets I know how he extracted a promise from Jacob years ago that we would give him first dibs if we ever decided to sell. "A man my age can't be too careful about who might move in next door."

I squeeze his hand. "I can't accept your offer to buy my house or move into yours. But thank you for it. It means more than you know."

"Are you afraid that people would think you are living off an old man who has nothing but his memories to keep him warm?"

"There's that. And what about when I begin to show?"

This brings color to his face. "Imagine the joy of a man of my years being accused of siring a child with a pretty woman?"

"What's all this talk about old age? Is there something you're not telling me?"

"Absolutely." His eyes roll dramatically heavenward. "I'm dying. Of something, I can't think what it is at the moment. So I need the comfort of a companion. A young woman who will bring laughter and joy into my failing life."

"And diapers and middle-of-the-night feedings and crying jags."

"I am almost deaf and half-blind. I won't hear or see much."

"What about your children?"

"To have this I will bear the anger of my children. Perhaps I shall disinherit them and give it all to you."

"The law won't let you do that."

He looks up, eyes bright with mischief. "So then, marry me."

Of course a conversation this light was heading this way. All the same, the words spoken have an unexpected response. I burst into tears.

"Hormonal," I assure Cy. All the same, the great breaths I take to ebb the tears draw the attention of others.

"You, go away!" Cy orders the waiter who bundles over to ask if he can do anything for us. Cy, in a mood, could have stood down the mutiny on the *Bounty*.

He is also an expert with a dinner napkin. He dries my tears with one corner and then straightens my smeared lipstick with another. "It was foolish of me to bring it up here," he says kindly. "I only wanted to make you smile."

"It's nutty me, not you, Cy!" I whisper furiously. "You'd think I'd never been proposed to before, or been pregnant before, or even had a kind word spoken to me!"

He takes all this remarkably well. "I've heard better excuses, and gotten better responses to my proposals."

"Oh, Cy."

"I've heard that one, too. You forgot to sigh on Cy."

I can't remain an emotional cripple before a man who's still waiting for an answer to his proposal. I smile and touch his arm. "If I were going to marry anyone at this point, it would be you."

He shrugs but takes my hand again. "That's a no. But a nice no."

He is silent for a while, a solemn, dignified man in a blue suit and silver tie and shiny lenses that reflect back a good portion of what he views. Then he sits up, becoming as stiffly erect as a drill sergeant. "I will speak with Jacob about his responsibilities. He will listen to me."

"No, thank you. I know this is an absolutely asinine thing to say, considering my circumstances, but I think I—" I look down at my middle. "We deserve better."

He nods thoughtfully. "I've always thought so."

Does Cy not like Jacob any better than Andrea? I don't think I want to know why.

"So, about this moving in."

I've swallowed so many tears I don't have the heart to dish out two *no*s in a row, so I let him talk for a moment while I try to remember if I was this touched when Jacob proposed. Why can't I remember?

"Better yet. I will buy your house and you can live there rent free." He leans in. "I make a hell of a landlord, let me tell you."

"You're putting me against the wall."

"That's my point. You can come and live on my second floor while I do the renovations. A mother-to-be mustn't be around paint fumes and wood stains and such. Better yet, you should have a bedroom on the main floor. I drew up plans for such a thing years ago. If Ethel had lived a little longer, she was going to need her own room downstairs. God rest her soul, the woman could snore. She worried about keeping me awake. We planned to convert our sleeping porch on the rear. Your house has the same arrangement. We'll take in the pantry you no longer need and backstairs closet and make a fine bathroom with lots of closet space. Of course, you still need a nursery. What about the kitchen nook? It's on the south, lots of sun and no drafts."

"Did I ever tell you how much I love you?"

"You love me so much you're going to share my house while I work for you." The tinge of sadness in his gaze says he knows he's just talking to make us both feel better.

Thankfully, the first of the appetizers arrive: scallops with black truffle sauce. This is only the beginning of a steady procession of some the best things I have ever put in my mouth!

To steer clear of Cy's view of my future I begin to talk about any and everything. Pretty soon it's clear my focus is motherhood, and I blabber about shopping for babies online and the weekly baby yoga classes I may look into.

After an hour and a half has passed, the headwaiter, seeing a lull both in the conversation and service, toddles over and says with a small smile, "May I recommend one of our desserts?"

"Something chocolate," we answer in unison. On that much, we can agree.

21

"There are three men in my house. I didn't invite any of them."

"Sounds interesting." Andrea rarely takes social calls at work, but I need to be humored. "Who are these daring males?"

"There's a contractor, who's searching for studs and talking about load-bearing walls. The plumber is looking for ways to tee off my main line to plumb a full downstairs bath. Cy is moving back and forth between them, with his sketch pad, drawing up plans."

"How is darling Cy?"

"About two minutes from being tossed out on his ear."

"That was your first mistake, letting him in."

"No. That was my second mistake. The first was to tell him I had an appointment with a real estate agent today."

"So how did it go?"

"It didn't. Cy waylaid her on the way to my door and then hung around. He was so rude that she finally asked me, 'Are you certain your father is ready to sell the family home?' I won't repeat what he said to her. I'd never heard it put that way before. Of course, I'll have to find another real estate agent."

Andrea laughs at my expense. "You're too nice. *Muy estupido,* and too nice. Now I got to go be an attorney. Big client's got a hard-on because the judge sent his case to arbitration. I should start a side business. Escort service for uptight clients who need to get laid before they come busting down my door!"

And with that felonious thought, Andrea hangs up.

I hear doors slam, followed by male laughter. Fine. Cy thinks he's going to renovate. Meanwhile, I'm learning how to clean up my act.

While Cy and I may have thought our evening was haute cuisine heaven, Baby put a whole other spin on the term "hellish experience." I will never ever again consume that much butter, salt and cream at one time!

It was 10:00 a.m. before I could sit upright in bed. Shortly after the agent stomped off and before men in work boots arrived, I browsed the neonatal aisles of my nearby bookstore. Every book and magazine that looked even remotely related to maternity health and nutrition came home with me. For the past two hours, I've been holed up in the window seat of my upstairs bedroom, ignoring the arrival of Cy and his cohorts, reading about eating for two. My grocery-shopping list is a healthy three columns long.

Another perk of *Five-O's* forward-thinking enterprise was that every worker, full- or part-time, could buy into the company health insurance plan. My next job may pay twice as much, but chances are generous health benefits won't be part of the package.

Which makes my walking out at *Five-O* even more of a kamikaze act.

I don't even look out to see who could be ringing my doorbell. It's 5:00 p.m. No doubt more of Cy's co-

conspirators who've signed out at their day jobs. If he wants to waste their time, let him. I haven't seen him this excited in years.

A few minutes later, I hear footsteps on the stairs and then a low knock.

"Come in!"

The door opens and Cy comes through. "Sorry to interrupt your—you're not napping?"

"I'm reading, almost as good."

"So then I won't bother you."

He is halfway out the door before I say, "Wait? Who rang the bell?"

Cy shrugs. "Some schlemiel. Says he's a photographer at *Five-O*. He looks like a hoodlum."

I'm out of my cushy window box in a flash. "Curran's here?"

"Maybe that's what he said his name is. Who can tell, the way the young speak these days? He said he's here to 'give props to my Boo.' Do you understand that boy?"

"Not always. But he's a good guy, Cy. Send him up." If Curran came to see me for any reason to do with *Five-O*, it will require privacy.

"His pants don't fit properly." Cy leans near to whisper. "I saw his shorts. They look clean. But that hair? In your condition, you can't be too careful."

My assurances that Curran uses conventional hygiene, and that dreads are not necessarily "infectious disease centers," send Cy away muttering under his breath.

After a couple of minutes I hear Curran taking the stairs two at a time, and then he's standing in the doorway. He's wearing a Rastafarian brightly knit baggy cap, a long white T with some sort of pieced-together knit vest, brand new baggy denim cargo pants and Jesus sandals with army socks. His attempt to grow a goatee has sprouted a few reddish hairs that he has twisted into tiny dreads about his mouth. He looks perfectly silly, and perfectly safe.

"Who's the old dude?"

"My neighbor."

"Pops needs to chill. He made me wash my hands before I could come up."

I'm so glad to see him I give Curran a big hug before saying sternly, "Did you really tell Cy you'd come to give props to your Boo?"

He grins.

"Well, save it for young women, like KaZi. She's your Boo."

Curran shakes his head. "Not after she went all Britney, 'I'm not that innocent' on me over this Marc poser."

I slide back into the window seat and point to the lounge chair that was once Jacob's. "Tell me."

Curran squats on the edge. "The mess got freaky after you did that Gloria 'Swansong' on us. Gwendolyn up and took some personal days. That was after this Marc poser asked if she would "ethnic up" her column for the more hip reader. She told him finances were finances, and you can't 'ethnic up' numbers. I didn't cop to what he asked Crescentmoon. But, damn, sistah's got a mouth on her! I was like peepin' notes."

I shouldn't be smiling. I shouldn't be happy that my actions caused a rift in the ranks. "Anything else?"

"Most def. Last three days, the shizz is thick. Tai's so ticked she can't let up long enough to get over it. Brotha can't live like that. Damn!"

"Okay, stop." My head is spinning. "I admire the linguistic virtuosity of hip-hop but I need standard English now. Okay?"

"Awright."

I frown in warning. "What are you doing here? Nobody at work knows my home address." Jacob had always said a column like mine needed a certain amount of distance from fans. I use a PO box for all business correspondence.

Curran grins. "You can put a cell phone number on the Net and come up with an address for just about anybody, you know how to look."

Now I feel really unsafe. "Okay, so this visit was your idea?"

Curran looks embarrassed, trying not to stare at my middle, but his gaze keeps tracking back. "So is it true? You're going to have a kid?"

I lean back so he can observe the curve. "Yes."

"That's phat!" It takes me a second to realize he's not talking about my belly. "You're way cool, Lu. At your age. Alone. Having a kid and, like, telling people to sit on it if they don't like it. You're, like, my hero!"

His earnest honesty reminds me that I'm now two for six in the happy-for-you department. Cy and Curran, bless them!

"Do you mind?" He points to his camera. When I shake my head, he whips it out. "I want to keep a photo journal of your progress. This is the most amazing thing!"

"What? Don't they make babies back in Omaha?"

He just clicks away, sliding off onto his knees to the floor to get a closer to me. "This is life. Only better. It's like Euro life. As you know, Catherine Deneuve had two children out of wedlock."

"Too bad we can't sell tickets. I need a job."

He grins and gives me some sort of bent-arm hand signal. "That's what I'm saying. I got your back, Boo—Lu."

I'm grinning, too, though I couldn't say why. "How so, bro?"

He lowers the camera. "I squared things with Tai. You can come back to *Five-O*."

Not that I believe him for a minute, but I say, "I'm all ears."

"I figure it like this. Tai needs you."

"Needs my head on a platter, maybe. You saw her face when I made that remark about her doing the column."

"Straight up." Curran smiles. "Only Tai's over that. Said that's when she knew you were telling the truth about being pregnant. 'Only some crazy—' Well, you know."

"You mean the crazy-pregnant-lady defense?" I think about all the things she might have said and decide I can live with that. "So she's not angry?"

He scuttles to my right side. "I didn't say that. Tai's got control issues. But Rhonda found out that Tai sold this 'New Lu' angle to her higher-ups on the guarantee of her bonuses, so they'd sign off on it."

"Wow." That explains why she was riding me so hard. "Guess my little stunt pulled the rug out from under her."

Curran's head bops behind the lens. "Yup."

Now, I feel bad, sort of. "I said at the beginning that it wasn't something I would do. Now that I'm otherwise oc-cupied, it's impossible."

"Exactly." He pauses and perches his camera on his knee. "Now, this is how I figure it. Tai can't go back to the higher-ups so easily and say, my gal Lu done a one-eighty on us, so deal."

"I wonder what she will do?"

"That's where yours truly comes in. I kinda had a talk with Tai this afternoon. I said, so what, we can't do the makeover? I thought that was whack. Anytime you see it on TV, it's so over for the market share. Except, sometimes TV's ahead of itself. Like with reality shows. Catch my drift?"

"Not even slightly."

"I've been at the magazine awhile. So like, what's a fifty-year-old woman's worst fear? Being dumped by hubby, right? But shit like that happens every day. Only with you we can go high concept. Sell it as a midlife 'survivor' sce-nario." He raises his hands as if he's framing headlines. "She's fifty…abandoned by her spouse! Left alone she must deal with a *real* shocker: The Big *P*!" Curran flushes with his inventiveness. "I call it 'The Pregnant Pause.'"

I have to admit, his thought process impresses me. I'm appalled by the idea, but impressed he thought of it. He may have a future in the Big Apple, after all.

"So you're suggesting I 'prime time' my very personal life? Who do you see as the audience for this tell-all?"

"Every woman, pro or con. I peep *People*. You've got your late-life pregnancies popping up everywhere. Geena Davis, again. Julianne Moore. Cindy Crawford. Joan Lunden had twins at fifty-two."

"She used a surrogate."

"But you're a signed check. The real deal. You can give Tai an exclusive behind-the-scenes, blow-by-blow look at a late-life birth."

"And Tai bought into this?"

Curran nods vigorously. "Tai bought into it. Totally. Well, mostly totally. She's willing to parley."

"Parley? As in I might need to crawl across broken glass to get my job back?"

Curran shrugs. "The way Tai sees it, you didn't quit. You just took a few personal days."

Me at Tai's mercy? I won't do this. Because I don't need the money? The job? The security of insurance? Okay, pride be damned! Solvency is not to be sneezed at.

"I'm making no promises." But my head is already swimming with column inches. "I have to think about everyone involved. This baby isn't a negotiating ploy. And I don't know that I want any part of a 'reality fix' for people who are long on free time and short on dealing with their own real lives."

Curran nods, but I can tell by the fixed expression on his face that he's dying to ask *the* question.

"And I have no intention of divulging the name of the sperm donor. Ever. Are we clear?"

"That's cool." I think my admiration stock just went up another notch. The young love mystery. "Whatever you decide, Lu. I'm there for you."

"Thank you." I am touched by his show of loyalty. "Facing Tai was no small thing."

His expression loses its playful quality. "You're really okay?"

"This is my life, Curran. I'm okay with it."

"Then let's get some reality on film. Right up through the delivery." He must read my expression because he adds, "Just think about it, Lu. That's all I'm saying."

Uh-oh. I've heard this before. "Think about what? You can't expect me to pose nude for you?" His expression gives him away. I'm out of my seat in a second. "You're nuts!"

"Not now, Lu, not now! In the ninth month. The Demis of the world think it's about a toned body and peekaboo sex. I want the earthy, gritty truth on film."

"The truth would be more like a 'Saggy Baggy Elephant' story. Forget it."

"Okay, okay." He rises from the floor. "Don't go off on me."

"What's going on?" Cy comes barreling through the door, looking like thunder. "He's bothering you, he's out of here." Cy points a finger at Curran. "Now."

Curran is half again as tall as Cy but he doesn't have *the presence.* He lifts his hands in mock defense. "Chill, dude. I just came to tell Lu she still has her job."

"Is this so?" Cy looks at me, and I nod.

Cy's expression alters to the pleasant one I know best. "Well then, sit down, young fellow. I was just about to order dinner. You like calamari?"

"Oh, no." I take Cy's arm and steer him back into the hall. "You've done quite enough for one day. Thanks. Be a dear and go home."

Cy cocks his head toward my bedroom. "You are putting that one out, too?"

"Eventually. We have work to do."

Cy cups my chin. "You will be careful?"

"He's a lamb, Cy. I know his girlfriend."

Cy shrugs. "I'll call you later."

"Now what?" Curran is standing with his camera ready. A flash from it hits me squarely in the eyeballs.

"You're going to drive me to the supermarket, because you've blinded me. Then I'm going to break my rule about not cooking for uninvited guests and make us dinner."

By six-thirty we've eaten plates of scrambled eggs and potatoes, fresh tomato slices and glasses of orange juice. Curran has burned up more film than any human being should.

"That's it for tonight, Curran," I say when the dishes are in the washer. "In the morning I'll make an appointment with Tai. We'll see if she even bothers to say no."

"Meanwhile, I'm here for you, Lu. Anything you need." Curran looks around. "Aren't you worried, living alone at a time like this?"

"Of course not. This has been my home for years."

"Still, wouldn't it be cool if I could get the full story on film, morning to night? I could move in with you, if you want. Paying rent, of course."

What's with everybody wanting to share my roof? Have rental properties jumped in price again?

I hand him his camera bag. "Good night, Curran."

As tired as I am, and unsure of my next step, I'm elated by possibility. This isn't like me, to think about stepping out from behind the screen of my column. I don't mind calling a fool a fool in print. But put myself out there? Well, I'm beginning to understand the whole image-conscious phenomenon. I've seen that secretly taped footage of fashion victims before their closets and tastes have been turned around. If Curran's camera is going to be a daily companion in my life, I need a facial and a hair appointment.

"And more clothes!"

The strange flutter low down catches me completely by surprise. At first I think it must be gas. I did try to eat bland. Acid in the OJ?

There it is again!

It's impossible to adequately describe the emotion when you feel your child move inside you for the first time. It's like being touched by an angel, from the inside.

22

The power of achievement can't be overstated. I've walked three miles today in under an hour. I feel so righteous I could crow. It doesn't matter that sweat that began in my armpits now pools about my waist. It doesn't matter that my T-shirt is plastered to my back and my leggings are wet in questionable places. It doesn't even matter that Andrea jogged circles around me the entire time, while she related details of her latest conquest. He owns a real-estate brokerage with offices in Bergen and Essex Counties. Dr. Yummy has been on rotation so she thought she should do the same.

Funny how you don't realize the world is made of pairs until your own equation changes. I don't mean romantic duets, but the basic-necessity kind.

Now that I'm sharing space, I see couples everywhere. There's Andrea and her self-involvement, chattering on and on while circling me like a happy blue jay. Curran and his flash camera. He flits in and out of my path like a deranged lightning bug. He's so dedicated about capturing my new life on film I'm beginning to worry that I'll meet him in my hallway during a middle-of-the-night hike to pee.

Oh, there in the park is a gentleman and his schnauzer, watching the do-si-do between a pigeon and a crust of bread. Farther on, two children walk to school. They must be brother and sister. Friends wouldn't punch each other quite so hard. The world's all coupled up. Bee and buttercup. Cab and driver. Even that street person pushing the grocery cart is not alone, even if she is talking to one only she can see.

I'm so pleased with my world that I'm even ready for my talk with Tai. One week to the day since Curran came to see me. Sweet Tum and I are going to see her at 11:00 a.m.

After that first flutter I could no longer think of my child in general baby terms. Sweet Tum came to me, and stuck.

I must admit it is a bit daunting to walk into *Five-O* after my *High Noon* exit. I can always gauge my anxiety level by how many times I change my mind about what to wear. Don't let anyone fool you, even a cerebral, tough cookie like Madeline Albright cares more on some days than others about what goes on her bod.

Babs is all smiles and sweet concern as she tells me to go right ahead, Tai is expecting me. Then she giggles. "You had us fooled, Lu. You seemed so steady."

I shrug. "Broke a leg leaping off my pedestal."

"Good for you!" Babs means it. How little we *know* the people we know.

Crescentmoon waylays me in the hall with a basket tied in green organza ribbons.

"It's all organic aromatherapy," she says as she presses the enormous gift into my hands. "Honey balms and herbal creams, nothing to irritate the expectant she person."

She person? That's a little too politically correct for me. But I relish the idea of quality body care.

Now I'm standing before Tai's door. Nothing to do but face the music.

Tai is standing behind her desk. I suspect she believes chairs are for the weak of mind and body. My sleeveless linen sheath is not technically maternity wear. But, if you know where to look, it isn't difficult to figure something is going on beneath its straight-line drop from shoulder to knee. She's eyeing me so closely I feel like Horton must have while sitting on the Who's egg.

Tai wears a casual Diane Von Furstenberg sweat-wear creation, a skimpy tennis dress that I swear is an abbreviated version of a little black cocktail number hanging in every woman's closet. I'm no longer disdainful. If I had legs like that, I'd show them off, too. They won't stay that flawless forever.

She offers me, the slack of mind and waistline, a chair. "So, then. Let's get to it."

She comes from behind her desk and picks up a trophy, the one from a London-based marathon that anchors her otherwise uncluttered desk. As she hefts the weight in her palm, is she thinking what I'm thinking, that it would make a wicked weapon?

"I don't give employees a second chance. If someone can't perform under pressure, I find someone who can. Why chance disappointment a second time?"

This is where I'm supposed to jump up and plead for that rarest of second chances. I decide to echo her instead. "I understand that would be a huge gamble for *Five-O.*"

Her gaze meets mine. "You have no idea."

"Of course." I look down first, because I know that backing down is what I'm supposed to do. And if I match her stare I might just decide that this isn't something I want any part of. *Baby needs new shoes,* or will one day soon.

"I imagine you're in a tough spot, without a husband for financial support at this rather awkward stage in your life."

"There are worse things. But, yes, I need my job." Damn! I'm starting to sweat.

She puts down the trophy, the heavy thump providing the imagery of a fist on the tabletop. "I expect full cooperation from my staff with whatever vision I project." She hasn't blinked yet. "No questions asked."

So she wants her own back. I can catch it as fast as she slings it. "What sort of new campaign do you have in mind?"

"I am weighing the merits of your unorthodox gestation as a possible focal point." She glances at me and—I swear—she shudders. "At best it's a gamble of immense proportions. But it's also a deliciously unpredictable tack for this magazine." She leans toward me. "Of course, I would need a doctor's affidavit stating that you are truly pregnant and capable of carrying the fetus to term."

"Certainly." I pat my middle for emphasis.

She recoils as if what I have might be contagious. As the chime of a new e-mail sounds, she turns to look at her monitor. She pushes a couple of buttons to check things before turning back to me.

"I like to play my hunches. So I took an impromptu poll yesterday on Fifth Avenue. Stopped women to ask if they were mothers. If so, what would be their greatest fear after age forty-five? Amazingly, it's not breast cancer or even wrinkles. It's that they might get pregnant again."

Tai leans forward, staring straight into my eyes. "It might be fun to give the *Five-O* reader a ride through her own personal nightmare!"

And using me to do it will be half the fun. Maybe I should give this another think.

Tai begins to pace. "I'd not be looking for namby-pamby, isn't-motherhood-all-warm-and-fuzzy. This would be tell-all time. I'd want copy that is daring, soul-baring, excoriating!"

"I understand." I search inside my purse for a tissue with which to mop my face. She's still using the tantalizingly conditional "would," yet we both know she's offering me a deal. "There's one condition we need to be clear about."

Tai freezes like a greyhound on the scent.

I pat my face before continuing. "There will be no speculation, no investigation, no assumptions about the father of my child. For the purposes of *Five-O,* this is an immaculate conception."

There's a pause before a very cunning smile stretches her mouth. "Aren't you the sly one? Yes, that will work for us."

Ah, we have crossed the language barrier.

"There will be conditions."

Here we go. "Of course."

"For instance, you'd have to work with Marc."

When my head whips toward her, she smiles. "He's agreed to be the visionary on the project. I know nothing about children or pregnancy."

He does?

I'm so glad I clenched my jaw when she began to speak or that question might have slipped out. "What does Marc have in mind?"

She puts up a hand. "First things first."

It takes only fifteen minutes for her to lay out her terms, which she basically sees as me handing my gestational life over to *Five-O,* 24/7, as she puts it. Curran will be my watchdog, recording any and everything he deems possible fodder for the mag. She's good at turning friends into adversaries. The CIA is missing a great operative. Marc will be the concept point person; Tai can't be bothered with that. But she has final say on every decision.

I balk only once, regarding marketing strategy. I want to be consulted.

"Absolutely not. We're taking enormous risks with you." Tai stares at me with a predator's interest. "We may have to be creative."

In other words, she won't hesitate to humiliate me any way she can.

Okay then, I need a very good reason to do this. "Since I'll be working, as you put it, twenty-four/seven for *Five-O,* I deserve a salary increase."

"No salary increase," she answers shortly, not looking my way as her e-mail chimes again.

She must hear me thinking, *Who needs this?* for after a moment of silence, she looks up. "I will consider bonuses tied to performance. Half a percent of your salary for every ten thousand additional issues sold over our basis figures with your new column in it."

I do the numbers in my head. This could mean an extra two to three hundred a month, with just modest increases. "Agreed."

She smiles again. "Fine. We're just in time for the board meeting." She's giving the smile a bad rap.

In full view of the other members of the editorial staff, Tai makes her announcement about my return in the emotionless staccato voice that she uses to reel off the monthly numbers. I'm back to do a "dissection," she calls it, of middle-age pregnancy. She announces that while I'm still on staff, read that as insured, I can be cut loose the moment things get dodgy. Tai's version of a short leash. Seems fair enough. Even I know she is taking a big chance.

Babs, Rhonda, Gwendolyn, KaZi, Crescentmoon and Curran act as silent witnesses to my capitulation. Thankfully, Marc is "unavoidably detained," whatever that means.

To signal we're finished, Tai offers me her hand. Curran takes a couple of shots for the magazine's personal album and then they all scatter.

I can't judge the others' genuine responses. With Tai, almost everyone nods and smiles and leaves as quickly as possible.

Not sure what to do next, I remain a moment, pretending to pack up my Blackberry and check my cell phone for messages. Tai, too, remains until there are only the two of us.

As she's about to leave she stops near me and points to my midsection. "I don't suppose you'll confide in me, off the record, how you did it?"

"Oh, I don't mind. After all, we're adult women." I lean toward her, brows arched and voice pitched in candid mode. "It all began with the birds and the bees. You are familiar with that story, right?"

She smiles and this time it almost seems genuine. "Aren't you terrified?"

"On alternate days."

"The rest of the time?"

"I'm petrified."

She laughs then. A real laugh. "I want all the juicy details. Every awful twitch. You're prepared to do that?"

"That which doesn't kill me will make me stronger?"

"Exactly. I don't want you dead, but I expect you to bleed like hell in print."

This is the moment when I realize that her hostility is not just personal dislike of me. Her arrogance is the general disdain of all narcissists toward others.

I leave with my pride and my nerve pretty much unruffled. As for the future, it's going to be a day-by-day thing.

Now for the scarier of the two tasks of the day, I'm having dinner with Dallas and Stephen. Her idea. I hope we achieve détente, if not an outright favored-nations agreement.

23

I see Dallas elbow Stephen as she catches sight of me crossing the dining room. I'm late. Pretty late.

The elastic in my most generous pair of panties gave out on the way home from *Five-O*. The dreaded panty hose I put on in place ruptured in strategic places as I tried to wrestle a shoe box from a high shelf. Then an old can of mothballs overturned as the box came free and left greasy streaks on my front. After I'd traded my dress for maternity slacks and top with beaded edging, I couldn't find my car keys. After twenty minutes, and more than my weekly allotment of curse words, I gave up and called a cab.

I'm limping only slightly. The rubber heel tip from one of my sandals is stuck in the revolving door of the building that houses the restaurant because some overanxious boyfriend shoved the door into my shoe while trying to hurry through. The scrape will heal. The shoe will mend. But my relationship with my daughter is in doubt.

"Sorry I'm late. Traffic," I say, the most polite kind of lie for a situation I don't want to rehash.

"So, you weren't planning to stand us up?"

I look around just to make certain Dallas isn't addressing someone who's come up behind me. "As I said. Traffic."

She looks annoyed but says no more.

"Hello, Lu." Stephen, who popped out of his chair as I approached, looks pleased to see me but nervous about it, as though he's been warned ahead of time about whose side he's on. He air-hugs me in one of those wide-armed loops that don't really touch a person. The kiss he lays high up on my cheek contains more nose pressure than lip action.

Don't get me wrong. I like Stephen. He's tall, smart and terribly earnest. He's a younger version of the sort my mother was pointing out at church socials and science fairs when I was fifteen to counter the suspicion that I, like my generation, was absorbed with dangerous types riding motorcycles or slinging electric guitars at amplifiers. In other words, Stephen is a nerd. A nice, attractive, smart, all-around-good-guy nerd. He's an actuary.

Once again, I Googled my way to knowledge. An actuary is one who is good at "Evaluating the likelihood of future events, designing creative ways to reduce the likelihood of undesirable events, and decreasing the impact of undesirable events that do occur."

Stephen's life is built around creating safety nets. No accidental, messy futures for him. My mother is very happy to welcome him into the family.

I set my purse and scarf on the chair beside me. One thing about a threesome, there's always that empty chair. "How's life, Stephen?"

"Can't complain. Well, I won't."

We all nod and smile. After two years' acquaintance I understand that this passes for humor in Stephen's world.

"Chardonnay?" he suggests as the waiter lifts the bottle from its icy bucket in anticipation.

"Absolutely not!" Dallas answers for me. "Not in her condition."

I smile at the waiter. "I got loaded before I came, just in case."

He gives me one of those vague eyebrow lifts, which could mean anything from "with this crowd, I don't blame you" to "what do you expect from me, I only work here?"

"Club soda with lime, please."

"How are you, Mother?" As she says this, Dallas looks pointedly at my midriff.

"Happy as a clam at sea."

"Why don't you tell Stephen all about it."

I get it now. This is my punishment. I'll have to explain what needs explaining to her young man. Where is that club soda? I'm going to need extra lime!

"Let's see. You know Dallas's father and I are divorced, Stephen. We made a last attempt at reconciliation back in February, before the decree was finalized. It didn't take. The reconciliation, that is."

"You clearly weren't thinking of that possibility at the time."

"Don't put words in my mouth, Dallas." I don't do contrite well, especially when my tendon still stings from the run-in with the revolving door. "I did not expect your father to change his mind. In fact, I was certain before we returned home that not to go ahead with the divorce would be a mistake."

I can see by her expression that Dallas isn't going to let me off that easily. "I don't see how you can now defend that point of view, in light of subsequent events."

"Was I defending myself?" I practically snatch up the drink the waiter places before me and gulp.

"Why don't we order?" Stephen suggests this, having no doubt evaluated the future of this conversation, and the likelihood that it will bring about an undesirable mother-daughter event.

Once orders are placed and everyone has had a time out, Stephen turns to me and says, "I've always meant to ask you, why did you choose the name Dallas? Were you a fan of the eighties show?"

"Yes, Mother, why did you name me after a stupid TV show?"

"You know very well I didn't. I never liked Larry Hagman. He always seemed so smug, in a creepy sort of way. I named you after one of my favorite movies, *Stella Dallas*. But I couldn't very well call you Stella. There would have been Stanley Kowalski catcalls following you all your life. Dallas seemed more subtle."

"Well, it didn't help that much. People still ask me who killed JR."

She doesn't join in the chuckle Stephen and I share. Sometimes I think my daughter was born without a funny bone.

Salads arrive and we gratefully dig in. Stephen and Dallas talk about their jobs and their at-home situations. I'm struck again by the fact that they live in separate states and don't really see each other that often.

We are well into our berries with crème fraîche and espressos—decaf for me—before Dallas again broaches the subject of what-to-do-about-Mom. "Your doctor is certain this is safe for you?"

"My doctor is planning to write a paper about me, I'm so okay. I just need to take it easy, exercise, eat right, get enough rest, the usual."

Dallas stirs her cup slowly. "So, then, you won't be working for a while."

"Not exactly." I smile. "*Five-O* took me back."

"What do you mean?" She leans closer so the next table won't overhear. "The last time we talked you said you'd quit."

"I thought I'd quit. It turns out I was just taking a few personal days."

"What about the ultimatum? And your boss's demands?"

"I gave her an alternative column idea."

Unlike Davin, who needs a few beats to catch up, Dallas is bang on the spot. "Mom, you didn't!"

"Didn't what?" Stephen's head lifts from a contemplation of his berries, looking like a buck sensing fresh danger.

"Mom's going to write about her…condition."

"A column?" Stephen's tone implies he's struck by the novelty of the idea. "That should certainly increase circulation."

"It won't have quite that sideshow freak quality," I say in a soothing tone. "It will be about alternative life choices. I doubt it will be on the radar of anyone under fifty."

"Well I think it's fine that you're having a child. Unconventional, unquestionably, but hardly shocking." He turns to Dallas. "You have to admit, Dallas, that it will be a good thing for your mother to have companionship in her old—er, declining—uh, her life."

"Most lonely people just get a pet!" Dallas mumbles.

"This dinner was your idea." I say it softly, but with a direct look at my daughter.

Dallas sighs like a much-put-upon parent. "I don't know what I expected. I should have known—"

My purse rings. Actually, these days it plays "Brahms Lullaby." As I reach for it, I say, "Excuse me."

"Lu?"

"William?" I am amazed I recognize a voice I've never heard on the phone before.

"You said you'd call."

"I did, didn't I?" Dallas is frowning at me. Is it because it's bad manners to talk on a cell phone in a restaurant, or the fact I spoke William's name aloud?

"Can you talk?" He sounds great on the phone, as if maybe he should have a job that requires him to speak on the phone. But Dallas is watching, and he wants to talk more.

"Okay." Does that sound neutral enough to throw off my daughter?

"I wasn't completely honest with you that night we were together."

Oh, goody. Every ugly thing I can think of runs like a news strip through my mind. He's married again. He has herpes. He's gay—uh, bi. "Really?"

"About Jolie, that is. Look, I'd prefer not to discuss it now. But her doctor found something in her amniocentesis. That's why she was here. That, and Jon. He's coming out here this weekend to discuss options with her, and I'd just as soon be somewhere else. I'm thinking of coming into the city."

"Come here." Before I can think better of it, I add, "You know the address? Good. Call me and I'll meet the train in Montclair. No trouble. Bye."

"You're having a guest?" Dallas's tone could make having one's teeth cleaned sound suspect.

"As a matter of fact, yes." I know I'm smiling, and I shouldn't be so transparent, but I can't do a damn thing about the happiness percolating through me in a way decaf can't.

"You're seeing someone, aren't you? A man."

"Would you be happier if I was seeing a *woman?*" Oh, dear. Now I've shocked Stephen. He's just shot what he says is a fine aged port out his nostrils.

As the cab pulls up to the curb I noticed two men sitting on my porch steps. They pop up when I exit.

"Where have you been!" Cy is practically shouting as I reach them. Curran is nodding in agreement.

"I've been out to dinner with my daughter and her fiancé." And when did they unite?

"Why didn't you tell me?" Cy demands.

"Most def!" Curran looks equally annoyed.

I survey this pair with what little self-control I have left as I fish for my key in my purse. "Friends I can use. Parents I've already got."

Curran gets it, but Cy just looks hurt. Must be the reference-to-age thing.

I put one arm about his shoulders and sling the other around Curran's waist. "Look, guys. I think it's time we get this straight. It's my little parade. You can't lead. You can follow—at a discreet distance. Otherwise, get the hell outta my way. Okay?"

William is coming to see me!

I lie in bed, wide-eyed and exhausted. Happy, and really scared.

Some moments are just so delicious that you—well, you can get by for a long, long time on just the memory without ever being tempted to want more. William was to have been one of those memories.

Now I suppose I'll have to readjust!

24

I'm sure I wasn't this nervous the morning after. But that morning would have been a month ago. A lot has happened since that afternoon turned night-of-wonder. As I watch him crossing the station platform I realize that no matter how right and familiar he looks, William is a stranger. So far, our relationship consists of a doctor-patient exam and a one-night stand. The mundane and the sublime.

It's the first day of summer, or will be at 7:10 p.m. He's dressed in a blue sport coat, white collared shirt, khakis, loafers, no socks, and carrying a duffel bag. It strikes me now as I wave to him from the curb where the car is running, that he's made the reverse trip of most summer weekenders, who crawl for hours through incredible traffic snarls to reach the eastern shores of Long Island. Speaking of which, Aunt Marvelle has called twice this week. She knows something's up. She's just not sure what.

Just this morning she said, "Your mother sounds strange on the phone. I don't buy that it's her dental work. My sister is hiding something. Now Dallas won't answer my e-mail. And I know you taught your daughter better manners. Am I going to have to take the Jitney in? You know how I hate Penn Station. And that New Jersey Transit service? If I have to come up island, I'll be staying a good while."

This is a threat.

I told my parents about Sweet Tum last week. They took it really well.

"Are you perfectly certain, dear?" Mom said. "Oh, well, these things happen."

"You're a bit long in the tooth to be knitting baby blankets, dumpling." Dad's laughter is always a little forced. "I wouldn't place too much stock in it."

Then they immediately changed the subject. As if, the Fates willing, this is not something they'll need to explain to anyone else. Like shingles or late-life acne, it should clear up on its own.

But I can't quite work up the necessary pique, because William is now making a beeline for me. His open smile makes me realize that I had been counting on seeing him again, no matter what my head was saying to the most unreliable of organs, my heart.

"You look good. How are you feeling?"

"Pregnant. Five months and everything's solid." I pat my tummy. While it's not as obvious as I tend to want to believe it is, it is obvious I no longer have a waistline.

He makes a motion to ask if he can pat. I nod. That pleases him.

After the firm medical touch he presses a huge bouquet on me. "I didn't know what you liked so I bought what looked and smelled the best."

I sniff the freesias, a very expensive and wonderful fragrance, and mock swoon. "So you knew it was me?"

"The public display of floral ecstasy?" He looks at me for a long moment. My toes curl up like straws held before a flame. "I knew, Lu."

Okay, we're past that hurdle.

A traffic cop shouts at me, "Move along!" breaking the moment.

"What would you like to do this weekend?" I've moved us into the line of city traffic.

"Anything. Everything." He chuckles and rearranges his large frame on the passenger seat for more comfort. "I haven't had a weekend off in over a year."

"Then you should be easy to satisfy."

He flicks my earring with a finger. "I'm in your hands."

That's intriguingly put. But I'm not ready to be alone with him, just yet. I know Cy has evening plans with his family. He left me his cell phone number, as well as those of his son and daughter-in-law. "Just in case." I'll bet Joseph didn't watch Mary this closely.

Thankfully, Curran and KaZi are spending the weekend at the shore. Dread care won out over what I promised him would be a boring weekend of DVD watching and column writing. Tai nixed my first effort. "Big yawn!" is how she put it. So, with any luck and a bit of good timing, I can insert and extract William from my weekend without either of my guardians knowing about him. Still, I need to give Cy's family plenty of time to pick him up before I head home with my not-ready-for-public-consumption houseguest.

"It's too beautiful a day to waste indoors." William smiles. "Where can we go and not be surrounded by other people?"

Think fast! "Are you hungry? I know a great place where we can pick up something and eat outdoors in a really lovely spot a little distance from here."

"Sounds good." He waits a second before saying, "How many times did you pick up the phone to tell me not to come?"

"Not even once." I approached the phone and I stared at it many times, but I never actually picked it up. It came down to this: if the stars are aligned in my favor for a change, why should I mess with the equation?

I swing by a Vietnamese take-away I love and order cold udon noodles and spring rolls with peanut sauce, then head out on the highway. Where do you take a person who lives in one of the most coveted beachfront property areas in the U.S.? The hills, of course! The Watchung Mountains, to be precise.

Northern New Jersey is beautiful on this early-summer afternoon, all dappled light and green spaces. Colonial villages set on winding roads follow paths laid down by the Raritan Indians long before this area was a British land grab.

William seems content to gaze out the window and ask the occasional tourist question. We are studiously not talking about pregnancy, Jolie's or mine.

Finally, I pull in at a narrow lane between trees that leads to a tourist stop of historic interest, the lookout point called Washington Mountain that allows a panoramic view southward of the plains of central Jersey.

Once we've gotten out and walked up to the summit, William whistles. "I've heard Jersey described as the Garden State. I always thought it was a joke."

"You think this is nice, you should see the area in autumn. That's northern Jersey at its absolute best."

He nods thoughtfully. "I hope to see a lot of Jersey in the future."

Okay, it could just be me. I'm reading all kinds of things into remarks that, if made by anyone else, wouldn't hang me up for a second.

William is now staring into space, and I wonder if we share the same qualms about our weekend. But then I remember Andrea's advice about men.

Sex was on his mind before you even agreed to this. He's a man. Sex is on his mind!

We spread out an old car blanket I've kept in the trunk

since the kids were small, in case we broke down in winter weather. Then we sit and eat with chopsticks, which I'm pleased to see William handles like a pro.

I admit it. I'm waiting for the disappointment. Last time was perfect. This must be the prelude to inevitable disillusionment. Only a really determined Pollyanna would think otherwise. I haven't gotten to my age without learning something about human nature and relationships. If he still looks and sounds this good, it's because I'm not seeing reality.

It's just that I can't help it, I like watching him, like the way his hands look. Doctor's hands, well-kept and smooth, but strong with well-defined tendons. Helpful hands. Healing hands. And his ears. And the way his hair lies against his neck in little Vs, damp with perspiration. I am fascinated by the way the sparse hairs on his arm glint red highlights as he reaches for another spring roll. The smell of his aftershave, faint and lemony, makes me want to lick his neck. I could be eating ashes. My senses are consumed by the man beside me.

"...slept here?"

I realize William is speaking and my mind has wandered. "What?"

"He slept here?"

"Who?"

"Washington." William is looking at me with a puzzled expression. "The historical sign I just read says General Washington stayed in many of the local colonial homes. It was actually his troops who kept watch up here for the British camped in the south. Do you have a sign that says Washington slept here?"

I roll my eyes. "If Washington slept everywhere people say, he must have had narcolepsy."

William laughs, and I feel like singing.

We finish eating and close our cartons, but neither of us moves to leave.

I lean toward William and he reaches out for me. His hand is firm at the back of my neck as he pulls me closer. I collapse forward, my cheek finding the hard curve of his shoulder. My lids flutter shut over unfocused eyes. I feel his arm come around me from behind and it feels so good, so just what I needed…a shoulder to lean on.

I wake in a half-prone position, my face pressed into his thigh. And William is taking my pulse.

"I was just checking. You were sleeping awfully hard."

I sit up, unsure of anything. "And?"

"You're fine. Pulse nice and steady."

I look away and surreptitiously wipe my mouth. Jeez! I hope I didn't drool on his trouser leg. I check my watch. Forty-five minutes. Yep, that's my usual afternoon interlude these days.

"Sorry about the nap."

He just smiles. "Are you ready to go home yet? Or do I need to look into booking a hotel room?"

Touché! "I'm ready."

He helps me pick up and then collects the blanket. "Mind if I drive?"

"Why, does my driving bother you?"

"Not at all. You just look so relaxed that I don't want the hassle of traffic to change that."

I hand him the keys.

I direct him onto my block, but I'm having second thoughts as I glance at my watch. Six-thirty-three. "Do a drive-by first, if you don't mind."

William glances at me. "Are we hiding from someone?"

"In a manner of speaking."

He frowns. "Your ex-husband?"

"No, two of my dwarfs, Doc and Dope." I make the "lifted elbows, hands angled inward at the wrists hip-hop" sign as I say *dope*.

William chuckles. "Why do I suspect you aren't joking?"

"Ever seen a redheaded Rastafarian from Iowa?"

"Do I have to?"

I'm too busy watching first Cy's windows and then the shrubs around my own house to reply. I don't mean to seem paranoid but I don't want to be caught, especially on film by Curran and his camera. "Looks clear."

"You never can be too sure." William speeds up and makes the turn at the corner.

"Where are we going?"

He rolls to a stop at the entrance to the alley. "I'll drop you off at your back door, then park up the block and walk back."

I don't quibble for an instant. I grab his bag. "If you're stopped by an older man in spectacles, or happen to spy a Rastafarian with a camera in the bushes, keep walking, circle round to the alley and come in the back way."

I'm out the door so quickly I catch only a vague glimpse of his startled expression. But I figure, hey, hang with me, you got to go through the motions of my life.

William's at my door in less than five minutes. But his smile is wearing thin.

"As a mature individual, I no longer assume the actions of the person I'm with are solely because of me. Therefore, I'm going to assume that this is your usual way of dealing with a long-standing problem."

It occurs to me for the first time that I may not be the one who's going to come out of this weekend disappointed by reality.

"It's a long story."

He follows me into my kitchen where we both sit at the table. I offer water.

"No, thank you."

Next I offer iced tea, then juice. He shakes his head. "I

think there's a bottle of unopened wine around here somewhere."

William reaches out and snags me by the hand as I rise to search for that wine. That touch is enough to hold me in place, for more reasons than one. "Know what I said about being mature? Forget it. I'm really going to need that explanation."

I relax back into my chair.

"My next-door neighbor is an elderly widower named Cy Schelgel. He appointed himself my guardian since Jacob walked out. Now that I'm pregnant he's morphed into this super-parental figure, part godfather, part Mother Superior."

"And Island Man?" He says this with a straight face.

"Curran has dreads. He's twenty-four and the staff photographer at *Five-O*. He's making a photo journal of my pregnancy for the magazine. The problem is, he likes spontaneous moments."

"This explains his hiding in the bushes?"

I nod. "Ready to go home?"

William shrugs, and it's really one of indecision. Good, a sane person should be having second thoughts. Then he smiles again. "I'm not bored around you."

"That could change."

I rise and head for the refrigerator. After a nap there's nothing I like better than a snack. I had just enough energy this morning to clean up Davin's room for William. I decided I shouldn't presume he came here to sleep with me, even if it's on both our minds. When I open the fridge I remember I didn't get to the grocery store. Hoping for a miracle of inspiration, all I find are two milk cartons, old cheese, OJ, eggs, assorted condiments and the remains of last night's pizza.

William comes to stand beside me and stares into the vast cool space.

Just as I think he's about to offer to whip up something

gourmet-ish and delicious from those eggs and air, William shakes his head. "You've nothing to eat. Where's the nearest grocery store?"

Fair enough.

William does a mean bag of salad, and burns the best sirloin strips this side of, well, damn good. He bought beer for himself, and something truly horrendous called near-beer for me. Thankfully, there's a can of frozen lemonade in the freezer. I contribute couscous—boiling water, I'm there—and lemon bars that Andrea brought me a while back and I froze.

We move through the kitchen as if we've done this many times before. William seems to know where to look for pans and utensils. This makes me proud. A sign of a well-laid out kitchen is one where things are where we intuitively expect them to be.

When dinner's ready, we eat like two ravenous bears.

Right in the middle of the thawed lemon bars, William reaches out and pulls me to him, and kisses me as if it's the first and only thing that's been on his mind all day. This kind of interrupts the dessert portion of the evening for a while.

When we resume our respective chairs, he's smiling again. "I would have called, but I didn't know what to say."

I do. "Jacob's not an issue. He thinks I shouldn't have the child, doesn't want to know about it. I've not given him much thought since."

"Your children?"

I grimace and tuck a graham-cracker-crust crumb into my mouth with a finger. Dallas called first thing this morning to demand that I tell her everything about "this man I was seeing" today. I refused. She threatened to call her father. I asked her if she really wanted to be responsible for what might happen then. "The short version is, no one, not *one* person who cares about me, thinks this is a really stellar idea. Cy and Curran are at least excited."

"Do you blame them?" William's expression is so gentle I could kiss him again. But I fight the urge as if his lips were laced with arsenic. After forty, pride counts for more than sex—some of the time.

"Yes— No, it's really none of their business. Not Jacob's, and certainly not my children's problem to solve. It's my decision."

"You put a lot of heat into that reply."

"Can I see your medical ID?"

"Sure. Why?"

"Because I don't remember seeing a doctor-of-psychiatry degree on your wall."

William sits back and crosses his arms, taking his lips out of temptation's way. "I'm an interested party, that's all."

"You're trying to figure me out. To see beneath the curtain of the half truths and bogus hopes I've erected to shield myself from the truth that, in about five months, I'm going to be sitting in this very kitchen, looking down into the eyes of a new life, wondering what I could have been thinking at this very moment five months earlier."

There's a new light in his eyes, but his serious expression hasn't changed. "Do you always bite the helping hand?"

"Do you always assume the high ground?"

A corner of his mouth twitches. "Are we having our first fight?"

"Sounds like it."

"Good. If we've gotten past being polite then we can deal with the truth."

"Such as?"

He drops his crossed arms and leans on the table toward me. "Since I met you, I'm suddenly afraid to die."

25

This is not your standard seduction line. At twenty, perhaps, it would be Swoon City. At this point in my life, it sounds suspiciously like it's still the best line I ever heard.

William looks to me to say something, but I wouldn't speak now under anything less than pain of death. He takes my hand and leans forward until his elbows rest on the table as he studies my face. "You're an unusual woman."

"You have no idea."

He laughs. "And I sound like an idiot."

I smile, "No. But if you need your heart jump-started, you should pick up a younger version of me, one who's life and space is not literally already spoken for."

"There. That's what I'm talking about. After seeing so many paths to death I'd begun to think, it's not so bad. On the whole, I'm ready to go. I've lived enough, seen enough, done enough." He pauses. "And then you walked into my office with all that drama and—and—"

"Wit?"

"No."

"Beauty?"

"That's not…"

"Tears?"

He grins. "You are just really *alive*. It never crosses your mind that it could at any minute all come to an end."

When men do get in touch with their emotions, they often don't know when to quit.

"William, I do love talking with you. I do. But if we're going to discuss the end of life, could we schedule an appointment for it?"

But the man has warmed to his subject. "Imagine my arrogance, thinking I was prepared to go."

"Is there something I should know?" Seems I just asked Cy a similar question.

"Only that I have been living half a life. Being with you has made me take a look around at my own situation. I have a grandchild on the way. A practice going full tilt. Hell, I haven't even cracked the half-century mark."

Uh, *what?* My eyes narrow in on his silver-tipped temples. "Just how old are you?"

"Forty-eight…next November."

He's got some nerve to sit there grinning at me. "You're a younger man."

"Not that much. Forty-seven, forty nine—"

"Fifty, next week."

"The French say an older woman makes the best lover."

I wish he wouldn't keep making it so easy to like him. "So then, you are here because you think you're going to get lucky again?" *I* should get so lucky again!

"Don't get the wrong idea, Lu. I just came to spend a little time with you. And, I admit, to ask your advice."

"About senior citizen benefits?"

"No." He sighs. "I'm a lousy mother." That sounds like my line. "Jolie needs someone to listen to her. She thinks I should be better at it. I try. But I only seem to get her back up. I don't understand. Patients love my bedside manner."

"They are mostly widows, and mostly senile."

He laughs as though it's forced out of him. "I wish that were the answer."

"You want to talk about it?"

I can see the change take place in his expression. "It's serious. Do you mind?"

I shake my head and settle back. I think I can handle daughter stuff—at least, someone else's daughter's stuff.

Spina bifida.

I hear William talking but it's taking my mind a few seconds to catch up. Oh, God. Poor Jolie!

He reaches for a paper napkin and pulls a pen out of his jacket pocket, and begins to draw a fetus's physiology. I try to adjust my layman's eyes to his deft strokes. He's good at explanations. But I have to admit the Latin terms mean nothing to me other than as signals that an unborn child's life could be in serious jeopardy.

Finally he sits back and rubs a palm across his mouth. "She should have been tested months ago. She and Jon don't have insurance so Jon vetoed any optional testing as an unnecessary expense. She was too proud to tell me until she left him. I was angry, of course. Didn't she know that I would have gladly paid? I convinced her that testing was still a good idea, although I was certain she had nothing to worry about." I can tell by the way that his voice has emptied of emotion that there's more.

His head dips a little. "She got back positive results the day we saw you in the Paradise."

I remember Jolie's red eyes and pinched expression when she saw my baby's sonogram picture, and I wished her well with her pregnancy. My heart feels tight as I think about it. My test results have been fine.

"Not that AFPs are definitive. There is a high potential for false positives. I told Jolie more than ninety-five percent turn out to be wrong." He doesn't make eye contact. "I should have said positive results indicate only one thing, the need for more testing. She had a level-two sonogram last week. It, too, was inconclusive."

"So now what?"

"The next step is an amniocentesis. I told her Jon should be included in the decision. The procedure poses some risk to both mother and fetus."

I look for the bright spot. "Isn't it a good sign that she agreed to talk it over with Jon?"

William looks at me. "I called him. He sounded so relieved to hear from me that I wanted to throttle him. Why the hell hadn't he come to see her?"

"Maybe because he thought you'd kill him." I smile, but William is having none of it. "And guilt. Guilt stuns the young."

"He's her husband, dammit!" He stands up. "Not that she's going to listen to him, after what he's done."

"Unless he's a complete idiot, Jon knows he made a huge mistake and is focused on his wife and baby. He's there to convince Jolie to have the tests, isn't he?"

William shrugs. "If the tests come back indicting severe defects, Jolie will have to make more choices. If it is spina bifida, she could be a candidate for an in utero surgery on the fetus. If not, she'll need a Caesarian delivery. There'll be specialists ready to start special care and reconstruction immediately after."

I can't help it. I shiver and wrap my arms protectively across Sweet Tum.

"There's another possibility. If she and Jon should decide on divorce, she'd be a single mother, with a child with terrible health problems…." The words seem to be moving out of him without the effort of his breath. "There are several private facilities where she can go where they ask no questions and assign no blame."

I get up and put my arms about him, but I can't tell him it's going to be okay. About halfway through this speech he turned to look at me, and I suspect he wasn't only talking just about Jolie.

"I don't need a choice, William. This is how life is sometimes. There's what you want and what you need. And then, occasionally, there's just what you have to do. A high risk pregnancy isn't what Jolie or I wanted. But we're both grown women. It's what we've got to deal with." I put my hand across my middle. "Her choice may be understandably different. I'm having my baby."

He nods and even smiles a little. "I knew you'd say that. I just wanted you to know, if you thought…I would disapprove of you ending the pregnancy, that I wouldn't." He lifts a hand as if flicking a thought away. "But I'm glad you want to have the child."

"So then, while you're being the absent parent, Jon will help Jolie understand the importance of the test. She's just scared. You hear stories about things that can go wrong with amnios. She needs to see it as a resolution to her fears. Or a way to take action to rectify the problem her child may have."

William looks at me. "You see why she needs a mother? You word things better than I can."

"I think Dad's doing pretty well. He hasn't murdered the wayward father, or even stayed to referee their first meeting."

For a moment, he looks grim. "You know what that cost me?"

"Tickets on Long Island Railroad and the New Jersey Transit?"

He smiles now. "I can't believe I'm here."

"I know. We sort of had a one-night stand. Those are by definition one-time things." I rise and head for the sink to put my glass in it.

He comes up to me. "Maybe it was something else." He puts his hands on my shoulders. "I think maybe we needed each other."

"And now? What are we doing?"

He pulls me in until we meet chest to chest. "We're being together for another while."

I lift my arms to his shoulders. "To keep from thinking about our real lives?"

"This is my real life." He leans a little away to better see my face. "Do you have another, with Doc and Dopey, perhaps?"

"Perhaps."

He kisses me softly. "You lead a busy life, for a woman your age."

"You should know by now that men can get into serious trouble when they try to talk about a woman's age."

"I guess you'll have to find a way to shut me up."

Half an hour later, I'm lying in William's arms, in my bed. I bought a new mattress the day the divorce became final. I steal a glance at the clock. He's been back in my life less than six hours and we've been through more emotional changes than many couples cover in a year. We're speed-reading through one another's lives. No need to be coy at this stage.

"What are you thinking?"

"That younger men have their uses."

His laughter jiggles my breasts under the sheet pulled over us.

"I've been little more than a doctor these last years." He reaches up and pats my stomach. "I'm just beginning to realize what I've been missing as a man."

"Enjoying rolling around in bed with women pregnant by other men makes you freaky, you do know that?"

He kisses the top of my head. "What if there's just one pregnant woman I want to roll around with?"

"I suppose then you only qualify as odd."

"Would it be odd if I said I could use another couple of those lemon bars?"

"A man needs his strength." I rise up to go get them, but he pulls me back against him and begins nibbling my ear. "I'll get them...in a minute...or five."

We are content just to touch and kiss and squeeze, learning the texture and feeling the limits of each other. I like his thighs. They are hard and nearly hairless, like the rest of him. Jacob had a lot of body hair. I didn't mind that, either. If William finds me too much or too little or too anything, he doesn't say, just seems to be enjoying sensation, as much as I am.

Yet I admit to a certain vanity. It's small of me and I despise myself for it. I have living proof that he likes me. So why am I even doubting...? While he says looks don't matter...what does? Maybe I can just do a little casual inquiry.

"I'm doing research for a piece for *Five-O* on what men find attractive in older women. The answers are sometimes refreshingly honest."

He takes my hand and licks the palm. "So now you want to know what I think?" Got to give him points for seeing through me. "Yes. I care what a woman looks like. Generally. The details, no."

And that's all I should need to know. But... "I did some research when Tai was pushing my column toward an extreme makeover byline. There are procedures for things I would never in a million years have thought of. What sort of woman feels she needs hand rejuvenation, toe shortening or—this I couldn't even believe!—a labia lift to attract a man's attention?"

William laughs. "Any woman showing her labia already has the man's attention."

I slap my hand across his middle. "You know what I mean."

He cups one of my breasts and kind of holds on, as if he really likes the feel of it. "A woman needs a good attitude, that's all. Everything else is gravy."

Must be the sexual energy, I can't keep my mouth shut. "Don't be disingenuous. Men judge women every day by how they look. I can practically give you the date men stopped looking at me."

He rises up and cranes his neck around so he can catch my eye. "I'm looking at you. And touching you. What else do you need?"

What else, indeed! I kiss him hard because he makes my heart pound, and that scares me a bit.

It's just that no one in her right mind would think this has any staying power. We're comforting each other in our need. Oh, boy, do we do that! Yet, my emotions, raging with the need to nest and cuddle, can't be trusted.

As for him, he admitted he'd been celibate since his wife died. Poor man! He's probably just forgotten what a young woman looks like with her clothes off. In his line of work, a woman my age must look pretty good by comparison.

And then I want to slap myself for all the snide, unnecessary conditions I'm putting on what is in actual fact one of the best things in my life.

I put a hand on either side of his face to stop his kisses. He doesn't give in easily. He licks the tip of my nose, and then each lip separately, before he lays his head back against my pillows.

"So what are you writing about in your column these days?"

He had to ask.

"Oh, midlife. Changes. Difficulties."

"You could publish a journal about your pregnancy, if you weren't too classy to peddle yourself in print."

"You think so?" There are still some topics we need to steer clear of today. "Say, weren't you hungry?"

A man's stomach is always ready for food. He hops out of bed, pulls on his boxers and walks out of my bedroom.

I follow him, after snatching a filmy floral wrapper with lace trim out of my closet. I stop to fluff my hair a bit, and run a finger under each eye to wipe away the mascara smudge beneath.

By the time I reach the kitchen, his mouth is covered in powdered sugar and cookie crumbs, and he's reaching for another lemon bar.

"Would you like some herbal tea?"

He nods, jaws locked in lemon-sugar delight.

I pick up the kettle from the stove and walk toward the sink. His eyes follow. I exaggerate my hip movements a bit to see what he'll do. The rest of him follows me to the sink, that's what.

As I turn on the water he moves in behind me and kisses my neck, just where the robe gapes away at my nape. *"Hmm,"* he murmurs. And then one arm comes around the front, powdered-sugared fingers splayed so as not to soil my wrapper, and his wrist hooks in low on my belly to pull me back against him.

The kettle is filling.

"Lu?" he whispers against my ear.

"Hmm?"

"Do you mind if I have another taste?"

I don't think he's talking about lemon bars because he's pulling loose my sash between the knuckles of his other hand.

The thing about sex is, if it's been absent awhile, it comes back in waves of remembrance of need. The need is mutual.

William's hands are something altogether different when they are being directed not by the physician's mind but the man's libido. Soon I'm remembering things I've only read about as those hands glide and slide and seek and slip into—oh my, I wonder if anyone ever used powdered sugar that way before?

Pretty soon, I feel him reach back and slide down his shorts and then he's lifting the back of my robe with the other.

Feeling what he's feeling, I wriggle back against him. "I've never done it standing up."

"Good. We have some firsts together."

A gasp at the right moment can be as distracting as glass shattering on marble. We are no longer alone.

One instant William is knocking on my door. The next, I feel the cool breeze of abandonment on my posterior. He's amazingly quick, a flash of naked man through the nearest exit, which is the dining room. And he didn't even trip on his boxers!

The blood draining from my head, my heart, my loins closes the world to a pinprick diameter as I turn to face our intruder.

Andrea. Standing in the doorway to the kitchen.

"I knocked. Nobody answered."

26

I need to collect my house keys. Far too many people have access to my house.

"Girl, you need to be more careful." Andrea has a hand on each hip. "I could have been anybody walking in here just now."

"You *are* anybody, Andrea. Go home!"

I've adjusted my robe but the damage has been done. It could have been worse, I tell my galloping heart. It could have been Cy or Curran, or—Davin or Dallas! Much, much worse.

"Who was that guy?" Andrea cranes her head around but I step in her way as she's about to follow the path William took as he sprinted off. "Tell me I didn't walk in on some sexual predator you're afraid to tell me about because he's got a gun pointed on us from the shadows?"

I fold my arms. "Do I look frightened?"

Andrea grins. "You look freshly fu—"

"Andrea!"

"He's cute. How come I don't know about him?"

I'm trying for poise here. I really am. I have never been walked in on in the middle of sex before. It takes a bit of effort to speak coherently.

"What the *hell* are you doing here, Andrea?"

She shrugs and, to my horror, goes to sit down at my kitchen table. "I saw your car parked up the street a couple of hours ago. Just now I came back and saw it still there. I wondered if you'd had car trouble. Then I called and got no answer."

"I turned off the ringer."

Andrea grins. "I can see why."

"What are you doing in my house?" I need the answer to make sense of an embarrassment so acute I feel a rash coming on.

"I rang the bell."

It's not that I don't believe her, it's just...I don't believe her. "It worked yesterday."

She crosses her legs as if I've asked her to tea. Tea! I turn to shut off the running water.

"Okay, so maybe I peeked through the window and it was so quiet and dark in here that I let myself in, thinking maybe you were sick or something."

"I was something."

"Next time you should like, let a sister know, so she can run interference for you."

"Andrea, I really don't want to talk about this. But if we must, can it be another time, like in four or five years?"

"Oh, right, you've got company." She stands up. Her head swivels toward the dining room again. "He looked pretty involved so I guess he's pissed at me."

"You could think that. I sure am."

"Listen, you should be thanking me. This could have been something else altogether. You got someone looking out for you." She prods her chest with a freshly manicured nail. "Don't forget that."

"At this point, I can recite a roster of people lined up to

look out for me. Maybe you could form a political party and elect me mayor." I point to the way out. "Home, Andrea."

"Okay, okay." She stands and takes long, cartoonish sneaky steps toward the door. "I'm proud of you. I told you, men are out there. Only answer this. Is he—good…?" She makes an obscene gesture with her hand.

I sling the first thing I can reach at her, a sponge.

At this point, it's about even odds that William has shimmied down the drainpipe and disappeared over the eastern horizon.

I give him plenty of warning that I'm coming, mounting each step with a heavy, reluctant tread. I know it's really me who's delaying the moment in which I must explain myself, and my friends, again.

William is standing in Davin's room, fully dressed. As in socks and shoes, and bag-in-hand dressed. "I'm sorry if it seems I ran out on you. I didn't know what— I thought maybe it would be better if I… Who was that?"

"The FBI."

"What?" Oh dear, at this point, he's ready to believe anything of me.

"The Fábregas-Prem Bureau of Investigation. Better known as Andrea, my best friend. She thought I was sick, or maybe you were a pervert who broke in. We sorted it out."

"Oh." William puts down his bag and looks at me with exasperation. "I don't want to tell you your business. But does it occur to you that you are managing a few too many parties in your life?"

I'm certainly not feeling like a party anymore, so I'll assume he means other people.

I sit down on Davin's bed and lean slightly forward, bracing my hands on my thighs to relieve the stiffness in my lower back. "I was a sensible middle-aged person until my husband walked out. I don't mean he held things to-gether. Far from it. But that's another story. Still, people never came and went in my house without warning. Well, Davin had that pack of friends who set up in the TV room his senior year and played Dungeons and Dragons pretty much full-time, when they weren't in school. And, of course, before that Dallas went through the stage where there were two or three guys hanging out all the time they weren't in school, either. But for me, basically, I've been a normal, relatively sane wife and mother, and journalist. Pretty much."

"I want to believe you." William comes up and sits down beside me. "But if that's true, perhaps you were sitting on a part of yourself you've never had a chance to know."

I give him a look. "No license to practice here. Remember?"

He smiles. "Okay. So what do you want to do now?"

"Go to bed."

"Now?" He looks alarmed, not lusty.

"Not sex. Sleep. I need my rest. Okay?"

"Okay." He chuckles. "Because I'm bushed, too."

And just like that, we set a pattern that will last the rest of the weekend. We don't answer the dead-bolted door. We don't go out. He takes some medical calls, and a few to Jolie. She and Jon seem to be managing to keep it together under one roof. On Sunday, William and I sit and read the paper, eat occasionally, make love when the mood strikes mid-afternoon, and I tell him each time I feel Sweet Tum within flutter. He's remarkably good at look-ing quite pleased about that, each and every time.

When Cy calls, he sneezes, bless his heart, and I put off his offer to visit with a "Not until you're sure it's just pollen. I have a baby to consider. Call me Monday."

27

There's one thing about drama. It juices the imagination. I've been typing like a fiend since William took a cab to the rail station an hour ago. I click the print button and smile. I have two hours left before I'm due at work. How I love deadlines!

In under forty-five minutes, I'm showered, dressed and out the door, a miracle of second-trimester tranquility.

The sight of Curran standing just outside my door, clicking away on the camera, leaves me unruffled. We made an agreement yesterday, by phone. From 6:00 p.m. Fridays until 8:00 a.m. Mondays, I'm a free agent. If anything really cinematic comes up, I will call. Otherwise, we all need time off from work, and one another.

"Hey, Lu!"

I smile and nod. "You look like a lobster."

Curran shrugs. "They say if you wear an SPF of 15, even a very white person can tan."

"They lied, Curran."

I slide behind the wheel of my car and he gets in on

the passenger side. I didn't volunteer to pick him up or take him home, but it seemed a bit much to expect him to pay an extra fare every day just so he can catch sight of me opening my door. This way, I know he knows he'll see me first thing. No scouting out my backyard, or surprise jumps from bushes. He gets his picture, and I get to drink coffee without closing all the blinds.

"Fun weekend?"

"The shore was stupid!" Since Curran's grinning, I assume he means he had a good time. "Your weekend see any excitement?"

I grin, too. "I have a secret lover. We had sex on every piece of furniture in the house."

Curran shakes his head. "Old movies and popcorn, huh?"

I shrug. Am I that dull?

We arrive at work a whopping fifteen minutes early. By now I'm almost accustomed to the fact that people I know will gawk at the sight of me. I suppose it's because I'm wearing maternity clothes more or less full-time. Various members of the staff catch my eye and wave, or give me a victory or thumbs-up sign. Well, not everyone.

KaZi is standing at the reception desk. When she notices Curran and me approaching, her eyes, rimmed in thick bands of black eyeliner, narrow into equal signs. Then she throws up a hand, palm out, and looks away.

I turn to Curran. "What was that about?"

Curran wheels around and, mumbling under his breath, "I gotta be somewhere," heads back out the door.

Evidently, the lovebirds are fighting. No need for me to take sides. "Hey, KaZi."

She gives me an I-don't-think-you-want-to-talk-to-me stare, then turns and walks away.

I shrug and look at Babs. "Hi. Please see that Tai gets this."

It's my revised column for "The Pregnant Pause." Before the day is over I'll know whether this is officially my first day back with a new column or my official last day at the old job.

"...wanted you to know." William's voice is low and soft with relief.

"I'm so glad." I shift the phone to my other ear as I reach to pause one of my favorite movies, *Dark Victory,* on my computer screen. "How soon will they perform the amnio?"

"A week. Jolie and Jon didn't exactly reconcile, but she agreed to go home until the time for the test."

"Which means you're released from parenting up close and personally." I hit the stop button to turn the movie off. Bette Davis's eyes are distracting even on Pause.

"I'm on call this weekend. So I was thinking that, if you're not busy..." The hesitation in his voice surprises me. "Come out here."

"Sunday's my birthday."

"What about your children?"

I fish a dried apricot out of my bowl of healthy snacks and pop it into my mouth. "Davin can't get away and Dallas probably won't try."

"Now, that's not right. What about your dwarfs and the FBI?"

"There is a small party planned for Saturday. I...er, how about you come help us celebrate?"

"You're not obligated to include me."

Damn! He heard the hesitation in my voice. Frankly, I am thinking about the repercussions. Even if Andrea has had an up-close and much-too-personal encounter with him, meeting Cy and Curran will be another thing altogether. I'd like to keep William to myself a little longer.

"Oh, then, forget it. You try to be nice to some people..."

His laughter, sharp as ever, cuts across the line and into

my frustrated day, laying open a sunshine center. "If I can switch part of my on-call weekend duty, I'll be there midday on Sunday. You stay put. I'll catch a cab from the station."

"Sounds like a plan." I look up and my voice changes. "Got to go."

Tai is in my doorway.

"Come in."

I know how it must look, curtains drawn, lights down, a DVD playing an old movie while I'm on the phone talking sweet and low—and I don't care. She's made me wait until three-thirty to give me the verdict on my column. Sweet Tum needed me to mellow out.

Tai's carrying my latest column copy between two fingers. "I read 'Knocked-Up But Not Out.'"

She practically purrs as she lays it on my desk. Is this a dead-rodent trophy or am I trapped like a rat? "I love it. It's got everything. Smarts. Sass. Controversy!"

I frown. "What's controversial?"

"The fact you say you will not name the father of your child. I've been thinking about that. Our readers are going to devour that tidbit. Absolutely devour it. And scour future issues for clues to his identity in your columns."

I sit back and smile. "There won't be any."

"There needn't be. You've flung down the gauntlet."

Tai folds her arms and leans her whippetlike body against my door frame. "Frankly, I wouldn't have believed a woman in your position could resist pointing the finger of accusation. Revenge is sweet, believe me. The possibilities of why you are resisting the opportunity to make the man squirm are too delish to ignore! Are you too noble? Too ashamed? Or won't say because you don't know?"

If she's waiting for me to offer up the real explanation, she can just go fish. "Always happy to make a positive contribution at *Five-O*."

Tai feigns disappointment that I didn't bite. "Got to hand it to you, Lu. It's positively genius PR."

"Thanks." I glance at my clock. It's still naptime. "Is there anything else?"

"Yes, actually. I've decided we won't be needing Marc's services any longer." She frowns slightly but it disappears in a microsecond. "He is not at all what I'd been led to expect." Her gaze comes back to me. "You, on the other hand, have unexpected depths, Lu Nichols."

So my job is secure because either I'm an example of nobility *ne plus ultra,* a fool or a slut. I can live with that.

My feelings are a surprise to me. Forty whizzed by on the tail of a comet so bright I didn't ponder it. I don't remember thirty. Seriously. But here I am, staring at the big 5-0 on the calendar of my birth date, appalled by where I am in my life.

The *Five-O* staff took me to lunch yesterday. I was ready for the usual gagfest of black balloons, tubes of Preparation H and denture cream. Instead, I got a "You Go, Girl" bash.

At Tai's behest, we took a train into lower Manhattan and celebrated at one of those no-oven, drinks-centric bars with an incredibly imaginative menu. Should have been a winner. But reality bites. Everyone happily drank themselves into stupors with Incredible Hulks and Tequinis while I sipped mineral water, scarfed down outrageously priced hors d'oeuvres and tried not to pout.

There were plenty of well-wishers in my corner. Tai had handed out copies of my first column for all to read as they came in the door. "A quick spot poll," she assured me. It quickly became a Rorschach test of the staff.

"My *She*-ro!" Babs trilled in delight when she had perused it. Then she gave me a raised-fist salute. "You go, girl!"

I'm amused that she knew this gesture.

Rhonda's voice was hollow with admiration. "I want you to know that we all think what you're doing is so brave. That takes such class, shielding a man who doesn't deserve it. Men can be such selfish bastards!" Then she slammed a fist into the palm of her other hand with the conviction of a veteran of the battle of the sexes.

A little later a combative-looking Brenda waylaid me. "Don't let him get away with it. He has legal responsibilities. And financial ones! My advice, get yourself a good attorney." When I suggested that there just are some mistakes a person doesn't want to deal with twice, she patted me on the back and said, "That 'mistake' has a bank account. This is your future he's messed with. Make him pay."

Curran just sort of stared slack-jawed at me, as if he had thought this protruding belly really was a spontaneous miracle of life. KaZi just glared—at both of us.

Yet for the first time, I've begun to wonder what kind of bargain I've made. Maybe I've let a seed be planted that I had not altogether thought through. Out there in the ether now is the persona of a despicable, dishonest and cowardly mystery man who got me in the family way then deserted the mother ship. As a result, I'm seen as the dupe left holding the maternity bag.

Even so, I smiled really hard when presented with a carved crystal *Five-O* logo to place on my mantel.

"Your survival trophy," Tai said as she presented it. "God! I can't imagine how it must feel to be you."

Me, neither. So then, I'm not as brave or blasé as I thought I would be.

That's why at half past ten on a Saturday morning, I'm lying in bed leafing through albums of Dallas and Davin as tykes, and wondering for the first time since my teen years, *why me?*

William seems to think I've kept a part of me hidden. If something was missing, I'm not certain I've yet found it. This new me feels a lot like the old me—only pregnant…and now fifty.

This is not how I envisioned this day. Where's my cruise on the Aegean Sea? My African safari? My getaway with gal pals for a shop till we drop on the floor of Van Cleef & Arpels? Not happening.

Dallas won't be coming home, after all. She has planned a weekend at Cape Cod. She swears it's a business boondoggle that she can't wriggle out of. I'm sure that's the truth. Yet she called a second time to explain, so I know we are still at odds. She did send flowers, a gorgeous bouquet.

Davin has to work parents weekend at summer camp. He sent me a picture of himself and the kids framed in a collection of twigs, nuts, seeds, pods and so forth, gathered and glued together by his "tribe."

I tell myself I'm not sad about this. It's to be expected that grown children would have lives of their own. To celebrate, Andrea, Cy, Curran and I are going to do lunch. A nice square number.

The sound of the doorbell drags me reluctantly out of bed. I look out the window and see a courier van parked on the curb.

I truck downstairs, wishing it were Fed Ex with some wonderfully elaborate birthday present from some smitten—

"Cy." Oh no, not from Cy.

No matter how wonderful, extravagant, perfect-for-me, delightful it is, it wouldn't be right to accept pure joy and bliss in a box from a man whose marriage proposal I rejected. I failed gold-digger class in fourth grade when conscience made me give back the Day-Glo eraser Jason

Hadley had offered me in exchange for a kiss, which I then refused to deliver.

When I've signed for the box, I realize the guy will expect a tip. "Just a sec."

"No need." The courier waves me off.

That's when I see Cy standing on his porch.

He gives me that old-fashioned tip-of-the-hat salute and calls, "Happy birthday, Lu!"

"Thank you," I call back. Why bother to say that he shouldn't have. Or even, what's in the box? He will just answer, "Don't deny an old man these small joys."

"See you later!" I shut my door, turning the dead bolt just in case he decides to come over to watch me unwrap something I suspect I'm really going to hate giving back.

When I've opened the outer box I discover a gift wrapped in heavy foil-embossed paper good enough to set with china. The silver-and-plum ribbon is a real silk scarf. Even before I open the card I'm smiling because I know this too-pretty-to-open gift could only come from one source.

The card reads, "Welcome to the best years of your life! Love, Aunt Marvelle."

It takes a few minutes to unwrap the wide flat box without spoiling the paper. Then I realize what I'm holding.

Still in its Cartier box, circa 1950, is a circlet of diamonds. I don't mean tennis bracelet chain-store type diamonds. These are individually chosen stones for the same color and clarity, graduated in size for artistic arrangement, and set in handcrafted platinum.

I know all of this because Aunt Marvelle first showed this necklace to me when I was six years old. Uncle Harvey was a U.S. attaché to some minor European country where embassy balls and state dinners and weekends on the Côte d'Azur were de rigueur. She sat me before a mirror and dangled the necklace before me, so I could see

what I might look like in it. Even then I knew I was out-
classed. All these years later, I've yet to attend a function
worthy of this necklace.

After washing my hands, I take the necklace out of the
box and lay it very carefully around my neck. It even
makes a cotton robe look good.

"Tallulah?" Aunt Marvelle sounds as if I've awakened
her with my call.

"Aunt Marvelle. I don't know what to say. I'm overwhelmed!" I'm preening in the mirror even as I speak.
"Are you sure you're ready to let go of them?"

"Wear them to your birthday party," she says matter-
of-factly, but I hear the satisfaction of my joy in her voice.

"There's no party worthy of this."

"Diamonds are the party! I wouldn't have thought I'd
have to say that to you, Tallulah. When you're my age,
waiting for a proper occasion is a waste of a good time.
Now, you just put on impossibly high heels, a flirty skirt,
and drink champagne until you can't stand upright without a man's arm about you!"

"You're absolutely right, Aunt Marvelle." Except about
the champagne, and possibly the heels. I'm going to have
to tell her about Sweet Tum soon. Tomorrow. "Thank
you!"

My Pity Party is over! I've got my health, my work, my
home and now a neckful of envy-me diamonds. And, if
he can get away, my lover will be here tomorrow.

Not bad for the middle of the journey.

29

Andrea is driving me home from my birthday lunch because, despite my sober state, I'm feeling that sudden exhaustion that occasionally comes over pregnant women. She has a nephew following closely behind in my car. Not that the occasion was any big blast that I hated to leave.

"Curran and Cy didn't say why they couldn't come when they called? And why did they call you and not me?"

Andrea is dancing in her seat to an OutKast tune on the radio. "You don't tell me everything. I don't tell you everything. Okay?"

The suspense of wondering what she could possibly mean is brief. As we pull up, Curran and Cy are sitting on my front steps. Pinned between their shoulders is William.

I don't feel surprise or even alarm. Instead of wondering how the hell I'll explain him to everybody, I'm thinking, *thank you, thank you, thank you, heavens!*

"This looks like fun." Andrea pops out of her low-slung vehicle while I extract myself more slowly. Way ahead of me, she hurries over to greet William with a big hug.

"You know this guy?" I hear Cy ask her.

"Oh, yes. I've seen quite a lot of him." Andrea winks at William, who shifts uneasily.

"Who is this guy?" Cy demands, as I reach the grouping.

I notice Cy's shirt collar is a bit askew and pat it back down. "I don't believe that's any of your business."

Curran pops up, his dreads wobbling. "It is when we almost hadda bust a move on him for trying break into your crib!"

"I was just trying to surprise Lu." I follow William's glance to his feet, where a large gift-wrapped package looks a little the worse for wear. "I tried your back door. It was open so I thought I'd wait inside. Then these two goons—guys jumped me."

"Yo! Don't be trying to perpetrate." Curran moves in recklessly close to William and crosses his arms high on his narrow chest. "You get jumped by the Cur, you will know it."

I grab Curran's arm and jerk him back toward me. "Down, boy. I've got it from here." I'm afraid to ask what Cy and Curran were doing in my house. I just want them gone. Quickly.

Despite his totally justifiable annoyance, William looks so good to me that I have to keep from bear-hugging him as I say, "I wasn't expecting you until tomorrow."

"So, you do know this dude?" Curran demands.

"Yes. This is Dr. William Templeton."

"The kind who makes house calls," Andrea adds unhelpfully.

Cy's gaze sharpens behind his lens. "Then why didn't he say so?"

"Yeah," choruses Curran.

Ignoring their questions, I lean in to kiss Cy on the cheek. "Thank you for taking care of me." I turn to Curran and tug the inch-long tuft of red beard on his chin. "Both of you. Now, go home."

Cy doesn't budge. "Not until you've seen your birthday gift."

I was afraid this was going too well.

It's a crib! A really pricey model made of New Zealand pine that goes from crib to junior bed. Exactly like the ones I have been drooling over in magazines. I have to blink back tears. "It's wonderful! But how did you— Andrea!"

"Cy needed a gift suggestion. This is much nicer than the one you said you could afford," Andrea coos.

Cy grins like a kid. "You wouldn't let me build a nursery. This is the least I could do. Curran and I set it up after you left for lunch."

"Oh, Cy. Thank you!"

He gives me a really tight hug. "My gift and my pleasure."

Curran picks up the lovely but empty pine frame leaning against the wall. "I'm going to do you a layette collage of pics of the baby for the wall," he says, and then gives William a smirky smile. "You know Lu's carrying a baby?"

"I am a doctor," William replies with remarkable subtlety.

"Just so you know," Curran grunts, "she's gots peoples looking out for her. Lots of peoples."

"The Village People," I say, and start to laugh.

William holds out his hand to Cy. "Despite our awkward introduction, I'm happy to know that Lu has such good neighbors."

Cy doesn't shake. "Did Lu tell you I've asked her to marry me?"

"What?" Curran yelps while Andrea whispers, *"Dios!"*

William withdraws his hand. "Can we discuss that another time? Lu looks tired."

Cy sends me a quick, concerned glance. I obligingly yawn.

"I keep an eye on things. You remember that." Reluctantly Cy turns toward the door.

Andrea gives me the "call me" sign. I give her a thumbs down.

It takes about ten seconds for Cy, Curran and Andrea to close the front door and descend the steps. All the while William stands with hands in pockets looking at me. He's not angry or unhappy or even annoyed anymore. He looks as if he's considering all his options.

Finally, he says, "Do you have any idea how fortunate you are to have such friends?"

"My padded cell will need to be a suite."

"Don't knock it."

And then he approaches and puts his arms about me. "Hi," he says against my ear.

"Hi, yourself." I hug him back hard.

He kisses my forehead. "So how's the birthday girl?"

I lean against his chest. "So tired I can hardly stand."

"That's too bad." He kisses my eyelids as his hands begin a gentle massage of my back. "I'm feeling the need to be very territorial at the moment."

"Because of Cy and Curran?" I don't laugh but, honestly, he can't be serious. William jealous of Cy or Curran? I try not to think too hard about that. "Now, about that slightly soiled box you brought in…"

He chuckles. "So, you are female after all. Fishing for presents after all I've been through."

I release him. "I'm so sorry about the earlier ordeal."

"You warned me." He shrugs.

"Even so."

"You're right. It's a lot to take in. So, you want to tell me about that?" He points a finger at my throat, stopping just short of the diamonds. "Is this from Cy, too?"

He is jealous! I smile. "It's Aunt Marvelle's welcome to the over-the-hill gang."

I watch him recalculate. He wants to believe me. Probably does. But then, what about Cy's proposal? That's the unspoken question swimming beneath the surface of his dark eyes. I'm not going to help him. Any reassurances on my part would be indirect encouragement for something I'm not ready to commit to.

He goes over to the box he brought with him and picks it up. "This did look better."

Since it's mangled, anyway, I tear the lid off the box and rip right through the paper. Inside is another box, and then another. I'm about to be really annoyed when I get to the fourth. Inside is a midnight-blue satin box studded with sequins. I smile. "Thank you. It's lovely."

"Don't stop now." He grins. "Open it."

I'm a girl. I pull it apart so fast the pair of dangling golden filigree earrings with blue glass spangles inside almost pop free. "They're gorgeous."

He looks pleased. "I saw them in a shop window and they looked like you."

"Me? They look like a party in a box." And ultra feminine and the very last thing I'd expected.

I turn to the nearest mirror and hold one up to my ear. "This is the sexiest present I've ever received."

"I can't take all the credit. The box was the saleslady's idea."

I turn back to him. "The box is cute. The earrings are the kind of thing that will get a man laid."

He looks even happier but says, "What's with the kid calling himself 'The Cur?'"

I laugh and respect anew his subtlety...or is it his confidence? Give me a man who enjoys the journey every time. "That's Curran's new moniker."

"As in mangy dog?"

I smile. "It's got a bite to it, *aw-ite?*"

William laughs, and I think, yeah, for now everything's all right.

30

"Hello, Lu."

"Jacob."

He looks quite natural framed in the doorway, though I never used to have to open it for him. Today, he's the very last person I expected to see. "Is everything all right?"

"Yeah. Just thought I'd drop by." He whips a hand from behind his back and produces a package with a bow. "Happy birthday, Lu."

"You remembered." I don't say this in giddy expectation, for Jacob was never big on birthdays, or holidays in general for that matter. Cheap and particular, I remind myself with lowering expectations. "Thank you."

He continues to stand there. Actually he's staring into the hallway behind me like a stray that hopes to be let in. I'm out of options without being absolutely rude. And, I admit, I'm touched that Jacob remembered the day. I guess fifty years is a milestone even an ex-husband is unlikely to forget.

"Would you like to come in for a minute while I open it?"

"Yeah." He looks relieved.

William has gone to the grocery store. I move to the circular table in the entry hall, one ear cocked for the sound of a garage door opening. Quickly I tear to shreds the wrapping paper, then pop the ribbons of tape by running a fingernail under the edge of the box lid. Clouds of tissue paper take flight as I dig for the item.

It's a crystal bowl, Mikasa not Steuben, but certainly nicer than the beer steins that were my first birthday present from him. (I don't drink beer but he does.) Last year's present was a pair of Calphalon oven mitts. He boasted that he thought to buy them because he remembered I had burned my arm trying to wrestle the Easter ham out of the oven. Associations with food are his strong point.

I hold up the bowl, noting the etched design, and feel my heart thaw a few degrees. "Why, Jacob, it's lovely. I didn't expect anything...."

"So nice?" His self-deprecating smile further disarms me. He's sporting a tan so perfect that, if I didn't know better, I'd suspect he's been going to a tanning salon. Naw! He's too cheap.

"Admit it. You aren't the world's best gift giver."

He takes a few steps down the hall and leans around the corner to peer into the dining room, looking around as if trying to discover what changes I've made. Maybe he thinks I'm selling off the furniture to pay the mortgage.

Finally he turns back to me. "So, I'm not the best shopper. You know how it is. Female things all look the same to me. And sizes?" He shrugs. "I had, uh, help."

"Sandra picked it out." I set the crystal piece down a bit hard. But, hey, at least I didn't heave it in his direction. "Well, thank you for the thought. I'm a bit busy, and since I wasn't expecting you, I really need to get back to work."

He shoves his hands into his pockets and rocks back on his heels. "What kind of busy are you on your birthday? You having a party, maybe?"

"Andrea threw one for me yesterday." I'm entitled to embellish the lunch.

He frowns at this. "I wasn't invited."

"You'd have accepted?"

"I might have." He points at the box. "I got a gift, didn't I?"

"Yes." And despite the fact that his new ladyfriend purchased it, I guess I have to give him some credit. Is that a car engine I hear in the back?

To my consternation, Jacob heads for the kitchen. "I need a drink," he says after the fact.

"I can get it," I say quickly, but I'm already trailing him. Oh, damn! Did I leave out the dishes from a late breakfast, two of everything sitting in plain sight?

Jacob enters the kitchen and stops abruptly, as if expecting something. Then he saunters over to the counter, opens a cabinet and stares as if his glass selection will affect some important event. When he's taken down a tall, clear tumbler, he carries it over to the refrigerator and pushes it into the slot for ice water. Every second of activity winds me a little tighter. It's as though he's playing for time. But, of course, it's just me who knows about William.

Jacob says, as he watches the glass fill, "So, what have you been doing with yourself?"

"The usual." I won't look at my watch. I won't!

He looks up, and suddenly amazement enters his expression. "My God, Lu! You're getting huge."

"You always had a way with compliments." My crinkle-cotton caftan makes the most of my evolving profile. I touch my middle. "We're both doing well. Thank you for asking."

He takes a long gulp of his water while I hang in the

doorway, hoping my reluctance to enter the kitchen suggests that he shouldn't tarry there, either. *Please don't let William find him here,* I fret. Or is it that I don't want Jacob to find out about William and me? Oh, what the hell. He's got Sandra. I just don't need a scene.

When he's well watered, Jacob runs the back of a hand across his mouth. "Jeez, Lu. I didn't think you'd do this to yourself."

I decide this time not to repeat how he had a helping hand in the matter. I simply cross my arms and give him what I hope looks like an impatient stare.

He leans a hip against the countertop. "The thing is, since you got into this situation, I just wanted to say that— well, I…" He's rubbing his hair and looking everywhere but at me. I haven't seen him this nervous since he told me he had filed for divorce, two days after he had walked out. That day I was in such shock I couldn't gauge the extent of his emotional distress. This time I can fully appreciate his discomfort.

"I've got some responsibility for things. I admit it, Lu." He looks at me with hound-dog eyes. "So, I'm gonna pay half the bills you got connected with the situation."

I suspect I'd be more impressed if I wasn't practically toe-dancing over the fact that I'm sure I just heard a car door slam. I move quickly to grab Jacob by the arm. "Can we talk about this some other time?" I tug him toward the hall. "It's wonderful of you to want to help. Really. Let me think about it."

"What's the hustle for?" He plants his feet, which brings us both to a stop. "What are you hiding?"

It's not what he says. It's the fact that he has any suspicion at all that tips me off.

I release him and step back. "Who have you been talking to?"

"So it's true." He juts out his chin. "You want to tell me who the guy is?"

I'm finding it difficult to draw breath. "Are you spying on me?"

"I am not." Jacob looks indignant. "Dallas might have mentioned you were seeing someone." Then, realizing he sounds as if he was hiding behind his daughter, he props a fist on each hip. "You should know you can't keep this kind of thing a secret. Might as well tell me."

"You must be joking. My life is no longer any of your business, Mr. 'Not-Meeting-My-Needs.'" Uh-oh, I'd promised myself as a New Year's resolution never to go there again.

He wags his head. "I thought you'd have more class."

Is that the garage door? As a kid I once ventured into a neighbor's chicken coop. Flustered by my inept groping for eggs, the hens took flight in the dim, nearly airless space. I thought I'd smother before I got out. That's how I feel now, cornered and lacking oxygen.

I march over to the front door and open it. "Just go, Jacob."

Bullheadedness is considered a manly trait in just about every country. When Jacob plants his feet apart, I know what's coming. "I'm not going anywhere until I know exactly what you're doing, and with whom."

Stubbornness runs through a significant portion of the female population, too.

I hurry over and pick up the crystal bowl and shove it at him. "You could have saved the girlfriend a shopping trip by making a call instead of sneaking in here behind that cheap excuse of a present just to check me out. I'm seeing someone. You're seeing someone. That's life. Now go."

He cradles the bowl like a huge egg. "What about the—uh…"

"Baby?" If he could just once say the word I might be able to forgive a lot. "Not your problem. I'm sole custodian, Jacob. I know how to look after us. Goodbye."

He takes a few steps toward the door and then whips around, a horrified look on his face. "You're having sex!" He just figured this out? "Jesus H. Christ! Have you lost your mind? You're pregnant!"

I point at the door behind him. "Out!"

His shoe squeaks as he digs a toe into the rug. "Lu, Lu. You're behaving like one of those sad, miserable women who screw around to get back at their husbands."

"I don't have a husband." I take several steps toward him, propelled by his arrogant assumption that I couldn't make a decision that didn't include a thought of him. "But yes. I'm having wonderful, unsafe kinky sex with a twenty-five-year old stud muffin." I feel muscles straining in my neck as I wave my arms for emphasis. "Now get the hell out of *my* house!"

I must be pretty impressive because Jacob backs up a couple of steps to the doorway. "Okay, Lu." He raises a hand to fend off my wrath. "We'll talk about this another time. You're too upset now. Think about the baby."

"Oh—my—God! You actually said the word. You said *baby.*"

His gaze shifts away from mine. "Okay, so maybe I had that coming. But who is going to look after you, and the baby, if you run me off?"

"No problem. Lu's in good hands."

Jacob and I both jump. For all the listening I had been doing, the sound of William's voice still shocks me.

I turn to William, standing in the entrance to the kitchen, and my expression is enough to raise his eyebrows. "Would you mind giving us a moment?"

But Jacob has spied his prey. He comes rushing back into the room and all but dumps the crystal bowl on the table. "Who the hell are you?"

"William, this is Jacob, my ex. Jacob, this is Dr. Templeton."

"Oh, yeah?" Jacob slides his hands into his pockets

and smirks. "I didn't know doctors still made house calls."

"There's a lot you don't know, Jacob. So just go away." I wave him off, but the gesture seems to throw me off center and I wobble.

"Are you okay?" Jacob asks as William moves toward me.

"I'm fine." But suddenly I don't feel so fine. The rage of the last few moments has left me woozy. I need a chair, but I'm not about to leave this hallway with two men squaring off against each other.

Jacob scowls at me. "We need to finish this, Lu. In private."

"Why don't you just come back another time?" William's tone is that of a physician dealing with a difficult relative of a patient.

Jacob cocks back his head, chin jutting upward because William tops him by three inches. "Who the hell are you to be telling me, under *my* own roof, that I should do anything?"

"It's my roof, Jacob." I make eye contact with him and say very deliberately, "And I'm asking you, nicely, to leave."

Jacob hunches his shoulders, his head sinking into his neck. He points a finger at my middle but he's glaring at William. "That's my kid, just so you know!"

"You've decided to own up to it?"

Jacob starts, as if poked. "Just what the hell is he talking about, Lu?"

"It's no secret that you aren't in favor of me having this baby, Jacob." I shift my weight to bring my body more fully between them. "You told the kids and Cy."

"That's family. And friends. What's it the hell to him?"

"He's my doctor."

"And *her* friend." William lays an arm across my shoulders. I'm not sure whether I should thank him or break it off at the elbow. This is clearly no longer about me. It's a pissing contest and I'm the tree. "Lu's made her decision, and I'm here to back her up."

"Nobody's talking to you." Jacob snorts and readjusts his attention to me. "What are you doing, Lu? No kind of real doctor would sleep with his pregnant patients." He smirks. "If word got around about this, he could get disbarred."

"I suppose you mean his license to practice could be revoked," I answer.

"Whatever." He looks at William. "It means I could make trouble for you, Doc."

"Don't make threats, Jacob." I slip out from under William's proprietary arm, which feels like the weight of Babylon, sins and all. "But since you brought it up, I no longer see William professionally. So there's no malpractice involved in our personal relationship."

I turn away and start unsteadily for the kitchen. "I don't feel so good."

"There, see what you've done by barging in?" Jacob says triumphantly. "Lu's feeling sick."

"She was okay until you started bullying her."

"What the fuck does that mean, Doc?"

"That you should leave Lu alone, permanently."

"The hell I will!"

I think I hear the scuffle of feet but, *hooo* boy, there's such a ringing in my ears!

Obscenities erupt behind me, followed by the sound a meat mallet makes when I pound chicken breast into cutlets.

I seem to be in slow motion. In the time it takes me to turn around, the two men I left in unfriendly confrontation have become an unsightly heap of flailing limbs on my hall rug. The hall table, an antique that's more rickety than valuable, is kicked. I watch, fascinated, as my birthday bowl slides to the edge and tumbles off, catching the midmorning light in its lead-glass facets and spraying dozens of miniature rainbows across the walls and floor.

And just like that, the lights go out.

31

"Tallulah? Tallulah Nichols?"

I reluctantly open one eye and then the other. There's a man in green scrubs standing over me. "The baby!"

"Your child is fine. Don't you remember?"

I nod slowly. I remember too much to think about. For instance, waking up on the floor with a ring of anxious faces staring back at me. Then the ambulance ride, and how my humiliation that two grown men I know personally could be reduced to slugging it out in front of me kept me from answering any of the medics' questions about how I was feeling. By the time I reached the ER, I was angry all over again, even angrier than before. That's when they gave me something to calm me down.

I blink at the doctor, all emotion defeated by the sedative. "I fell asleep."

The doctor smiles. "You needed the rest. Your blood pressure was up."

"Where is everybody?"

"There are several people in the waiting room hoping

to see you. One claims to be your husband. Another your doctor. After that I'm afraid I'm a bit fuzzy. Something about a neighbor and your...ah, official photographer?"

"Guy with red Rastafarian braids?"

"That's the one."

"We work at the same magazine."

"I see." But by his expression, I can tell that this doctor doesn't see a thing about me clearly. Who can blame him?

"The one claiming to be my husband? He's my ex-husband. But I suppose you should send him in first."

The doctor nods but hesitates. "Is there anyone else you'd like me to call first? Someone less involved?"

That's when I know that he's heard about the fight. Can I sink any lower? "I suppose I do need a female influence." I give him Andrea's number. "Tell her to come as my attorney."

The doctor looks up from making notes. "Are you planning to press charges?"

"What?"

"There's a policewoman waiting outside. I think she'd like to speak with you before you see anyone else."

"Why?"

"It's routine procedure in domestic disputes," the policewoman tells me, smiling a smile that doesn't quite reach her unblinking gaze. "The responding attendants called the police. Do you wish to file a complaint against either man?"

"For stupidity?"

"For injury. Reckless endangerment to you and your child." She flips open her pad. "How many times were you struck?"

"I wasn't—"

"Shoved or pushed or...?"

"No one laid a hand on me! Really, no one. I fainted."

She looks at me, her uniform so clean and crisp and professional I feel like a cornered felon. "You're not alone, ma'am. This sort of thing happens all the time, even in the best neighborhoods. You've nothing to fear. We can find you shelter. Get you counseling. Don't protect a man, or men, who'd hurt a pregnant woman."

Okay. Where is the rock I can crawl under?

It takes about five more minutes to convince her that I merely fainted. And the two fools in the brawl were blessedly aiming blows only at each other. Thank goodness I had the presence of mind to grab the edge of the table as I went down. No bumps or bruises show to counter my claim.

Finally, she flips her notepad closed and offers me her card. "If you change your mind, or at any time in the future feel unsafe, don't hesitate to call this number." She cocks her head toward me. "Ex-spouses can be the worst."

I ignore her, though Jacob probably has the scare coming. "Speaking of which, please send in my ex-husband."

I'm not feeling happy about mediating a smackdown from an emergency-room examining room, but I seem to have no choice.

Jacob arrives in the doorway a minute later, looking positively smug for a man with a blackened eye and puffy lip, and torn shirt. "Hey, Lu. How are you doing?"

"The police suspect you of domestic violence. I'm only glad your poor mother's not here to witness this day." It's a low blow, the lowest I can think of. He responds by blanching. "To think that you would do this to me, in my condition…" Hey, I'm pretty good at guilt trips. Guess I learned something from my mother-in-law, after all.

He rushes over and takes my hand, then begins to stammer like a kid. "Now, now, Lu. Y-you know I'd n-never do anything to hu-hurt you and…and…"

"Yes. That's what I told the police, but—"

"That's why they're here?" His head whips toward the door. "To arrest me? Jeez, Lu. What am I going to do?"

"Go home, Jacob. And don't come back to my house unless invited."

"What about your condition, Lu?" He winces from the effort to speak. Is that a bandage peeking through the tear in his shirt? No, I won't feel sorry for him. Not after what he's put me—I reach down to pat Sweet Tum—us through.

Yet, as he nervously fingers his raw-meat lip, he seems to remember what started all this. "You scared the hell out of me! Dropping like that. Didn't you think of the kid? You could have done some damage—!"

"Shut up, Jacob. You started a fight. In my house. You struck a guest!" I'm up on an elbow now, feeling as light-headed as before I went down for the count. "You broke my birthday gift!"

My raised voice is all that is required to bring a nurse to my door. "What's going on here?" The tone of her voice says the police aren't but a crooked finger away.

"He's leaving. After an apology."

Jacob reddens before the nurse's gimlet eye. "Yeah, I'm sorry, Lu. Really sorry. I'll call tomorrow. Or, when you say. Okay?"

"Let me do the calling. Now please send in Curran."

Curran looks as spooked as Davin did when he was a little kid and I was too sick to get out of bed. Hanging in the doorway, he's fidgety and pale. "Hey, Lu. You and the kid okay?"

"We are marvelous, Curran. How are you involved in this?"

"I'd cruised by your place to get a snap of the birthday girl. That's when I, like, peeped the ambulance and all. You sure you're okay?"

"I just fainted. Sorry to frighten you."

He hoists his ever-present camera.

"Stop! I said I'm fine. But I'm not in the mood for photos." I hate to halt him in mid-focus, but there are limits. "If you take even one photo in this room, I will never *ever* speak to you again."

"Sure, Lu. Whatever you say." He lowers his camera until it dangles from his neck strap, lens pointed downward, impotent. But do I dare trust him?

"Go home. Destroy your film. Speak of this to no one. Ever. Under any circumstances. I will know if you do. Swear to do this upon your secret desire for Catherine Deneuve."

His head droops like a puppy that's sighted a rolled newspaper. "Aw, Lu."

"Destroy the film, Curran."

He winces. "Deal."

When he's gone I elect to speak to Cy.

One look at his exhausted, harried expression and for the first time I feel like I'm the one who deserves to be chastised. "I'm so sorry you had to be involved in this, Cy."

He comes close and grips my hand. "Why sorry? You think I couldn't break up a fight? You forgot I was a marine. Saw action in Korea. Two bozos going at each other? I've seen it dozens of times. There's a technique to breaking up a brawl." He grins, though he is still too pale for my liking. "Knocked some sense into them. But you? Lu, why bring those fellows under the same roof?"

"Believe me, it wasn't planned. You broke up the fight? How did you know about it?"

"Didn't I see Jacob arrive? And when William returned without Jacob leaving, I thought I'd better come over, see if you needed any help."

"I won't say you shouldn't have. All the same, it's beginning to creep me out, Cy, the way you watch my place. Know what I mean?"

"You tell me you didn't need me today, and I'll back off."

There's nothing like the truth to take the wind out of a good gripe. "Thank you."

"So how's our little tot?" He's frowning hard as he looks at the slight mound under the sheet. "She's okay?"

"She or *he* is fine. I just got excited. Hadn't drunk enough water today. When the fellows lost it, my blood pressure kinda went wonkers on me."

"For this you need a keeper." He swipes his brow with a hand. "I can do only so much from next door. Like I said before, you should come and live with me."

I squeeze his hand hard. "You're the sweetest guy on the planet, you know that."

"But you got the hots for the doc." He says this kindly.

"It's not what you think, Cy. He's just…"

"What you need?"

"What I need now. That sounds awful, doesn't it?"

Cy shrugs. "What do I know? But I do know you shouldn't expose your child to the kind of emotional roller coaster that lands you in the emergency room. You're too smart not to know that, too."

"You're absolutely right. I promise here and now not to ever allow anything even remotely like this to occur again."

"So, you'll come home with me?"

The man doesn't let a thing go. "I've seen Jacob. How bad off is William?"

Cy snorts. "I'd like to be there to see him explain the stitches over his eye to his patients tomorrow." My gasp brings his sharp gaze my way. "What's a couple of bruised ribs? Neither of them has bragging rights. They felled a pregnant woman."

All too true. "Can you see about getting me out of here?"

Cy brightens up. "You got it, kiddo!"

If possible, William looks more worried and contrite than any of the others. Oh, and his poor eye!

He rushes over and takes my hand, to feel my pulse. "Are you okay? Any pain? Nausea? Cramping?" His hands touch me lightly, professionally. "Did you hit your head, hip? Any heart arrhythmia? Are you spotting?"

"I'm fine, Dr. Templeton." It's all I can do to keep from reaching out and cradling his face in the most unprofessional manner. In addition to his stitches, he's got a bruise the size of Cleveland on his chin. But I'm angry and disappointed that any man this wonderful could be reduced by a few ugly words to a brawler. Oh, but he looks like he needs kissing. Even at a moment like this, I'm wired as a comfort-giver. This is the kind of thing that gives femininity a bad name.

When he's satisfied that I'm in good order, he bends and kisses my forehead, the physician role abandoned for lover. "They wouldn't tell me a damn thing or let me see you, even after I showed my credentials and said I was your doctor."

I smile, but it's not a nice smile. "Maybe that's because you are under suspicion in a domestic dispute."

The accusation drains the hubris from his face. "Jacob and I could be arrested for fighting over you?"

"Or with me." I'm still so mad at the pair of them I can't resist turning the screws. "I've been asked if I want to press charges against the pair of you."

For a moment he looks appalled. I can see him calculating the effect a criminal indictment would have on his patient roster. In his battered condition, the mug shot alone would make me think twice, and I sleep with the guy.

But then he has the grace to murmur, "Whatever you say, Lu. I'm just so damned sorry. I don't know what came over me. I haven't been in a fistfight since high—well, the boxing club at college."

"You should be sorry." He was a boxer? What happened to his technique? No, I can't ask questions now. I'm hurt and indignant, and grateful Jacob isn't mincemeat. "I can't imagine what you thought you were fighting over. Last time I checked, I was a completely free agent."

"You're right. All that's important is that you are okay." He frowns, studying my face once more. "You are certain you are okay? And the baby?"

"Both fine. Both tired. And both ready to go home."

He brightens. "I'll take care of it. I'm prepared to pay for everything."

"No." I put up a hand to cup his bruised jaw. "Cy has everything under control. I've had enough excitement for one weekend. You should probably go home and take care of that eye."

He hangs his head. "You're entitled to be as angry with me as you like, Lu. I more than deserve it. All that's important is that you and the baby are okay."

Another time, when I'm well rested and feeling more like myself, I'm sure I'll look back on this moment with sympathy. But for now, all I can think of is how much I want to go home to my own bed.

He reaches the door before he looks back. "Happy Birthday, Lu."

I'm home in my bed, with Andrea and Cy keeping watch downstairs, before it strikes me that not every woman can boast or whimper that she spent her fiftieth birthday in the emergency room because two men started a fight over her. I'm still furious and yet, dare I admit it even to myself, strangely titillated by the idea.

This must be what they mean when they say popular entertainment is coarsening our culture.

july

Who decided life—like furniture—should have a style?
As if we could pick our lives out of a showroom,
and accessorize with the "right" man, child, car and/or dog.

—"I Don't Do Country, French or Danish Modern!"
CUE LU!

32

"Aunt Marvelle!"

"Hello, Tallulah." She brushes past me trailing the powdery fragrance of Arpège. A chauffeur follows her. I'm not nearly as surprised by the limo parked on the curb as I am by the amount of baggage the man brings through my door. She's dragged out the vintage Louis Vuitton. And there's a vintage hatbox from Bonwit Teller.

Once inside, she pauses to pat her forehead with a linen handkerchief. "This is exactly why I never travel up island in summer. There's no sense in all this heat without sand and sea to make up for it."

"I'm delighted to see you, but why are you here?"

"I've come to look after you." She pats my shoulder, bracelets sounding like an armful of wind chimes, and then turns and hands the limo driver several bills. "Thank you, my good man." When he's gone she smiles at me. "I ordered a limo to meet the Jitney because I cannot bear the stink of Penn Station in July. Never mind all those rattling trains."

I've had five whole seconds to think about this unexpected turn of events. "Dr. Templeton called you."

Aunt Marvelle's perfectly penciled brows lift. "Is that coffee I smell? I hope it's decaf, Tallulah. In your condition, it should be. I'll have mine with ice, lots of ice."

It's a little past 2:00 p.m. on Tuesday. The doctor advised several days of rest, no stress. Nice job, if you can get it.

For the past two nights Cy has slept on my downstairs sofa. Andrea has spent the same two nights in Dallas's old room. Thankfully she has to get up and go in to work each morning. Cy I have to eject each day. I called work and told them I'm on bed rest. The idea that my pregnancy might be in danger upset Tai so much that she actually called me. I had to assure her that I was fine, this was just a precaution because my blood pressure was slightly elevated. She promised that there'd be no pressure at work when I came back. My silver lining?

Curran comes by every day. This morning he waited on the porch until Cy invited him in for breakfast while I sulked in my room. No pictures this week.

William calls every evening, to make certain I'm okay. He talks to Andrea more than I like, if I don't beat her to the phone. I hate being "managed."

When we have seated ourselves at my kitchen table and decaf is steaming up glasses of ice cubes, I look at my aunt. "I've got some news about me you're going to find quite amazing."

She gives me an owl stare. "You're pregnant. I'm hurt, Tallulah. Hurt that I had to hear the truth from a stranger."

"I wanted to tell you, Aunt Marvelle. Things have been moving so fast. I just didn't know quite how."

"So you leave it to the most eligible man I know to call me to say my niece, whom he's seeing, needs my help because she's having a baby. And, by the way, her husband is giving her hell."

"William said that?"

She picks up a packet of sugar substitute, thinks better of it and reaches for the sugar bowl. "He didn't say nearly enough, for my liking."

"It's Jacob's."

She makes a moue and shoves the sugar bowl aside. "Go on."

Very quickly I give her the scenario of last February.

Her mouth is puckered like a prune by the time I'm finished. "I suppose this means you once hoped to win Jacob back."

"Definitely not. And it's mutual."

She checks her perfectly manicured nails, then squeezes the tip of her left pinkie, as if to put a better curve in it. "Are you very sure?"

"So sure that I've told no one except you and William that he's the father. And the kids. And Mom and Dad. And Andrea and Cy. And Curran."

"That should insure secrecy."

"They had to know. At least the family. There's going to be a new member, whether they like it or not."

"I hope you aren't now going to try to tell me that Dr. Templeton's interest in you is purely platonic."

I can't find the words to lie about it.

Reluctantly I relate the story of William and me, ending with Sunday's fiasco of William and Jacob struggling like beached octopuses in my hall. My aunt limits her responses to the occasional "He didn't?" or "Child, child, child" while I confess all.

When I'm done, a smile tugs her straight-lipped expression off center. "All these years I've waited to see the reason why your mother named you Tallulah."

"Yes. Being named after a woman with a thick vein of wanton stupidity and self-destructive tendencies tends to take a toll."

"Tallulah, if that's the way you felt, why didn't you just change your name when you reached legal age?"

I slump forward, elbows on table and my laced fingers making a hammock for my chin. "Because I always hoped that an unusual name would insure an unusual life. How sad is that to admit to at my age?"

"Yes, I do see your point. Until now you've lived an absolutely unremarkable life. Much as I'd like to say so, Jacob's not to blame for that. You are." My aunt fingers the top of the half-and-half carton then pushes it aside. "After a brilliant start as a journalist, you let circumstance sidetrack you. Thankfully, you're again breathing the air of the discovered woman."

"Discovered? It feels more like I've been exposed."

She is quiet for a moment as she stares at her iced coffee. "I don't suppose you have any Baileys about?"

I go in search of the Irish cream whiskey.

When I return, Marvelle has powdered her face, and looks as cool as one of those slices of cold cucumber she uses to eliminate puffy eyes.

"You must learn to pace yourself, Tallulah." She says this as she pours a very indiscreet amount of liquor into her glass. "I believe in a woman keeping her private business private. However, you find yourself in a situation that won't allow that. So then, how do you propose to keep your dignity?"

It's moments like this that remind me that my aunt maintains a more sophisticated, pre-reality-TV attitude. Dignity is a thing one works to preserve. Nowadays celebrities and presidential candidates trip over one another in the rush to prove they lack any shred of self-respect, hawking everything from Depends to Viagra.

And then I realize that I better explain why I am about to be publishing's newest gossip item, if my editor has her way.

I quickly outline *Five-O*'s take on my pregnancy. "One thing I'm adamant about is that, for public consumption, this baby has only a mother. I know that's inviting speculation. I thought, at first, I was shielding Jacob. Now I realize I'm doing this for me."

Aunt Marvelle puts down her iced Irish coffee after taking a satisfying sip. "Do you think people wasted their time in lurid speculation on how Jodi Foster got pregnant, not once but twice? No. The press couldn't heap enough praise on her for simply saying paternity was nobody's business but her child's and hers. She got lots of positive press."

"Didn't you remind me not long ago that I should keep my private business private?"

She waves away the thought with a tinkle of her bracelets. "That was when you were living a conventional life. Now you've got other priorities, like earning a living. In this instance you need notoriety to do that. That's not the same as caring what strangers think. Are you asking any of them to raise your child, feed it, educate it or even change a single diaper? So then, let them wonder. Celebrity life is about attitude, Tallulah. Once you make up your mind about how you feel on a matter, that will dictate how you handle it."

Aunt Marvelle looks away, crosses her legs and then, with a huff of impatience, uncrosses them. "Doctors! Telling me that I shouldn't cross my legs because it cuts off circulation to the extremities." She bends forward and traces an imaginary seam up the back of one trim calf. "At my age my legs are one of the few good parts left."

I sip my sugarless iced decaf. "I wish things were that simple for the kids. Davin is afraid of competition if I have a boy. Dallas is furious because..." I shrug. "She's just been angry with me for a while."

"They are young." Aunt Marvelle looks up from rearranging her skirt. "The young think life should be orderly and reasonable, even when they aren't. But no woman worth calling herself female arrives at your age without a few skeletons. Attitude determines whether you hang them in the closet or put something fashion-able on them and stick them in your front window as tro-phies."

I can't long be unhappy around her. "I love Mom, but she's never quite understood me. How do I get to be you?"

"Stay awake in life." She reaches for her purse and pulls out lipstick and mirror with practiced ease. "It will keep you from making some mistakes, and repeating those you do make." She pauses to roll up a tube of Revlon Red. "For the rare instances when you might want to repeat a mistake, you'll remember how it's done."

She applies color to her lips, blots them with a napkin. "Now then, tell me more about your Dr. Templeton. Can he dance? I love a man who can dance."

33

Tai tried being a caring and indulgent boss. It lasted a week. By nature she's a heat-seeking missile, and we are all warm-body targets. No staff person has spoken above a whisper in days. We're like ghosts, appearing and disappearing in silence, all but reduced to wearing Uggs in July to keep our footsteps a muffled secret. The August issue of *Five-O* hits the racks next week. But there's a more immediate reason for nerves. The issue starts showing up in subscribers' mailboxes today.

There was no lead time for the usual "sell" before the launch of "The Pregnant Pause." It is going out with all the fanfare of a late-breaking bulletin—on the WE Cable channel.

Unfortunately, I didn't keep that opinion to myself. Yesterday's brainstorm session for next month's column went from bad to worse. Tai had worn the nap off the carpet before turning snide, saying that it was too bad I'm so damn healthy, after all. The suspense of a disaster pregnancy would make for more sexy copy.

When I suggested that we have time for interest in "The Pregnant Pause" to build, she went postal.

"Build? A piece like this has to explode into popular consciousness. People have to feel they *need* to know more, and better yet, talk about it with everyone they meet."

"A good steady climb—"

"Explode!"

And so forth.

She's the hammer. I'm the nail. Her last words to me were "It's your ass on my bottom line."

Right now I wish my bum were anywhere else other than in this photo meeting with Curran. We're looking over a range of Tai-initiated maternity fashion photo-op sites.

Tai decided we needed to look at me as a TKO, technical knockout, in the ring of life.

"Lu's wounded, lost a few rounds," she said as she handed Curran the sketches. "She needs a method to cope. Equipage."

"Harnesses and halters?" Curran ventures uncertainly. "Is S and M bondage in the *Five-O* demographic?"

Tai's frowns last no longer than the bat of her lashes. "Equipage means accoutrements, Curran, darling."

The puzzlement doesn't vanish from his incredibly open face.

"Provisions, Curran. Supplies. High-end comfort items."

"Ah! Run up the credit cards!"

Tai nods. "Madly expensive items, real perfume…silk pillowcases…mohair booties. Furs. Jewelry. Our tagline, "'Unlucky in Love? Be Lucky in Lux!'"

After observing the sketches, Curran pushes a handful of dreads back from his forehead. "Diesel!"

"Are you joking? Tai wants me to pose at a pro-choice clinic, an adoption agency and a home for unwed mothers, to show off expensive shoes, bags and jewelry."

"It's edgy."

"It's freaky." I push back from the table with a sigh. "I never thought I'd say this, but I miss Marc's metrosexual approach to life. At least he would have been about the clothes, not the message."

Curran idly twists a dread. "I think Tai's ideas are da bomb! Camera angles a-poppin'... The one of you in the stirrups, showing only the shoes on your feet? That's phat!"

"I see this getting out of hand. Next thing, Tai will want me in my ninth month in a full-length fur on the cover saying, "Daddy's a Hound So We're Dressed in Fox!"

I turn to the next sketch and groan. It's one of me standing on the railing of the George Washington Bridge. "Oh, bother! I mean, what do you wear to a drowning?"

Curran grins. "Ralph Drown-in? Nine Vest? Chan-*nel* wear?"

"Bad, Cur. Bad!" I pick up the notes to swat him. He retaliates by trying to tweak my nose. We are halfheartedly struggling when the door opens.

"Oh." KaZi's gaze cuts like a laser between us. "I came to talk about makeup options. I didn't know *he* was here."

"Come in." I'm determined to be friendly with KaZi. She's been avoiding me for weeks. But before I can add another word, she's gone, the door shut behind her.

I look at Curran. "What's going on?"

Curran ducks my look. "She's just trippin'."

"That much I got. You're a man. I can think of a dozen good reasons why she might be annoyed with you. But why is she angry with me?"

"She's not, exactly."

I grab a single dread and tug it. "Don't make me torture you."

"Gotta be all up in a bro's business—ouch!"

"That's for switching syntax on me. Now, tell me, in boring English, what's going on."

He looks put out. "She's mad on account of the time I spend with you."

"I can understand that. I'm annoyed, too, by the amount of time you spend following me around with your camera. So knock it off." But Curran's not meeting my gaze. "There's more?"

"Girl's outta control. Says you're always on my jock."

I release his hair. "That better not translate as obscenely as it sounds."

"It mean's like flirting."

"Me flirting with you? That's what KaZi thinks? You told her that's ridiculous, right?"

"Damn straight. I tried." Curran tests his dreads for smoothness. "She says it doesn't matter what I say 'cause what I do is follow you around like I'm jonesing."

The idea isn't totally a shock. I'm smart enough to know that a lonely young man is likely to develop inappropriate attachments. That's why I've tried to keep things light between us. But I thought, with KaZi to take up his time...

"Curran, you don't...?" I pick my words carefully. "You aren't...?"

"No, 'course not." Oh, damn. Curran isn't looking me in the face, and if his ears were any redder, he'd need first aid for burns.

For a second I'm nonplussed, but I know if I don't stomp on this right now it will smolder like some sad secret until Curran and I won't be able to be in the same space anymore without the specter of unauthorized affection threatening our friendship. So I do what impulse drives me to.

I put a hand on the back of his neck, and when he turns to look at me, I kiss him hard, on the cheek. "Thank you. You've made my week. And tell her if she doesn't treat you right after this, she's definitely going to lose you to the better woman."

Curran just stares at me. I know he doesn't know what to think. I don't, either, but I just nod and grin and keep on grinning until he begins to smile back. "So, what's it going to be first? The bridge, or the home for unwed mothers?"

Tai joins us a little later. Curran tries to steer her away from the Planned Parenthood clinic. I cite the average age of our readership to try to skip over the home for unwed mothers. But Tai's adamant.

"Our new advertisers are looking at us as a fresh but one-time market. We need to deliver a spread that will make a lasting impression."

I check out of the debate to glance at my watch. I've got fifteen minutes to get out of here and meet Andrea, or I'll be late for my second ultrasound. It's chancy but I decide, for the welfare of the magazine's vested interest in me, to mention this to Tai.

She looks annoyed. "Can't you take care of that sort of thing after hours?"

"I'd be fine with that, but the clinic keeps regular office hours."

"God! I've got to get back to the city where people have priorities!" Tai tosses her notes on the table and stomps out, practically knocking over Brenda, who's passing by in the hall.

A few minutes later, Brenda joins me to wait for the elevator. "Let me guess what's eating Tai."

Rhonda, who's already standing there with an armful of mail, says, "Maybe that's the problem. No one is."

I'm caught off guard by this observation. Crude, but shrewd. Tai does seem like a woman without any joy in her life. Is that possible?

She has all the diva dimensions of sex appeal. Yards of leg, lots of tanned, toned torso, impossibly luxuriant hair, coupled with a temper of tsarina proportions and a hot job. Okay, not as hot as her last. But, six figures can cushion the loss of a Big Apple business address. I imagine her apartment in Manhattan is some comfort. She's still in the society pages on a regular basis, schmoozing with some Euro celeb or boyish executive type. Yet I must admit, I never think of Tai in terms of romance.

"I don't recall hearing who she's dating."

"She isn't." Rhonda leans in to whisper. "Not since Marc."

"Marc and Tai?" I ask, and am immediately shushed by my companions, who glance warily over their shoulders.

I vaguely recall Rhonda hinting at this before, but I was in the midst of imploding, career and all, and it didn't register.

"It could just be rumor," I offer. Why I should feel loyalty to Tai is beyond me. Maybe it's the single status we share.

"No one ever dared ask her," Rhonda admits.

"Some of us didn't have to," Brenda says as the elevator doors part. "I almost stepped in her business. Literally."

She waits until we've entered the empty elevator before erupting in deep chuckles. "A few weeks back Tai asked me to deliver this article the minute I was done. The door to her office was shut so I knocked. It swung open, exposing more than I ever wanted to see of people I need to respect in the boardroom."

"Get out!" Rhonda shrieks in laughter.

I, too, try to picture it. Two fabulously dressed image-conscious people going at it like a pair of hormonally inflamed teens. The image won't cue. In my imagination they are much too sophisticated and put-together to ruin the "image" with sweating, sticky, messy sex.

Brenda bends a seriously sober gaze on us as the elevator doors open one floor below. "You did not hear that from me. Un. Der. Stand?"

Rhonda and I nod in unison. If I had to pick a side in a fight, Brenda's my girl.

★ ★ ★

"The doctor says everything is going quite well," I say into my cell phone. "Gotta go now, Aunt Marvelle." These cell calls to Alaska better be on my one-price, all-calls-all-the-time minutes.

As good as her promise, Aunt Marvelle's friend Jane came up with last-minute fares for an Alaskan cruise. After five days of smothering, Aunt Marvelle was as ready as I was to see her turn her talents to other, more interesting ventures. She's accustomed to brunches and lunches and bridge parties and afternoon cocktails. These days, after a day on the job, all I'm good for is supper and bed.

Because I feel in need of more down time, I decide to play hooky after my appointment long enough to have lunch on my own. It's a beautiful summer day, the kind that makes you want to have lunch in the park. I order takeout and walk over to sit on a bench near a pond to watch the ducks, and the toddlers feeding the ducks, and the mothers herding the toddlers feeding the ducks.

I can see myself doing this next summer, and many summers to follow. I might not have been the best wife ever, but I am a good mother. Even if Dallas hasn't completely forgiven me for having a life. She called me the day after Aunt Marvelle arrived. I suspect Aunt Marvelle called her first. Not even Dallas would stand a chance against her.

Since then, our calls are frequent, short and oh so polite. We don't talk baby and we don't talk Jacob. There have been a lot of wedding details to share. As long as I listen and say soothing things, we're okay.

The wedding is in exactly eight weeks. On most days I manage to ignore that fact. Not because I don't eagerly anticipate seeing my daughter commit to wedded bliss, but because it means I'll have to be pleasant to Jacob for a whole day.

There's been no word from the man since I ordered

him out of the ER, and my life, a little more than two weeks ago. I should be grateful, but I'm suspicious. Jacob doesn't like to lose, even if he's not particularly interested in playing the game.

By the time I return to my office, I've mellowed out to the point that not even the sight of Tai can derail my giddiness.

"Oh, there you are!" She sashays her way over to me in impossibly high heels she's donned since lunch. "Babs has called you a dozen times but keeps getting your answering service."

"I turned my cell phone off during lunch."

"Well, get your head back at work. We've had calls. Lots of calls. And e-mail."

My heart skips a beat. "What kind of calls?"

"From subscribers." Tai makes me earn every word with a drop of sweat.

"Positive ones?"

"Not all. Thank God! There are some indignant ones, and better yet, a couple of really bitchy, snide ones. That's the best. Polls indicate that the unhappy reader is also a vocal one. She will be spreading her opinion to all her friends. A fair number of them will buy *Five-O* to read the column just to trash you! Our decision not to name the father was a brilliant hook. Of course, the real test comes when we hit the stands next week."

And then, to my shock, Tai actually pats Sweet Tum. "How was the checkup for our little golden egg?"

"Brilliant!"

Isn't it always the way? Now that there's a market share up for grabs, my problem has become "our" success.

34

I spent the weekend in seclusion. My e-mail bottomed out within twenty-four hours of the subscribers' delivery date. Now I'm back at work, wading through a fate worse than failure. Success.

Copies are flying off the newsstands and generating the kind of mail usually reserved for political tell-alls. Tai says we need to stay close to the reader on this one, give her personal attention, as in answer every one of the e-mails "The Pregnant Pause" receives. Even if I could type sixty words a minute for a solid week I could not keep up. Never mind that I don't have the medical or psychological savvy to deal with letters "Dear Abby" would hesitate to tackle. For instance:

> "Don't we have enough problems without encouraging self-indulgent middle-aged women to bear genetically morbid children to justify their egotistical whims?"

Or this one:

"At last! Someone who understands. Even though I detest men, I'm meant to be a mother. Given the chance, I'd rear a male child to be the kind of man I've never found."

Or:

"Thanks to your columns on self-acceptance, I had come to embrace my childless state as natural. Now you flaunt your late-life fertility in my face. I will never forgive your betrayal. Please cancel my subscription.

Or, even better:

"No rational woman wants to give birth to her grandchildren."

And so forth. Tai is jeté-ing down the halls. She brought in champagne for a toast I had to forgo. The reason for her elation? The blurb in the *Montclair Times* is only the beginning. I'm to be interviewed by the statewide *Caller-Times* tomorrow. Right now, the staff's gone to lunch on Tai. I said I needed a nap. But I'm really sitting here trying to figure out exactly what my next move should be.

Cy thinks I should back out. "There are crazy people out there. Not like before, when nutzo fans just wanted to catch sight of the object of their desire. Today crazies want to take you home and bury you in the backyard for safekeeping. You should install remote-camera surveillance of your property. Think of your child."

This, of course, makes me feel very safe and happy about my decision to be a more public persona than usual.

I came home yesterday to find two men wiring my house with an alarm system. Cy had the sales slip in hand. I didn't say no. But I don't feel happy about it.

William wants to come into town on Saturday. I don't know. I'm falling for this man. Really falling, as in love, commitment and ever after. But, as Andrea so colorfully put it months ago, I've just been let out of jail. Do I want to commit another crime—and get caught?

William's the marrying kind. A woman can just tell. He's a planner, and a natural at couplehood. I'm not an afterthought in his life. Only last night he said I shouldn't live alone the last two months before delivery. He has been talking to an obstetrician friend. The last trimester is "when things can get dicey for a woman my age." If he can't convince me to come out and stay with Aunt Marvelle, he says I should consider letting Cy move in. I know he has a bias toward the Aunt Marvelle solution. So do I. But—I'm afraid to hope for happy ever after.

"Mother!"

The appearance of the young woman in a Donna Karan suit at my office door is so singular that I don't for a moment think it's my daughter Dallas. She would have had to come in from the city, blowing off work on a Tuesday morning. The extremity of circumstance that would force her to such radical irresponsibility escapes me. Then I see her expression, a volatile mix of hurt, fury and high dudgeon.

I'm not often reminded of the word dudgeon, only in connection with Dallas, and always when it's way too late to head off her eruption.

"What were you thinking?" She closes the gap to my desk in two strides, and slaps a copy of *Five-O* on my desk. "Are you trying to ruin my life?"

"Is any of that rhetorical?"

"Do you know what I found when I arrived at my office this morning? This!" She bangs the cover with a fist. "It was taped to my door with a marker conveniently tucked into your column page." She sniffs. "To say that the child you carry is a bastard! In print! How could you?"

"I don't recall that phrasing. I believe I said I'm going to be a single mom, something short of Immaculate Conception but with the result there's no Baby's Daddy."

"Why would you put that in print?"

"Because it's true? It's a column, Dallas. My column, my life."

"If only that were true." She pauses, her chin trembling as she fights to maintain her dignity. The sight affects me, but not for the reason she might assume. I'm reminded that her tantrum tactics haven't changed since age two. "I'm the one being humiliated. My e-mail is jammed with notes from friends and colleagues who think your pregnancy is hilarious or a hoax."

"I had no idea *Five-O* was so popular among the under-thirty crowd."

"They're e-mailing your column to one another. It's been posted on my alumni college class bulletin board."

"Isn't that copyright infringement?"

"I can't believe you! You make a fool of yourself—of your family—and all you can think about is yourself. You never think of us anymore!"

I'm not unmoved by her misery but strive to stay calm. The family has been through enough stressful scenes in the past month to last us a decade. And there's Sweet Tum's emotional well-being to consider. But Dallas, too, is flesh of my very tired flesh. "I love you, Dallas, want the best of everything for you. But if you think how I appear to your friends is numbered among my priorities, you are mistaken."

"I should have expected this. After all, you let your new man friend beat up my father!"

I rise from my seat and move to shut the door and pull

the shades over the panels on either side just in case someone comes back early from lunch.

As I approach Dallas the crisp scent of Pure Tiffany
perfume tickles my sinuses. I gave it to her on her last
birthday. "You told your father about William. Don't think
I didn't figure it out before your father admitted it. Did
you encourage him to come snooping with the pretext
of bringing me a gift?"

Dallas pales. "I didn't think that man would actually be
there."

"Didn't you?"

She shrugs.

"As long as we're on that subject, don't ever go tattling
behind my back to members of this family again."

She gapes at me in utter disbelief. "You're just so, so—
I don't know who you are anymore."

I indicate the chair for her to sit. "Who, exactly, did you
think I was?"

"You were my mother." She sits. I offer her a tissue from
my desk box. "My role model."

"I'm still modeling, dear." I rest my hips against my
desk. "I just modeled the higher ground while you and
Davin were growing up."

She takes a moment to blow her nose. "You certainly
have taken the low road this year."

"Yes, I can see how it might seem that way to you."

She looks at me in confusion.

I reach out and put a hand on each of her shoulders.
"Dallas, parenting is a role seen through a telescope held
up to the eye of a child. That distance gives both parent
and child the comfort of a focussed but narrow view. You
saw what your father and I wanted you to see in order to
grow up to be the best person you could be. One day you
will be at the other end of the telescope."

Dallas exhales a long breath. "That sounds ominous."

"In ways you can't yet imagine. If you do it right, the

labor to produce a fully functioning adult lasts a good eighteen years." I shake her shoulders lightly. "Terms are negotiable."

She smiles at me for the first time in months. "Have you always been this unconventional?"

"Probably not. I'm changing." I release her and lean back. Sweet Tum needs more of my room everyday. "It's one of the things that bothered your father."

Her brows draw together in annoyance. "Dad's changed, too."

"He may not welcome that observation. But, between you and me, of course he has."

Dallas is silent a moment. "I never told you, Mom, but when I was thirteen, my girlfriends voted you and Dad most likely to remain married."

"Is that like being voted most popular?"

"I thought so. I know it sounds dumb, but I always believed if my parents stayed married, I could. But now—" she looks up at me "—if you and Dad couldn't make it, what chance do Stephen and I have?"

I tell her the only truth I know. "The fact that your father and I didn't make it to the 'until death do us part' part doesn't mean it was a mistake for us to spend twenty-seven years together. If you and Stephen are happy now, you have a very good chance of being very happy at least that long."

"That's just it." Dallas looks away. "I'm not sure that I want to marry Stephen."

"That's natural. Prewedding jitters."

"You're right." She gives her head a quick shake, as if to throw off the thought. "I've invested too much time and money into making everything perfect."

I notice now that her hair, though pulled back, is dramatically longer than it was just a few weeks ago. She's had extensions put in.

That's when it hits me. All her efforts toward this

wedding are really an elaborate incantation. Sort of wedding voodoo. She thinks that if the ceremony is big enough, grand enough, it will somehow magically seal the marriage.

"Want to talk about it?"

She shrugs. "Stephen's not the man I thought he was." The lament of every woman, sooner or later. "He went canoeing upstate with college buddies instead of opting to spend a weekend at Cape Cod with me." She looks up with an expression of utter insult. "Can you believe that?"

Yes. Because I can think of a perfectly reasonable reason why Stephen preferred the chilly waters of the Finger Lakes to the temptation of Dallas in close quarters: S-E-X.

"Are you two still celibate?"

"Yes."

It's so pitiful a reply I can't resist a smile. "And whose idea was this?"

"It was mutual." She shrugs. "I had read this article that said if two people who are sexually active become celibate in the months before their wedding, it makes the honeymoon more special."

There's an awful lot of stupidity parading as wisdom in print.

"I never thought I'd say this to a child of mine, but throw the damned books and magazines away! Life isn't a test you cram for."

Dallas seems to shrink in her chair. "I just wanted everything to be perfect."

That word again. "Do yourself another favor. Delete the word perfect from your vocabulary. Some of your happiest memories will be of times when things were far from perfect."

"That's it?" She looks annoyed. "Edit my vocabulary and reading list. That's your advice in my time of crisis?"

I smile and nod. "Advice is easy. Living by it is the hard part."

She takes a moment to collect her alligator portfolio and stand up. When she does, she meets my gaze with her guard completely down. "Have I ruined my marriage before I've even had my wedding?"

It's been a long time since my daughter looked to me with such complete trust. I can't blow this moment, for either of us.

I give her a hug, a great big Mama Bear hug. This is my firstborn, the reason I am a mother. I love her the way I love blue skies, sudden summer thunderstorms and ripe tomatoes eaten warm from the vine. I couldn't imagine the world without her.

I brush a hair from her cheek. "I wouldn't cancel the caterer just yet. Try spending a lot less time on the day and more time on Stephen first. Your future happiness depends on the answer to this question. When you turn out the lights at night, is Stephen the only thing in the dark you care about? If not, cut Lucy the consultant loose."

"But the cancellation costs?"

"Cheaper than a mistake. Your crazy mama will be right there to back you up."

She nods. "Thanks, Mom."

Dallas and I head out for an early lunch. She didn't have breakfast and I'm ever in need of a food fix. She's not exactly comfortable about the fact that I draw a few stares of recognition in public, but she makes no comment. I do warn her that if she hated this month's column, she will want to burrow underground for the September issue.

I'm finishing a fudge bar when I arrive back at *Five-O*. I didn't know they still made them until I stopped to peer into the ice cream case in the deli downstairs.

Babs flags me down as I'm about to head for the darkroom in search of Curran.

"There's someone waiting for you in your office. Someone official."

"How official?"

Babs smiles. "She hinted that she was from the press."

Tai catches up with me halfway there. "Now, remember, give her sound bites. And you're going to do something with your hair, right? Is that chocolate on your chin?"

We sidestep into the ladies' lounge. Five minutes later, I'm as presentable as I'm going to be under the circumstances.

The official-looking stranger stands up as I enter my office, bright of smile and crisp of linen suit. "Mrs. Lu Nichols?"

"Yes. Can I help you?"

"You certainly can." She offers to shake my right hand and simultaneously offers me an envelope with her left hand.

She's so swift she's halfway out the door before I can say, "Is that it?"

She barely pauses. "Yes, thank you."

If the stranger disappeared swiftly, Tai appears even more swiftly. "What kind of interview was that?"

"It wasn't an interview." I open the envelope and pull out several thick pieces of paper, the kind only attorneys can afford.

"What's that?"

I feel my chin moving but thankfully the words won't come out.

It's a petition from Jacob. He's filed for joint custody of Sweet Tum.

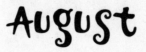

August

The most frequent answer to the question,
describe a sucessful marriage, was
"The partners stay married until one of them dies."
This doesn't sound as much like victorious love as grim survival.

—"Sentenced Unto Death?"
CUE LU!

"I hate her."

"Transference." Andrea hands me a double scoop pistachio ice-cream cone. "You're redirecting your anger because you won't face the source of your real rage."

"I know her name. *Saaandra.*"

Andrea plops down beside me beneath the outdoor umbrella table with a scoop of fudge caramel nut. "Not enough information for genuine hate."

"She's seeing, make that *sleeping with,* Jacob."

"And this makes you care, why?"

But I'm so into conjuring up my nemesis that I can't be bothered with reason. "I bet she has a concave stomach decorated with a tattooed garland." I make a circular motion with my fistful of ice cream cone. "It's probably pierced with a gold ring containing a diamond."

"Can we say *obsessing* here?"

"It's difficult to keep a good gripe going around you."

"You're an amateur. My sister Nina can peel paint just complaining about her visit to a nail technician." She takes a long slow sensuous lick of her ice cream. "You need reassurance just to stay mad at the man who's threatening to take your child."

She's right, as usual, dammit! "It's just that I psyched myself through the divorce with the consolation that at least I didn't have to deal with the other woman. I should be spared that now, you know." I indicate five-months of Sweet Tum.

"Then kick her to the curb." After catching the eye of the man she knows is secretly watching her, Andrea turns her cone upside down to catch a few melted drops on her tongue. "The most powerful being in the world is the female. The only being more powerful is a pregnant one."

"I thought she was the most vulnerable one."

She wags a finger side to side. "Why does Cro-Magnon man's oldest sculpture depict a pregnant female? He knew that the hand that rocks the cradle should rule the world. Renaissance women knew the power of the rotund belly. Have you ever really looked at the clothes they wore? In Italy, young maidens were coached to walk as if they were in their ninth month to attract an eligible gentleman's attention."

"How do you know all this?"

"I took a course in Shakespeare. Juliet waddled like a duck. That's how she snared Romeo."

"And I thought I was broadly educated."

Andrea cuts her eyes to the side and then attacks her ice cream like an XXX starlet in her first film. As she wipes her mouth with a napkin she says, "You've got this Sandra on the run. Believe it."

"Do you have to do that!"

Andrea gets big-eyed. "What?"

"Pole dance with your ice cream. There are children about."

Andrea feigns hurt. "Just because you're miserable you don't want me to have any fun?" She shrugs and picks up a plastic spoon. But no sooner has she transferred ice cream to the spoon than she's sucking on it for all its worth.

I reach out and snatch it from her. "Concentrate on me a minute. I need to figure out how to get Jacob to rescind his custody suit."

"I thought you wanted him to be part of the baby's life. Only a month ago you were lamenting the fact that he had made it clear he wasn't going to take his fathering duties seriously."

"Exactly. Something's changed. And it wasn't anything I said."

"Maybe he had a change of heart."

"Then why not come to me instead of serving me with papers?" When Andrea can only shrug I know I'm on to something. "The only reason I can think of is he's under some other influence. Jacob's insisting that I meet Sandra. That's why I agreed to dinner with them tonight. We go to court next week. I need to know what I'm up against."

Andrea looks up sharply. I follow her gaze.

The man she's been flirting with has decided he is bold enough to approach her. When he gets within range, Andrea subjects him to a furious frown, her "Medusa" stare I call it. He veers away so suddenly there's a breeze in his wake.

"How do you do that?" I ask in annoyance and admiration.

She shrugs. "He's a man. You just have to understand that."

"That's my problem. I don't know how I'm going to handle Jacob."

"No, wait!" Andrea looks up from her melting ice cream. "*Mi ja!* You're right. This business of shared custody must be Sandra's idea."

"I didn't say that."

"No?" Andrea frowns in concentration, her ice cream forgotten for the moment. "So then maybe this is about the fact that you publicly called his manhood into account."

"You mean because I didn't mention Jacob as the father in my column?"

Andrea chuckles. "You told the world you didn't need a man to have a child."

"I was trying to give Jacob a graceful out."

"You outed him, all right. Right out of his paternity."

"For a child he doesn't—didn't want."

"Maybe introducing this Sandra is just an attempt to help salvage his pride. She must be so afraid of your power over him that she's willing to share him with her worst nightmare, the ex-wife's child."

"Let me get this straight. I, the pregnant pudgy wife he discarded, am the greatest threat a nubile twenty-something can imagine?"

Andrea grins. "Ain't love a bitch?"

Personally I think Andrea is nuts. Why would a young woman with a middle-aged man friend want any part of joint custody? I see traces of Jacob's William-hammered ego all over this ploy.

Yet as I dress for dinner with Jacob and his ladyfriend, I begin to see reason in the old adage, you play the hand you're dealt. And then there's the adage, if you can't beat 'em, join 'em. Andrea says use my assets.

I had planned to wear a slimming black linen sheath with pricey sandals, to show I still understand fashion even if I can't get into it. Instead, I try on one of those no-belly maternity capris that cut me off in a most unforgiving way, and a white top with rows of vertical tucks. Mom sent it to me, thinking, as she said, that in the ninth month I will want something that doesn't touch me anywhere below my shoulders. I guess she thought I'd be blind to fashion by then, too. The tucks accent curves in a way no woman could love.

I make up my face, do my hair and slip on my sandals. For luck, I'm wearing William's earrings. I'm not a complete fool. If I look too sad, the jig will be up. Oh, and I discovered that if I walk like a duck, I look an extra two months along. It's true. Shakespeare is timeless.

I'm no contest for young, svelte and tanned. What I've got going for me is maturity, wits and the rotundity of maternity. Why not play to my strengths? I don't want Jacob back. I just want him off my back.

36

As I pass customers waiting to be seated—people who on another occasion I would like to have impressed with my sophisticated style—I notice they gawk at me. But no matter. I've sighted the enemy. I smile hard as I approach them. The game has begun.

Sandra stands up, a number-two pencil in lemon-custard linen crop top and narrow-legged pants. She's young, with a waterfall of shiny dark hair and wide-open eyes. The contrast between us couldn't be more pronounced.

"Hi. I'm Lu." I stick out my hand stiffly at shoulder level because I'm afraid if I don't keep a grip I might swing back and slap her.

"Hi, I'm Sandra." She takes my hand and it's like shaking hands with a plush toy.

Yeah. I hate her. It's not right or rational. But if you want rational you don't go to a pregnant woman.

It's not that she has Jacob, or vice versa. It's that she represents something he found lacking in me. The fact that

William seems to think I have enough of everything he's interested in can't, at the moment, balm this hurt.

"Hi, Lu." Jacob leaves his place to buss me on the cheek, something he's never done before, and pull out my chair, which he has to practically wrestle away from the waiter.

I check out Jacob's face as I sit. It looks normal, except for some chalky stuff that's— It's make-up to hide the last traces of his black eye!

He's smiling hard as he takes his seat on her side of the table. "This is good of you, Lu. But like, wow, you've changed so much in just four weeks."

"It's water. Retaining like crazy. You should see my ankles by 10:00 p.m." I make a basketball shape with my hands while the waiter tries to drape my lap with a napkin.

"Isn't that a problem?" Sandra sounds appropriately concerned.

"Not yet. Gestational hypertension doesn't usually appear to be a significant problem until about the twenty-eighth week." My cheeks hurt from maintaining a smile. "Of course, there's the chance that it's gestational diabetes, which could become life-threatening at some point."

Sandra's eyes widen. "I never heard of such things."

Jacob is frowning. "Are the doctors worried about the baby?"

"Oh, no, not the baby. Only about me." I let my gaze fall from his. "But as I said, we aren't there yet."

"But if you're ill?" Jacob says.

"Dismiss the very idea!" I reach for my water.

As I take a long sip, I watch the pair of them over the rim of my glass. They look nervous as they catch each other's eyes for cues on what to do next. Make that three of us.

"Ah, that's much better."

"Would you like something from the bar?" Jacob asks.

"A double martini with a twist." I don't have to force laughter, for Jacob's expression is priceless.

"Bring her a Perrier with lime," he tells the waiter. "I ordered hors d'oeuvres for the table."

"Nothing greasy, I hope. It gives me—" I lean forward and catch Sandra's eye, "Gas."

"Don't they make pills for that?" she asks, the soul of sympathy.

"I'm sure they do. But these days, pregnant women are advised against taking even over-the-counter drugs. At my age, I'm in an extra-delicate condition. My doctor is being very cautious."

Jacob knocks back the last of his Manhattan and waggles the glass at the waiter. I notice two cherry stems on his butter plate and smile.

I pick up my menu. "Can we order? I'm famished. Eating for two is such a joy—no tiny salads for me." I smile at Sandra, who has opened her menu. "Have you chosen?"

"I was thinking of the salmon rounds with endive." She blushes because, of course, this is a salad entrée. "But I'd really like to try the gnocchi." She half turns to Jacob, as if to beg a boon. "I hear it's wonderful here."

"Potato pasta! It is." I smile meaningfully at Jacob. He looks constipated. "And I'll have the rack of lamb."

I see Jacob wince, but he's not so cheap that he'll tell his pregnant ex-wife that she can't have the specialty of the house on the night he's forced her to break bread with his new paramour.

I don't know how I manage to swallow a thing. But we achieve conversation and eat, and even amuse one another. Sandra is bright and smart. A real estate attorney. She and Dallas could have been classmates, I'm thinking. So it comes as a surprise to hear her say she'll be thirty-three in October.

"I was born on Halloween. Isn't that something?"

"It is. Something." Okay, so Jacob's robbing junior high, not the day care. He's still got twenty years on her. That's a generation gap that won't get any easier with time.

Midway through my lamb, I decide it's time to pick up the pace.

"Let's talk custody. Now, if it should come to a matter of my health, the doctor may need to take the baby early. Much as I hate the very idea of joint custody—" I point my steak knife at Jacob for emphasis "—I can appreciate the comfort to be had in knowing that while I recuperate from the ordeal of a Caesarian, should I require it, you and Sandra are willing to be there to care for a preemie."

"We'd love it!" For the first time, Sandra touches Jacob, sliding a hand through his arm. "We have talked about doing up a nursery. Isn't that right, Jacob?"

"Yeah. Right." Jacob is fidgeting with his fork. "But wouldn't the doctor most likely want to keep a preemie in the hospital until you're released?"

"Ordinarily, yes. But since we're discussing joint custody, and you are right here in the area, I'm sure they would allow you to take the baby home. After all, those every-two-hour, around-the-clock feedings take up a lot of staff time. Sometimes preemies are sluggish eaters. It can take an hour to get two ounces down. So, lots of time for you and Sandra to bond with junior."

"Oh." Sandra has wound her arm more tightly about Jacob's. Her free hand is rubbing up the side of her neck. "Well, perhaps we won't interfere at the very beginning. Babies need to bond with their mothers, right? I was reading about that."

"Reading about 'what to expect'? You? Really?" I notice Jacob's eyes flash in warning but this is too good to pass up. "Then you know all about the symptoms of thrush, colic and pinkeye."

"Well, no…" Sandra looks to Jacob. "I thought newborns can't catch diseases because of the immunities transferred in the mother's breast milk."

"That's for communicable diseases." I'm in my element. "But babies can be plagued by a whole host of ailments. Remember Dallas's cradle cap? Poor tot. She had a head of crusty scabs for weeks. We had to carefully wash her hair with this stinky tar shampoo. And it's really intimidating with a new baby because their scalps are soft. The bone hasn't closed over their little brains. It's nerve-racking to touch it and comb out these loose pieces of skin that come off in huge flakes—"

"Come on, Lu. People are eating here." Jacob looks a little green in places the makeup cannot conceal.

"I'm sorry. But Sandra seemed so interested."

Sandra is transfixed, like a bystander to an auto accident. "I had no idea. What other kinds of things do babies get?"

"Thrush. That makes little white spots on the inside of their mouths. It's a fungal growth. Oh, it just hurts so much. I would just cry and cry when Davin had it. Didn't I, Jacob? He did, too, of course. We just walked the floor at all hours. Colic, well, almost every parent deals with a touch of colic. Even breast-fed babies can have it. And, as I'm sure you've read, breast milk is best. I suppose that means I'll have to keep you supplied. They have these containers you can freeze it in for transport."

Okay, even I'm getting a little embarrassed by my obvious pandering. Yet I'm willing to talk about blocked milk ducts and sitz baths if it will derail Jacob on the issue of joint custody.

I smile at Jacob. "So what were you thinking? Weekdays with me, weekends with you? After all, my work schedule is so much more flexible than yours."

"I'm not sure." Jacob stabs a piece of steak. "I gotta think about it."

I look across at Sandra. "Did I mention constipation? If you do decide to use formula, for those times when I haven't pumped enough, you can expect constipation."

I switch back to Jacob. "Remember that time we left Davin with my mother and she gave him the wrong formula for three days? Poor baby, he was backed up so bad. But the doctor recommended ear-syringe enemas."

For a moment the two people on the other side of the table stare at me, she in frank alarm, he in consternation. Then Sandra pushes back her chair and says in a muffled voice, "Excuse me. I need to find the ladies'."

It's working!

However, the victory is bittersweet because now I'm really ashamed of myself. I've used anecdotes of my children to offend, disturb and repel someone. I'm exhausted, out of ideas and so close to tears that I'm afraid to look at Jacob.

"This is not like you, Lu."

I look up and meet Jacob's gaze. "As you said, I've changed."

He shrugs. "But you know what? I do remember that constipation routine. Jeez, Lu. Were we ever that young and naive?"

"About twenty years ago."

He nods and forks in a jumbo bite of steak. As he chews, I drink water, trying to swallow the sense that I'm a bad, bad person.

Finally, he says, "So then, here's the thing, Lu. I've been asked to consider a change of location. For working purposes."

"You're going to turn it down, I suppose?"

"That's what I'm trying to tell you. I don't have many options, career-wise. I'm over fifty. I leave a job now, I'm practically asking to be retired permanently."

"Okay." I have to pinch myself under the table to keep hope from rising. "So where are you going? Upstate?"

"A little farther. Lima."

"Ohio?"

"Lima, Peru."

"I see." I don't feel the total triumph of the moment. I feel...sick.

"This just came up. This morning." I stare at him, trying to hear the nuance in every word. "But I was thinking even before today that maybe I was a little hasty about this joint custody." He smiles. "I'm being honest here. But then I saw you with that guy…!" I can see Jacob start to get angry all over again.

"I understand how you feel," I say quickly. "I'm having dinner with your date, remember?"

He hunches his shoulders. "Right. I guess I kinda lost perspective."

"So then, let's just forget it."

I hold my breath as he takes his time before answering. "I just want my name on the kid's birth certificate, Lu. That's what I want."

I smile. "All you had to do was say so."

He nods. "Okay then, I'm asking. I want the kid to know I'm the dad."

A dozen questions crowd in on me. I want to know whose idea it was to file for joint custody? And why he did it, to punish me or to run William off? But just as suddenly, I realize those answers don't matter. As Tai likes to say, *it's all about the bottom line.*

"How do I know you won't change your mind again, about custody?"

He looks grim again. "Can I share custody from Peru?"

"I'm serious. I'm seeing William. I may very well go on seeing him, even after the baby's born. If not him, then, eventually, there will be another man. You can't jump in and out of my life, depending on whether or not you approve of every person who's part of it."

He looks at me with deep sadness. "You want papers giving you full custody?"

The good, altruistic, generous, believe-the-best-of-people me wants to say, "Of course not. I trust you." But this isn't about me. It's about that person with the hiccups inside me. "I think it would be best."

He nods. "Have something drawn up."

Which means, you pay the attorney this time.

"You also need to know I won't back off the focus of 'The Pregnant Pause' column. The magazine has bought into the single-at-fifty-unwed mother angle big time. I'm going to be in a fashion layout next month." I bite my lip. "I advise you not to look."

He looks down. "Do you hate me that much?"

I have to think about that. "No, I don't hate you. Maybe early on. I'm human. But now? No."

He grins, and for the first time in a while it doesn't put me on my guard. "Truth is, I was thinking, even before Peru came up, that maybe after the kid's here, we should try again."

Now that's the one thing I had never in this lifetime thought he'd say. Sandra, his sweetie, just left to powder her nose.

Yet I see in his eyes that he's serious. Maybe he's just staking out territory again, because I've mentioned William. Or, perhaps, he's having second thoughts because I just brought up all those fun times we had as parents.

I touch his left hand. "You don't want to be with me, Jacob. It's just familiar. I know I'm practically irresistible in my pregnant 'Sweet Potato Queen' finery, but I won't look this good forever."

He chuckles and shakes his head. "What is that you're wearing?"

"It's from Mom. Don't ask."

"Look, Lu, I—I—" Suddenly he looks like he's about to cry. "I don't want to start over as a parent. That's the God's honest truth. You're fearless. Always have been. You just take life as it comes, on the chin. You don't need me, haven't needed me for a while."

"That's not—"

"Be honest, Lu."

I don't know how to tell him he's right…but not entirely accurate.

"We changed, Jacob. We're looking for different things. Some couples endure great pain and expense to keep things from changing. They wear down the enamel on their teeth, eat bran to keep their bowels from impacting, and pop pills to quiet the hammers in their heads. I think we both deserve better, don't you?"

He looks defeated. "I'm feeling my age and, I gotta tell you, it terrifies me."

"And whenever you look at me you see the accumulation of all those years, time that you can't recapture."

He blushes but nods. "Something like that."

"You can't outrun aging," I say gently.

"I know. But I want to live to the fullest whatever time there is left. Even if it means leaving some of my old life behind." I hear a counselor's voice in his phrasing, but this time I agree.

I withdraw my hand because I see Sandra making her way across the room toward us. Poor kid. She doesn't know how many times the world has turned in her absence. She's already a footnote in Jacob's biography.

I lean forward and say in a low, honest voice, "I love you, Jacob. But we both know you can't be part of my future, or my child's."

"Yeah." He looks…relieved.

Sandra alights on her chair with a big smile. "Did I miss anything?"

I smile. "Not even dessert. How about a chocolate soufflé?"

37

The second issue is flying off the stands. Not as fast as the sleazoid headlining, "I Had the President's Secret Love Child," but *very* respectable numbers. The photos of me surveying my "options" boosted interest. Score one for Tai. My next paycheck should be nearly as plump as I am.

"...the projected numbers for next month's issue look even better." Tai is not pacing for a change. "Lu's local interviews gave us a boost. It's a start."

I smile. We all smile. From Tai, this is tantamount to an oracle's declaration of peace and prosperity.

Not one to rest on her elegant haunches, Tai continues. "The most frequently asked question about 'The Pregnant Pause' is how Lu got that way. Crescentmoon will answer that question in next month's issue in her health column."

"Did she interview the sperm donor?" Rhonda is feeling very frisky. We've all noticed it.

"Did she interview the sperm?" KaZi, on the other hand, is not. If funk had a persona, she would be it.

"Don't interrupt," Tai answers shortly. "The question

of paternity is running a close second. We're also getting tirades against the sanctity of the traditional family unit. *Bo-ring!* I want to take a page from the tabloids, and do a tongue-in-cheek poll for nominees for Lu's baby's daddy."

"How about the ex?"

Tai shakes her head. "Too obvious."

The others look at me. "I'd have to agree. It is a cliché."

"The mailman?"

"Harassment lawsuit!" Tai snaps.

"A neighbor?"

Again, heads swivel my way. "My neighbor's a seventy-two-year-old widower. I have it on good authority that he'd be delighted."

"Gawd! This is fantasy time, ladies." Tai glances at Curran. "Apologies to our lone male, but who do the rest of you secretly want to do the nasty with?"

Rhonda chuckles. "A much younger man."

Tai gives her a quick glance. "Such as?"

KaZi smirks without looking up. "How about Curran?"

I don't know if I should be grateful that the table instantly erupts in laughter, but it defuses any possible interest in pursuing the subject.

Curran, however, has turned radish-red. He stands up, camera on shoulder and heads for the door. "Later!"

Without missing a beat, Tai says, "Now, then."

There's a lot of giggling and ribbing as the staff indulges their libidos at my expense. Everyone from Rodrigo to the kid who delivers takeout from the Vietnamese place across the street is fair game for speculation. After this issue, I doubt I'll be able to enter any of my regular haunts without scaring off the male staff.

When the list of potential dads has been whittled down to ten, Tai puts Rhonda in charge of getting signed releases from the "real" men for use of their photos and names. "We'll fill out the list with a few celebrity hotties.

After readers pick the top three, we'll have Lu's face morphed with the candidates and print the 'offspring' photos in the October issue. Lu can write a column about each fantasy lover to go with it."

"Not on your life," I say sweetly. "This child will be born with enough baggage attached. Mama's not going to do soft-porn columns over the conception."

"Then you better think of something else equally entertaining," Tai responds with her usual edge.

"Naturally." I shut my eyes and repeat under my breath, "Baby needs new shoes, baby needs…" Poverty is a great spur to inspiration. I'll think of something.

Rhonda waves at me as I enter the deli for lunch. I nod and point to the hot buffet line. As I approach, I see two other familiar faces in the adjacent salad-bar line.

I have to admit dreads are beginning to look good on Curran. The carefully sculptured facial hair gives his features some added dimension. He's dressing better, too— baggy but better. Today, KaZi's channeling Patti Boyd sixties retro, in thigh-high skirt, knee boots, a mane of stick-straight brown hair with bangs to rival Tai's, black eyeliner, fake lashes spiked with loads of black mascara, and pale lipstick.

As I watch, Curran says something to her. Predictably, she turns her back. He reaches for her tray but she slaps his hand. He backs up, before he turns away.

I know it's none of my business. People fix and ruin their lives every day without any help from me. But after what Curran has told me and KaZi's remark this morning, I can't help but feel that one big boulder in this rocky relationship has my name on it.

I veer away from the pizza slice/lasagna line and fall in next to KaZi, reminding myself that greens are good for baby and me.

"Hi, KaZi."

She doesn't look up from picking the frosted polish off her short nails. After a moment, she shoves a handful of hair over her shoulder and picks up a tray.

Seems a more direct approach is called for.

"You eating here, or what?" I look back to see a man in a delivery uniform bending an unkind eye on me. "Take a tray, lady. I ain't got all day."

I pick up a tray and follow down the opposite side of the salad bar from KaZi. When I'm across from her I say, "I want to thank you again for the great makeup job you did for this month's photo spread. Despite my mum-to-be moon face, Curran says you made me look sultry and luminous."

"That's his drama." She continues reading the ingredients on a yogurt label. When she's made her choice, she moves on. She passes bowls of conventional lettuces and grabs the tongs for the organic mesclun mix. While she's fishing for greens under the glass hood, I start piling up spinach salad. We finish making our choices at the same time and reach the end of the table where the dressings and condiments are.

"I seem to recall a time not so long ago when if you'd asked Curran to paint his tongue black and wear a nose ring, he would have."

She looks across at me. "Talk to someone who cares."

"But—"

She throws up her hand, flipping it palm outward. "Slap to your forehead, Lu. I have a mother. Okaaay?"

And I guess that puts me in my place.

When I've slunk away, trying to keep from tripping on the tail tucked between my legs, to join Rhonda she says, "What was that about?"

"Young love."

She looks down, smiling. "I can relate."

It takes me a second to register her tone. "Are you trying to tell me something?"

Rhonda nods. "Remember that article I offered to re-search when Tai first came to *Five-O?* Well, I've been free-lancing."

"And?"

"He's younger. Much younger." She leans in. "Did you see the episode of *Sex and the City* where Samantha meets this hot…?"

William calls almost nightly. Occasionally he wakes me, but that's not difficult any time after 7:00 p.m. Tonight he talks about a patient he lost earlier in the day.

"Some patients just get to you."

"I'm sure you did everything you could for her, William."

"That didn't make it any easier when I had to tell her that my best wasn't going to be good enough. You know what she said afterward? 'Well, Doctor, if you've done all you can do, all you know how to do, that's all anybody can ask.' And then she held my hand while I shed a few tears." He's silent for a moment. "Does that sound like I'm patting myself on the back?"

"It's a bit Sarah Bernhardt. But, remember, I've seen you in action with Aunt Marvelle."

"And that's why you love me." His voice catches for a second. "You think I'm going to be that nice to you in thirty years?"

Every dozing brain cell zaps alert at the word "love," even though it was buried in a throwaway line. For one crazy nanosecond I wonder how to respond, but the treat-it-lightly habit is hard to break. "Oh, I plan to outlive you."

He laughs. The moment passes. I swear I can smell ozone as my overstimulated synapses cool. And my heart could pump oil it's still hammering so hard.

After we hang up, I get up and get a bowl of Jell-O with pineapple because I'm too stoked to fall asleep. Like a fifteen-year-old, I replay in my head every word of tonight's conversation, trying to figure out from his in-flection and word choice, what he meant by inserting the *L* word in our exchange. And why I'm so frightened by it.

"Don't be an ass!" Andrea says impatiently when I can't resist calling her. "You know what it means. I know what it means. Even *he* knows what it means."

She's right. We all know it means this is getting serious.

"He needs a place to lay his weary head. And I like it a lot that he comes to me. We are good as friends."

"Excuse me. There's sex involved."

"It's friendship sex. But, Andrea, I'm not ready for serious. We've got issues."

"Who doesn't? Did I tell you that heart doctor kid is calling me again? You know how I feel about being crowded. Men! They want to be in *looove*. All this talk about men who don't want to commit. Where are *these* men?"

When we've finally worn ourselves out and I'm shuffling back to bed, I realize that I should simply let the matter go. The *L* word may never come up again.

As I pull the sheet up I can't help but think about KaZi's ability to put an end to a relationship without breaking a sweat. And Andrea's avoidance that masquerades as keeping her options open. But I really like being part of a couple. Like it so much, in fact, that I know I'm going to have a very hard time letting go if the *L* word doesn't come up again.

September

Not long ago I called my mother to complain that my
grown children still call regularly for help and support.
When exactly, I asked, do they make the transition into
independant, freethinking individuals?
There was a pause before Mom said,
"You're on the other end of my line, sweetie.
How long do you plan to live?"

**—"Mum's the Word"
CUE LU!**

38

To our collective female family consternation, tonight's rehearsal dinner has a theme, *The Great Gatsby*.

Hungover from the bridesmaids' Girls' Night Out the night before, Dallas slept most of the day. At the moment, she's come to my bedroom to try on the "perfect for you" 1920s Boue Soeurs creation her soon-to-be mother-in-law, Marj Pascal, borrowed from a friend's vintage-dress collection for Dallas to wear at the rehearsal they're hosting. As it was just sent over by car, this is the first time any of us have seen it.

It's made of lace with satin rose garlands. It's pale pink. It's...hideous.

"Holy Christ!" Dallas cries when the full-length mirror reveals the awful truth.

"It isn't the most becoming shade," my mom, who has arrived for the wedding, begins tactfully. "And the drop-waist gathers..."

"Tell the truth, Leila. It's vile!" Aunt Marvelle clicks her tongue. "She looks like a giant pink fig."

"Mo-*ther*." Dallas's expression is brittle as glass. One wrong word and she will shatter into a million vibrating pieces, which I'm much too ungainly to pick up.

I pat her shoulder. "Take it off, Dallas. We'll think of something."

One week out from the wedding, my assertive, forthright, take-charge daughter moved back in with me for refuge. I am the calm center about which she spins, quakes and erupts as she negotiates the intricate web of exhausting last-minute wedding details. I am the om of the wedding weekend. I am...really tired.

I try to calculate the devastation to the in-law relationship my idea may create. Jacob and I have met the Pascals exactly once before, just after the engagement, and just before he walked out.

Marj is the principal of a private school. She's attractive and forthright in the manner of one whose job includes the ability to tell parents who pay way too much for the education of their offspring that said progeny are deficient in things like math and manners. Husband Preston is a CFO for a venture-capitalist firm. Casually elegant in that Ralph Lauren Black Label way, they own a horse farm in an area of Bergen County where money and prestige needn't announce themselves. The assumption is we are all equal, aren't we?

Yes and no. I have a nice home. Marj and Preston have an estate and grounds, where they occasionally host galas for hundreds. "We've got a perfectly good indoor arena and horse barn. Why not hold the rehearsal and the dinner here?" Stephen asked his parents to keep things intimate. Marj agreed, sort of. The idea of a theme came later. Along with the decision to wear costumes.

"Someone should have told the mother of the groom that she is supposed to wear beige and keep her mouth shut," Aunt Marvelle says as she sips her afternoon martini. "I don't see why we have to dress up like fools for a woman who wears jodhpurs and thinks a barn is a swell place for a party. Well, Tallulah, what's the child to do?"

Dallas watches me like an acolyte who expects her Goddess Mother to turn disaster into Roberto Cavalli. At this late date there's really only one possibility. "There's always the family heirloom."

Dallas immediately stops quaking. "You don't mean…?"

"Mother's beaded dress!" Mom and Aunt Marvelle chorus as if cued.

We head for the door at the same time, but Mom and Aunt Marvelle quickly outpace me. My size is not the problem, it's my blood pressure. It's low so I'm slow. It helps me keep a perspective. No one beyond my inner circle knows my secret, of course. The weekend isn't about me.

There's a cedar closet in the guest bedroom that we call "Aladdin's Cave." It's where we store all the clothing that no one wants but doesn't want thrown out. Davin and Dallas once loved to dig around in the cave to find things for Halloween costumes. We don't have to dig for the gown. It is stored on a shelf in a silk-lined suitcase, wrapped and rolled in yards of tissue paper so that it won't crease or stretch from weight. Once I locate it, Mom and Aunt Marvelle reverently unroll it. The twenties-era dress consists of two sleeveless panels of silk netting covered with jet beads in art deco patterns.

Dallas sloughs off the offensive pink-lace dress, then Mom and Aunt Marvelle slip their mother's old gown over her head. She takes a few tentative steps as the sheer silk panels sway about her calves. "Well? What do you think?"

"I think you need a slip, or at least black panties. The pink thong? Too much." But she can see by the look on my face that I think she looks fabulous.

She looks at herself in the mirror and smiles. "I feel just like Cinderella!"

Thank goodness, Grandma had a sense of style.

We group-hug, careful not to snag the eighty-year-old gown. Nothing bonds four generations of women faster than a fashion crisis.

"I think we should have had that second martini, just in case." My mother, usually a rock on social occasions, says this as she blows a feather from her sister's headdress out of her face.

Five of us are crammed into the back seat of a Lincoln Town Car because the limo we reserved a month ago was unavailable at the last moment. The bridesmaids are following in another car.

"Who is up for a lemon-drop stop?" coos Amanda, Dallas's maid of honor and the fifth member of our select group.

"If it contains alcohol, I am," Marvelle answers. "Ask the driver if he knows of an establishment nearby. We've time for a short libation."

"Mother!" Dallas's voice rises in alarm at the mention of such mutinous action.

I pat her knee and say, "We don't want to be late, Aunt Marvelle. After all, we have the bride." But if Aunt Marvelle is feeling the strain we could be in trouble.

From the moment I haul my body out of the Lincoln, I am put in mind of Gatsby. The paddock lawn is a lovely, almost surreal shade of green. There are flower-strewn tables beneath white umbrellas. Surrounding them are people—lots of people—dressed in variations of "twenties" fashion. It is a *Vanity Fair* moment, with a whiff of manure.

As I enter the white fenced area I'm enveloped in a hug I didn't see coming.

"Oh *gawd,* Lu! I've been reading all about your pregnancy. How tragic!" Thelma Lawson, my divorce attorney, has thrown her arms about my neck. "Was it your hormone therapy?"

"What are you doing here?" I ask in astonishment.

"I was invited, of course."

And now the numbers on the lawn begin to make sense. I look around and realize Marj and Preston invited the entire wedding guest list, and then some.

"Mom! Do you believe this?" Dallas looks furious as she surveys the scene. "They are going to steal my thunder," she whispers in a tight voice.

I smile serenely. "No one can do that. You are the bride." But I cross my fingers behind my back because it's just possible I've told my child a lie.

"There she is, our little bride!" Marj is opulence itself in a silver bugle-bead dress that ripples like water along her lean flanks as she crosses the lawn toward us. Stephen, looking natty in a white dinner coat, is her escort. "But, Dallas, dear, where's the Boue Soeurs gown I borrowed for you?"

Dallas looks vague in a way Davin would approve. "Didn't fit. Luckily my great-grandmother's did. It's perfect, don't you agree?"

"Yes, I suppose…." I imagine Marj is frowning but not a line creases her brow. The Botox party must have been a success. "You look fine, dear. Fine."

"You look so hot!" Stephen says in a way that makes this mother's heart swell with relief. Going braless has assured Dallas of *his* attention. He practically vibrates around her. He grabs Dallas's arm. "Come on, I want to show you off."

Marj gives me a tight smile. "And this is your family?"

I quickly make introductions. Mom and Marvelle are dressed in costumes from an off-Broadway production of *Thoroughly Modern Millie,* thanks to the ever-changeable KaZi, who volunteered to use her theater connections after she overheard me talking to the Radish about my need for vintage garb. They wear pastel handkerchief-hem dresses with matching headbands with jeweled feather ornaments.

I opted for the black-lace number with the ostrich feather hemline Andrea talked me into putting in layaway back in May.

"And Lu! How clever of you to come as a pregnant flapper." Marj pats my stomach but then jerks her hand away. "Oh! I thought— That's a really firm pillow."

Unlike Thelma, apparently Marj isn't a reader of *Five-O*. Equally obvious, neither Dallas nor Stephen has said a word about my condition.

Aunt Marvelle gives me the fish-eye and says to her sister, "Come on, Leila. It's definitely time for that drink."

Before I can begin the necessary explanation, Stephen's dad arrives at Marj's side, Scotch glass in hand.

"Hello, Lu." Preston's smile is wide and his eyes are bright, really bright. "Sorry to hear about you and Jacob." He hugs me a little too hard and a few cold drops of his drink splash down my back. "Say, maybe you better cut back on the Ben & Jerry's comfort therapy. Huh?"

"Preston!" Marj admonishes in embarrassment. To me she says, "Preston started celebrating early."

"Oh, come on," Preston says, patting my cheek. "We're all family here, or soon will be."

I remind myself that perfectly nice people can get a bit weird when a wedding is involved.

I slip an arm through one each of theirs. "Since you're both here, I have a little announcement to make. It's not a problem. It's not an issue. It's just a fact. I'm pregnant. Six and a half months."

Preston bursts into laughter but I watch Marj's gaze focus on the bump beneath my dress. Preston quickly sobers, after a fashion, aware that he's missed something huge. For seconds the silence is absolute, as the mathematics of gestation becomes a lawn game.

"Well, well. Isn't that wonderful?" Marj says finally. "Right, Preston?"

"Oh sure. Wonderful." Preston is busy checking his shoe, for he's stepped in a pile of manure.

It's clear Marj and Preston are shocked. Shocked.

I smile and slip free before they can think of the obvious follow-up questions.

I'd been warned that wedding rehearsal dinners fall into two types. The first launches joyful festivities that won't end until the couple is on their honeymoon. The second involves dealing with situations that quickly remind you why you don't see these people more often. It seems I've been dealt the second hand.

Jacob arrives shortly after this with Davin and, regrettably, Sandra. She wears a thigh-high chemise that looks more like an undergarment, but who's judging?

Davin gives me a big hug. "Wow, Mom! You look hot." Thank goodness for sons who like feathers.

"Yeah, you look nice, Lu." Jacob's face is bright red as he kisses my cheek, and then I get a whiff of gin. Seems like the whole gang thinks being stinko is a good idea.

Sandra and I smile at each other. I thought she was history. I'm sure she wishes I were. I suppose Jacob didn't want to show up without a date, in case I had one.

Funny, I feel no real angst. William wasn't able to get away. He's promised to make the wedding. Andrea, alas, had other plans, too.

Soon after, Cy and Curran arrive. Cy latches onto my elbow. "So, how bad is it?" I give him the look. "I would have escorted you. But you must be the independent woman."

"I was wrong. The Pascals don't approve." I pat Sweet Tum.

"They've got taste," he says, "just not good taste."

As we make our way through the throng, Curran follows. His camera should be surgically attached. It's like having my own portable paparazzo.

Despite the fact that this is Dallas and Stephen's evening,

I find I'm the reluctant focus of attention among many guests. Once Aunt Marvelle makes off with Cy, claiming she needs his help with some arrangement, my late-life fertility becomes a pretty good gauge for the mind-set of one's acquaintances as they greet me with monologue reactions.

"Well, la-la-palooza Lu!" Dill Graves, my dentist, flashes me a white-porcelain smile, which reminds me I'm overdue for a checkup. "You're looking quite, quite something I can't put my finger on."

I just smile.

A moment later I get a big wink from Jacob's podiatrist. "So, you're still in the game, huh, Lu?"

"There goes your retirement," offers my CPA.

"I've been reading all about it in your column, Lu. You're so brave. So very brave." This from a woman whose youngest has just flown the nest.

Men with exes say things like "Poor Jacob. How's the old boy handling it? What's the poor bastard going to do?"

One of Jacob's golfing buddies leans in to whisper, "A big girl like you should know better. Now, if you'd come to me, I would have taken care of business."

Some men just leer. Really leer, as if my expanding tum is the most embarrassing turn-on since Bob Dole started hawking Viagra.

Then there are the distant, less sympathetic utterances.

"—just ridiculous."

"—at her age."

"Showing off, that's all."

Through it all I smile and behave as if I'm not ready to bolt. Whenever I catch Dallas's eye, I nod and wave. But finally I decide that if getting drunk is out then a sugar high will have to do.

Yet as I make my way over to the sweets table, Dallas's godparents, Jeff and Sarah, waylay me.

"Lu, Lu!" Jeff begins in mournful tones like the start

of a homily on the prodigal child. "How the hell—*aw*— *ouch!*"

Hmm. That's going to leave a bruise. Sarah never spanked her children growing up. She just pinched them into submission.

"Lu knows what I meant." Jeff looks leery as he glances from his wife's poised right hand to me. "Right, Lu?"

"Sure, Jeff. It's a shock. To all of us. Still, we must be brave and do the best we can, under the circumstances." I quickly step away from Sarah, just in case she's thinking I'm being a bit too glib. I bruise very easily.

I smell shrimp, lovely broiled shrimp! I can't drink, but I can certainly eat.

Unfortunately, Ellen Jenkins, the spreader of last year's "clap trouble with hubby," meets me at the buffet table. "Just between us girls. Who are you seeing?" She says this with the avid expectation she usually reserves for news of a new stylist at a Manhattan salon.

Thelma, hovering nearby, joins us. "God, yes! Tell us. Is he here?"

I shake my head and take a large bite of the shrimp on a skewer. Food in mouth will possibly keep me from having to say more.

"Your news frightened him off." Ellen doesn't sound at all saddened by the idea.

"Men can be such bastards about these little accidents," adds Thelma.

Ellen nods. "It doesn't matter how many tricks you know. Men just won't stick around if you're past forty and not rich."

"Get a boob job," Thelma suggests, for abundant reasons. "Men don't care about wrinkles if you keep a good rack."

Ellen swings around on her. "Is the clinic in Jersey?"

I munch my shrimp and wonder, why do I know these people?

★ ★ ★

The rehearsal itself is predictably awful. While lining up, two groomsmen get into a heated discussion—work issues. The flower girl gets sick and barfs into her basket. Then the ring bearer, Stephen's sister's timid son, can't be persuaded to take even two steps down the makeshift aisle. I keep reminding Dallas that a lousy dress rehearsal is the harbinger of a great opening night or wedding day. It doesn't help matters that through it all, I remain a constant source of speculation.

"But if they're divorced, who's the father?" I overhear Stephen's grandmother ask Aunt Marvelle.

"A fine young man," she answers, and moves quickly away.

A little later, Grandma Pascal buttonholes Cy. "Who's the father?"

"I am," he offers.

She gives him a look of consternation. "I'm not impressed."

When it's time to walk down the aisle Jacob can't be found. Dallas is frosted. "Why can't I have friggin' normal parents like other people?"

I make no comment about the fact that Stephen's father is piss-faced in the corner. Instead I join the volunteers to locate her father.

We find Jacob with Sandra behind the barn having an argument over "that pregnant cow," his ex-wife. Nice to know I made that good of an impression.

"You're needed for Daddy duty," I say, startling them both. "Not new-daddy, old-daddy duty."

But Dallas has had it. She won't walk down the aisle with Jacob, she won't even make a show of it. She screams at him something like "Hate you" and "Grow up!"

Then Davin, feeling protective after all these months, lights into his father for bringing Sandra. "What were you thinking? In front of Mom!"

In the midst of this impressive family moment, Stephen and Dallas slip away, not to be seen again for the rest of the evening. It's too much to hope they have decided to elope. No, we'll all have to gather together again tomorrow and do this all over again.

When we can reasonably head for our car without seeming to bolt, Aunt Marvelle wobbles up and grips my arm for support. "Tell me. How the dickens did I get so drunk?"

"I know I wish I were."

She nods, her feather bobbing over one eye. "It was too much to take in sober."

39

Dallas returns home at 6:15 a.m. as I am making tea for Aunt Marvelle and me. She has on sweats, a baseball cap and the biggest smile I've seen since she slipped on Stephen's engagement ring. She hands me Grandmother's beaded dress, carefully rolled up in a shopping bag, kisses my cheek and says, "The only thing in the dark!"

"I suspect S-E-X," Marvelle says when Dallas has floated off to bed.

"You think?" I answer, and then we both break out in a fit of giggles.

There are some things I'd rather shave my head than do. Right now facing wedding guests is one of them. But at least I'm visually prepared thanks, again, to Andrea.

"It's a loan from a client," Andrea said the day she brought it for me to try on. "His third wife was pregnant when his son from his first marriage married in Honolulu in April. She was a cow by then. Not that I think you are, okay? She was this petite thing before the pregnancy. You are taller and big-boned." What are friends for?

Mother-of-the-bride is wearing a three-piece suit of deep rose silk. The jacket has a swing-away cut, the skirt pencil-slim to mid-calf. The bodice is strapless, fitted over the bosom, then flares like an umbrella over Sweet Tum. I hate to admit it, but we are just too cute!

I'm even wearing heels, open-toed, in case my feet swell like yeast buns before the end of the day.

The wedding is what all weddings are, lovely. The fans and cascades and trelliswork, the drape of greenery, bows, swags and sprays all mesh to give the impression one has stepped into a hothouse love chapel.

And the bride is radiant.

Dallas is still smiling, even when laced into a gown with a waist size I'm sure I haven't seen since I was ten. She's a glorious bride, and her happiness makes all the mess and the fuss and the bother and the expense—okay, most of the expense—worthwhile.

As we line up to be escorted into the church I start to chuckle.

"What?" Cy is keeping me company because William has yet to make an appearance.

"Marj is wearing beige." And so, by the way, is Preston. At least that skinless baked-chicken complexion of his is a comparable shade. The chuckle becomes giggles.

"What?" Cy's expression is now serious.

"Stephen's dad is—is a chicken-bone pastel," I sputter. "Pastel, not Pascal. Get it?"

"Nerves."

Cy's brows lift in warning, as in I better quit before I get started.

I sniff hard to sober up, and look away as the mother and father of the groom start down the aisle.

On the bride's side of the church, Aunt Marvelle, Mom and Dad—who had the sense to avoid the rehearsal—and

Davin and his ladyfriend of the moment are all seated near the front pew. I notice that Jacob is alone today, but then he gets to walk Dallas down the aisle.

"This is like, so cool!" Curran murmurs repeatedly as he clicks away at everything and everyone for a change.

He looks super-good in a tux. I've often thought every man in the world should be photographed in a tux. It makes the short tall, the skinny brawny, the broad robust and even the ugly passably cute.

I try not to think about William, who called earlier because he's stuck in traffic somewhere on I80 East. I've decided that I have to tell him that some things, like the rest of this pregnancy, are better done alone. So I suppose I should get used to his not being there for me.

As the music swells to signal the beginning of the procession, Cy offers me his arm at the same moment Curran comes up and does the same.

For a second I'm tempted to say, "I can do this on my own," but the truth is, I'm not alone. I'm surrounded by love and friendship and loyalty. I take one arm each, smile at Dallas, and head down the aisle.

We make a good-looking trio. How do I know? The groom's side of the aisle is twittering. And it's not just over Aunt Marvelle's diamond birthday gift winking wickedly at my throat. Sweet Tum looks good in rose silk.

Halfway down the aisle, I hear a door slam behind me and then voices and then the sharp click of heels. When I look back over my shoulder I see a very handsome man in a tux rushing up the aisle. It's William. He smiles as he nears, picks up the back edge of my jacket as if it were a train and nods for us to continue.

"Now, that must be the father!" I hear Stephen's grandmother say in that carrying voice peculiar to the hard of hearing.

I should be so lucky!

★ ★ ★

I dance until I can dance no more. I dance with Stephen and Jacob and Cy and Davin—even Curran. But when I'm at last in William's arms, I realize that if I don't sit down soon, I'm going to drop like a rock.

"I guess that answers the question of my appeal," William says as he begrudgingly pulls out a chair for me.

I smile and cup his cheek when he's sitting beside me. "I prefer you horizontal to vertical. But just for the record, you do dance well, don't you?"

He grins. "Turn horizontal to vertical. Now, what do you think?"

Ooh, baby, baby!

And then I remember my decision, and that I'm really rather hot and sweaty already. I slip off my jacket, revealing the pregnancy-enhanced proportions of the strapless bodice. William just stares at me in a way that makes me wonder who I was before I met him.

Of all the times I should have been embarrassed when I've been with him, I suddenly feel a deep flush creeping up my neck. "I could use a cup of punch."

He sees right through me. "Hold that thought. I'll be back."

But he's gone awhile. And I notice Cy and Aunt Marvelle on the floor, and Mom and Dad, and Andrea and…that's Dr. Yummy!

Then I remember something that I forgot to tell Dallas.

I rise quickly and start across the floor. Only I don't go in any direction but down. A leg that suddenly has no feeling in it folds under my weight, and I slip toward the floor.

I hear cries of alarm but, really, all I've done is sit rather hard on my bum. Suddenly Cy and Curran are bending over me. William appears and then Jacob.

"Lu! Are you okay? Are you hurt?" they all ask at the same time.

"No!" I'm only horribly embarrassed that I've drawn even another eye-flicker of attention my way.

William bends down to bring his face on a level with mine. "What's hurt?"

"My pride." I lean forward and whisper, "Please, get me off this floor!"

That requires me being lifted front, both sides and rear by four men. If that doesn't make a girl's day I don't know what will.

"Drinking." I hear someone whisper.

I whip my head in that direction and bark, "No, pregnant!"

When I'm rather inelegantly seated again the hovering continues, joined by Dallas, Stephen and Davin. "Mom, what's wrong?"

I give them a thumbs-up. "The baby's just getting heavy," I say, dimly recalling a similar incident with Davin that revoked my driving privileges during the last two months. "Leg went numb. Sweet Tum must be sitting on a major nerve or blood vessel."

"Maybe we should call an ambulance," Cy suggests.

"Absolutely not! One thrill ride per pregnancy, that's my limit."

William is watching me like a doctor. "You're sure?"

"Where's my punch?" I scowl at Curran because he seems the easiest of the group to intimidate. "I—*wow!*"

I grab my middle in amazement. Instinctively, other hands mimic my reach for the tum.

"What's the matter, Lu?" William says anxiously.

"Nothing." I look up with a big smile into camera flashes that leaves me blind. "Sweet Tum just did a Rockette high kick."

40

It must be a really slow news week. The picture of me with "hands on" Curran, Cy, Jacob and William was picked up by wire services nationwide. That has been enough to keep my phone buzzing since the first paper hit the first porch eastern daylight time Monday morning.

I had to wait for nearly an hour to see the source of the controversy. The kid who delivers the paper must be down with something because his grandfather, a careful (as in slow) man, always picks up his route. Ever since I received a belated copy, I've been saying a prayer of thanksgiving that Dallas is on her honeymoon, and Davin doesn't read anything but the front page unless it's assigned in class.

There in the Lifestyles section of my paper is a photo of me sprawled in a chair, looking about eleven months gone, while four very upset men in tuxes reach out to pat, catch or—depending on your point of view—generally feel me up. That they were only trying to help me is completely overlooked. Below this undignified photo op is the caption "Who's Your Daddy?"

Who knew the wedding photographer freelances as a paparazzo?

At first I thought it was amusing. I can take a joke. After three days of calls from minor talk shows, wanting "the guys" and me to come on and tell all about our unusual relationship, it's gotten to be annoying.

Tai doesn't like me passing up these opportunities to "pitch future issues of *Five-O.* " Easy for her. She doesn't have to face questions like, "How many men have you slept with since you learned you were pregnant?" Or try to explain to her dentist or her beautician, or her son's high school English teacher, a Cue Lu! fan, why I won't talk about "him" when I seem to be willing to expose every other aspect of my pregnancy.

So, I'm avoiding Tai as I slurp a decaf latte in the deli below *Five-O* and try to concentrate on the three-day-old *New York Times* Sunday crossword puzzle.

I look up as the waitress serves me a toasted bagel with a smear. "What's a six-letter word for 'unanticipated affair'?"

"Crisis?"

Of course.

I don't even bother to check caller ID as I answer my cell. "Who's the Daddy? Yes, that is the question, isn't it?"

"Lu?"

"William? You sound funny." I sigh. "Don't tell me. You've had enough. I'm sorry. I warned you. Next time pick a woman without her own laugh track."

There's a short pause. "Obviously something's going on. Can it wait?"

"Sorry. What's wrong?"

"Jolie." He sighs. "She went into false labor last night, and then, after Jon took her home from the hospital, she bolted."

"As in ran away?" He's got my attention.

"Yes. We found her, thank God, at the municipal airport."

"Where was she going?"

"She said something about going to find her mother."

"Oh, William."

"She was absolutely hysterical. The doctor says it could just be hormonal but, Lu, she's claiming now she won't deliver her baby. She says she's changed her mind about having it. For the first time in my life, Lu, I don't have a clue as to what to do."

"I'm on my way."

I don't know what I think I can do for Jolie. I'm not exactly a model of decorum and right thinking. I gave what I'm sure was a critical piece of my mind to the guy who tried to take the last seat on this Long Island railway car. He claimed he beat me to it but—excuse me!—who makes the pregnant lady stand? The conductor intervened and I imagine he's still cooling off while standing in another compartment.

Hmm. Maybe I will have something to say to a young woman who thinks she can escape giving birth by skipping out on the delivery room.

Once he picks me up William tells me Jolie's begun to dilate and under the circumstances, he pulled some professional strings to get her admitted into the hospital where he practices even though, technically, she's not in true labor yet. He says she's been given a very mild sedative, that she's not to be upset, nor made to talk about what's bothering her, and especially not anything about Jon, who left the hospital after she threw a pitcher of water at him and hit him in the head.

I completely block out William's advice. Who's going to take seriously a man who looks like he slept in his clothes? There are wrinkle lines in his face from his corduroy jacket, which he must have used as a pillow in the hospital waiting room.

"She'll be fine," I repeat anytime he seems to come to

the end of a distracted paragraph on our drive to the hospital. "She'll be fine."

I repeat this one more time as I push open the door to Jolie's room.

Sitting in the middle of the hospital bed playing cards with herself, she seems even younger than the woman I remember. Her black hair is loose, flowing down her back like Snow White's did in books before Disney gave her a thirties coif. Then I notice her belly. Her striped hospital gown covers a globe the size of a Volkswagen. She looks up and sees me about the time I'm thinking, she looks so peaceful I should not be here.

"Are you the shrink?" Her voice is curiously calm but her gaze is alert.

"No, but feel free to call someone to scoot me out if you'd like." I take a few steps toward her. "I'm Lu Nichols."

"I remember you." She smiles, but it's automatic politeness. "You're Dad's ladyfriend."

I'm completely surprised by how happy her words make me. "Your dad talks about me?"

"Only constantly." She's so pretty it makes me a little jealous, shallow creature that I am, for surely this is how stunning her mother must have been at this age.

I touch my bouncing baby, who seems to be practicing the cha-cha at the moment. "I'm surprised your father's been so open, considering."

Her gaze shifts to my bump and her smile dissolves. "Dad thinks you're brave and honorable." *Unlike me,* is the unspoken codicil. She goes back to playing solitaire. "Are you in the hospital for a checkup?"

"No, I came just to see you."

I watch it dawn on her that maybe I'm not a benign visitor. "Dad sent for you?"

"No. I volunteered. Since we share a condition I thought maybe you could use an ally."

She stops playing. "What kind of ally?"

"Do you mind if I sit?" I indicate a chair by the bed.

"Of course. I should have offered. Are you in pain?"

"Only the backache kind." I ease my rear into a high-backed chair. The train may be posh, but in my state it felt like one step up from schoolbus. "If I could just put Sweet Tum down for a couple of hours a day, I could happily stay pregnant another six months. Know what I mean?"

She cocks her head to one side. "You're trying to handle me." Smart, like her dad. I should have known.

"As long as I'm here…" I point to the cards on her food tray. "Do you play Hearts?" She shakes her head. "It's easy to learn."

I pick up the deck and begin shuffling. "Here are the fine points. It's a game of matching suits and winning tricks with the highest card. Hearts are trumps. But you don't want to take a trick that leaves you in possession of the queen of spades. Okay?"

She shrugs.

I quickly deal a hand and then hold my breath until she picks up hers.

I want to say things, such as we don't have to talk about pregnancy, or the baby, or her marriage, but I know if I bring up any of those things I could be asked to leave. So I talk about anything that comes to mind, mostly Dallas's wedding. I feel like a Talking Head who's been told to fill airtime for a no-show guest. My audience is mostly silent.

"I don't want a baby." Jolie says this after we've played two hands. She crosses her arms over her enormous belly. "I should have had an abortion. I'd have one now, if I could." She sends me a hard glance. "Does that shock you?"

"A bit." I keep shuffling cards. "Mostly because you've done all the hard work."

"It's going to be defective." She shakes her head as I start to deal. "Did Dad tell you that his grandchild is going to be a gimp or a cripple, or something worse?"

"No. I had heard you had tests." I pile up cards between us, anyway. "After the amnio I thought the doctors discounted the possibility of serious problems."

"What do they know?" She turns her head away. "First they said it was spina bifida, which is a horrible thing to tell an expectant mother. Awful! And then they change their minds after some tests? But I know it's going to be defective."

I'm amazed that she's talking so much. I expected to find a partially catatonic young woman in the fetal position sucking her thumb. Yet, this is not exactly the state of mind one wants for an impending mother-to-be. "So screw them."

She looks back at me in surprise. I pick up my hand, pretending I'm interested in arranging the cards. "Screw the doctors! Doctors are people and, if you want my opinion, overrated when it comes to having all the answers. I like your dad but he can be a perfect prat at times."

She says nothing, but I notice her fist tightening on the tabletop. A contraction?

"Having this baby is the wildest thing I've ever done in my life. Fifty and no husband? I'll tell you the secret I'm not making public. I'm having my ex-husband's child, and even he didn't want me to have it. But I said, my child, my business. What kind of crazy is that? And then along comes your father, a supposedly smart man, and he hits on me." I look up with a smile. "Your dad did tell you all this?"

She shakes her head. "He said you had a situation that the two of you were handling discreetly."

"He said discreetly?" I play a card. "So, you don't know about the fistfight?"

She blinks. "What fight?"

"My ex-husband was being a royal pain a couple of months ago when your father walked in on our discussion. I suppose he thought he was doing the honorable thing by coming to my rescue. I didn't need rescuing, but then it wasn't really about me. They started with accusations but it quickly degenerated into fists."

She snorts. "I knew Dad was lying about running into a door! He's never clumsy. I just thought he was too proud to say he'd been mugged."

"Both came out of it pretty evenly banged up. Men!"

She nods. "Men." And quite unexpectedly she bursts into tears. "I hate them! Hate everyone!"

"Especially Jon." My hands tremble as I pull a few tissues and hand them to her, but one of us has to keep a grip. "You're still furious with Jon."

She takes a moment to mop up. "You know about Jon and me?"

"I know he made a huge, unforgivable mistake, which only a woman who really loves and knows him well enough to believe that he really means it when he says he'll never do it again would forgive—one time."

She sniffs herself back into control. "Was your husband ever unfaithful to you?"

I put my cards down and look her in the eye. "I don't know."

Her expression droops. "You mean no."

"No, I mean I don't know. I never had a reason not to trust him. But I will never know if that trust was ever broken. It's like a not-positive test."

"Mine was. Positive."

"Right!" I say with genuine anger for her. "Jon's a bastard. The bastard!"

Jolie jumps at my tone.

I lean forward, my heart brimming for this lonely

frightened young woman. "I don't know Jon. Maybe he's a generally good guy who got his head stuck in a crack because he was drinking and being an ass, as only a man can. Or maybe he's a coward who thinks bagging women is a male sport alternative. You know him. Only you know whether he'll be a good father and husband, or only drag you down if you let him. Give yourself credit for that, whatever you decide. Know that your instincts are right."

She looks infinitely sad. "I wish someone would fight for me. Jon says he loves me, but he isn't even here." The tears start to flow again.

Right about now I want five minutes alone with Jon so I can box his ears and pull his nose, and yell until he's cowering on the floor! *You asinine human being! This is as good as it gets! This is your moment to be more than you ever thought possible, and you're blowing it! Grow up!*

Since I can't do that, I decide that I, no, *we* need a change of environment.

I stand up. "Are you under bed arrest or can we go downstairs and get a snack?"

The nurse says we can go to the cafeteria but only if Jolie's in a wheelchair, and eats only liquid things. The arrangements are made. Fifteen minutes later we're tooling down the hall when we meet a stunned grandfather-to-be.

"Where are you going?" William stops us just outside the door of the maternity ward, looking like he's interrupting a jailbreak.

"To the best place for girl talk, anywhere that serves food and drink." I push him gently aside. "Go home, or go take care of someone else. We have this covered."

"Yes, Dad." Jolie sounds annoyed to be interrupted. "We're fine."

The look of gratitude he gives me weakens my knees.

Above Jolie's head, I pantomime "Call Jon."

His eyebrows rise. I nod in the affirmative.

★ ★ ★

Once she warms up, Jolie is very much like her dad: interesting, funny and quite smart. I notice her wince once in a while, and surreptitiously watch the clock, but neither of us says a word about what's going on.

We have eaten bowls of red Jell-O and shared a vanilla yogurt, chased by mini cartons of milk, when Jolie suddenly gasps and looks down. We hear a soft *splash* as liquid spills from her wheelchair onto the floor.

I pop up with a big smile. "Congratulations, Jolie! You're going to have a baby."

Her eyes widen with panic. "But I don't want a baby!"

"Sure you do. You want a nice, healthy, happy baby." I stop a passing nurse, point to the wet spot. "Please tell Maternity Jolie Katz is on her way."

I start to push her back the way we came. "Now say to yourself between contractions, 'I'm having a healthy, happy baby. I'm having a healthy, happy baby—'"

"Boy."

"You know it's a boy?"

Jolie nods, but grabs my hand. "I don't think I can go through with this. I can't!"

I stop and move to stand before her. "I know. I felt the same way the first time."

"It's not the pain." She blinks back tears from eyes that are dark with dread. "I know millions of women deliver babies every year. It's not the pain."

I take her face in my hands and say, with the absolute conviction of my own situation, "You're scared because you don't know what to expect. But you do know your life is not going to be quite like it was before. And you'd just as soon stay where you are awhile longer while you try to figure it all out."

She's blinking really fast. "I wish my mother were here."

My heart breaks on those words. "That's how it is. Once you're a mother, someone always wants you. This is your chance to love and protect and be for your child the mom you need."

I must sound hokey as anything but, amazingly, Jolie smiles at me. "I can see why Dad likes you."

"He's had a lot of practice with the irrational, has he?"

There's a bit of a flurry once we return to the maternity wing. Then I'm left sitting in the waiting room while William plays doctor. I skim through piles of useful issues of *Baby, Modern Mother,* and *Child.* Then I skim through adult fare like *Gourmet* and *Architectural Digest.* After that I read whatever comes to hand. After a bottle of water and a package of peanut butter crackers, I realize my work is really done. If I wait on William I could be here until dawn. I should just take a cab to Aunt Marvelle's.

As I reach for my bag I see a young man enter the waiting room. Ordinarily I don't stare at strange young men, but he's something to look at. He's one of those sun-streaked blondes, with a darker sketch of beard that hollows out his cheeks and accentuates the jut of his jaw. His turtleneck sweater hugs a lean torso. His jeans hang on the rim of hips and cup a decent butt. Finally, he realizes I'm staring, and gives me that sort of half smile of recognition for a woman charmed.

I rise, lifted by an impulse too strong to be denied. I approach with a half smile of my own.

He digs his hands into his pockets as I near, head leaning to one side, the whimsy of self-deprecation in his expression, signaling that he's had this happen before, and often. He is about to handle an overture from a smitten woman.

"Jon?" I say in a breathy voice.

His smile widens at my use of his name. "You know me?"

"I know Jolie." I whip back a hand and slap him as hard as I can.

As he yelps and reels away, I sail through the doors that *swish* open at my approach.

"I'm going to need ice for this," I murmur, holding my throbbing palm as I head for one of the cabs parked out front.

41

It's a boy! A perfectly healthy six-pound, eleven-ounce boy.

"Jolie wants to name him William Cuffey Katz!" William's joy sails across wireless space into my ear. "He urinated all over the delivery nurse. Plumbing works. That's excellent!"

"I'm so glad, William. How's Jolie?"

"She was a real trouper. She surprised the doctors and nurses, all of us. I don't know what you said to her, but it worked. When the pains got rough she even refused anesthesia, in case, she said, the baby would need help after delivery. But he didn't. Can you believe it? A first-birthing time of five hours and ten minutes."

"I remember eighteen hours and forty-seven minutes with Dallas. But, who's counting? I knew she could do it."

"There's a few other people I need to call, and then I'm getting out of here. Is it too late to drop by?"

I look at my watch. "No, of course not. I'll be up."

Though it's midnight, Aunt Marvelle and I celebrate

the news by toasting with cups of cocoa. Yes, hers had a dash of Baileys, for medicinal purposes.

"That young man's serious about you," Aunt Marvelle says as we sit listening to the late September wind.

"I like him, too."

"You more than like him, Tallulah. You need to decide, and quickly, what you are going to do about that." She stands up. "Now I'm going to act like an old lady whose bedtime is long past due. Lock up after he leaves. If he stays, lock up, anyway."

Aunt Marvelle is right. It's time I told my feelings to William.

And just like that my joy nosedives.

I overplayed my hand by coming out here uninvited. So what if I did a good job with Jolie? I stepped over that vague but distinct line of noncommittal friendship. Until today, I was simply William's ladyfriend. We were each the person in the other person's private life. The attachment was companionable, simple, easy.

Until today, I had not made it obvious.

I'm in love.

I wince as the weight of my cup hurts my hand.

I love William so much that I'm willing to picks fights in the Maternity waiting room in the name of somebody he loves.

It's so easy to mess up easy.

William's hug lifts me off the floor, baby and all. The kiss is the kind that in the middle of it I think I can't bear for it to end. Only, this time, there has to be retreat. For one thing, I've entered my seventh month. And even I feel funny about sex with an unmarried man under my aunt's roof. Besides, I seem to vaguely recall an earlier resolution to cool off this hot time.

William is over the moon. I sit and listen as he elaborates about the perfection of his newborn grandson, how brave his daughter was, and how happy and relieved he is.

"The obstetrician says Will is small but well formed, and scored nine on his Apgar. He'll grow quickly. I'll bet he walks early."

"He's only a few hours old and you're ready to buy him shoes. Can he just lie there and coo for a few days?"

William laughs. "He can to anything he wants. He's perfect, Lu. Perfect." With him, there's no impossible expectation baggage that usually accompanies that word. This is the ten-toes, ten-fingers garden-variety kind of miracle.

"Now, about you." He stretches his arm along the back of the sofa and smiles at me in a way that makes me want to slide into him. "I don't have the words to thank you for what you did for Jolie. You should have stayed to see Will."

"A good fairy knows when to make an exit."

"You made one hell of an impression on Jon, too!"

I gasp. "How do you know about that?"

"It was pretty obvious something had happened when he walked in with a handprint blazing on his face."

I flex my still-swollen hand and feel again the thrill of my reckless act. I hope he remembers it the next time a woman smiles provocatively at him. "What did Jolie say?"

"Not a word. But you know how it looked. Then Jon started explaining how a pregnant woman in the waiting room attacked him. It was so pathetic that I was ready to put both hands around his neck and squeeze, until Jolie started to laugh. That's when it occurred to me that he'd described you. I went out to look for you. Why did you leave?"

"Righteous retribution doesn't work if the messenger hangs around."

William wags his head. "He's going to have that mark for at least twenty-four hours."

"Sometimes you have to communicate with people on

the level they understand best. Even so, I was tactful. If Jon were *my* son-in-law, I've have used my knee."

"Remind me to never get on your bad side." William reaches for me again. "Right now I want all your good sides showing."

I find myself kissing him back, but we finally pause with mutual understanding that now is not the time for more. When I'm tucked under the protection of his arm he says, "I'll be a wonderful grandfather, don't you think?"

"I think William is the luckiest kid in the world."

"I make a pretty good Dad, too." His expression changes in a way that lets me know he's thinking now about me and only about me.

Antsy about that, I turn out of his arms and reach for my cocoa. "So then, how did Jon behave when he saw his son?"

"He looked stunned and stupefied, as if he didn't know Jolie was pregnant."

"Some men can't make the leap until it's a done deal."

"I hope you're right. There he was when I left, cuddled up with Jolie and Will as if nothing had ever happened between them."

I arch my back, straining to relieve tension in tired muscles. "I'm glad, for all three of them."

William grunts. "We'll see. Just before I left, I pulled him aside and told him if he planned to stay with Jolie and the baby in the hospital, then he better be prepared to take on that responsibility for good. He's a father. It's time he acted like a man."

"And he said?"

"He said if Jolie can forgive him, I ought to." William starts a slow rubbing of my back, low down where I need it most. "Looks like my life and my house are my own again."

It's too good. I move a little away, as though I've had

enough of his magic massage. "I hope you'll enjoy your well-deserved solitude."

"I don't have to be alone to be happy." As his arms slide around my belly from behind, I feel every inch of me respond. It's not sexual, exactly. It's more intimate, as if I know I'm being touched by something fundamentally good and right. The urge to merge is more amoeba-like, cell into cell, asexual mating. That's probably bad biology, but I swear it feels as if our skins dissolve a little one into the other each time we touch.

He leans close to press his lips against my ear. "I'm thinking it's a good time for us to get a few things straight."

"William, it's not really—"

"Lu, marry me."

Whoa! Wait a minute! He skipped steps two, three, and four; mutual declarations of love, living together perhaps, at least one breakup and reconciliation. One of us has to be practical. But I have to leave his persuasive embrace before I can think even halfway straight. I stand and move a few feet away. "William, that's just euphoria talking."

"Okay." He grins at me and stands up. "Maybe I'm jumping ahead. But we know where this is going. I love you, Lu."

"Me, too." I can't help smiling. "I love you." But as he advances I hold up a hand to fend him off. "But that's beside the point."

"That is the point." He smiles so tenderly I want to smack him. "We're good together. We've known it from that first night in May."

"That was just sex. Very good—okay, incredible sex. And it's all been good ever since." I wish he would stop grinning as if he'd like to prove to me again right now. "But that's just sex, William."

"I like you even when you don't sleep with me."

Because I can't think of a good defense for that, I begin

to pace. "You're forgetting I have a weird life. I'm doing a tell-all in a magazine. And I have Dwarves."

"They'll back off once they see I'm in charge of the Care for Lu department."

"What about our families? Dallas and Davin haven't completely accepted the divorce. Now there's a new family member on the way. If I announce I'm remarrying, they may just revoke my mother license."

"They're adults. Eventually they will accept that you're entitled to a life, like any other person. After what you did for her, Jolie already thinks of you as family."

He's so reasonable. I pace harder, hoping active leg muscles will squeeze the blood back up into my brain instead of letting it seep down into more treacherous regions. "I've been divorced less than a year. What makes you think I want to marry again?"

He spread his arms. "Maybe it's the way you look at me. Or the way you back up against me in bed in the middle of the night and then pat my thigh when you find me. Or the way you smile in your dreams."

"How do you know I do that?"

"I watch you sometimes." He reaches out to hold me in place. "I feel like an ass telling you that. But I don't know how to be careful around you. With you it's as if I've woken up from a bad dream that's consumed a lot of my life."

"Maybe what you feel is just rebound." The blood is going both to my head and loins so fast that I feel woozy. "We've both had a couple of tough years. We could simply be having a mutual gratitude affair. And then in a few months, we'll look at each other and go *yeech!*"

"Never going to happen." He touches me "that way" again, placing his finger on that spot just below my breastbone just like he did that first night. "There's nothing to keep us from being very happy together, Lu."

Just as I'm about to say *You're absolutely right! Screw the world!* Sweet Tum sneezes, or hiccups. And I remember the best reason of all for not giving in.

"I'm having another man's child."

"Yes, I noticed." He looks down at my belly and says, "I'll adopt your child."

I wrest free of his hands. "See, that's what I mean. You don't even know what you're saying." I fold my arms atop my bulge and say, "You've been surrounded by pregnant women for months. No wonder you think you're in love. It's a reaction to all that maternal nesting, hormonal fall-out. You've got estrogen poisoning."

He laughs. "And you just stopped making sense."

"Aha!" I'm grabbing at straws and I don't even know why. "One of the things I like best about being divorced is that at the end of the day, I can be totally irrational without apology under my own roof."

At last he looks a bit doubtful. "Maybe it wasn't a good idea to discuss this tonight. It's just that you came out here without me even asking to help my daughter through the most difficult day of her life. Then, slapping Jon around—" I watch him try to make sense of it all, but he just ends up smiling again. "I thought we had something that didn't need rules or schedules or logic or any of that crap that makes life miserable."

I want to fly into his arms and sob that I love him so much it makes me stupid, and how I don't want to be ir-rational all alone. That I pat his thigh in the middle of the night because then I know he's solidly there, not just a wish in my head. That I need him desperately, and will prob-ably die lonely, unloved and pathetic if he's not with me.

But I'm scared.

I know from hard experience how even with the best intentions the day-to-day slog through modern life can pervert feelings. I'm scared of becoming another mistake that we will have to live with. The new Lu is too new. She's gelatin. If I'm not careful she will melt away.

My anxiety crystallizes into one complete thought. "What if you are the one I chose just because you were there at the time?"

For a moment he looks stunned. And I know this is a thought he's not had before, but one he's too smart not to consider now that it's on the table.

But he doesn't ask. He just rubs his forehead as though he's wearier than dirt. "I guess I got carried away with the moment. I should go. You need to be in bed." He kisses my cheek quickly. "Good night, Lu."

I hope he didn't see me tearing up before he walked out because I'm in overflow as the door slams. Too tired and miserable to take it all to the privacy of my bed, I sit on Aunt Marvelle's sofa and sob out loud like a six-year-old.

What kind of woman throws away a declaration of love from the right man? A deranged pregnant one.

But I'm so very tired of being there, and being what other people need. I'm good at it. I'm just tired.

After a few minutes I hear footsteps, and look up to see Aunt Marvelle crossing the room to the front door.

"I'm not saying a thing about that. Not one thing. But I could." She flips the dead bolt and turns back the way she came.

42

"That's right. A spa vacation. I came in for a checkup yesterday and requested a physician's permission slip to fly! I needed it today. T-o-d-a-y. Can't you people get anything right?" I slam down the phone.

I'm cranky. Ask anyone who's had to deal with me this past week. Even Tai backed off lobbying for the "nude" photo shoot Curran had the audacity to mention to her. Since his artsy pictures of me started appearing in *Five-O*, he's had some overtures from other magazine and photography agencies. His boat has been launched. Now he wants more, of me, just when I'm feeling the need to hide away from the world.

When he arrived just now for our formal weekly photo session, I wouldn't let him in.

He did a really good job of making me feel his pain. It's one of those drizzly early-fall days with an icicle feel in the wind. Yet there he was, in a cotton shirt that flapped about his rangy body like a flag. "Come on, Lu! Let me in."

I twitched the living room curtain aside and beckoned

him closer with a curled finger. When he was practically nose to glass, I said, "Curran, dearest? Go to hell!"

I hear knocking again. I'm sure he went to enlist aid from Cy.

Sure enough, when I stop practicing a drum-line rhythm with my pencil on the tabletop and concede I will have to answer the onslaught at my door, I see the silhouettes of two men in the glass.

I smile as I hear them fiddling with my lock. Ever-vigilant Cy doesn't know everything. His key no longer fits. I had the locks changed after they accosted William.

"You, old man!" I shout from ten feet away, "Go home! You, young man! Get lost!"

"It's the eighth month," I hear Cy tell Curran. "Mothers-to-be start getting testy about this time."

Testy is scarcely the word. I'm furious! With myself, with my world, with—oh, joy, my hair! The reflection in the hall mirror is of a robed woman who slept hard, and didn't brush afterward.

"The pregnant woman's on strike!" I shout as I move nearer the door, my cow booties *mooing* with every step. Hey, when you go to seed, I say go all the way.

"Step away from the door. There are no more gal-pal, buddy-buddy, social-escort services available on these premises. I free you! Flee! Find women your own ages to harass!"

Curran puts both hands to the glass and tries to peer in. "Lu, don't be trippin'. You're messing with a brother's future."

"This is my world, squirrel! You're just trying to get a nut." I'm not certain I got that expression quite right, but I like the way it sounds.

"She's gone all diva on us. Think like she's sick or sumthin'?" Curran asks in a worried tone. "Maybe we should drop a dime on that doc."

I press my nose to the glass opposite his. "Stop annoying this demented diva, and drop that dime on a female who wears hip-huggers and a navel ring. Faint heart never won fairly weird maid. Get thee gone, forsooth, the soother the better!"

Cy raps on the glass, as if I'm not already paying attention. "Lu, this is Cy. Open the door. Otherwise, I'll have to take action, for your own good."

He means he'll call Aunt Marvelle or Dallas, or worse, William.

"You leave the newlyweds alone. Have you no decency? And Aunt Marvelle has a cold. Call Dr. Templeton, and I will put the house on the market. I'm going away, far away, where there's sun and sand. And I swear, if you don't both scrambola this instant, I'm never coming back."

"She must have got Tai to okay the spa deal," Curran says to his co-irritant.

"So, maybe we should back off?" Cy answers.

"Yes. Be a mensch, Cy, and back off. Take—" I hear my phone.

I shuffle back to the kitchen to pick up, checking the caller ID. It's Tai. This call I want.

"It's a lock, Lu. Your reservation at the resort is set. Ten days of absolute decadence in the desert. A courier is running the plane tickets over. Enjoy!"

"Thank you. Oh, and don't bother to contact me. I won't respond!"

I sit back and prop my feet on a chair. My ankles aren't what they used to be. If I don't watch it they balloon by noon. But I'm too pleased by Tai's news to stay in Cruella DeVil mode. Tomorrow I'm going where no one knows me, and better still will expect nothing of me.

43

Resort means hope, to have a chance, where to turn for help, where to seek refuge, the ultimate means of relief. I've resorted to the desert, and it becomes me.

Every woman I know has done the occasional spa day at a mall store. This is altogether different. I'm nine days into a sustained body-and-soul experience meant to alter one's view of life. I've been strategically slathered, steeped and basted, and generally made to feel my flesh is my best friend.

This spa even offers a specialized regimen for safely pampering the expectant mother and child. In addition to being loofahed, waxed and buffed, I've lain supine on a massage table built for the body of a mother-to-be while an expert in such matters has massaged me into a spreadable-on-toast state of relaxation.

Sweet Tum loves it, too. I'm certain she will be born a total Epicurean. Yes, it's a girl. I had a dream the third night here. Sweet Tum is a she.

More than that, I know that she and I will be our own happy family unit.

It was simple. All I needed was a time in a place to think only my thoughts. Even a thing as miraculous as love can be an intruder at certain times in one's life.

In the middle of the night after I ran William off, it dawned on me that I've been thinking of myself as the consummate adult, coping and moving forward in my life. What I've really been doing is walking on eggs, trying to maintain a version of the status quo. You know you're in trouble when you need Latin to describe your life.

From the moment Jacob disconnected, I tried to address the feelings and concerns of everyone even remotely connected to me. "It's okay. It's all right. We're fine." By now, I've probably said this to pieces of furniture and my car.

First there were Davin and Dallas to coddle through the divorce. Then Jacob's need "to be sure," followed by his desire not to be a father again. Let's not forget Tai and her expectations. And then, of course, there's Curran, Cy and even William. Within the past fortnight, I've married off a daughter, and talked someone else's child through birth. Who haven't I tried to please in the name of good human being?

Me.

I hadn't a clue about what I wanted because I haven't been able to shut out the voices of those dear sweet others. Here, alone, it was so easy.

I do love William. Maybe he's the best XY-chromosome combination to ever walk through my world. But at the moment he's not the one to whom I owe my full-time allegiance or all-out efforts. Neither are Dallas and Davin.

I cannot hope for better results than my first two kids. What I have this time around, in place of plenty of youth and a partner, is experience.

For now and the immediate future, my full-out interest will be showing this being I carry the "aha" elements of this world. I've lots of plans for her. For instance, monthly trips to Manhattan when she is old enough…two sounds like a good beginner's age. We will visit aquariums, zoos and museums. Later on, perhaps age three, art galleries and stage shows. We will shop and trek and have lunch in trendy places, ignoring the stares or envy of others. We will learn Japanese and Spanish, and then travel to places where we can use it, like Kyoto and San Antonio. Life will be an adventure, because I have time now to do more.

I've begun making notes. And I often smile because what I write is gleaned from grandparents and aunts and uncles, and all the other wonderful ordinary life-size household human deities who have made my life a wonder. I even jotted down a few of Aunt Marvelle's Marvelous Matrons' witticisms. Some won't be appropriate for Sweet Tum for years. But they'll be there when she most needs them, even if I'm not. That's not being morbid, that's being real.

Now, about me. I will continue to dye my hair. Vanity is good when it's on a leash. To lift or not? Who knows? I say no, but in a decade or two I may want to open my eyes without needing props like toothpicks. I can't tell from here.

And it's a relief to acknowledge that. If I don't know, I've got options!

Meanwhile, at the spa I'm content to sit and watch the world of the shamelessly indulged pass by. I often go all day without speaking to a single soul who isn't directly connected to enhancing my pleasure zone. That suits me.

October

I know he's a good man.
You know he's a good man.
My bad days are when *he* knows he's a good man
—Katherine Hepburn, *State of the Union.*

**—"Katherine, The Oh-So Great"
CUE LU!**

44

"Lu, I know you're angry. I don't know why you're angry. Just be angry at me in a way I can understand."

I smile as I punch Delete and move on to the next message. There are fifty of them. Far and away, William's outnumber all others combined.

"So, I guess you're not back yet. I talked with Cy. I'm sorry. I don't know what—"

I punch Delete.

"This is ridiculous. We're both grown-ups. At least give me—"

"For God's sake, Lu! I—"

"Look. I'm sorry, I—"

I hang up.

This record of pain bothers me. I've been rude, callous and selfish, deliberately refusing to ease the suffering of someone I love. Of that I'm now certain. But I'm not sure what I should do about that. I'm in flux. I've been home two days. It took me that long to decide to listen in on the world I left behind. Today I'm going into

work with a new outlook, and a new plan. I need time
to adjust to this new sense of me.

The phone rings as I turn away. I hesitate and then push
the speaker button but don't speak.

"Lu? It's William. I care. I'll wait."

"Thank you." I hang up. Good man, my William. I hope
he'll be as understanding when he learns about what I'm
planning to do next.

I scarcely have both feet off the elevator before I register the mortuary silence. There's not a soul anywhere to
be seen in either direction except for Babs, who never
deserts her post. "Did I miss the fire-drill announcement?"

"It's a three-alarm blaze!" Babs zooms up to me with
a *shrrrr* and then a small squeak of her brakes. "Haven't
you seen it?"

"Seen what?"

She motions me to follow her over to and behind her
desk. She picks up and unfolds a daily tabloid, out of sight
of anyone who might pass by. Slim chance of that. The
hall echoes with absence. "This is about our fearless leader.
You won't believe it."

She looks both ways before whispering, "It seems our
sweet young thing, isn't."

"I never thought Tai was sweet." Still, I take the paper
and scan the page until Babs points out the column.

Ever wondered why *Bling,* the essential magazine for
the style-consumed urban influential jettisoned its
twentysomething guru, **Tai Leigh**? Here's a clue.
That purveyor of forward-focus, youth-obsessed editorial style just celebrated her *(shush!)* **fortieth** b'day!
But who's counting? And that's not all…

"Whaddaya know?" I might have read this bit of nas-
tiness four months ago and not blinked. But I've learned

a few things since about Tai. We will never be close, but she did give me a chance to save my career when not twelve other editors in a dozen would have done the same. She has class, and the kind of savvy this backstab is meant to undercut.

I look up at Babs. "How's she taking it?"

Babs's eyes roll. "She's in her office. Told me if her phone rings, I'm fired."

"That doesn't sound like all-access all-the-time Tai." I hand the newspaper back to Babs. "Who needs to be thirty again? Right?"

Babs shrugs. "What do I know? I wish I were sixty again." Then she blinks. "But you. You look...so different!"

I wink. "Desert heat."

"No, I mean you look 'so different' good. You're younger, thinner, prettier."

"All for the reasonable price of ten Gs at a first-class spa."

"On you, it looks like a million!"

Who knows what makes a person think she can offer aid to someone she doesn't know well enough to ring at home? Tai's worse than a total stranger—she's my boss.

This debate with myself goes for a whole five seconds while I stand outside her office. Then I hear, "Get away from my friggin' door!" Sounds like an invite to me.

I knock lightly and turn the knob. Just in case she's waiting to heave a heavy object, I call out, "Incoming pregnant woman!"

Tai is, as usual, standing. She looks, as always, glorious in a slim miniskirt and a one-button, cut-away jacket that leaves her navel bare, and no doubt about the fact that she's not wearing a bra. The thick, wild bangs are more ruffled than usual. Otherwise, nothing is different. Even her superior smirk is in place.

"That isn't the reason I left *Bling*! Bastards!"

"I didn't think so." Interesting. After a two-week absence, she assumes I'm here about her. She's right, of course. "Does the truth matter? You got column inches."

"What?" I guess she was expecting sympathy.

I slide myself into the narrow wedge of one of her modern chairs. "I'm genuinely curious. What's wrong with being forty?"

She lunges forward, both hands flat on her pristine desktop. "It's as simple as this. No one looks at a woman of forty."

I can't help it. I laugh. "I look at you. We all look at you. Every day. With great green envy. And that's just us hens. Men? Men get whiplash looking at you."

"That's because they didn't fucking know how old I was."

"So, you're eight, nine years older than everyone thought. So what?"

"I recently went out with a guy who's twenty-seven. He teased me about being an older woman. Can you imagine he'd even have spoken to me if he knew the truth?"

"Sorry." I shake my head. "I'm channeling Demi and what's-his-face."

"Demi has had everything lifted, tucked, vacuumed and buffed. And she's got leverage in Hollywood. But you're the lifestyle editor for accepting the inevitable." She folds her long, lean arms. "You tell me. How do you remain smug when all you have to look forward to is wrinkles, sagging boobs and old men—if you can find them."

"Did you know that if an Australian widow is young and sexy, her accidental-death compensation can be reduced because she's supposedly more likely to remarry? That's a scary precedent, and a reason for married women to let themselves go. And, contrary to rumor, many men like older women, even the un-engineered kind."

"Yes, you would say that. You have no choice. I do—did." She makes a sound like a sob. "They even printed my real name! Bertha Leighton."

Bertha? I suppose I should have finished the column. And to think I have issues with Tallulah.

Tai resumes pacing, and it's like watching a kettle coming to a boil. I swear I see a whiff of steam before she boils over. "That bastard Marc told them!"

There's no point in asking why Marc would be so vicious. People who do these things don't need reasons, just opportunities. More to the point, "How did he find out?"

Tai runs her fingers through her bangs. "It had to be that he read the birthday card my mother sent me. It's one of those awful cards that says 'Happy 40th' right on the front!"

"That's unfortunate."

"Exactly, which is why I left it at my apartment." She reaches out to smooth the top of her teakwood desk, as if it had a wrinkle. "In a bedroom drawer, between the layers of my underwear."

"But that's awful!" I'm referring to Marc digging through her undies, not her need to hide a birthday card.

"Bastard!" Tai begins again. "He waited a couple of months to try to throw me off, but I know it was him. I fired him. So sue *Five-O.* Sue me. Why kill my career?"

"Jealousy?"

"Of course that. If you want to reach the top you need to have more secrets than the competition." She comes around in front of her desk. "I knew Marc bloodied the waters wherever he went, but in doing so he brought attention. Unfortunately, his ability to generate a buzz is overrated. Completely. He wasn't even good in bed."

"He's a first-class bastard!" I say in support of womanhood scorned. "But there is truth in that old saying, Tai. 'You knew he was a snake when you brung him in.'"

Tai blinks. "I've never heard that."

"You've heard similar. Play with fire... Dance with the devil... If you lie down with dogs...?"

She folds her arms across her bosom and leans back in that impossibly swayback stance that only the long and lean can achieve. "Your cozy comments aren't helpful."

"You have a point. The milk's been spilt." She nods. "So how are you going to handle this?"

"I'm not. I can't respond without confirming that the story is true."

I stand up. That chair is so uncomfortable that being on my feet is preferable. "Of course, it's your life. But I would just hate it if everyone's last thought about me was that I'm a coward."

Tai tosses her head at that word. "I suppose you're now about to bore me with some other shit piece of disgustingly uplifting and wise advice."

I smile. "Did you ever hear the one about taking your skeletons out of the closet and setting them in the front window as advertisement?"

She just stares at me.

"Then let me confess this. I know how sorry everyone has felt for poor old screwed and abandoned Lu. There hasn't been so much head-shaking over a lost cause since little Ollie North thought he should run for president. The truth is, none of you know a thing about the real me." I smile big. "Since I became pregnant, I've taken a lover, been proposed to by another man, and had a guy in his twenties following me about like a puppy."

Tai smirks. "You've obviously been fantasizing while reading your e-mail."

I smile. "If it's spun right, not even the truth will be believed. So tell your truth and see where it gets you."

Tai actually takes a moment to think. "You're saying a great offense is better than a great defense. Therefore I should—"

"Actually, I was thinking more of—"

"I could leak it that poor Marc hoped to sandbag his drooping rep by screwing me, but—news flash!—he's a lousy lay. I bet I can get backup for that. I know a woman he dated—"

"That's not—"

"Oh, but that's good!" Tai has a really nasty laugh.

I think my work is done here.

As I'm leaving she calls out, "Lu! You look fabulous! But I don't believe that crap about your boyfriends. Still, if you put it in your column, I'll print it."

45

I've decided to pose "starkers" after all, as they say in Jolly Olde England.

The word to describe this act is important to me. "Nude" invokes taut, nubile flesh. "Naked" sounds like every super-sized pore and ingrown hair will be featured in 3-D Technicolor. In the case of its country cousin, "nekkid," kegs of beer are involved. "Bare" can only truly be effective when applied to a baby's bottom. "In the buff" has a mellow groovy vibe, such that mind-altering drugs may be involved.

No, only "starkers" works, as in stark raving mad, but joyous about it.

I've told only those it immediately involves. Curran, obviously. And KaZi, for makeup, prop placement and artistic value. Curran's hired the studio and a lighting specialist because he has ideas that require exacting standards, he said. Said person is required to be female, I replied. I told Dallas to keep the sisterhood of mothers and daughters tight. She was silent. I consider that a victory.

"Thanks for everything," I say as Cy pulls up before the photographer's studio. I asked him to drive me because the numb-leg problem that floored me at the wedding has returned with more frequency. My doctor revoked my driving privileges until after delivery.

"I'll find a place to park and be right up," he says as he helps me out.

"Oh, you don't need to wait around here. I'll call when I'm ready."

Cy shakes a finger at me. "I'm no Peeping Tom, but someone should be the chaperone, to keep things professional. You can't run around in the altogether alone with a young Tom like Curran. People will talk."

"I'm not alone."

"And you're not going to be!" Which means Cy will sit on the studio steps in the rain if I don't let him in.

"Fine. But, Cy, not one word. No matter what you see or hear or even think. Understood?"

Cy shrugs. "What do I know about nudie pictures? I'm an old man."

"Not that old." I feel myself blush. "You really want to do this?"

He looks positively eager. "When will I get another chance to risk being picked up in a police raid?"

"I don't have to tell you how weird this feels, having someone put makeup all over me."

"All actors do it for nude scenes," KaZi says matter-of-factly, as she applies opaque makeup to my torso with a chamois-like puff. "Men are more insistent about it than women. Talk about ego. I could name names of the A-list actors who won't even take their shirts off without time in the makeup chair first. Contoured pecs and all. It's a psychological trick for confidence. You know you're covered head to foot, yet everything shows."

Not quite everything. Strategic covering will be required. For instance, I'm holding a towel to my front, which she's finished, while she does my back.

"You're in pretty good shape for your age," KaZi says as she stands back to get a perspective on her work. "You've got a nice strong back, not much cellulite on the thighs and really nice calves."

I'm really touched by her generous statement. "Thank you."

"Squat," she commands, and begins to shellac areas I don't even put suntan lotion on. "This is super-good stuff. It's used as a surgical cosmetic. It'll cover every kind of defect: scars, burns, freckles, moles, tan lines, stretch marks, birth marks, age spots, even those big blue veins on your breasts. Pregnancy is, like, so weird!"

It occurs to me that we're not after reality here, but rather a state of mind. As with all photographic efforts, like prom photos, what the poser really wants is a record of the essence of the moment. My body, only better, as it will seem in retrospect.

When she's done, I'm dusted with anti-aging powder. "For that natural look. Now, give yourself about fifteen minutes to dry and you can put on a loose robe. But don't sit or tie the sash. That will rub off the makeup."

"You ready?" Curran calls from the other side of the door after a few minutes.

Am I ready? The adrenaline rush is instantaneous. I begin to hyperventilate.

"Breathe slow, slower," I hear KaZi say at my shoulder.

I take a deep breath, a really deep breath. But I only get about half inflated before Sweet Tum thumps in protest. "Okay, okay," I say, and smooth a hand over the area.

"Watch the makeup," KaZi warns.

I remind myself I'm doing this not for any reason but that I want to. It's not vanity. It's not an act of defiance, or provocation, certainly not sleazy titillation or even simply to be outrageous. It's a conscious decision to put me out there, on the line, in the light. Just me. And Sweet Tum. In about twenty years she will understand. Or, just maybe, she will need to be on the upside of forty to fully grasp the audacious joy of Eve before the fig-leaf police arrived.

"I guess we're as ready as we're ever going to be."

The studio is the typical slant roof loft with a wall of high windows for natural lighting. Curran has set up a series of backdrops and props—like a crib, a rocker, gigantic blocks and a desk. "Desk?"

"You are a writer, after all," Curran says as he leads me to the chair behind it. "Now, take your time, Lu. I need you to relax. See the heaters? They will be turned on the moment you disrobe. You don't want goose bumps or a case of the shivers. Just take your time. Feel your way into the moment, into the space."

"Uh huh. You just go over there, on the other side," I say, for suddenly my teeth are chattering like castanets.

It's not only me. Curran is speaking Standard English, and chewing his soul patch as his gaze darts from me to KaZi as if he's watching Ping-Pong. She shrugs and turns away.

Cy sits in a corner opposite me, pretending to be reading the paper. It's a cliché, but it really is upside down.

I try to think positively as I slowly push aside one corner of my robe, exposing a shoulder. How bad can it be? If the pictures stink, only we four will ever know they existed. Tai hasn't a clue!

The staccato raps on the studio door send us all to our feet in alarm.

"Police," I hear Cy mutter. It's so improbable that even I release giddy laughter.

Curran goes to see and comes back moments later with— "Dallas?"

She comes across quickly to me while I hurriedly cover my naked shoulder. "Mom! Am I too late?"

"No. But what are you doing here?" I told her about the shoot. No more evading my truths, but I never expected her presence.

"I thought you might need a few things." She holds out a large wicker basket. "I've brought bottles of water, grapes, your favorite Brie and crackers, a shawl and slippers. Oh, and a bottle of Black Cashmere. Its spicy scent is the kind you like."

"That's so sweet, Dallas. But I thought you didn't approve of this."

She gives me a "duh" look. "I don't. But I have to, do I?"

She smiles. I smile. "No. You don't."

"So, then. I thought you should know that I do support you, even your right to be inappropriately outrageous."

"In that case, I guess we're ready."

Dallas looks around. "Where's the music?"

"What?"

"You can't have a shoot without music," she says with great authority. "Everyone knows that."

Curran looks sheepish. "I thought Lu wouldn't want it. Do you?"

I shrug. "What have you got?"

It turns out he's got a lot. He has a portable Bose and about a dozen CDs, everything from old-school Luther to Floetry to OutKast. Their cut, "I Like the Way You Move," quickly becomes a favorite of the day.

The first poses are a bit awkward, as I try to get into the Zone while keenly aware that all that stands between my ta-tas and the two gentlemen in the room is a copy of "What to Expect When You're Expecting." Sweet Tum bulges beneath the book until the desk cuts her off, hiding my draped lap area while the keyhole allows my bare crossed legs to show.

For a while Dallas is very restrictive about Curran's area

of operation. He's accustomed to spinning around me at all angles as if he wears skates. Today, he's kept at a latitude of about forty-five degrees. Even then she *"uh-uhs"* him whenever he bends too low or rises too high for her comfort. As a result, I don't have to worry about covering my rear, literally and figuratively. Pretty soon, I'm laughing and smiling and giving Curran what he calls the "money shots."

As we move from desk to rocker, I discover that Dallas's oversize crocheted shawl offers me better coverage and does less damage to KaZi's artwork than the wrapper. Yet it is October so the portable heaters are never far from me.

Before I know it the music has thawed the room. Curran and KaZi are trading friendly insults, and Dallas is dancing with Cy, who, by the way, does a mean cha-cha.

I get frequent breaks, drink lots of hot tea—sorry, Dallas, no ice water. The grapes and cheese are another matter. I consume them as if I haven't eaten in a week. I guess bodaciousness burns a lot of calories.

At the end of the day, my little covey of friends has bonded. Dallas has offered KaZi advice on stock options. Cy and Curran, already like father and son, are discussing art galleries in SoHo and NoHo.

And me? I'm just so giddy-girl pleased I kept faith with my ambition to risk it all. Just because I could.

46

"Oprah?"

"Her people." Tai says this in a tone that makes clear the distinction.

"They've been keeping up with your column. They want to know if you're going to continue it because they're thinking of doing a show on late-life motherhood after the first of the year. With you as the journalistic authority. *Five-O*'s very own Lu on *Oprah!* Wouldn't that be fabulous?"

"That would be fabulous." The winning lottery ticket would be fabulous, too. Maybe it's just my size, but I feel very anchored to reality these days.

I shift the phone from one ear to the other. "After the first of the year, you say? I couldn't possibly agree to come back to work until my maternity leave ends in February. That includes traveling to Chicago."

"I told them. They are completely okay with it. They need time to book celebrity late-life moms. They mentioned Geena Davis and Julianne Moore. And they want the baby to come with you. Which is fabulous! I hear Oprah treats all her guests so well."

"Chicago in February. Isn't that a lot like Anchorage in February?"

"We'll get a *Five-O* advertiser to loan a fur coat. Two furs, mother/child furs."

Sooner or later, I just knew Tai would get around to putting me in fur.

"Speaking of which, how is our little cash cow? No offense, Lu."

"None taken." I've seen my reflection in the bathroom mirror. "She's fine."

"Here's one other little tidbit for you to tuck away. As you must know, *Five-O*'s parent company owns, among other things, both new-mother and pregnancy mags. I've gotten requests to loan you out as a guest columnist."

"And you said?"

"I told them they'll have to pay. *Always* make them pay." And that's why she's the boss. "I've put the higher-ups on notice, too. We've improved market share, widened our demographics—and that's just the beginning. You should be getting a bonus check this week that will make you smile. I had no idea the size of the market for schmaltz among the over-forty set...." She goes on in this vein for a short while.

She finally winds down. "Thanks to that 'Little-Smoky' Marc, *Five-O* and I were mentioned recently on *Leno,* something really snide and dismissive about my age. But, Lu, *Leno!* I faxed them a clever comeback, and they've asked me to be a plant in the audience next week!"

"Marc must be making wee-wee in his shorts because he can't take credit."

"Exactly! You were so right. So, if there's anything you need, anything at all..."

"I'll think about it. The columns. *Oprah.* After."

"Lu, I think you're fabulous! Absolutely brilliant!"

After I hang up I take a deep breath. What I really am is down for the count. On maternity leave for two weeks already, I've got about two weeks to go to my due date.

"You're not a youngster," my doctor said the other day. "You need complete relaxation. No trials or strain, no stress. You've come this far without trouble. Let's keep it that way."

It's Halloween. It's clear but cold, with a sharp north wind and the smell of unseasonably early snow in the air. It's the kind of weather that used to make Dallas and Davin very nervous, because coats and hats and mittens might be involved after dark, ruining the fear factor of really great costuming.

These days, the weather doesn't affect me. I'm more or less under house arrest. Against my wishes, but to be perfectly safe, Andrea has moved in with me until further notice. Mother wanted to, but we'd drive each other nuts. Aunt Marvelle offered, but the relief in her voice when I declined confirmed my right thinking. Cy, bless him, is my chauffeur. Well, actually, his chauffeur is my chauffeur. I place a call, he comes to get me. Cy does the grocery shopping. I go to the doctor. I'm living large, in more ways than one.

So most days, I sit and read, watch movies Curran brings by, along with bags of Kettle Korn and steaming cups of decaf mocha java. Occasionally I jot down a brilliant statement.

I'm writing a book. Sort of. Most days I feel too dumb to do more than breathe. Eventually it's going to be a kind of reference guide for "late bloomers," women over fifty who now have the time to search for the meaning of their lives.

Today I'm pondering a lecture I once heard by Joseph Campbell. If I remember correctly, he said that the quest for individual freedom once belonged to the aged. In other words, for millennia, the search for self-fulfillment by a "me" generation was conducted by the arthritic and gray. And then marketing got involved.

I'm pondering the modern juxtaposition of "quest now pay later" when the phone rings. Usually I check to see who's calling, but Campbell has a way of taking you away, rather like Calgon, only better.

"Hello, Lu."

"William." William! "How are you? Is everything okay with Jolie and Will?"

"All okay. I called to ask about you."

"Oh, absolutely divine. Eating bonbons, drinking champagne, lying on the deck sunning myself. Expecting a few close personal friends in for dinner. Jack, Julia, Denzel. The usual."

It's good to hear his laughter. We talked, finally, the day after the infamous photo shoot. I told him I needed space, and he needed to get out there, date someone else. Get a perspective. Then in about six months, if he wanted, we'd talk again. I've tried not to think about what I'd do if that call didn't happen.

"You sound the same, Lu. But how are you really?"

"I'm fine. Really." I pause to suck in a breath as a false labor contraction reaches its peak. I've been having them on and off for a week. "Doctor has me on rest, basically. I'm due in two, but it might be sooner, as I'm bigger than a humvee."

"You sound a little weird now."

"Just a muscle spasm." Ouch! That sucker hurts! "I get them a lot lately. Eating bananas for potassium."

"In that case, I've called to report in."

"Let me guess. You've been dating." Why I think this is amusing I don't know. Lately, my emotions are random. I cry while watching comedies and laugh hysterically at tragedy.

"Yes. I've been dating. A lot. Speed-dating, uber-dating. Three, four a weekend."

Why am I chuckling? "Good for you."

"Yeah, that's what I thought." He sounds annoyed. "I hate it."

I get such a kick from that statement that I have to take a breath to calm my voice before I say, "Oh, I'm sorry to hear that."

"I'm glad you're sorry. It's your fault. I see this really great woman, beautiful, rich—"

"Younger?"

"Always younger. Sometimes decades younger—"

Okay, I deserved that, after the way I treated him.

"And all I can think about while staring into her baby blues, or almond browns, is that she isn't you."

"That must make the sex really boring." I hold my breath to smother the giggling. I'm gonna need a shrink before this is over.

"No, the sex is good."

"Oh." There was sex! For some reason my laughter still pours forth in frothy teenage ripples. I put him out there. I kicked him to the curb. I can't rant and rave just because one woman's trash is another woman's treasure. Except I knew he was wonderful, funny, sexy, smart and an all-mine treasure.

"You certainly are taking this well." He sounds really ticked now, the person having all the sex.

"Sorry. I'm sure you'll find the right woman soon." And I will hate her with everything in me for the rest of my life.

"I already have. A really great woman. She was a friend to Linda. Not best friend, but the same-type friend." And familiarity is so very seductive to a man who wants to be a twosome. "She's invited me to go with a few friends to Fiji in February."

"Oh, now that sounds like fun." If only I weren't gagging on my words. The giggles are gone.

"I don't know. Will is still so young. I'd miss a lot if I were gone a month."

A month! The heifer! She wants to close the deal while they're gone. She plans to come back engaged-to-be Mrs. Templeton. "Sounds like a long time to lie on the beach."

"Oh, we won't get there for weeks. We're sailing."

Not she's sailing, or they're sailing, but "we're" sailing. I feel nauseous. "Be sure to take Dramamine along. Even experienced sailors get seasick from time to time."

"Okay, well, maybe this call wasn't a good idea—"

"No, I'm really glad to hear from you. Glad—"

"Because I was going to suggest dropping by."

"You're in New Jersey?"

"At a medical seminar. And I thought, if you weren't busy, I'd drop by afterward. I've got pictures of Will I thought you'd like to see."

"I'd love to see the pictures." And—*I love you*. Can't say that. So I better get off in a hurry. "What time?"

For about two minutes I run around in all directions. But the clutter is more than I can manage. I waddle to the phone, punch in the number for what I call emergency housekeeping. Two minutes later I've agreed to pay double the usual amount to have service complete before 5:00 p.m.

I bath, dress and call the chauffeur to take me to get my hair done. I've been meaning to do this, anyway. Didn't want to go to the delivery room looking like a bag lady. I even get my legs waxed while I'm there. It's a holdover from the spa experience. I've come to believe that a certain amount of pampering is just what every woman needs. Add to that the fact that I can't see my toes, let alone trim and paint them, pedicures just fit into my lifestyle.

By five o'clock I look like a very well groomed, delicious-smelling pregnant elephant. I forgot to eat but I'm not feeling especially hungry. I'm kind of queasy and sort of achy. The practice contractions have slowed and no longer hurt, but getting up and down and in and out takes concentration and effort. I'm exhausted.

Doorbell. Curran.

"Happy Halloween, Lu." Curran's dressed as a Rastafarian.

"Trick or treat yourself. I'm fresh out of Snickers."

He holds up a large manila envelope. "I brought the treat. Thought you'd like to see the results of your work and my weeks of artistic efforts."

"You brought the nude photos!"

I have to admit, I'd completely forgotten about them. Lately, any topic more than twenty-four hours old is subject to predelivery dementia.

"You're going to love them," he assures me as I follow him into the dining room, where he pulls them out and spreads them on the table.

I don't know what I expected. But this is totally different. Some are in black and white, others in color. The overall tone of the collage before me is a cross between Georgia O'Keeffe and Anne Geddes. They are in soft tone, some actually blurred. The sharp images pop, oversize and astonishing. My body has become curves and valleys, wind-swept mounds and deep, dark caverns. Very few are of all of me. Instead, shapes and images, forms and color and texture supersede the exact image or personality of the subject. Yet there is one.

It's a full frontal of Sweet Tum exposed, my thighs strategically wrapped in a shawl beneath, that tells the truth about me.

"I don't remember this one," I say, mesmerized by the fearless thrust of pregnancy and the ripe melon weight of the breasts— "My breasts!"

I whip my head toward him. "I didn't expose my breasts to you."

Curran shrugs. "You didn't officially. But about that last hour, you really loosened up, stopped worrying about things. You became an artist's subject, not a friend."

Hmm.

"Look at it, Lu. It's perfection. And I didn't include your head."

"No, only the rest of me is very much on display." I'm feeling queasy again. And the false labor is crimping.

"It's a great shot. The best of the bunch." Curran smoothes the edges of the image lovingly. "The rest of these could sell baby diapers. But this one." He picks it up. "And this one." He pulls another shot from the pile, one of me from the side, cradling my breasts. "These are art."

He's right. And I just have to get over being intimidated by the fact that that's my pear-shaped butt in the other. "They are good, Curran. No, they are great!"

"*Olla,* all! Look who I found on the doorstep." Andrea always makes an entrance. This time she's led William through the front door.

She, who has no scruples, marches right over and picks up a photo. "What's this? You do these, Curran?"

He nods, but he's suddenly as tight as a clam.

"They're good." Andrea fans a few more of them out while I make eye contact with William. "Hi."

"Hi." But I can't hold his gaze. He's spied the photos, too, and it's too late to back down. I watch his expression change from happy to horrified.

"You posed nude for this guy?"

"It's okay, his eyes were closed."

"*Jesus, Joseph and Maria!*" Andrea cries. "This is you!" Imagine that. It is possible to shock Andrea.

"You posed nude for this guy!" William's voice is loud, big bad loud.

"Nobody forced her," Curran says hurriedly, as if he's been accused of harassment, or worse.

"No, no one forced me. In fact, it was my idea. I need to sit now. Can we carry this conversation to the living room?"

Not waiting for agreement, I waddle over to the nearest seat.

William follows, holding a picture he picked up. "I can't believe this. I knew you were a little out there. I like that about you. But that you'd actually do this." He's waving around the photo of my breasts.

"It doesn't have my head in view."

"I don't need your head to know it's you. Andrea didn't. How many other people will put two and two together and know it's you?"

"Practically everyone, since my name will be underneath."

For a second he's speechless.

I heave belly forward onto my feet, with Andrea's unobtrusive aid. Anger requires a standing position. "If you expected me to remain like that hysterical clingy woman you met in your office back in May, you better cut your losses and run. I'm changing, and I'm going to keep on changing until I can't remember where I left my false teeth."

"You'll get implants," he answers. Then as if he's just remembered there are other people in the room, he turns to Curran and points. "Get out." His gaze moves farther to Andrea. "You, too."

We all hear footsteps and the noise of happy children on the hunt for candy and gum just before the doorbell rings.

Andrea grabs the candy bowl I filled in preparation for trick-or-treaters. "I'll just take this with us. Okay, Lu?"

"Out!" I guess William is in charge because they flee for their lives out the front door.

When he turns back to me, he looks as if he's trying to decide how to tell me to go to hell. He rubs his brow. "I don't know what's going on with you. And I don't care. But if you think you can run me off by acting crazy, you don't know beans about me, either."

He begins to pace. I guess a certain kind of energy moves us all about. "I'm not happy you're pregnant by another man. I'm not thrilled you've been writing about it for the world to read in ways that, frankly, make me squirm."

"You read my column?"

"Don't interrupt. I hate that I haven't been able to have a private moment with you for weeks. I'm jealous as hell that you spend more of your time with Cy and Curran than you ever did with me. I want to beat that little knot-headed kid into a bloody pulp for taking those pictures of you." He pauses to catch his breath. "They are damned sexy, by the way. Which must make me some kind of pervert, or truly in love with you."

He swings around at the sound of the doorbell. "And I swear I'll flatten the next person who tries to come between us."

But he's started this and I'm stoked up for Round Two.

"First of all, I don't have to answer to you. We aren't a couple. Secondly, you're having sex with other people!"

"That was your bright idea."

"Yes, well, these days the blood supply to my brain isn't always what it should be."

"No argument from me on that." He's smiling again. "But why do you care who I'm having sex with?"

"I don't." I feel another Braxton Hicks coming on, and this one's a doozy.

"Really?" He looks quite pleased with himself. "Then why did you bring it up?"

"B-because…b-b-because…." I'm sputtering like Porky Pig. I look like Porky Pig! "Because I suspect I'd be in love with you—dammit!—even if I wasn't pregnant."

"Good, because I've got issues, too." He crosses his arms. "And I'm not moving from this spot until you say it plainly. You love me."

I flinch, but not from offense. I take a deep breath. "Can I get a rain check on this argument. I have a rather more pressing need that's just come up."

I look down quickly. When I look up again I see that William's gaze had followed mine down to where a puddle is forming on the floor between my feet. My water just broke.

47

I think there's some discussion of who my Lamaze partner is when I arrive at the hospital. Andrea and William have an argument I vaguely take in outside my door. I'm pretty sure I told the doctor to go screw herself when she asked me to decide. It's true that birth pains don't stay in the memory. But they do fully occupy one's mind at the time.

"I'm too old for this," I tell my doctor after a while, and after I've apologized half a dozen times for my outburst.

"Do you want an epidural?"

"No, thank you. I've earned this. I'm not going to be numb through the miracle part. But a vodka gimlet wouldn't go amiss about now."

She pats my hand and offers me ice shards.

After that things get kind of rough.

They don't call it labor for nothing. And I'm out of practice with pain. But I also have my little village to keep me company. It feels more like a royal birth, where you have to prove you actually delivered the heir apparent.

The troops are arrayed around my private room in

gowns and masks: Cy, Curran, Andrea and William. Dallas has called. She's on her way. Meanwhile, William talks about his grandson, Will. Shows pictures all around. Brags about how he's become proficient at disposable diapering, instant-formula feedings, and baby-sling carrying. Generally they have a tête-à-tête, while I lie groaning and moaning and sweating and thinking evil thoughts about all of them.

We're wheeling down the hallway toward the delivery room when William leans down low and says, "There was no sex, Lu."

I blink sweat out of my eyes. "You don't have to say that."

He nods. "I know."

"Are you lying?"

He smiles. "Does it matter? I love you, Lu."

I look up at him, through the sweat and tears and blinding overhead lights, and say, "What about Fiji?"

"Screw Fiji!"

That's when I grip his hand and hold tight for the rest of the night.

"It's a girl!"

"Her name's Hermione," I say with a big fat grin as she's placed in my arms.

William leans in. "Like in *Harry Potter?*"

"No. Of course not! As in Gingold."

September

Not all of us want to lead the charge in life.
For some that early bird's worm comes way too soon.
Yet we emerge later in the day, still full of promise.
The night may come too soon for some.
But for most, the sun will burn late into our evening.
We're okay with that. Call us what we are, Late Bloomers.

**—*Late Bloomers*
by Tallulah Nichols**

Epilogue

It's William's grandson's first birthday. The perfect day for it, too. The sky is bright blue with summer clouds in a September sky. The breeze off Sag Harbor bay is the kind that carries white sails briskly along at a distance without knocking over the umbrellas of the lawn tables ashore. Jolie looks radiant in a simple print voile dress that swirls about her ankles. Jon, too, who seems to have eyes only for her. I know because I sent Andrea over to flirt with him. Either her brand of sex on stilettos is showing its age or he has developed a healthy leeriness of the forward approach by a strange, however lovely, woman.

William's buying a house near the water, with all the privileges that that implies. Today he's borrowed a fellow physician's home on the water's edge for this gathering.

I watch as he lifts his giggling grandson aloft and admire his tireless enthusiasm for "ah'p'n, BopPa, ah'p'n" as Will spread his arms like wings and his grandfather swings him around in circles as if he's an airplane on a string. It doesn't bother him that his hair is ruffled or that his coat is creased. He's never more happy than when surrounded by family.

There's laughter and toasting on the patio, where there are far too many balloons and grown-ups present for a baby's first birthday. In fact, there are enough guests for a wedding, which is exactly what we decided should take place between the magician's act and the cutting of the birthday cake. The wedding cake, by the way, is a choo-choo train with one big fat candle in the middle and a tiny bride and groom on the caboose.

I smile at Dallas as she hands me my bouquet. It's a bunch of Hampton hydrangeas, so deep a blue it seems that you should be able to squeeze the color out of them.

"Are you happy, Mom?"

"The only thing in the dark." It's become our shorthand for "deliriously pleased with life."

Flanking me for the journey to the arbor where the ceremony will take place are Davin and Dallas. Just as the music begins, my youngster starts to fret in Andrea's arms. She twists and fusses until she locates me, a few feet away, and then her two fat little hands make grabby gestures for me.

"I'll hold her, Mom," Dallas offers.

"Oh, no, you won't." I hand her my bouquet. "It should be clear to one and all by now that we do things a little differently in this family."

I gather up my ten-month-old daughter, Hermione, and hold her before me. Dressed in a pink satin and tulle dress, she looks exactly like a live bouquet.

We're not quite sure where the red hair came from. The pink makes it shine as if gold thread was spun into the bodacious color. I think it was all the love she received during the nine months of her journey to us.

Or maybe it was all the good sex.

I wink at William as I start down the short makeshift aisle. His grandson is his best man.

I think we're going to be very happy together.

Tai is there, with Curran, who is up for a prestigious award for his photography, thanks to his boss's encouragement and connections. Those pictures of me hang in a gallery where, believe it or not, they sell.

Even Jacob came. With him is Midge. She's no Sandra but, at a settled forty-five, she does look like wife material. Aunt Marvelle is here, and the Marvelous Matrons, along with many of William's patients. And, of course, my parents and William's dad.

Only Cy declined. He's in Israel with his son and daughter-in-law. He said he's an old man. Weddings are not good for his heart.

Now that my book, *Late Bloomers,* is about to be published, I'm scheduled to begin doing a monthly tie-in with Oprah on late-life parenting.

Will I be the next Dr. Phil or Iyanla? Only time will tell.

What is certain, the new Lu has never been happier or more alive!

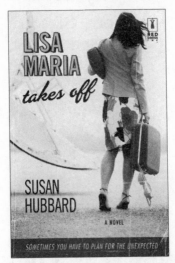